# A
# THISTLE
# BEYOND
# TIME

## BY
## JENNAE VALE

## Acknowledgements

Thank you to my husband, David, my children, my extended family and friends for your support and encouragement throughout this process.

Thank you to my editor, Deb Williams - The Pedantic Punctuator, for all your help and for making the editing process a fun learning experience.

# ONE

The silence surrounding Jenna was as all encompassing as the thick blanket of fog, which had just settled in around her. A shiver travelled up her spine when she noticed she was suddenly and completely alone, where moments before the Marina Green had been filled with people walking their dogs, running along the pathways, and otherwise enjoying the morning. Movement caught her eye and as she watched, the fog began to swirl and move towards her, as if it were a living, breathing entity.

"Chester, come," she called. Her cousin Dylan's massive Rottweiler trotted her way. "Time to go, boy."

As she finished leashing the dog, the wind picked up and Chester began barking and leaping at the approaching fog. They were in the middle of some kind of whirlwind. Jenna brushed her wayward locks out of her eyes as Chester barked happily, his little stub of a tail wagging along with his entire hind end. Why was he greeting the fog, which continued swirling their way?

Curiosity held Jenna in place. The fog was alive with movement, and sparked and popped with mini lightning strikes of color. She knew she should get out of there, but her feet were frozen to the spot. Moments passed in slow motion as the fog began to dissipate, leaving in its place a very tall, kilted man with long, dark hair and mesmerizing blue eyes that were trained on Jenna. He smiled and walked her way.

"Ye must be Jenna. I've come for ye lass."

Jenna forced herself to speak. "Do I know you?" Her voice quivered only the tiniest bit. She wracked her brain, trying to remember if she'd met this guy before. Jenna imagined if she had, she'd remember him. He wasn't someone she'd easily forget.

"Nay. We've not met."

That voice and that accent were affecting her ability to move. She really needed to get away from him, before she turned into a puddle of mush at his feet.

"Then how do you know me? Where did you come from," she demanded, as she quickly surveyed the surrounding area.

"I dinna know ye, lass. Edna sent me."

He said the last, as though she should know who Edna was.

"I don't know anyone named Edna. You must have me confused with someone else." She began backing away. He followed.

"Nay. Ye dinna know Edna, but she knows ye. She said ye'd be the first lass I'd set eyes on when I arrived."

Jenna was trying her best not to freak out, but the intimidating stranger who was wearing a kilt and pacing towards her, wasn't making it easy.

"So, this is San Francisco." He looked around and his eyes lit on the Golden Gate Bridge. "'Tis an amazing sight."

The fog was completely gone and people were visible once again. Jenna breathed a sigh of relief.

"And who is this?" he asked, as he bent to pet Chester - who was doing a pathetic job of protecting her.

"His name's Chester. He's not usually very friendly with strangers." She couldn't believe it. The dog was all over this guy. One thing was certain, to this point Chester had always been an excellent judge of character. If someone was not to be trusted, he reacted with growls and raised hackles. It was a shame that today was apparently the day he'd decided to lower his standards.

"Look, Mr.—" Jenna started.

"My apologies, lass, I forgot to introduce meself. Me name's Cormac MacBayne."

"Well, it's been nice chatting with you, Mr. MacBayne, but I've got to get going."

"I'll come with ye then."

"No. No, you won't." Jenna cursed the fact that she'd left her cell phone at home.

"Aye. I must. I'm here for ye, Jenna."

"What exactly does that mean," she snapped. Jenna's eyes narrowed in disbelief.

"Edna sent me to bring ye back with me. Yer to be me wife."

"Okay, I don't know what drugs you're on, or which one's you should be on, but you need to leave me alone." Jenna assessed the situation and decided she needed to get home as quickly as possible. There were plenty of people out and about now, so if he tried anything, she'd scream. This guy was obviously a nut job, but oddly, she didn't feel threatened by him. Too bad he was delusional, because otherwise, he was a fine specimen of man.

She quickly turned around and started walking away. He hurried to catch up with her. Jenna surveyed the area for the quickest way to lose this guy. It didn't look hopeful.

"Don't you have somewhere you need to be?" she said.

"Nay, lass, I'm here—"

"I know, I know, you're here for me," she growled.

"I've nowhere else to go," he admitted in a somber voice.

"So you're homeless. Is that it?"

"Nay. My home is far from here."

"Do you have any money?" Jenna asked, her initial wariness turning down a notch.

"Nay, I dinnae." he responded, with a curious look on his face.

"Okay. Since you insist on following me, if you leave me alone and don't try anything, when we get to my place, I'll give you some money and I'll have my cousin, Dylan, drive you to the homeless shelter. There are people there who can help you." Why was she leading him right to her front door? She kept telling herself that Chester wouldn't let any harm come to her and Jenna simply didn't get a bad vibe from him.

He continued to look as if he couldn't understand why she thought he needed help. "That won't be necessary, lass. If ye come with me, we'll tell Edna we're ready and she'll bring us back to my home."

"I can't argue with you about this. You obviously have issues that need to be dealt with and I don't have the time or the patience to do it. So, please, don't say another word about me going anywhere with you. As a matter of fact, don't say anything else at all."

"As ye wish, lass."

Jenna kept her eye on him as she walked. She had been accosted by strangers in the past. San Francisco was a big city and there were many roaming the streets who needed help. None of them had ever followed her home though. Some would ask for money and some only wanted someone to listen to them for a moment. Cormac MacBayne didn't utter a single word, but she noted his head on a swivel, turning from side to side. He looked at the cars and buses with immense curiosity. Everything seemed fascinating to him.

Jenna was relieved when she finally reached her house, a neat little Victorian with lots of gingerbread trim, in a row of similar multicolored houses. It may not have been the wisest decision to lead him straight to her front door, but something told her she had nothing to fear from this strange man.

"You wait here. I'll send Dylan out to help you."

"Jenna, lass, I—"

"No. Don't say another word. Zip it." She motioned to her lips like she were zipping them shut.

Cormac wrinkled his brow and looked confused at that, but he did not speak.

"Come on, Chester." She had to pull the dog away. *He must be wearing bacon cologne,* she thought, as she climbed the stairs to her front door. She took one more look at gorgeous, but crazy and then unlocked the door and went inside.

~~~

"Dylan," Jenna called as she closed the front door. "Dylan, get up. I need you. We've got a problem and he's waiting for your downstairs."

"Morning to you, too, cuz." Dylan stretched and rubbed his eyes as he emerged from his room, wearing nothing but a pair of jeans. "Coffee." He pointed as he made his way to the kitchen and poured himself a cup.

"So, what's up? Jonathan back?"

"No. Some crazy guy followed me home from the Green. Oddly, he knows my name. Some lady named Edna sent him, or so he says. I'm supposed to go with him and be his wife."

"Well, you better get packed then. You probably shouldn't make him wait too long. He might leave without you." Dylan chuckled at his own joke.

"Very funny. You're just a riot, first thing in the morning, aren't you?"

"I do believe I am." He tossed his golden blonde curls back out of his face and reached for a shirt tossed over a nearby chair. "Between that, and this face and bod, it's a wonder I don't have women beating down the door to be with me."

"I don't want your head to swell, but they do."

Dylan grinned. "Oh, yeah, you're right."

"Come on, Dylan. Get serious. We need to do something about this guy. And when I say we, I really mean you."

"Should I bring my baseball bat?" he teased.

"No. He seems pretty harmless," Jenna related. She found her purse and pulled out her wallet. "Here's some money for him. I thought you could drop him off at a homeless shelter."

"Okay. I'll take care of it." He looked out the front window. "That him?" he asked.

"Yes."

"He's a big dude. I wonder if he played football."

"I wouldn't know. I didn't ask him," she replied sarcastically.

"I'll bet he did. Probably got hit on the head one time too many. Concussions, you know."

Jenna rolled her eyes. "Dylan, not everyone plays football."

"I do."

"I know, but he's Scottish."

"Oh, yeah, he's wearing a kilt. That should have been my first clue."

Jenna was pushing him towards the door now. "Go, go, go."

"Okay, I'm go, go, going."

Jenna slammed the door shut behind him and went back to the window. She took her phone with her just in case she needed to call the SFPD.

~~~

Cormac leaned against the light post and waited as he had been instructed by Jenna. He hoped Edna hadn't led him astray. This woman was quite bonnie, to be sure, but she had a sharp tongue, which was in great contrast to her angelic face, golden locks, and liquid brown eyes. She was petite. Her head only reached the top of his chest and though she was slight of build, she was quite shapely.

His eyes were drawn up to the windows above his head. He could see movement there and knew he was being watched. Moments later the door slammed behind a tall, light haired man, who looked down the stairs at him.

"Hi. My name's Dylan. I'm Jenna's cousin. She asked me to come down here and help you."

"Good day to ye, Dylan. I be Cormac MacBayne. Edna sent me to find me wife. She told me Jenna was the one, but Jenna doesnae believe it."

"I see." Dylan was baffled, but he wanted to get to the bottom of this for his cousin's sake. Taking this guy to a shelter wasn't going to answer the questions he had.

"Cormac, are you hungry, by any chance?"

"Aye. I am."

"Me, too. Let's go get some breakfast and you can tell me all about Edna and this wife thing."

As they headed off down the street, Cormac took one last glance up at the window and caught Jenna spying on them.

~~~

"Where is he going? I told Dylan to drive him to the homeless shelter, and instead, they've headed off down the street like two old friends," Jenna muttered irritably.

It occurred to Jenna in that moment, that Dylan might be pulling a prank on her. It certainly seemed like something he would do. That must be it, because nothing else made sense.

This Cormac was very handsome. He dressed oddly, but it was kind of sexy. Who didn't love a man in a kilt? The t-shirt, leather jacket and boots were icing on the cake as far as she was concerned. She wondered where Dylan had found him. Did he know him from college? She liked the Scottish accent and wondered why she'd never visited Scotland. If the men there looked anything like Cormac Mac-Bayne, she was going to have to put it on her bucket list.

Her best friend, Ashley, had gone off to Scotland the previous spring and she'd ended up getting married and staying there. *God, I miss you, Ashley,* Jenna thought. *I can't even call you. Who lives someplace where there's no phone service, anyway?* If Ashley were here, they'd be busy cooking up ways to get back at Dylan. A good practical joke always deserved a response.

Her walk with Chester was supposed to help her relax and instead it had added a whole new list of things for Jenna to mull over in her head. Sometimes it was too hard to turn off all that mindless chatter. The thoughts that made her feel like everything that had happened in her life recently had been her own fault. The thoughts that told her she'd made the biggest mistake of her life when she married Jonathan, and that if she'd been paying attention, she would have known better than to trust him. Jenna looked down at her now-fisted hands and grimaced at her own inability to let things go. She made a conscious effort to relax her hands and took a deep breath, expelling it and all of the obsessive thoughts floating through her brain.

"Come on, Chester. Let's go get something to eat. I'm not going to solve all my problems right now."

# TWO

Cormac and Dylan made themselves comfortable in a corner booth of Joe's Diner, a local watering hole.

"Let's order some food first and then we'll talk," Dylan suggested.

"Aye." Cormac looked uncomfortable as he examined everything - from the booth, to the glasses, to the floor and ceiling.

"Here." Dylan handed Cormac a menu, but instead of reading it, he just held it in his hand.

"No diners where you're from?"

"Diners?"

"That's what this place is. It's a diner."

"Nay. I've not been to a *diner*." Cormac carefully pronounced the word.

"Okay. Well, that's the menu in your hand. You order your food from it."

Cormac took a deep breath and continued to look around.

Dylan wasn't sure what was going on. "I'll order for both of us. I'm pretty hungry and I'd guess you are, too."

"Hey, Dylan, long time no see." A pretty young waitress stood at their booth ready to take their orders.

"Oh, hey, Sophia. How's it going?"

"Okay, I guess. You never called me," she said, staring daggers at him.

"Oh, yeah, I'm sorry. I just got really busy helping Jenna out, you know."

"Right." She didn't believe him. He could tell. "Who's your friend," she asked not hiding her interest.

"This is Cormac."

Cormac stood and gave her a slight bow. He took her hand, brought it to his lips and said, "'Tis an honor to meet ye, lass."

Sophia's legs appeared to go wobbly and she looked a little flustered, so Cormac steadied her to keep her from falling. She fanned herself with the order pad and started to walk away.

"Aren't you going to take our order, Sophia," Dylan asked.

"Oops. Sorry. What can I get you, Cormac?" She smiled and batted her lashes at him, ignoring Dylan.

Dylan ordered enough food to feed a family of six and as they waited, he decided there was no time like the present to find out what Cormac was all about, but before he could ask his first question, Cormac had one of his own.

"What have ye done to that poor lass that has angered her so?"

"You picked up on that, huh? I made the mistake of going on a date with her. She's really pretty, you know, but we didn't have any chemistry. So I never called her for a second date. I guess she expected I would."

"Chemistry. What is chemistry?"

"Really?"

Cormac continued staring at him, waiting for a reply.

"Chemistry is like when you have this immediate connection with someone. You just hit it off right away."

"I'm sorry, Dylan. I'm not verra good with yer twenty-first century American language. Ashley speaks it all the time and I've come to understand most of what she says, but there is always something new to learn."

"Did you say twenty-first century American language?"

"Aye. I did." Cormac looked like he was weighing his options as to what to say before he continued. "Edna told me to be careful what I say and not to look puzzled by all the strange sights I would see. She thought it might frighten Jenna, but I believe I already have."

"Yeah, she was a bit freaked out when she got home. But explain to me… where are you from?" Dylan got the feeling something was not quite right here; hopefully he'd figure it out soon.

"I be from Scotland. Edna sent me. She's a witch, ye ken."

"You mean a witch who casts spells?"

"Aye."

"So, Edna sent you to get Jenna and bring her back to Scotland?"

"Aye. She told me Jenna would be me wife, but I'm nae so sure. She isnae sweet like me brother's wife."

"Who's your brother's wife?"

"Cailin is newlywed to Ashley. She is a twenty-first century American lass, like Jenna. She lived here in San Francisco before she met me brother."

"Ashley Moore?"

"Aye. That's her. Do ye know her?"

"Aye. I mean, yes. She is Jenna's best friend. She went to Scotland on a vacation and called to tell Jenna she was getting married. We haven't heard from her since."

"'Tis not likely that ye will."

"Cormac, you need to tell me everything. I can't help you if I don't know the whole story."

Just then, Sophia returned with two huge plates of food and a steaming pot of coffee, which she placed on the table in front of them.

"Here you go." She focused all of her attention on Cormac, leaning over him and pressing her ample bosom into his arm as she poured him some coffee. "You let me know if you need anything else. Anything at all." She winked at him and gave her hips a little extra sway as she walked away.

"Are all of the women in San Francisco like Sophia? I've seen many beautiful lasses in the short time I've been here. Mayhap I can find someone else to bring back with me. Someone more like Ashley."

"Believe me, Sophia is nothing like Ashley."

Dylan began to eat, but Cormac looked a bit confused by the utensils and the food. *This is really odd,* Dylan thought. *He seems like he's never seen a fork before.*

"Hey, dude, you alright?"

"Dude? Who is dude?"

"You. It's twenty-first century American." Dylan showed Cormac how to use the fork and with a smile he dug right in. He tasted the coffee and made a face.

"You should put cream and sugar in it. It can be kind of bitter otherwise."

"Cailin told me of this coffee. He had some when he visited yer time."

That caught Dylan's attention and he put his fork down and focused on Cormac.

"What do you mean, my time?"

"Edna will be angry with me, but I must tell someone. Ye must promise to say naught to Jenna about Ashley. 'Tis important she come with me because she wants to, and not because of Ashley."

"I won't say anything about Ashley. I promise. Now tell me what you meant, by my time."

"You see, Dylan, I be from the year 1514 in Scotland. Edna sent me from that time to bring Jenna back to Breaghacraig with me."

Dylan's mouth was hanging open at this revelation. Being a huge fan of sci-fi, he was more than willing to believe Cormac. He was open-minded on most topics and believed that just because he hadn't seen it with his own eyes, it didn't mean that something didn't exist.

"Whoa, dude! That's amazing. How did she do it?"

"I dinnae know. I stood at the bridge as she told me to do and when the fog came, it whirled around me for a while and then left. I opened my eyes and I was here and I saw Jenna, just as Edna said I would."

"What about your clothes. You're wearing a kilt, but you have a t-shirt and a really cool leather jacket on. I don't think they have those things in the sixteenth century."

"Yer right. She told me that the lasses here would find me irresistible in these clothes."

"I think she was right. Every woman we passed on the street did a double take when they saw you. I might have to copy your look."

"It did not impress Jenna. She couldnae wait to get away from me."

"Don't give up on her yet. I'll see what I can do to help you. You gotta understand, she just got out of a bad marriage and she's mad at the world right now."

"Jenna was married?"

"She was. She married this guy named Jonathan. None of us, her family or friends, liked him. We thought she was making a huge mistake, but she didn't want to hear it. It turned out he was just interested in her for the family money. Once she found out, she dumped his ass and got her marriage annulled. She felt really betrayed and she's still getting over it."

"She is lovely to look at, but she has a viper's tongue," Cormac observed.

"Sarcasm is her weapon of choice, bro. She's really a great girl. She's kind of hard on the outside and this whole Jonathan thing hasn't helped with that, but she's a sweetheart once you get to know her. You'll see."

"I trust ye, Dylan. Will ye be unhappy to have yer cousin leave yer time?"

"Nah. I'd be happy for her... *if* she really wanted to go. *I'd* want to go to. Do you think that would be possible?"

"I dinnae know. We'd have to ask Edna."

"How do you communicate with Edna? Do you use mental telepathy? Or does she materialize right in front of you?"

"I'm sorry, Dylan, I dinna ken *mental telepathy*. If ye want to know how I talk to Edna, it's in me head. I dinna think I can explain it any other way."

Dylan was finishing up the last of his food and he was grinning from ear to ear.

"We're going to have to find a way to get Jenna to let you stay at the house. Leave it up to me. She'll be pissed at first, but she'll come around. You'll see."

Sophia brought the check. "Can I get you guys anything else?" Again, she was totally focused on Cormac, who was having a hard time with the slang.

"We're good to go, Sophia." Dylan handed her some cash. "I think that covers it."

"Do you want change?"

"Nope. You keep it."

"Hope to see you again, Cormac. I work most mornings. Just ask them to sit you at my table."

"Thank ye, lass. I'll be sure to do that."

As they left, Sophia followed them to the door. Dylan watched with interest as she blew Cormac a kiss and then nearly fell over when he returned it with a devilish smile.

# THREE

J enna was running the vacuum cleaner when Dylan returned with Cormac. She didn't hear them enter and when she finally did look up, she jumped, clutching her chest.

"You scared me!" Her heart was racing in her chest.

"Sorry, cuz," Dylan apologized, with a sheepish grin on his face.

Jenna looked around Dylan and an angry scowl lit across her features as she spied Cormac.

"I thought I told you to take him to a shelter! What didn't you understand about that?" She snapped.

"I couldn't do that to him, Jenna. He's from another country and he doesn't know anyone here. He's a good guy, really. We just spent the last hour having breakfast and getting to know each other."

"Dylan, I know what you're up to, so you can stop right now." Letting go of the vacuum, Jenna crossed her arms over her chest.

"I don't know what you're talking about," Dylan replied.

"I know this is all a practical joke. I don't know how you pulled it off and I don't know where you got this guy from, but I can't believe you would do that to me. You know how upset I've been lately and when *he* appeared out of nowhere, well… I thought he was a serial killer or something."

"I would never harm ye, lass." Cormac said, as he peeked around from behind Dylan.

"I know that now, but at the time I was pretty scared."

"I apologize to ye. I didnae mean to scare ye."

"It wasn't a practical joke, Jenna. This guy, Cormac, is from Scotland and he was sent here by a witch. That's the Edna he mentioned. Anyway, he's not even from this time. He's from the sixteenth century. Can you believe it?" Dylan asked excitedly.

"No. I can't believe it and I don't. Nice work trying to convince me of something completely impossible. Have you been taking acting classes lately, Dylan, 'cause you're pretty good. If I didn't know you better, I might even believe you."

"It's true, Jenna. I'm not making it up. Tell her Cormac."

"He's telling the truth, lass. Edna sent me from the year 1514. She said ye were to be me wife."

"Now don't start that again. You both need to give it up. I don't believe you. There's no such thing as time travel. Period. The end."

"Okay. I won't mention it again, but we're not lying and time travel is totally possible, you'll see," Dylan insisted.

Jenna got a chill down her spine. How could she possibly see? Something was off here, but she couldn't put her finger on it. Best just to let Dylan have his fun and ignore his Scottish friend as much as possible. She stood there, vacuum cleaner in hand once again and looked from Dylan to Cormac, where her gaze rested. He was truly an amazing looking man. He could have stepped out of one of those fancy men's cologne ads. He was definitely not hard on the eyes. Speaking of eyes, his were the most beautiful shade of blue. The word cerulean came to mind. Although why, she couldn't say. It wasn't a word she ever used. *I guess I've read one too many romance novels.* His face was perfectly constructed - the features were bold and angular from his straight nose, to his strong jaw line. He was definitely all man. His mouth revealed very kissable lips and she wondered if they were as soft as they appeared. His body was next up for examination as she continued her perusal. He had broad shoulders, strong arms and hands. His chest was straining the bounds of his t-shirt and tapered to narrow hips and really nice legs. That kilt he wore was so sexy. She wondered if it was true that nothing came between a man and his kilt. Jenna suddenly became aware of the fact that the room had gone completely silent. She raised her head and was embarrassed to see two pairs of eyes watching her. A slow, sexy grin spread across Cormac's face and she thought she might just faint from embarrassment and the devastating affect that grin was having on her heart.

"I'll get the guest room set up for Cormac, since we're the only people he knows here and we can't just put him out on the street to fend for himself." Dylan broke the uncomfortable silence.

"He looks pretty capable of taking care of himself, if you ask me. Can't he just stay at a hotel?" Jenna asked.

"Don't be like that, Jenna. We don't want Cormac going back to Scotland with stories about how rude Americans are, do we?"

"I guess not. Okay. He can stay, as long as he doesn't mention taking me back to Scotland to be his wife. Understood?"

Both men nodded in agreement.

"Come on, Cormac. I'll show you to your room."

"Jenna, lass, thank ye."

"You're welcome. I think."

~~~

Cormac followed Dylan to what would be his bedroom. It was small in comparison to his bedroom at Breaghacraig, but there was plenty of room for him to be comfortable. The bed was large and the windows let in enough light to keep the room bright and cheery.

"This is it." Dylan extended his arm as he presented Cormac with the room.

"'Tis verra nice. I will be most happy here."

"Well, don't get too comfortable. We'll be heading to the other house in the East Bay tomorrow."

"Ye have another home?"

"Yeah. They both belong to Jenna's parents, but they've more or less given them to her."

"Where do they reside?"

"They have homes all over the world. They never stay in one place very long and they haven't been back to San Francisco in years. The bathroom's in here." He led Cormac to his own private en-suite.

"Dylan, ye may need to explain things to me. We dinna have rooms like this where I come from."

"Right. I almost forgot." Dylan showed Cormac how everything worked in the bathroom. He showed him how to turn the lights on and off in both rooms and where he could find towels and soap. "You look like you're about my size, so if you need any clothes, you can borrow mine."

"Aye. Ye are most generous, Dylan. Thank ye."

"No problem. Tonight we're going to a karaoke bar in Hayes Valley. You should be okay wearing what you have on. It's been a winner for you today. Why mess with success?"

Cormac just shook his head. This was almost too much for him. He could barely understand what was being said around him. Why had he let Edna convince him to come here in search of a wife? Jenna had not been verra happy to see him and she had tried to get rid of him, almost immediately. She had, however, given him quite the once over when he came back with Dylan. She was attracted to him. Cormac knew that look. Many a lass had looked at him the verra same way. As she examined him from head to toe, Jenna looked like she was planning to devour him for dinner. That thought alone had the blood rushing through his aroused body. She was a comely lass and he wondered what it would be like to hold her in his arms, to feel her hands on his body, her lips on his lips. He groaned aloud at the thoughts wreaking havoc with his brain.

Dylan cleared his throat, "I'll leave you to it, then. You might want to rest a bit. I'll bet time travel really takes it out of you."

"Aye. I believe yer correct. I should rest." Cormac was feeling a bit drained, but it was unusual for him to lay abed during the day. He would never do that back at Breaghacraig, as there was always so much that needed doing.

Dylan closed the door behind him and Cormac lay down and closed his eyes. He had no sooner done so than he heard Edna's voice.

"Cormac. Can ye hear me?"

"Aye, Edna. 'Tis ye?"

"Who else would it be? How many people talk to ye in yer head, dear?"

Cormac smirked, despite knowing Edna couldn't see the reaction. "Only ye, Edna."

"Yes, well, how is everything? Have ye met Jenna?"

"Aye. She is quite a lovely lass, but she doesnae care for me I'm afeared."

"Don't ye worry, dear. She'll come around. Remember ye only have a week to get her to agree to return with ye. Then, at that time, ye need to go back to the exact same spot so I can bring ye back."

"Her cousin, Dylan, has been helping me, else I'd be staying at something she called the homeless shelter."

"Oh, my. Thank goodness that didn't happen. Be patient with her. She is not a happy young lady. She has had a life lesson at the school of hard knocks and it will take her time to trust ye."

"Are ye sure she is the one for me?"

"I would not have sent ye otherwise, now would I?"

"Nay. I would hope not."

"As I told you, try to fit in. Don't act surprised by anything you might see."

"'Tis been difficult, but I dinnae believe anyone has noticed. I told Jenna's cousin about Ashley. He willnae tell a soul."

"Good. I'm glad you have someone to confide in. If ye need me, just call to me."

"I will."

And then she was gone and Cormac decided it wouldn't be such a bad idea to sleep for a while.

~~~

Jenna was perplexed beyond reason. She had been puttering around the house for the last hour, cursing Dylan. She didn't think she was going to be able to deal with having Cormac under her roof. The last thing she wanted was to find herself attracted to him. She wasn't ready for that. She was still reeling from the deception she had been living with during her marriage to Jonathan. Romance was not high on her 'to do' list. As a matter of fact, it wasn't on there at all.

"Damn, damn, damn," she muttered.

"Damn what?" Dylan had just walked into the kitchen to find Jenna, holding her head in hand, cursing soundly.

"Dylan, what were you thinking?"

"Huh?" Dylan cocked an eyebrow in her direction.

"Inviting Cormac to stay with us. I'm not sure how I feel about having a total stranger sleeping right next to my bedroom."

"Afraid you'll accidentally end up in his room? Or him in yours?" Dylan teased.

"You know what I mean. And stop that. No one's going to end up in anyone else's room. I don't have time for that."

"Jenna, of course you have time for that. It might be the best thing for you. Don't let Jonathan mess up the rest of your life, just because he was a scam artist."

"I'm not ready yet, Dylan. So, don't push me," she snarled.

"Okay, okay. You win," Dylan conceded. "I told Cormac he could come with us to karaoke tonight."

"I don't know if I want to go." Jenna continued cleaning, and avoided eye contact with her cousin.

"Why? You were fine with it earlier," Dylan protested.

"I'm just not feeling very sociable."

"Jenna, you can't become a hermit. You're going and I won't take no for an answer. You need to lighten up and have some fun."

Jenna wrinkled her nose and stuck her tongue out at her cousin. He was right. She really needed to get out of her own way and start living her life again. "Okay. I'll go, but I'm not singing."

"We'll see about that," Dylan chuckled.

Jenna ignored Dylan and continued her cleaning rampage through the kitchen. Not that it needed to be cleaned, but it kept her busy and it was somewhat therapeutic for her.

"You missed a spot," Dylan was not about to leave the kitchen without making her laugh.

"Where?" she asked, seriously, eyeing the granite counter top from all angles.

"Jenna, hello... I'm kidding. Can I at least get a smile out of you?"

She forced a smile to her face. Dylan grabbed a wet towel and flicked it in her direction, spraying her with water. "Dylan... don't! You'll mess up the kitchen."

"Then you'll really have an excuse to clean," he teased, as he ran past and poked a finger in her ribs.

"Dylan, stop!" Jenna shrieked with laughter and chased after him.

"Not until you promise me you'll smile more often."

Dylan grabbed her around the waist and tickled her.

"I will... I promise."

Dylan let go and she swatted at him as he ran across the kitchen, laughing. He turned to head for the doorway, but was blocked by a large Highlander leaning against the doorframe.

Jenna's laughter stopped abruptly as she took in all 6'4" of Cormac MacBayne, looking hotter than hot with a sexy half smile on his very handsome face.

"I'm sorry for interrupting yer fun. I was hoping to find something to drink."

"Oh, I'm sorry... sure..." She was stumbling all over her words and worse yet, she could feel a blush creeping up her face. "What would you like? Beer? Water? Milk?"

"Get him a beer, Jenna. He could probably use one."

Jenna went to the refrigerator, retrieved a bottle, and handed it to Cormac who looked at it as if it was the most puzzling thing he had ever seen.

"Is that a twist off, Dylan? I didn't look."

"No. He needs a bottle opener."

Cormac was still looking bewildered when Jenna handed him the bottle opener.

"What do I do with this, lass?"

"Are you serious?" she questioned and when he didn't answer her, she took the bottle out of his hand and using the bottle opener, removed the cap. "Here you go."

Dylan had retrieved a bottle for himself and took the opener from Jenna. He nodded at Cormac and took a swig from the bottle.

Cormac followed suit, finally realizing what he was supposed to do with the bottle.

"Don't they have beer in bottles, where you come from?" Jenna asked.

"Nay, not like this."

"You'll have to tell me all about... Scotland. The part you're from, that is." Jenna's curiosity was piqued and she hoped to catch him in a lie and then this crazy practical joke would be over.

"Aye. Mayhap another time, if ye dinnae mind."

"Of course. I think I'll go get dressed for our night on the town."

Jenna was relieved to walk out of the kitchen. It was getting a bit awkward in there, and hot. She felt like she would spontaneously combust at the sight of Cormac in the doorway. She hoped the evening would be fun and that she'd be able to relax around him. The way he looked at her made her feel a bit shy, which was an emotion she seldom suffered from. It was as if he was looking into her soul. She didn't know how she felt about that, but she planned on treating him just like she did all of her other guy friends. *Yeah... right!*

Cormac and Dylan exchanged knowing glances as Jenna left the kitchen.

"I think you're getting to her, dude."

"I would have to agree with ye. She turns a lovely shade of pink when she looks at me."

"Keep up the good work. Although you're not really doing much. I wish I had that effect on the ladies. Maybe you could teach me a few of your tricks."

"I dinna use tricks, Dylan," Cormac chuckled. "'Tis just me curse to be attractive to the lasses."

"And that is the unfortunate truth, my man." Dylan slapped Cormac on the back. "We'll see how I do tonight. Maybe there'll be a trickle-down effect from hanging with you."

"A what?"

"I'm hoping some of your charm will rub off on me, and the ladies will be all over me, like bees to honey."

"I'll be sure to send them yer way, as I only have eyes for yer cousin." Cormac was starting to feel that there might be some hope. Jenna had not been quite as prickly as she had been when they first met. Mayhap Edna was on to something.

"Thanks, I appreciate the help. Do you need to get ready to go out?"

"Nay. I believe I'll keep the clothes Edna gave me for tonight. Jenna seems to enjoy them."

# FOUR

The night air had grown chilly and a misty grey fog was settling on the city as Jenna, Cormac and Dylan made their way into the bar. EJ, the bartender, looked up as they entered.

"Jenna! Good to see you back. It's been a while." He smiled, giving her an appreciative once over.

"Hey, EJ, nice to be back." She felt Cormac inch closer to her back and she said, "This is Dylan's friend Cormac. Cormac, this is EJ."

EJ gave him a quick nod of the head and Cormac did the same.

"What can I get for you?"

"Can I get a Margarita, EJ? Dylan, Cormac, what do you want to drink?"

"I'll have whatever's on tap, EJ," Dylan said.

"Whiskey, please," Cormac requested.

They settled in at the bar. Jenna and Dylan both took stools and Cormac leaned his tall frame against the bar as he surveyed the room. Jenna couldn't help but notice the women at nearby tables giving him the once over. For some reason she couldn't name, she reached out to touch his hand. She was surprised by the warm sensation that made its way up her arm at the feel of his skin. Cormac looked at her, head tipped, questioning. Was he feeling it too?

"I just wanted to make sure you were okay," she lied. She could feel the warmth making its way up to her face and knew she was blushing… again. Thankfully, the lighting in the bar was dim and she hoped he wouldn't notice.

"I be fine, lass. What of ye? Are ye well then?"

"I'm fine, thanks."

EJ arrived with their drinks.

"Dylan says you're from Scotland. I've given you the finest Scotch Whiskey we have. I hope you enjoy it."

Cormac took a sip, appearing to savor the flavor of the drink. "'Tis verra good. It rivals the finest I've ever had. Thank ye."

Jenna couldn't help noticing that Cormac and EJ were sizing each other up. She knew EJ had a bit of a crush on her and Cormac was under some delusion that she was going to marry him. They were doing that posturing thing that guys did. The testosterone flying around the bar was palpable and was making things somewhat uncomfortable for Jenna.

A group at a table near the stage started waving and calling to her.

"Jenna, Jenna!"

"Oh, no," she muttered under her breath. "Hi." She reluctantly smiled and waved back.

"Who are they?" Cormac asked.

"Some friends of my ex."

"I take it yer not happy to see them?"

"No. I can't say that I am."

Dylan had wandered off and was talking to a group of girls at the far end of the bar. Cormac picked up Jenna's drink and smelled it. "What is this drink?" he asked.

"It's a Margarita. It's made with tequila. Taste it," Jenna offered.

Cormac did as she suggested and she could see from his facial expressions that he was searching his brain to identify the taste. "Hmmm…" was all he said.

"Don't you like it?" Jenna asked.

He lifted his glass. "I prefer the whiskey."

Music was playing in the background and people were filtering up towards the stage, to take their turn at singing.

"Cormac, you have a horrified look on your face. You're not enjoying the music?" Jenna observed.

"They sound like yowling cats, lass. I've never heard the like. Those people shouldnae be singing. They be verra bad at it."

"That's kind of the idea. People come in, have enough drinks to get their courage up, and then go up and sing their hearts out. Sometimes they're good - and sometimes they're pretty awful."

Cormac appeared skeptical. The song ended and there was a slight smattering of polite applause. Dylan sauntered onto the stage and the bar patrons erupted in cheers. Dylan chose to sing *'Living On A Prayer'* by Bon Jovi. Unlike most people who tried singing that song, Dylan did it justice. He belted it out and had a swarm of women dancing at the foot of the stage.

Jenna was laughing as she watched.

"He sings well, lass," Cormac pointed out.

"Yes, he does. It's one of the reasons he likes to come here. He's a frustrated rock singer. That, and the girls love him."

"I can see that they do. What of you? Do ye sing?"

"Not usually."

Cormac was about to speak when Dylan's song ended to whistles and applause. He bowed and left the stage, accompanied by his little band of groupies.

"Jenna, Jenna!" Her ex's friends were calling out to her, much to Jenna's chagrin. "Jenna, sing! Come on, please!"

Jenna just shook her head at them. They weren't about to take no for an answer and started chanting her name. She rolled her eyes and stood up.

"I guess I'm singing," she said to Cormac, who offered her a brilliant smile.

As she approached the stage, someone in the group called out, "Sing *'Rollin in the Deep'*, by Adele."

Cormac watched appreciatively as Jenna made her way onto the stage and stood behind the strange metal pole the people sang into. He had noticed it made their voices louder. When Jenna opened her mouth and began to sing, he was in awe. She had the most beautiful voice. She sang like an angel. Other people in the bar stopped what they were doing and paid attention, obviously enjoying her ability. People in the bar applauded and cheered when Jenna finished singing. She had a happy smile on her face as she made her way back to the bar and Cormac and settled on a barstool.

"Ye sing beautifully, Jenna," he said with admiration. "I've never heard such a wee lass with such a big voice."

Jenna laughed and Cormac thought she was the most beautiful woman he'd ever seen. She was looking at him differently than she had earlier in the day, and he began to think he might stand a chance.

The door opened and a tall, lanky man with spiky brown hair entered. He walked up behind Jenna, poked her in the ribs, and leaned in so his mouth was right beside her ear.

"Hey, babe, miss me?"

"I'm afraid not, Jonathan." Jenna eyed him suspiciously and Cormac moved a little closer to her. He felt an urge to shove this man away from Jenna, but he waited to see what this was all about. Edna had warned him that things were different in this time.

"Aw, come on, not even just a little bit?" Jonathan tugged on a lock of her hair.

"Knock it off, Jonathan." Jenna's face, which just moments before had been happy, was now looking very angry. Cormac put his arm around her shoulders, effectively blocking Jonathan from further contact with her.

"Who's this? Is he your new man?" Jonathan sneered, as he looked Cormac up and down.

"Aye. Yer right. I am and I suggest ye leave the lady be."

"Lady? That's a good one. When did people start calling you that?" he asked Jenna. When she didn't respond, he continued. "She's no lady and you're welcome to her. She'll make your life miserable, just like she did with mine."

"Cormac, really, you don't have to protect me from this jackass." Jenna glared at both men.

"Aye. I believe I do. 'Tis my duty as *yer man*." A slow smile spread across Cormac's lips and he looked directly into her eyes. Jenna began to feel a bit warm under his scrutiny, finding his gaze hypnotic.

"Jonathan. Go bother somebody else." Jenna dismissed him, keeping her attention on Cormac.

"Jonny, man, it looks like there's an empty stage and a microphone with your name on it," EJ said, attempting to diffuse the situation.

"Thanks, EJ. Don't mind if I do. This one's for you, Jenna." Jonathan blew her a kiss as he headed for the stage.

Jenna closed her eyes and shook her head.

"Lass, ye dinna need to listen to him," Cormac offered.

Jenna looked up at him and smiled tightly. "Thanks, but I'm fine."

Jonathan made his way onto the stage and announced, "I'm dedicating this next song to my ex, Jenna. I hope you all enjoy it, as much as I will."

Jonathan's friends began to cheer and laugh. Jenna could feel their eyes on her, waiting for her reaction. She refused to take her eyes off Cormac, wouldn't let anyone know how anxious she was. Jonathan began to sing Hall and Oates, '*You're A Rich Girl*', with a slight change to the lyrics. Jenna stood and clenched her fists. Cormac could tell she was about to head for the stage and he wrapped his arm around her waist and drew her back against his chest. He held her delicate hand in his and using his thumb massaged the fist away. Jenna sank into him and Cormac liked the feel of her body as it relaxed into his.

~~~

Jenna was so angry she was seeing red. She wanted to punch Jonathan so badly, but Cormac must have read her thoughts, because he pulled her into his embrace. Her first instinct was to fight it, but she didn't, because it felt good to lean into the warmth of his body. It instantly relaxed her and she forgot all about Jonathan and his *You're a Bitch* song. Sure, his friends were all laughing at her expense, but they were his friends, not hers. It obviously had been a mistake to come here tonight, but how could she have known he would be here?

Dylan headed her way with a concerned look on his face. "Don't worry, Jenna. I'll take care of him."

"No. Nobody's going to take care of him. Not you, and not Cormac. I'm just going to ignore him." Jenna reached out and grabbed Cormac's whiskey and drank the rest of it in one swallow. "EJ, can we get two more whiskeys, please."

"Sure thing. Coming right up."

Against her better judgment, Jenna downed the second whiskey, with Cormac giving her a puzzled look as he did the same.

EJ served them another drink and as Jenna sipped the whiskey, she explained to Cormac that Jonathan had been a successful musician, and she had sung back up for his band. That was before they got married, and before he decided Jenna would be his meal ticket. While Jenna was talking, Jonathan concluded his song and sauntered in their direction.

"Not cool, man," Dylan said, drawing himself up to his full height. "You shouldn't have done that."

"It's a free world. I can sing whatever I want." Jonathan directed his next comment Jenna's way. "I can't help it, if that song is perfect for you, Jenna." He laughed and looked towards his friends for their approval.

Jenna struggled to get out of Cormac's embrace, but before she could move, he had lifted her up and placed her behind him. He grabbed Jonathan by his shirt collar, lifting him off the floor.

"I think ye owe the lady an apology," Cormac growled.

He was a menacing figure and Jonathan looked worried as he hung in the air. Jenna watched him as his expression morphed from triumphant to terrified. She couldn't help but smile.

"Cormac, man, put him down," EJ ordered. "I think it would be best if you all left. I can't afford to have any trouble in here."

Cormac dropped Jonathan, who fell to the floor gasping for breath and desperately trying to steady himself.

"My apologies, EJ," Cormac said.

"Come on, let's go." Jenna took Cormac by the hand and led him towards the door. "Dylan, you coming?"

"I'll catch up in a few minutes."

As they headed for the door, Jenna was shaking. She was so angry that tears were pricking at her eyes. Jonathan was trying to humiliate her, and she'd be damned if she was going to let him get away with it.

"Cormac," Jonathan yelled as they walked through the door. "Watch your back, man."

Cormac turned and scowled at Jonathan, who, seeing he was in imminent danger, decided to turn tail and run back to his friends.

Once outside, Jenna broke down, anger overwhelming her. She stiffened her spine as Cormac took her into his arms, to soothe her as best he could. He spoke soft words in a language she didn't understand, but they were melting the ice she had built up around her heart. The whiskey she had downed warmed her insides, but Cormac was stoking the flames. Jenna felt herself softening and enjoying the close contact with Cormac. She really needed to get a grip here. She couldn't let what happened in the bar affect her, to the point where she might throw herself at Cormac just because he was there - and she was undeniably attracted to him.

~~~

Cormac wanted to tear Jonathan's head off and he knew that if the man did anything else to hurt Jenna, he surely would. He stood with her, wrapped in his embrace, and did his best to calm her. He suspected Dylan would have a word with Jonathan and then he would join them outside. Cormac moved to lean on a street post and he took Jenna with him. She went along willingly, much to his surprise. Jenna was a very spirited woman and because she was, he knew how hard it must be for her to let someone else take care of her. He wanted to be the one who did the caring. The thought surprised him. Cormac's feelings for her were growing, despite her sharp tongue and cool demeanor. He hadn't had much hope earlier in the day, but he could see the softness in her eyes and feel it in her arms as she let down her guard and wrapped them around him, so he could hold her close and protect her from the hurt she was suffering. She needed him, even if she didn't know it yet.

Dylan joined them, moments later.

"Let's go," he said.

They headed off down the street in search of another bar.

"Jenna, what about O'Reilly's? How does that sound?"

Jenna sniffled a bit and wiped at her eyes. "Yeah, that should work. Cormac might like it better, too."

Cormac smiled at her when her eyes met his. They continued their walk in silence and he looked around in amazement at the streetlights and the buildings, all lit up from within. At Breaghacraig, the clan didn't go out at night, unless it was absolutely necessary. It was much too dark to be able to see, unless one carried a torch. Here, it seemed everyone was out, with no worry at all for the dangers of the night. The cars and buses constantly passing by were also a source of many questions for him, but he dare not ask. As Edna had instructed, he wouldnae appear shocked by anything he saw.

They reached the second pub and went inside, to the sounds of Irish music being played by a live band. The atmosphere was loud and raucous in comparison to the karaoke bar they had just left. Everyone seemed to be truly enjoying themselves, as they clapped and stomped along with the music. Cormac wasn't sure why, but he felt more at home here than he had anywhere else he'd been, all day long.

Jenna ordered more whiskey for the three of them, seeming determined to drink the men under the table. They found an empty booth to sit in and Cormac became very aware of the fact that Jenna was quite into her cups. If she were sober, she wouldnae be leaning into him and have her hand resting on his knee. Not that he was going to complain about this development. Dylan winked at him and nodded in his cousin's direction. Cormac simply shrugged his shoulders. He wished there was something he could do, to make this night better for her. Drinking the amount of whisky she had consumed was not going to help.

"Cormac," Jenna was starting to slur her words. "I jush wanted to thank you, for shticking up for me back there."

"It was me pleasure, lass."

"I like it when you call me lash. Did you know you are probably the mosh handsome man I've ever sheen?"

"I didnae know that." Cormac chuckled.

"You are… really. I mean it."

"I ken ye need to stop drinking, lass." He decided it was time to intervene, before she got sick.

"No… I jush want one more, pleash."

"Jenna, Cormac's right. You're going to regret this in the morning. Why don't you let Cormac take you back home? I've got some unfinished business I need to take care of."

"Shtay away from Jonathan, Dylan. I mean it."

"I'm not talking about Jonathan. I met a pretty girl earlier, and we're going to meet up at her place."

"Oh… okay. Cormac, lesh go." Jenna swayed as she tried to stand up and Cormac steadied her before she fell over. "You're so sweet," Jenna giggled, clutching his sleeve.

"She's pretty drunk," Dylan observed.

"I ken it. Dinna fash. I'll be sure she gets home and to bed."

Dylan gave Cormac a questioning look.

"Alone." Cormac reassured him.

"I'll get you guys a cab." Dylan offered, and then headed outside to flag one down.

"Come, lass, let's get ye home."

As they hit the fresh air outside, Jenna swayed even more.

"Weeeee!" she cried.

Cormac was concerned she was going to fall, so he did the only thing that made sense and picked her up to carry her to the waiting cab.

Dylan paid the driver and told him the address. He handed Cormac his house key.

"Here, you'll need this to get into the house."

"And what of ye? How will ye get in?"

"Don't worry. I've got a spare," Dylan winked, as he prepared to close the cab door.

"Thank ye, Dylan."

The cab dropped them off in front of Jenna's house and Cormac lifted her into his arms again, carrying her up the stairs to the front door. Opening the door, he carried Jenna across the threshold and she began to giggle.

"What's so funny, lass?"

"You carried me, like I was a bride." She continued laughing, as if it was the funniest thing she'd ever heard.

Cormac was puzzled, but Jenna was in no condition to notice. Closing the door, he found the light switch and headed for Jenna's bedroom. Chester, who had been soundly sleeping by the front door, lifted his head in greeting and then promptly went back to sleep.

Jenna was resting her head on Cormac's chest and she reached up to caress his face. "Cormac... would you kiss me? Please?"

He nearly dropped her at the sound of her sweet voice requesting something he'd never dreamed would happen. She looked up at him with such longing that he couldn't speak. He reached her room and put her down by her bed.

"Come on... kiss me." Jenna stood on her tiptoes and brushed her lips across his. Fire shot through Cormac, from head to toe and all the places in between. He let her kiss him and found that he could not resist kissing her back. He wrapped his arms around her and let his hands wander over her back and hips. They slid up her sides and brushed her breasts. Jenna moaned softly. Her lips were soft and warm and he wanted more than anything to crawl into bed with her and explore her beautiful body. Being a gentleman, however, he would not allow that to happen.

Her breath was mingling with his and the kisses were becoming more and more impassioned. He had to end this now, because if he didn't, he wouldn't be able to stop.

"What's wrong?" Jenna asked, when he abruptly stopped kissing her and placed her away from him.

"Nothing is wrong, lass. Ye've just had too much to drink and I dinnae want to take advantage of ye."

"But I want you to make love to me."

"Not tonight, Jenna love. When I make love to ye, I want ye to remember it."

She giggled at that.

"Will you lie down with me? Just for a little while."

"Aye. I will happily do that."

He helped her take her boots off, examining the black leather and high heels with a smile on his face. Cormac then got her into bed, pulled the covers up over her, so he wouldn't be tempted, and then he lay down next to her.

"Whoa! The room is spinning," Jenna cried.

He pulled her in close and she rested her head on his chest.

"Close yer eyes and try to sleep. I'll be right here. I promise."

She did as he told her and drifted off to sleep, almost immediately. Cormac took the opportunity to examine her, while she was unaware and didn't have her guard up. She was truly beautiful. Her skin was soft and smooth and her lips were pursed into a pretty little pout. Her golden tresses lay strewn across the pillow and he couldn't help himself and curled a lock around his fingers. She was perfect in every way, as far as he was concerned, and he knew that starting tomorrow - he had a chance with her.

# FIVE

Jenna's head was throbbing and her mouth was as dry as the Sahara Desert. She tried to move, but couldn't. Something was anchoring her tightly in place. Her head rested on the hardest pillow she could recall sleeping on. Realizing she didn't have any pillows like that, her eyes shot open and the pain in her head increased tenfold. She tried to sit up. No luck. There was a very large, very masculine arm holding her down.

"What the…" she muttered.

The arm moved and she discovered it was attached to a fully clothed Cormac, who was just opening his incredible eyes to look at her.

"How be ye this morn, lass?" he asked as he stretched and sat up.

"What happened here? We didn't— did we?" She nervously awaited an answer, while simultaneously trying to remember what had actually happened last night.

"Nay, lass, dinna fash. Nothing happened, but not for lack of trying on yer part," Cormac chuckled.

"I'm sorry, but I don't remember inviting you to sleep in my room with me," she snarled.

"Well, ye did, lass. I wouldnae be here otherwise. I believe ye had a wee bit too much whiskey last night."

"Yuck. Don't remind me. Ooh, my head feels like it's going to explode." Jenna's hands went to her head as she groaned.

"Wait here, lass. I'll get ye some water. A verra wise woman once told me that ye need to drink lots of it, when ye feel as ye do."

"Can you bring me some aspirin, too? It's in the cabinet above the glasses, in the kitchen."

"Aye. I'll return quickly, lass."

Cormac left the room and Jenna replayed the night's events from the beginning, trying to piece it all together.

"What on earth did I do? I hope I didn't embarrass myself too much," she said to herself.

Bits of memory were making their way into her brain. She remembered Cormac carrying her up the stairs to the house. *That was nice of him.* He carried her into her room where she kissed him. *Oh, my God, I kissed him! He must think I'm easy - or worse.* But the kiss, as she remembered it was incredible, all soft, and warm. A very solid wall of man had wrapped himself around her and she'd liked it, very much. She was drunk, though. Maybe it seemed better than it really was. Just thinking about it was doing crazy things to her body, so it must have been pretty damn good. *Oh, no! I asked him to make love to me! It's official - I am never going to be able to look him in the eye again.*

Cormac walked back into the room to the sight of a very red-faced Jenna fanning herself with an old magazine. She immediately lowered her gaze, as if she had just found something very interesting to read.

"Are ye well, Jenna? You look a bit ill."

"I'm fine," she barked. That felt better. She needed to reestablish the boundaries she'd set yesterday. She definitely didn't want him thinking she was interested in him. Although he was very sweet, and protective of her, when Jonathan was being an ass. *So, he's a nice guy. What difference does that make? I'm going to stay as far away as possible. I don't need this right now. I used to think Jonathan was a nice guy, too. Hell, I married him!*

Cormac handed her the aspirin and the water.

"Can I get ye anything else, lass?"

"Yeah, you can leave me alone and get the hell out of my room." Yelling at Cormac was making her head hurt worse, but it was also allowing her to take back control of her wayward emotions.

"I'll leave ye, then. I can see that yer back to yer prickly self." Growling under his breath, Cormac turned on his heel and strode from the room, leaving Jenna to nurse her aching head and sort through her conflicted feelings.

~~~

Cormac soundly closed the door to Jenna's room. He was having a hard time understanding how she could be so sweet last night, and so thistle-like this morn. Could drinking all that whiskey have turned her into someone she was not?

The front door opened and Dylan walked through, looking a bit disheveled.

"Hey, dude, how was your night? Did ye get Jenna back here without any trouble?"

"Aye. There was no trouble," Cormac scowled.

"Your words are saying one thing, but your face is telling a different story. What happened?"

"Nothing happened. Yer cousin is in a verra bad mood this morning."

Dylan took a seat and motioned for Cormac to do the same. They eyed one another, both waiting for someone to speak.

"She was pretty out of it last night. Thanks for making sure she got home in one piece," Dylan finally announced.

Cormac nodded and continued to scowl.

"It couldn't have been that bad," Dylan said.

"It wasnae, until this morning. She was a different lass last night, sweet like honey and this morning, she's as prickly as a thistle. I dinna ken what changed."

Dylan grinned. "She sobered up, that's what changed. She always has her guard up, especially around men. She's been dealing with Jonathan for a while now and it's made her very skeptical of any man's motives. Plus, my guess is, she's a bit embarrassed about last night."

"Aye. I ken what ye speak of." Last night he'd thought there was hope for them, but this morning all of his hope had been thrown out the window. Why on earth did Edna think that Jenna would agree to be his wife? A better question yet - why would he *want* her to be his wife? A brief glimpse into the softer side of Jenna had him curious to find out.

~~~

Jenna was feeling badly about how she had treated Cormac. He hadn't done anything wrong. As a matter of fact, he had been a perfect gentleman. She should apologize to him for her behavior and leave it at that. The wall was back up and she wasn't planning to let it be knocked down any time soon.

As she was about to enter the living room, she could hear Cormac speaking with Dylan. He sounded hurt and confused by her ill treatment.

"Ahem." Jenna cleared her throat to announce her presence and both Cormac and Dylan glanced in her direction. "Cormac, I just wanted to apologize to you for my behavior last night and this morning. I was angry with my ex, and I took it out on you. I'm very sorry." She hoped she didn't look as embarrassed as she felt.

Cormac looked up in surprise at her words, a relieved smile spreading across his handsome face. "Apology accepted, lass."

"Good. I promise not to be all 'prickly like a thistle'." Jenna did her best to smile through her embarrassment.

"I'd like that verra much," Cormac said, ending Jenna's awkward apology. Chester had curled himself up into a ball at Cormac's feet and looked up adoringly when Cormac bent to pet him. "Yer a good dog, Chester. Do ye know that last night when we returned, he didnae even stir?"

"That's because he trusts you," Dylan said. "He's not like that with everyone. Chester hates Jonathan. Never warmed up to him."

"I cannae understand why," Cormac joked.

"Hey, let's go get some breakfast. Same place as last time. Okay?" Dylan asked.

"Aye," Cormac agreed.

"You just want us along to protect you, from that waitress who's in love with you," Jenna accused. "I'm on to you, Dylan."

"She's in love with Cormac, now," Dylan laughed.

"Cormac?" Jenna repeated in disbelief. Why did she suddenly feel jealous? She shouldn't. She had no claims on him; Cormac could see whomever he wanted.

"Yeah. She was all flirty with him, when we were in there yesterday. Told him to come back and ask for her table."

"Well then, we wouldn't want to disappoint her, would we?" Jenna tried to make her voice light and carefree, but somehow it didn't come out that way. Both Cormac and Dylan were watching her skeptically. "Come on, let's go," she urged.

~~~

Cormac was quite amused by the two ladies both vying for his attention. Sophia was obviously not happy to see Jenna with them when they arrived at the diner. She did everything possible to exclude Jenna and Dylan from her conversation with Cormac. As for Jenna, she was showing signs of jealousy and doing her best to pretend Sophia was invisible. They were both speaking to him at the same time and it was all Cormac could do to keep a straight face and answer both of them. Dylan was very amused by the whole situation, and constantly snickering under his breath.

"Ladies, I cannae possibly speak with ye when ye both talk at the same time." He purposely focused his attention on Sophia. He was enjoying this little game with Jenna. "Now, Sophia, what was it ye were saying to me?"

Sophia gave Jenna a triumphant smile.

"I was wondering what you were doing later today. I get off of work at four."

Jenna was just about to speak, but Cormac beat her to it.

"I'm afraid I willnae be able to see ye at that time, lass. Dylan tells me we're going to someplace called the East Bay."

Sophia giggled. "Cormac, you are so funny." She batted her eyelashes at him and positioned herself in such a way that he couldn't avoid seeing her cleavage when she touched his arm.

"Mayhap we can meet some other time." He winked and gave her a cocky grin.

Sophia was fanning herself with the menus. "I'd like that."

"Can you take our order please," Jenna said, her tone clipped.

"What would you like, Cormac?" Sophia asked, in the sweetest voice.

"I'll have what I had yesterday, lass, if ye dinna mind."

"I don't mind at all. Anything for you." Sophia continued ogling Cormac.

"Oh - My - God. Could you hurry it up already, Sophia? This is a restaurant, not a dating service," Jenna fumed.

Turning to Jenna with a growl, Sophia said, "What do you want?"

"I'd like a Denver omelet, please. And an orange juice."

Sophia didn't say anything in response.

"I'll have what Cormac's having," Dylan offered.

Sophia turned and winked at Cormac as she walked away.

"You really shouldn't encourage her, you know." Jenna said angrily.

"There's nothing wrong in flirting with a pretty lass," Cormac answered.

"You'll be sorry when she starts stalking you," Jenna testily offered.

"I'd have to agree with Jenna on that one," Dylan confirmed.

The restaurant was crowded, but Sophia managed to get them

their food in record time. She poured everyone coffee, again ignoring Dylan and Jenna.

"Grrr. She is really getting on my nerves," Jenna confessed as Sophia walked away.

"Why would she be annoying you?" Dylan questioned.

"She's just so obviously ignoring you and me. It's like we aren't even here, and if we say anything to her, she acts like we're disturbing her."

"The lass is working verra hard, Jenna. Ye shouldnae judge her." Cormac hid his grin.

"Never mind. We need to finish breakfast and get back to the house. I'd like to be across the bridge by noon."

They ate their breakfast in silence, interrupted only on those occasions when Sophia was fawning all over Cormac.

Of course, Cormac was no fool. He knew exactly what he was doing by encouraging the waitress.

"Jenna, ye have no reason to be jealous of Sophia," Cormac said.

She gave him a look of sheer disbelief. "I'm not jealous. Don't flatter yourself, MacBayne," Jenna snarled.

He laughed, "Aye, ye are jealous. I'm not a daft idjit. I know what I see."

"You are out of your mind, if you think I'm even remotely interested in you!"

"Ye and I both know the truth, Jenna, lass." He gave her the smile he knew made the lasses weak in the knees. He wasn't sure it was working on her. Now, she just seemed angry.

"Can we get out of here, please?" Jenna snapped.

Dylan was watching the interplay between Jenna and Cormac with an amused expression on his face. "Sure, let's go," he said.

Cormac stopped to thank Sophia and lifted her hand to his lips. She looked like she might faint and out of the corner of his eye he watched Jenna's reaction.

"MacBayne, we don't have all day here," she spat angrily. "Do your flirting on your own time."

With that, she stormed out through the door, with Dylan close on her heels.

Sophia was smiling triumphantly and Cormac felt a bit bad about using her to get to Jenna, but he'd probably never see Sophia again, so he didn't think he'd done anything terribly wrong.

# SIX

Back at the house, they loaded up Dylan's truck with everything they needed. Chester sat in the back with Jenna. She let Cormac sit up front with Dylan, for the simple reason that he wouldn't have fit in the smaller rear seat. Chester rested his head in her lap and sighed contentedly as they drove off.

Cormac appeared to be fascinated with the truck and was asking all sorts of weird questions. If he was trying to make her believe his crazy story about being from another time, he was doing an admirable job. The two men were preoccupied with each other, so she used the opportunity to examine Cormac without him knowing. He really was gorgeous and she sighed contentedly as she continued to give him a thorough once over. She couldn't believe she had propositioned him last night. Well, maybe she could. Any woman in her right mind would find him irresistible. That obnoxious waitress, Sophia, certainly had. Jenna couldn't understand why it had bothered her so much, to see Cormac flirting with the other woman. She didn't need another dead-beat man in her life. Jonathan had been enough and she was not going to repeat that mistake, ever again. Jonathan had only wanted her for her money. That was another reason to steer clear of Cormac. He didn't seem to have any money or even a place to live. He had somehow weaseled his way into their home and was taking advantage of their good graces. They'd been paying for all his food and drinks. If Dylan really didn't know him, just what was he up to? She'd better be careful. Letting him hang around might be a huge mistake.

"Cormac?" Jenna said, using her sweetest voice.

"Aye, lass."

"Where you come from, what do you do for work?" She needed to get a clearer picture of exactly who Cormac MacBayne really was.

"I be me brother-in-law's captain," Cormac answered.

"Your brother-in-law?"

"Aye. Robert MacKenzie. He's married to me sister, Irene."

"I see. Does he pay you to do this?" she wondered aloud.

"Aye. Why do ye ask, lass?" Cormac questioned.

"I was just curious. You don't seem to have any money."

"Edna said me coin would be of no use here."

Edna again. Who was she and what was her part in all of this? "And where did you say you lived?" Jenna asked.

"I live at Breaghacraig, with me family," Cormac replied.

Jenna was chewing on her bottom lip, wondering how she could discover if he was lying. So far, he seemed to be telling the truth. He wasn't evading her questions and he didn't hesitate with his answers. The fact that he claimed he was from another time troubled her. To top it all off, he expected her to believe his story.

"Cormac?"

"Aye, lass."

"You said you're a captain. Does your brother-in-law have an army, or something?"

"Aye."

"Wow. Really? Why does he need an army?" An army of his own, in this day and age, seemed highly suspect. *Cormac's story is getting stranger and stranger by the second.*

"To protect his family, his home, and his lands," Cormac responded.

Jenna sat quietly in the backseat, petting Chester and pondering

Cormac's answers.

"Is all well with ye, Jenna? Ye seem to be full of questions. Have I answered them to yer satisfaction?"

"Yes. I'm sorry. I'm just curious about where you come from. That's all."

"'Tis fine. Ye may ask me anything, and I will always tell ye the truth."

"I appreciate that, MacBayne." She dismissed him by focusing her attention on the dog and let him go back to quizzing Dylan on the way everything in the vehicle worked. She had decided she would maintain her distance, by referring to him as MacBayne. She would reserve the right to call him Cormac, for times when it worked to her advantage.

~~~

Sitting next to Dylan in the front of the truck was an education for Cormac. He was happy that he could ask anything of Dylan, and it would be answered without judgment. Jenna, on the other hand, was a puzzle he was having a hard time deciphering. One moment she was all sweetness and light - and the next she was calling him MacBayne and snarling at him. Rather than dwell on it, he focused his attention on the wondrous bridge they were crossing. He had never seen any-thing like it and he was craning his neck in all directions to get a better look, as they passed beneath the grey steel towering above their heads. He would have such amazing tales to tell, upon his return home.

As Cormac turned to watch the view through the back window, he noticed Jenna staring at him with a most unhappy expression on her face. He caught her eye and she smiled half-heartedly in his direc-tion.

"What time is everyone coming over, Dylan?" she asked.

"Some people are coming earlier, around six. The one's with kids - you know. Then everyone else will be there later."

"You have everything arranged, right?"

"No worries, Jenna. It's all taken care of. The only thing I have to do is get a keg delivered and we're good to go."

Cormac wasn't sure what they were talking about, and he raised an eyebrow in an unspoken question to Jenna.

"We're having our annual end of summer party tonight," Jenna explained.

He nodded in response somewhat worried about dealing with a lot of new, modern strangers he didn't know.

Jenna seemed to realize he was worried, and reassured him. "It's a lot of fun. You'll have a good time, I'm sure."

"Lots of beer and babes, my friend," Dylan chimed in.

"Beer and babes?" Cormac repeated.

"Mmhmm… you'll see. We have to get home in time to let the caterer and party planners into the house. We'll be there in no time."

"I dinna doubt it. This carriage travels verra fast," Cormac observed.

"This is nothing. You should ride in the Porsche, if you really want to see fast," Dylan boasted.

"I hate to break up the bromance you two seem to have going on, but Dylan, I don't want any trouble tonight. I hope you told your friends they're going to need to behave themselves. I don't want the neighbors calling the cops."

"Don't worry, I invited them," Dylan announced cheerfully.

"The cops? Or the neighbors?" Jenna retorted smoothly.

"Funny, Jenna."

"Dylan, what is a bromance?" Cormac asked. From the way Jenna had said the word, he couldn't imagine it being anything good.

Dylan laughed. "It's just what they call it, when two guys enjoy each other's company. Don't worry, it's nothing bad."

Jenna was snickering in the back seat as they pulled into the driveway of a large house, set at the very top of a hill on a narrow and curving road. There were other houses close by, but this house was, by far, the grandest of them all. As they were getting out of the truck, a heavy set, dark haired man walked up the driveway and waited to speak with Jenna.

"Hi, Jenna."

"Hey, Travis, what's up? I hope you're coming to the party to-night."

"Wouldn't miss it. I just thought you should know that Jonathan has been hanging around here. I've seen him coming out of the drive-way, a couple of times. I don't know if he's been in the house or not, and I wasn't able to stop him before he left, to ask what he was doing here."

Jenna looked worried. "I knew I should have changed those locks."

Cormac came over and stood by her side. He put an arm around her waist and surprisingly, she didn't resist.

"Thanks for letting us know," Dylan offered. "We'll see you later, Travis."

The man waved as he walked down the driveway and returned to the house next door.

"I can't believe Jonathan's been here. What are we going to do, Dylan?" Jenna anxiously ran her fingers through her hair.

"Don't worry. We'll get a locksmith out, first thing in the morning and change the locks. In the meantime, I guess we should go inside and see if he's done any damage to the house."

Cormac kept his hand on the small of Jenna's back as they mounted the steps to the front door and entered. To Cormac's eyes, everything looked very neat and orderly, but there was no way he would know if anything were wrong.

~~~

Jenna and Dylan made their way from room to room, checking to see if anything was missing.

Relief swept through Jenna when they found everything was ex-actly as it should be. *What is he up to?* She had a very uneasy feeling about the situation. Jonathan had been extremely angry with her when she got the marriage annulled, and he'd walked away with nothing. He obviously wanted her money and when he hadn't gotten it, he'd made his displeasure known in lots of different ways. The events at the karaoke bar paled, in comparison to some of the stunts he'd pulled since their divorce.

She didn't have too much time to worry about it however, as the doorbell rang and Dylan opened the door to the caterer and party planners. An army of people made their way into the house, to prepare for tonight's celebration. Food, decorations, flowers and serving trays made their way from the front door to the kitchen in the arms of the catering staff. The DJ arrived and set his equipment up, out on the back patio by the pool and the people who would be serving the food were getting lengthy instructions from the caterer.

"We should probably get out of their way and let them do their thing," Jenna suggested. "Dylan, why don't you show *MacBayne* around."

"Jenna, ye can call me Cormac," he responded, with a twinkle in his eye.

She ignored him, "Dylan?"

Dylan nodded. "Okay. I'll take care of it."

Jenna headed towards the stairwell. "I'm going to go upstairs and try to take a nap. My head still hurts, after last night."

"No worries. I'll handle everything down here," Dylan reassured her.

~~~

Cormac watched as Jenna made her way up the stairs. He wished there was something he could do, to win her trust. He knew she had just been through a terrible experience with her ex-husband and he could see the pain etched on her face whenever Jonathan's name came up in conversation. While he was more than capable of protecting her, Cormac could tell she wasn't going to let anyone else take care of her. Particularly him. He would have to work on that. She needed him, even if she was unaware of it.

"Cormac, let's go check out the pool," Dylan suggested, once Jenna disappeared.

"Aye."

They went out through the floor to ceiling doors, which folded open, exposing the entire back of the house. Cormac couldn't believe his eyes when he saw the pool. "What is this?"

"It's a swimming pool," Dylan answered.

Cormac bent down and put his hand in the water. "'Tis warm," he announced, surprised.

"It's heated. Nice, huh?"

"The water is so verra clear." Cormac touched the outside wall of the pool. "I've never seen anything like it. Ye have yer own wee loch."

Dylan grinned. "It's a man-made loch. You'll have to go for a swim later."

"Aye. I'd like that."

Dylan showed him around the house, which was filled with the most wondrous items. The kitchen fascinated Cormac. At three times the size of the verra nice kitchen at the other house, which he'd not had the time to explore, this one opened into the rest of the house. The ceilings were vaulted, giving the whole first floor a feeling of spaciousness. He loved the box Dylan called a *refrigerator*. It kept everything so verra cold. He knew his sister Irene would love it. The cooking was not done in an overlarge fireplace like it was back home, but in an oven and atop a stove. Water came out of a faucet - already hot, or cold. Cormac wondered where it came from. Did they have a well? He could spend all day trying to understand all of these things he had never seen before. Dylan was most helpful and answered most of his questions, but there were some things even Dylan didn't know. Jenna had so far refused to answer any of his questions, saying that he knew very well what everything was and to stop pretending he was from a time in the past. Cormac chuckled, thinking about her. He'd convince her yet. It was just a matter of time.

~~~

The doorbell started ringing at about 6 p.m. as Jenna and Dylan's married friends began to arrive with their babies and small children. The plan was for them to enjoy some time at the party and then be heading home before the rowdier crowd arrived at around 9 p.m.

The children were all enamored with Cormac. They seemed to think he was a giant, and they all stood and stared up at him. To put them at ease, he squatted down to their level and introduced himself. Jenna thought his Scottish accent made him seem all the more magical in their eyes and before long he had children crawling all over him. Cormac had become the perfect baby sitter.

"Where did you find him?" Jenna's friend Emily asked, with an envious look in her eyes.

"On the Marina Green," Jenna honestly offered.

"He's a keeper. Look at him, with those kids."

Jenna couldn't help but smile as she watched Cormac with the children. He even had Emily's baby boy tucked into his side. The kids were climbing over him, as if he was a jungle gym. He didn't seem bothered by it at all and in fact, encouraged their play. He took the children out to the barbecue area en masse and saw that they were fed, and then sat and told them stories about faeries and magical beings in the Scottish highlands. They were fascinated and their parents were happy beyond belief to have some uninterrupted time to chat with their friends.

"Are you okay, MacBayne," Jenna questioned at one stage. "I can see that you're a hit with the children, but if you need a break, I'd be happy to take over."

"I'm fine, lass. I miss my sister's children back home and these bairns are easing my heart a bit."

"Auntie Jenna," called a little tow-headed boy.

"Yes, James, what would you like?"

"Auntie Jenna, I like the big man," James said.

"His name is Cormac and I'm happy you like him." Jenna smiled warmly at the boy.

"Will he be here next time we come visit?" the boy asked.

"I don't think so. He lives in another country, very far away," Jenna answered.

"Awww…" All the children moaned at once.

"Don't worry, he'll be here all night," she assured them.

"Aye. I'm not leaving yet." Cormac gave Jenna a sweet, sexy smile that melted her heart.

"Well, I'd better get back to my other guests. Thanks for keeping them busy." She hurriedly crossed the room to a large group of laughing women. She didn't want to give him the impression that she might be falling for him, because she was determined she wasn't.

The other women were all talking about Cormac - and how handsome, sexy, and strong he was. They were speculating about what he might look like with his shirt off and about what might be under that kilt.

"Jenna?" Emily asked with an inquisitive smile.

"Don't look at me. I haven't seen him with his shirt off, and you ladies need to stop ogling him as if he's a Chippendale's dancer," Jenna protested.

"Okay, if you say so miss, but I think I might wrap him up and take him home with me," Emily laughed.

"I think Ben might object to that," Sarah chimed in. "So, I'll take him home with me."

"No one is taking him home with them." Jenna sounded a bit testy, even to her own ears.

The other women simply giggled and eyed her jealously. She had to admit, she was having a difficult time keeping her emotions in check where Cormac was concerned. *Keep your distance. He's luring you into his web of sexiness. Grrr…*

Cormac watched Jenna from across the room and completely enjoyed the sight of her turning from a very becoming shade of pink to crimson red. Whatever those lasses were saying to her, was making her verra uncomfortable. He was pretty sure they were talking about him. The surreptitious gazes sent his way were a sure giveaway. He had been enjoying the little ones verra much, but it was time for them to go and they all lined up to give him hugs and kisses goodbye. Some cried at having to leave and others yawned sleepily in their parents arms. Everyone thanked him profusely and offered him something called babysitting jobs. He guessed that was what he had just been doing.

The families had no sooner walked out through the door than another crowd of people started arriving. They were loud and boisterous and the greetings ranged from handshakes, slaps on the back, to kisses, and hugs.

"Cormac, I want to introduce you to my former team mates," Dylan said proudly. "I was on the football team in college, until I blew my knee out."

"Football?"

"I know you don't know what it is, but it's the greatest sport ever. The guys are going to go downstairs to the game room and we're going to play some video games. I'll explain it all to you while we're down there. Come on."

Dylan led the way, spouting off names as he passed a group of verra large men. "Sam, Tony, Diesel, JoJo, Tank..."

Cormac couldn't possibly remember all their names, but it really didn't seem to matter. They all greeted him with firm handshakes and a few slaps on the back as they headed downstairs to a room Cormac hadn't yet seen.

"This is the game room, Cormac. You can play pool over there," he said pointing at a large table, the top of which was covered in green fabric. The table had holes in the corners and in the sides and there were many different colored balls set within a triangle and sitting atop it.

"This is an air hockey table. And this... this is foosball."

Cormac was both amazed and confused by all he was seeing.

Dylan pointed out another area of the room. "But this, over here, is the best of all. This is our video game system. Don't worry, we'll show you how to play."

"Don't they have these things where you come from in Scotland,

Cormac," Sam asked.

"Nae, we dinnae have anything like it."

"Well, you're in for some fun. We'll go easy on you, don't worry," Tank chimed in.

"Thank ye," Cormac said, wondering just what was about to happen.

Upstairs, Jenna was busy greeting more friends, who were coming through the front door in a steady stream. Everyone was eating, drinking and generally having a very good time. The caterer had the food under control. Trays were being presented to the guests with various hors d'oeuvres, beautifully created in easy to eat portions. The barbecue had been fired up out on the patio and lanterns, candles and small outdoor lights cast a magical glow over the pool and waterfall. Those who brought their swimsuits were enjoying the hot tub, as well.

A commotion at the front door ruined Jenna's dreams of a trouble-free night. A few of her male friends were trying to prevent someone from entering. Her neighbor, Travis, called downstairs for Dylan, and an army of oversized football players, followed by Cormac, made their way upstairs to help.

"What's going on?" Jenna called.

"Jonathan's here," Travis answered, as he headed her way.

"What? Why?" Jenna was nearly beside herself. She could feel her blood starting to boil. *The nerve of him, to show up here!* She pushed her way through the crowd, which had formed near the entryway.

"What are you doing here?" she calmly asked, when she came face-to-face with her ex. She couldn't believe she had her voice under such control, because the adrenaline coursing through her veins had her shaking like a leaf. Cormac was at her side in a heartbeat, and put a steadying arm around her waist.

"I heard you were having a little soiree tonight, and I assumed my invitation got lost in the mail. I didn't want you to miss me, so here I am," Jonathan casually announced.

"No one invited you," Jenna responded.

"Really? I'm surprised. I've been invited to all the other bashes."

Jonathan raised his eyebrows as if he couldn't believe what he was hearing. "Now that I'm here, I guess I'll just have a little something to eat and drink, and then I'll be on my way," Jonathan announced, pushing his way through the door.

"No! Get out now," Jenna barked angrily.

The crowd of big guys surrounded Jonathan instantly, and he backed up towards the door, lifting his hands in surrender. "Okay. Okay. I'm going. You'll be seeing me around though. Don't you worry about that, Jenna. I see you've got your new man candy standing guard, but I'm not afraid of him." Glaring at Cormac he snarled, "I still owe you, dude. You'll be hearing from me."

Cormac started towards him, but Jenna grabbed his arm. "Just leave it. The sooner we get him out of here, the better."

The crowd of men followed Jonathan out of the house and watched him get into his car and drive away. The group came back inside, slapping each other on the back, proud of themselves for handling the situation and muttering about kicking Jonathan's ass.

"I'm hungry," Dylan announced. "Let's get something to eat."

He was like the pied piper, followed by his entourage; they descended on the trays like a flock of starving seagulls and then headed out to the barbecue area.

"Are ye alright, lass?" Cormac remained at Jenna's side, and she hated to admit it, but his concern was sweet.

"Yeah, I'm fine. I've come to expect this kind of thing from him. I wish he'd find someone new to torture and leave me alone."

"Dinna fash. I am here. I will protect ye."

Despite the fact that she had been very happy to have him by her side during the commotion, she responded rather sharply. "I don't need you or anyone else to protect me. Now, if you'll excuse me, I have guests to see to." She stormed off across the room and didn't look back to see the look of hurt she knew would be on Cormac's face.

# SEVEN

S hocked at her own behavior, Jenna gave herself a good talking to. *Stop being so rude. What is wrong with you? Jonathan is the one you should be angry with, not Cormac.* She was typically not a mean-spirited person, but she was having such a hard time controlling her mood. One minute she was calm and the next she was ready to explode - and she was afraid she was taking it all out on poor Cormac. She didn't know how she could make it up to him, without giving him the wrong impression, but she'd try. She checked in on her guests, making sure they all had enough food and drink and then she went off in search of Cormac. She found him outside seated by the pool, lost in thought.

"Hey," she said, as she sat down next to him.

He didn't say anything. Instead, he continued to gaze out over the water.

"I'm sorry. I don't know what's wrong with me and I certainly don't know why I keep yelling at you. You've done nothing but try to help and I'm grateful for that." She tipped her head to the side, so she could get a look at his face. Receiving no response, she touched his arm and felt a head to toe rush of wanting him, which left her weak at the knees. He felt it too, she could tell by the way his head jerked up and his eyes found hers.

They were so blue. How was it possible for anyone to have eyes of such a brilliant color? She could see the hurt she had put there, and her heart ached for him. Cormac placed his hand over hers, where it rested on his arm and before she knew what she was doing, she leaned forward and softly brushed her lips over his. His response was immediate - he reeled her into his arms and kissed her back, gently at first and then more passionately. Jenna allowed herself to let go of the control she usually so carefully kept in place, throwing her arms around his neck and tangling her fingers in his silky black locks. His tongue played at the crease in her lips, asking to be let in. Lost in passion, Jenna allowed it. He tasted salty and sweet all at once and he also tasted of beer. His hands settled on the curve just above her backside, pulling her closer. Jenna didn't resist, melding her body to his, in order to be as close as she possibly could. The sounds of the party had faded into the background and she didn't care what other people might think of her as she placed herself fully in Cormac's hands. Coming up for breath, they looked longingly into each other's eyes. There was an unspoken agreement passing between them and then the spell was broken by Dylan and his friends, as they grouped together to pick up both Jenna and Cormac, and threw them into the pool.

Jenna sputtered to the surface and could barely see, with her drenched hair hanging into her eyes. Cormac came up right next to her and pulled her close, gently brushing her hair back from her face. They looked at each other and simultaneously laughed.

"Dylan! I'll get you for this," Jenna shouted at her cousin, although secretly, she couldn't think of anywhere she'd rather be than in the grasp of Cormac MacBayne, whose muscular arms held her securely against him.

A tidal wave washed over them as everyone began removing shirts, shoes, and diving in beside them. Cormac's facial expression was one of horror as he watched Jenna pulling her very tiny little dress off. He tried to stop her, but she was having none of it.

"Don't worry. I've got my bathing suit on under this," she smiled. "You might want to take that kilt off. It must be pretty heavy with all that water it's soaking up."

"Are ye sure, Jenna?" Cormac questioned.

"Yeah, go for it."

Cormac unwrapped the length of plaid fabric around his waist and Jenna suddenly remembered what the appropriate attire was beneath a kilt. Absolutely nothing. He pulled his t-shirt over his head, grabbed her dress, and then swam to the side where he deposited everything. His tight backside emerged as he dove under the water and swam back to her. She was speechless to say the least, when she found herself up against a very naked Cormac MacBayne.

The rest of the crew in the pool decided they'd join in on the skinny-dipping and Jenna found that she couldn't find a place to look, amidst the group of suddenly very naked men and women. There was plenty of laughing and splashing, but no one, other than Jenna, seemed the least bit uncomfortable.

"I'd better get out and make sure everything is going smoothly inside." Jenna excused herself as she disengaged from Cormac's embrace and swam to the steps. As Cormac began to follow her she shouted, "Stay where you are, Cormac. I'm fine, really." She didn't look back as she headed for the house. "I'm just going to get towels for everyone." *Good excuse,* she thought. She needed to get away from Cormac, for long enough to distance herself from emotions that were pushing her 'I'm-not-getting-involved' attitude to the side, in pursuit of the lusty agenda her body had in mind.

~~~

Needing to cool his ardor, Cormac swam to the waterfall and let the icy water splash over his body. Watching Jenna walk away in the odd little bits of clothing she called a *bathing suit* had him more than ready to follow - partially to cover her from the view of the others, and partially to find out if that kiss they shared would lead where he hoped it would.

Closing his eyes, Cormac tipped his head back and enjoyed the feel of the water coursing through his hair. The sounds of feminine giggles from nearby alerted him to the fact that he was not alone, and upon opening his eyes, he was surprised to see he was surrounded by a number of naked women, all smiling, and observing him with obvious admiration.

"Ladies," he nodded. As he attempted to move away from them, the circle around him tightened.

"You're a cute one," the red-haired lass with the emerald green eyes said.

"Cute?" Cormac repeated, not knowing what she meant.

"I'm Amy. And you are?" she asked.

"Me name is Cormac. I'm pleased to meet ye."

The girls all giggled.

"I love your accent," the dark haired girl on his right said, as she moved closer.

"Thank ye," Cormac replied. "Are ye a friend of Jenna's?"

"No, we're here with the guys."

He wasn't sure which guys, so he looked around to see if anyone was missing them. No one seemed to notice his dilemma.

"Dylan's friends," yet another girl said.

"No one told us there was going to be a hot English guy here," Amy said.

"I be Scottish, lass," he replied, feeling insulted.

With that, they all started oohing and aahing in chorus. Cormac was getting a bit nervous. That was not his usual reaction to women who were interested in him, but this time he didn't want their attention. In the past, he would have enjoyed the company of the lot of them, but now he suddenly and inexplicably wanted to be out of the pool. Where had Jenna gone? He moved to swim past the girls, but the redhead wrapped herself around him. She had her arms around his neck and her legs around his waist. She was looking him right in the eye, with her nose touching his. Of course, Jenna chose that very moment to return, along with some of the catering staff. They all carried armloads of dry towels. Jenna took one look at Cormac, and stopped in her tracks, before she dropped the towels and ran back inside.

"Hey, Amy. What do you think you're doing? You're supposed to be here with me," the man Dylan had introduced to Cormac as Tank yelled, from across the pool.

"Just having some fun, babe. Nothing for you to worry about." Amy disentangled herself from Cormac and swam across to Tank, giving him a kiss on the lips and putting herself in the exact same position she was just in with Cormac. The other lasses followed, latching on to the rest of Dylan's friends.

"Jenna's pretty pissed," Dylan said, as he swam up to Cormac. "What did you do that for?"

"The lass threw herself at me! I didnae ask her to. I need to find Jenna and explain to her," Cormac was worried; Jenna had seemed extremely upset.

Dylan laid his hand on Cormac's shoulder. "I'd leave her alone for now, if I were you. Let her cool off. I'll talk to her later for you."

Cormac shook his head ruefully. "Dylan, I cannae ask ye to intervene for me every time something goes wrong with Jenna."

"Okay, but I'm telling you, she's not going to want to hear it right now."

"I'm going to go find her," Cormac said, and he could hear the determination in his own voice.

"Don't say I didn't warn you."

"Dylan, I'm nae afraid of yer cousin. She's but a wee lass, with a big temper." Cormac swam for the side of the pool and grabbed a towel, which he wrapped around his waist before beginning his search for Jenna.

~~~

Jenna couldn't believe her eyes. She had just started, stupidly, to think Cormac might be what she needed in her life, at this moment in time. She wasn't out of his sight for more than five minutes and he was already glued to some girl she didn't even know! *Typical man.* Well, she wasn't about to let that happen again. To think, she had kissed him! What was wrong with her? She couldn't seem to keep her lips to herself when he was around. *I hope you learned your lesson this time, Jenna. Men are not to be trusted, no matter how good they kiss.*

"Jenna, I must speak with ye." Cormac appeared in the doorway to her bedroom.

"Not interested." Jenna shut him down immediately. "Please leave my room." She walked to the door, waiting for him to leave and prepared to close the door and lock it behind him.

"Nae. I'll not go until ye've heard what I've come here to say." Cormac stood with his hands on his hips, filling the doorway and looking very determined about speaking with her.

"I already told you, I'm not interested. What don't you understand about that?"

"Jenna, yer eyes saw something that was not as it seemed."

"Oh, really! Well, my eyes sure saw you and your hands full of that busty redhead and I'm pretty sure I wasn't imagining it." Jenna refused to look at him. All she could see was a naked Cormac and a naked redhead in each other's arms. It made her furious.

"Yer right, but 'tis nae what ye think. I was trying to swim past her and the other lasses when she wrapped herself around me. I couldnae believe it. I told ye I would not lie to ye and I havnae. I would never do something like that to hurt ye. I want to spend my time here with ye, nae with anyone else."

Jenna was not good with confrontation. She hated it. There was always confrontation with Jonathan and she couldn't deal with it anywhere else in her life.

"I really don't need this right now. I'd appreciate it, if you'd leave me alone so I can think."

Cormac looked totally defeated. He just stood there, not moving.

"Please," Jenna softly said.

He sighed and dejectedly left her room. She closed the door behind him and wondered for the millionth time, what had gotten into her.

Cormac spent the rest of the party downstairs in the game room, avoiding the amorous lasses in attendance. He had never met a group quite like them. Back at Breaghacraig, the ladies could be forward, but never so many all at one time. He wanted nothing to do with it. He was trying to prove to Jenna that he only had eyes for her and if it meant isolating himself in the game room, then that was what he was going to do.

He could hear people leaving upstairs, as he lay sprawled across the sofa. The party had wound down and there were only a handful of Dylan's friends left. As far as Cormac knew, Jenna had not left her bedroom after she closed the door on him. He had seen two different sides to Jenna. The soft side and the hard side. He knew the hard side was her way of keeping people at a distance. He also knew that he had the power to turn that hard side into soft, yielding Jenna. The Jenna who had kissed him, after she had yelled at him. He was so confused. He had never cared enough to let a woman baffle him before, but Jenna was proving to him that he did care. He just didn't know what he was going to do about it. His days here were going to come to an end. He still had time left, but it certainly didn't appear that Jenna was going to go anywhere with him, at least not willingly - and he was not going to force her. He came here to make Jenna his, and so far he was failing miserably.

"Cormac! What are you doing down here all by yourself?" Dylan asked when he came down the stairs, after showing the last few stragglers out.

"I'm attempting to stay out of trouble." Cormac felt miserable; he couldn't even muster a smile.

"I believe you are already in trouble. I don't think you would have made it any worse by staying upstairs and enjoying yourself," Dylan responded.

"Dylan, how is it that your cousin is yelling at me one minute, kissing me the next and then angry with me again - all in one night?" Cormac was exasperated and he flung his arms in the air as he spoke.

"Dude, relax. It's Jenna we're talking about. She won't stay mad at you. I guarantee by tomorrow morning she'll be all apologies. Believe me, I've been on the receiving end of her temper on many occasions, and she hasn't thrown me out yet. I don't think you have anything to worry about, bro."

"I hope yer right, but I'm only here for five more days and I'm not making any progress."

"I beg to differ. She was kissing you tonight, wasn't she?" Dylan asked.

"Aye. She was." Cormac smiled thinking about it. "And *she* kissed me. I didnae initiate it. It was just like last night, when she had too much to drink."

"Well, she is definitely into you. She doesn't do that with just any-one," Dylan reassured him.

Cormac began to feel more hopeful as he stood and clapped Dylan on the back. "I be verra tired and I'd like to go to bed."

"I hear you. I'm just going to make sure everything is locked up and that the alarm is on, and then I'm going to hit the hay too."

"The hay? Do ye nae have a bed, Dylan?" Cormac asked.

"It's just an expression, bro. I have a very comfy bed and some-one up there keeping it warm for me." Dylan raised his hand in the air and Cormac looked confused. "High five?"

"I dinna ken."

"Let me show you. Put your hand up in the air, just like mine. Now we're going to slap hands." Cormac did as Dylan instructed. "That's a high five. In this case, it would be like congratulating me on my good luck at having a hot babe waiting for me in my bed."

"I see." Cormac said. "Well, enjoy yerself then, *dood*." Cormac tried the word he'd heard Dylan use so many times.

Dylan laughed and said, "You're catching on, dude, I like it."

They headed up the stairs and Cormac was happy to have Dylan here with him. He reminded him of his brother, Cailin. "What will the day hold for us tomorrow, Dylan?"

"Maybe surfing. I want to be sure you experience things you don't have back home."

"Surfing?"

"You'll see. I'll check the weather in the morning and we'll go from there."

Cormac shook his head in disbelief. He was having a hard time understanding a lot of what was being said around him. It wasn't that he didn't understand English, but these words were not what he was used to. He really needed to lie down as he was feeling overwhelmed by the events of the past two days. He was happy when his head finally hit the pillow in his bedroom and oblivion overtook him.

# EIGHT

Cormac rose bright and early, as he always did back at Breaghac-raig. He made use of the shower and marveled at the fact that hot water was shooting out of the wall. The bathroom steamed up and he thought this had to be the greatest creation of all time. He made use of the various soaps and when he was done, he felt refreshed and ready to conquer the day and, if he was lucky, Jenna. He found himself, once again, only wearing a towel. He didn't know what Jenna had done with his plaid and he didn't have anything else to wear, so he left the room to see if Dylan was up yet. *Mayhap he will have something for me to wear.*

The smells of breakfast cooking hit his nose and his stomach began to grumble, reminding him that he hadn't eaten verra much last night and he was now ravenous. He followed his nose to the kitchen and peeking in he saw Jenna, with her back to him, working at the stove. She was singing, and the sound of her sweet voice melted his heart. He walked up behind her and peeked over her shoulder, to see what she was making.

"Oh!" Jenna exclaimed. She appeared frightened by his sudden appearance.

"I'm sorry, lass. I didnae mean to scare ye."

She was clutching her chest. "The least you could do is make some noise when you come up behind me like that." She was gasping for breath.

"Are ye well this morning, Jenna?"

"I was fine, until you scared me half to death." She smiled, letting him know she wouldn't hold it against him. "I thought I'd make you some breakfast this morning. Are you hungry?"

"Aye. Verra hungry. Ye can cook?"

"Of course. I don't eat out all the time, you know. I like to cook and I think I'm pretty good at it."

"I'll be the judge of that, lass." Cormac teased her with a wink.

"Sit. I'll get you a plate." Jenna reached into the cupboard to get out plates and cups and then opened the silverware drawer to get utensils.

Cormac sat at the counter and watched her every move, appreciating the look of her, with her hair still wet from the shower, and wearing a short robe and barefoot. She caught him watching her and smiled shyly.

"Cormac, it seems I'm forever apologizing to you. I got a text message from Tank this morning. He told me Amy was to blame for the incident in the pool. I'm sorry I didn't believe you, and I'm embarrassed by my behavior. It's just that I've been lied to a lot lately, and I immediately think the worst. It's not fair to you. You're obviously not Jonathan, but he's colored everything in my world and made it a little darker. I guess I'm just not seeing through that darkness very well."

Dylan had been right about Jenna. He knew her so well and Cormac knew her very little. He would have to start taking Dylan's advice where she was concerned.

Jenna laid the food on the counter and handed him a serving spoon. "Here you go. Help yourself. And if you don't mind me asking, why are you still wearing a towel?" She arched an eyebrow and nodded in the direction of his hips.

Cormac helped himself and savored a piece of bacon, closing his eyes as he did so. "I dinna have me kilt and Dylan is not awake yet. I thought to ask him for something to wear."

"Oh, I'm sorry. I should have realized that you didn't have anything to replace the kilt. It was soaking wet last night. It's wool, so I didn't want to put it in the dryer and have it shrink on you. It'll take some time to dry. I put it outside in the sun."

"Dryer?" Cormac was repeatedly puzzled by these unfamiliar words and items.

"Sooner or later, you and Dylan are going to have to stop pulling my leg," she laughed and continued eating. "I think Dylan has some clean clothes in the laundry room. After we eat, I'll get them for you."

"Thank ye. The food, 'tis verra good, Jenna."

"I'm glad you like it. Tell me more about yourself, Cormac."

"What would ye like to know, lass?"

"The usual. Where you're from, your family, why you're *really* here."

"Hmmm… I've shared some with ye already and I can tell ye more, but I dinnae think ye'll believe me."

"You won't know for sure, unless you give it a try."

"Fine, then." He took a deep breath and began. "I be from Breaghacraig in the Scottish highlands. I live there on Clan MacKenzie land with me family, me brother Cailin and his wife, and me sister, Irene. Irene is married to the Laird of Breaghacraig. His name is Robert MacKenzie. 'Tis a beautiful place. I'd love to show it to ye, Jenna," he said hopefully.

Jenna was listening carefully. "Did you say your brother's name is Cailin?"

"Aye, I did. Why do ye ask?" Cormac hoped he hadn't said too much.

"That name sounds familiar to me, that's all. I don't know why though." Jenna looked perplexed. "Oh well, go on with your story. It'll come to me."

"Well, there's nae much more to tell."

"Why are you here? You didn't answer that part of the question."

"Ye willnae like me answer, Jenna and I dinnae wish to make ye angry with me again."

"I'm trying to be open minded this morning. I won't get angry, I promise."

She looked to be telling the truth, so Cormac said, "I'm here to find ye, Jenna. I told ye that the first time I saw ye. Ye see, I wanted a wife and Edna said she could help me, but that I'd have to travel to San Francisco to find you."

"So, this Edna said I was the one you were looking for?"

"Aye."

"And she knew my name?"

"Aye."

"So, if I'm to believe you, I have to believe that a woman named Edna, whom I've never met, knows me by name and she somehow sent you here through the fog to find me."

"That be true. Dinnae forget that Edna is a witch."

"That's right and you're also from the sixteenth century, correct?"

"Aye. I know it seems daft, but do ye nae believe in magic?"

"Not really. I need proof, I have to see it with my own eyes."

Cormac took another forkful of pancakes. "I've never eaten anything like this before. I like it verra much indeed."

Jenna smiled at him as if he was a daft fool. How was he ever going to make her believe him? He'd need to ask Edna. Dylan believed him and Cormac didn't even have to work verra hard to convince him. Dylan believed in magic - *that* was the difference. How sad that Jenna's world was so black and white. Cormac knew he had his work cut out for him, but he was starting to believe she could be worth it.

"I know ye believe that Dylan is playing a trick on ye, but try to think differently of it. What if it were true? Do ye not see that I am different from the people of San Francisco?"

"Wow! That's a loaded question. You're not from around here, obviously, but if you spent any time in San Francisco, you might know enough not to use the people here as your guideline to what's normal." She giggled at her own words and then sipped her coffee. "I'm okay with the Scotland part of your story, but the rest of it is just too weird. However, I am willing to go along with it, just to see how far you two will take this."

Just then the flat box that Jenna always kept with her, buzzed on the counter. She picked it up and laughed. She poked at it with her fingers and then put it down.

"Jenna, what is that?" Cormac asked pointing at the object.

"Testing me already, I see. Okay. It's a cell phone. Dylan just texted me from his bedroom to see if I made enough breakfast for him and his overnight guest. They'll be down shortly."

"Everyone has these *cell phones*?" Cormac asked curiously. "Are they important?"

"I guess you could say that. Most people walk around with them in their hands all the time, or at the very least in a purse or pocket."

"What do they do?"

Jenna raised a disbelieving eyebrow. "Seriously? They keep us in touch with each other. Don't you have cell phones or land lines where you come from?"

"Nae. We visit with each other, or write letters and send messengers with them. They can take days or weeks to reach their destination."

"Wow. Sounds like a lot of work, if you ask me."

"Are ye using *sarcasm*? I believe Dylan said it was your weapon of choice."

At that, Jenna burst out laughing and couldn't seem to stop. Tears formed in her eyes and Cormac wasn't sure how to respond. He hadn't seen her enjoying herself this much since he'd met her. She came to a hiccoughing stop and Cormac reached out to brush a happy tear from her cheek and then continued caressing her skin with the back of his hand.

"Ye are a beauty, Jenna, and even more so when yer happy." He hoped he hadn't said the wrong thing, because she stopped smiling, stood up abruptly and began removing their dishes from the table. She rinsed them off in the sink and put them in what Dylan had called the dishwasher.

"Dylan says we're going to head to the beach today. Let's go find you a pair of board shorts to wear and then I'm going to pack some lunch to take along."

Cormac stood and followed Jenna into the next room. It was lined with shelves and there were stacks of neatly folded clothing everywhere.

"One of these days, Dylan is going to put his clothes away, but I guess we should be happy he hasn't yet, because now we can find you something to wear." Jenna went through the stacks and pulled out an armful of clothing which she handed to Cormac. "Hopefully they'll fit, because even though you're looking pretty good in that towel, we don't want to have the women around here fainting at the sight of you."

He stood there, staring at the pile in his arms, and when it occurred to him that Jenna had just said she liked the way he looked, a satisfied grin lit his face.

"Is something wrong?" Jenna asked.

"Nae. Will I wear them all?" he asked with a puzzled expression.

"You're pretty funny," Jenna laughed. "I'll play along. Here, put these on, and this." She handed him the board shorts and a t-shirt. "I guess you need shoes, too. Dylan will have to get those for you. A pair of flip-flops should do. Go get dressed and then come back. By then Dylan and his *lady* friend should be here.

~~~

Jenna was proud of herself. She had managed to apologize to Cormac without kissing him again. The sight of him in that towel this morning had put thoughts into her head that shouldn't be there. Thankfully, she hadn't embarrassed herself by *accidentally* causing the towel to drop to the floor. A surge of warmth covered her from head to toe and she didn't need a mirror to know she was quite red from blushing. She hurried down the hallway to her room where she found her sexiest bathing suit. She put it on and looked at herself in the full-length mirror that created her closet doors. *Not bad, Jenna. This one will work nicely.* She checked herself out from all angles and when she was satisfied, opened the closet to remove a pretty flowered sundress. She finished her look with a pair of sandals, a floppy hat and sunglasses.

She wasn't sure whom she was trying to impress, but the one thing she knew for sure was - it was not Cormac MacBayne.

Arriving back in the kitchen, as predicted, Dylan was sitting there with a pretty brunette woman.

"This is Samantha. Samantha, my cousin Jenna." Dylan made the introductions and Samantha looked a bit embarrassed.

"Nice to meet you, Samantha," Jenna offered.

"You, too." Samantha said. "Dylan, I really need to go. Would you mind walking me to my car?"

"Sure," he said as he put an arm around her shoulders.

As they got up to leave, Cormac returned. He looked amazing in Dylan's shorts and t-shirt. Jenna gulped and quickly turned to open the refrigerator and stick her head inside. She needed to cool off. Spontaneous combustion seemed like a distinct possibility.

"Good morn to ye, Dylan," Cormac said, as he smiled at Samantha.

Jenna pulled some things out of the fridge and watched as Samantha gawked at Cormac. *Put your eyes back in your head,* was what she wanted to say, but instead she just stood there and watched the show.

Dylan reluctantly introduced Samantha to Cormac, who bowed in her direction.

*Who does that?* Jenna thought, as she slammed her refrigerator finds down onto the counter. Everyone turned and looked her way. "Sorry. They slipped out of my hands," she lied. Jenna stood there like a zombie as Dylan and Samantha left the room. *What am I getting so worked up over? I already decided I wasn't interested in Cormac, right?* Wrong. She was more than interested.

"What are ye thinking in that pretty wee head of yers?" Cormac was right beside her, touching her forehead with his finger *and burning a hole in it.*

"Nothing. I… just…" she stammered. "I was going over the list of things we need to take with us." She pressed an unopened package of cold cuts to her face. "Whew! It's warm today. I guess it's a good thing we're going to the beach."

"'Tis nae so warm," Cormac said. "Are ye well?" He reached out to lay a hand on her forehead.

"I'm fine." Jenna dodged his hand, before he managed to make contact. "Would you mind coming with me into the garage, to get the cooler?"

"Aye. I'd be happy to help ye."

"Follow me," Jenna ordered as she made her way from the kitchen to the garage. Cormac was right in step behind her. She pointed out the cooler, which he picked up. "Bring it over here to the freezer, so we can fill it with ice."

Jenna opened the freezer and Cormac's eyes grew wide. "This is just a bigger version of the one in the kitchen," Jenna pointed out. "You look like you've never seen one before."

"I havnae. We have none of these things at Breaghacraig."

"Sounds like you live in the Stone Age," she teased. "Can you grab those two bags of ice and we'll put them in the cooler."

Cormac hesitated for only a second and then did as she asked. Jenna signaled him to follow her again and he brought the cooler into the kitchen.

"Set it here by the sink, please," she requested. "I'm going to make some sandwiches. Do you like tuna, egg salad or cold cuts?" From the expression on his face, she figured it might be all, or none, of those. "I'll just make some of everything," she suggested.

Dylan entered the kitchen looking happy. "Jenna, I'll get the chairs into the truck. Anything else you want me to grab?"

"The beach bag, towels… the usual. Cormac, why don't you go help him with that?"

Cormac nodded and followed Dylan back into the garage.

Jenna got to work making the sandwiches and filling the cooler with water, sodas and beer. She had some nice, late season peaches she had purchased at the Farmer's Market at the Ferry Building when they had been in the city and she packed those as well. Jenna looked in the refrigerator for anything else that might be good to bring along. She knew Dylan was a big eater and she assumed that based on the size of him, Cormac was as well. She didn't want anyone to go hungry. As the final items were placed in the cooler, Dylan and Cormac reappeared to take it to the truck.

"What have you got in here, Jenna?" Dylan grunted as he picked the cooler up and Cormac grabbed the other end to help him.

Jenna just rolled her eyes at them. "You know how much food you eat, Dylan. I wasn't sure even that was going to be enough."

They finished loading the truck and Dylan secured his surfboard to the roof. Chester, who had been out in the backyard, was barking at the sliding door to be let in. As soon as Jenna opened the door, he made a beeline for the truck, beating everyone as he dove into the backseat.

"Well, Chester, it looks like you and I will be sharing the backseat again," Jenna said. Chester answered by licking her face and panting heavily in her ear. "Thanks for that," Jenna laughed.

"We're outta here," Dylan hooted. "Dude, I can't wait to teach you how to surf."

Cormac was looking apprehensive and Jenna teased, "Don't worry, dude, you'll probably be a natural." She smiled to let him know she was joking.

"She's right, Cormac. I'll bet you pick it right up," Dylan said, as he backed the truck out of the garage. He hit the button in the truck to close the garage door and Jenna watched the wonder on Cormac's face as he reached for the button and sent the door back up. He pushed it again, closing it and looked like he might give it one more try, when Dylan stopped him. "It opens and closes the garage door, bro. Let's leave it closed, okay?"

"Dylan, did you set the alarm? We still need to get the locksmith out here, you know."

"Don't worry, my friends and I got the key away from Jonathan when we tossed his ass last night. He'll have to break in, if he really wants to get in and I've got the alarm set. Besides, the neighbors know that if they see him around they need to call the police."

Jenna was relieved. She had worried he would come back while they were out. Their neighbors were the best and she could always count on them to keep an eye on things when they weren't around. She let out a long sigh. Now she could relax and enjoy her day at the beach. She just hoped she didn't do anything stupid, where Cormac was concerned.

# NINE

Cormac still couldn't believe the pace at which they were travelling. The scenery was whizzing past them so fast he could barely take it all in. Back home it would have taken them days to travel this distance. The hills they had been travelling past on their journey were a velvety golden brown and had obviously not seen rain in quite some time. There were many other cars and trucks travelling the roadways with them and he wondered, were they all going to the same place? The truck left the flat black road and they climbed uphill through densely forested land. It was the first real greenery he had seen since his arrival. Cormac couldn't believe his eyes when they drove past two eight-foot tall cat sculptures guarding an entry gate. His head whipped back to catch another glimpse as they swiftly faded from sight. Jenna must have noticed, because she was quick to explain their presence.

"Those cats have been guarding Poet's Canyon since the early 1920's. Their names are Leo and Leona." Jenna offered a bit of local history to Cormac, who merely nodded in response and silently went back to watching the road curve its way to the summit.

"Don't worry, Cormac, I've driven this same road too many times to count. You're in good hands," Dylan reassured him.

"I'm nae worried, Dylan," Cormac lied - he'd be daft not to fash.

"Good. We'll be there in no time flat. You're gonna love surfing, won't he, Jenna?"

"I wouldn't know, Dylan. I've been asking you to teach me for years, but you've never had the time," Jenna retorted with her usual sarcasm.

"You got me there, cuz. Maybe today will be your lucky day."

Cormac glanced back at Jenna in time to see her shrug at her cousin's words. She looked so beautiful back there, with the sunlight streaming through the windows creating streaks of gold through her hair. She was focusing all of her attention on Chester, who was sound asleep in her lap. He wondered if the dog knew how fortunate he was and he tried to imagine what it would be like to have Jenna focus that kind of loving attention on him.

"Jenna," he asked. "Do you mind having to sit back there with Chester?"

"Of course not, Cormac. Chester is a good travelling companion. He never complains and he's been asleep since we pulled out of the driveway," she smiled.

His heart nearly melted at the sight of it.

"The question should be, do you mind sitting up front with Dylan? I have to admit that sometimes when he drives I get a bit nauseous," Jenna continued, and she wrinkled her nose.

Was she trying to drive him to insanity? The way she was looking at him was completely mesmerizing and had him forgetting about the breakneck speed at which they were travelling.

"I be fine, Jenna, lass. Dinnae fash," Cormac said.

"What beach are we going to, Dylan?" Jenna asked.

Cormac noticed the shift in her demeanor, as she switched her focus to Dylan.

"I thought we'd go to Manresa. If I were doing this with more seasoned surfers, I'd go to Steamer Lane, but I don't want to kill anyone their first time out."

"I hope the surf's good," Jenna said.

"We'll know soon enough. We're just about there," Dylan said, as he slowed the truck and turned onto another smaller roadway.

Cormac turned back towards the front to watch where they were going, wondering less about the surf and more about whether he could convince Jenna to kiss him again this day.

~~~

It was all Jenna could do to maintain her cool. Cormac had a maddening way of making her feel things she didn't want to feel. She had to keep reminding herself that he was not for her, but damn it, every time he looked at her with those amazing blue eyes, she almost jumped into his arms. Speaking of which, those arms were so strong and muscular, she kept imagining them wrapped around her, holding her close to that equally muscular chest.

"Stop it, Jenna."

"Stop what?" Cormac asked, sounding confused.

Had she just said that aloud? She couldn't recall being this embarrassed in her entire life. Cormac was still eyeing her curiously.

"Oh, it was nothing. I was just talking to myself," she said.

"Aye. I ken ye were, since ye mentioned yer own name," he teased.

She laughed a little too loudly at his comment, probably because she was feeling self-conscious at being overheard talking to herself.

"Really. It was nothing for you to worry about." But it was definitely something for Jenna to worry about. Maybe a dip in the ocean and a surfing lesson would help.

They managed to get all of their stuff down to the beach in one trip, although not without complaint from Dylan.

"Jenna, what on earth did you pack? There are only three of us, you'd think you were planning to feed a pack of hungry wolves," Dylan teased.

"Sorry. Better to have too much, than not enough," she pouted.

They found a good spot near the water and set up their chairs, blankets and a small beach tent for Chester, so he could get out of the sun. The temperature was perfect and the sun was reflecting brightly off the deep blue of the ocean making it sparkle as if it was covered in sequins. Waves crashed onto the beach and sea birds roamed the shoreline in search of food, while a light breeze blew just enough to keep the warmth of the sun from becoming uncomfortable. Jenna watched as Dylan prepared his surfboard and put on his wetsuit.

"Hey, aren't we going to need one of those?" she asked.

"Not unless you're planning to spend a lot of time in the water," Dylan said, before he waved and headed for the waves with his surfboard.

Cormac had planted himself on the blanket and was observing everything going on around him, and when Jenna pulled her sundress off, he jumped up so rapidly that she didn't even have time to react before he was trying to wrap her up in a towel.

"Cormac, what are you doing?" She was irritated by the crazy way he was behaving.

"Jenna, should ye take yer dress off, lass, for the entire world to see?"

"Cormac, look around you. Every woman on this beach is wearing a similar version to what I have on. It's okay. This isn't a nudist beach. I promise I'll keep the bathing suit on."

He still looked concerned, but he allowed her to put the towel down as he tried to conceal what was obvious to Jenna - she had aroused him. She secretly smiled at the obvious response he'd had. So, she was apparently having the same effect on him, as he was having on her. She cleared her throat when she sat on the blanket beside him.

"Cormac, would you mind putting some sunscreen on my back?" Jenna asked as she handed him the tube of sunscreen. He stared at it, as if it was something he'd obviously never seen before.

"Don't tell me… they don't have sunscreen where you're from," she stated matter-of-factly.

"Nae, lass, they dinnae."

"Here." She took the cover off and squirted some into his hands. "Now, you rub it into my back until you can't see it anymore. Okay?"

"Aye."

She could feel the heat of his hands before they even touched her back. If she had been thinking clearly, she would have realized what a bad idea this was. His large hands covered her back easily as he applied the sunscreen to every bit of exposed skin. He was very thorough in his ministrations, stopping only momentarily to squeeze more sunscreen into his hands and then he went to work on her legs, gently covering them from top to bottom. She couldn't tell how uncomfortable he might be, but she was starting to feel an aching sensation between her thighs as his hands lightly brushed near the source of her sweet discomfort. She snuck a peek and was pleasantly surprised to see that he was looking at her with an unusually pained expression on his face. He wiped his hands on a nearby towel and then dove face down onto the blanket. She thought she might know why and smiled as she glanced over at him. His lustrous ebony locks were covering his handsome face and Jenna was surprised by the fact that she had a desire to see his eyes.

"Cormac, let me do something with your hair. It can't be comfortable all over your face like that." She sat up and reached for the beach bag. She searched through the pockets and came up with a hair tie and a brush. Jenna motioned for him to sit with his back to her and she brushed his beautiful hair into a ponytail and then into a man bun at the base of his neck. She couldn't help observing that he was quite tanned, from head to toe. He must spend a good deal of time shirtless and the mental image practically made her drool. "Do you want me to put some sunscreen on your back for you?"

"Why would I need *sunscreen*, lass."

"Oh… well, it's to keep you from getting sunburn. Too much sun is not good for your skin."

"'Tis not?"

"No. It can cause skin cancer, age spots and wrinkles." Why was she taking the time to explain this to him? He had to know all of this already. It wasn't a secret, but somehow she almost believed he didn't know. His reactions seemed so very genuine.

"Aye, then I will nae stop ye, if ye wish to put it on me."

Jenna went to work covering his back with the sunscreen and relishing the feel of his warm skin beneath her palms. She skimmed over the hard planes of his back and had to bite back the groan that played at her lips. She ran her fingers down the corded muscles of his arms as he sat stock-still. She didn't think he was even breathing.

When she was finished, he turned to face her, asking less than innocently, "Would ye like to put some on me chest?" The twinkle in his eyes gave him away and she pursed her lips, shook her head, and handed him the sunscreen.

"You can handle that yourself," she said.

"I dinnae believe I can, lass. Yer much better at it than I," he teased, holding the sunscreen out for her to take.

"Okay. If you insist. I guess it wouldn't hurt to help you with it, especially since you have so little experience with this kind of thing."

Jenna sat on her heels, facing him. She took a deep breath. This was going to take a lot of self-control on her part, but apparently she had none as her hands began to shake when she placed them flat on his chest, rubbing the lotion all over him. She looked up and directly into his deep blue eyes. He had a smoldering expression on his face and she quickly lowered her gaze back to his chest. She wasn't sure which was worse - the rock hard chest or the unbelievably gorgeous face. There didn't seem to be anywhere else to look, because when she lowered her eyes they aligned directly with his lap and the hard, projection of desire that taunted her. Jerking her head back up, she directed her gaze towards the ocean and mentally started counting the waves. Cormac didn't seem content to allow that to happen and he placed his fingers under her chin and turned her to face him again.

She took one look into his eyes and true to her nature of late, Jenna jumped up from the blanket and ran towards the water. "I'm going in to cool off. It's getting too warm for me," she shouted over her shoulder as she ran.

~~~

Cormac watched in wonder as Jenna ran full tilt for the water. He laughed to himself. She really was quite smitten with him. No matter how angry or frustrated she became with him, she wanted him. He knew that look and he'd never been happier to see it on any lass's face before this. Her sweet little legs carried her quickly to the water where she dove in to the waves, disappearing for a moment before emerging like a goddess from the sea, water sparkling like diamonds as it coursed over her body. His aching manhood could probably use a dose of that same water about now. Making his way down the sand and towards the water, Cormac kept watch on Jenna. She was his to protect and he made sure she kept safe as he proceeded. By the time he reached her, Dylan and another young man were beside her and obviously discussing the waves. They were pointing away from the shore and in deep discussion when Cormac approached.

"Cormac. Ready to try some surfing, my man?" Dylan asked.

The number of different names Dylan had for him was baffling. *My man, dood, bro…* "Aye. I'd like to try, if ye'll show me."

"Okay. Jesse here is going to show Jenna and I'll work with you."

Cormac was really not *okay* with it, but since he was only learning himself, there wasn't much he could do about it. He watched as Jesse smiled broadly and gave Jenna an appreciative glance. He spoke quietly to her and Cormac strained his ears to hear, but to no avail. Jenna was laughing as she stood beside him. Much to Cormac's dismay, he watched as Jenna laid on the board and Jesse climbed on, laying partially atop her. They began paddling out further into the water. Dylan was talking to Cormac, but he didn't hear a word he said. The rush of jealousy and anger filling his head prevented it.

"Dude. You really need to pay attention. Forget about what they're doing."

"But why must he lie atop her like that?"

"Don't be jealous, bro. It's just Jesse. He's only sixteen years old. You've got nothing to worry about in that department."

Cormac knew that a sixteen year old could be just as dangerous to a woman as an older man could. He wanted to swim out to them and pull Jesse off her, but controlled the urge and did as Dylan suggested. This was not his time, he had to remember, people acted differently here.

Dylan, thankfully, did not get on the board with him. He gave him instruction and told him to watch Jesse, to see how he did it. He explained paddling out, sitting and waiting for a perfect wave and getting to your feet and riding it in. Cormac watched some others who were out on surfboards and saw how they did it. He was a quick study and didn't think he'd have a problem. He might fall a time or two, but he knew he'd be able to ride this *surfboard* before too long.

Cormac paddled out and sat beside Jesse and Jenna. Jesse gave him some words of encouragement and when a good wave came along, Jesse had Cormac go first and give it a try. He did surprisingly well. He rode almost all the way to shore before toppling off and into the churning waves. He stayed where he was and kept watch on Jenna and Jesse. He watched closely as their wave approached and they quickly paddled into position, Jenna stood with the help of Jesse and he held her waist, damn him, as they rode the wave. They didn't make it quite as far as Cormac before they fell, but he was relieved to see Jenna's head pop to the surface wearing a huge smile. She swam in his direction full of excitement.

"That was amazing, but I am so cold. I need to get out of the water. Are you coming?" she asked, as she stood shivering in front of him.

Dylan approached, full of praise for them both and asking if Cormac would like to try it again, but Cormac's only concern was getting Jenna warm. He pulled her into his arms and started for shore.

"Thanks, Jesse," Jenna called back and Cormac held her a little tighter.

Once they reached their blanket, Cormac grabbed a towel and wrapped Jenna snugly inside. He continued to hold her, rubbing her arms and back to get her warm. She was still shivering, but not as badly.

"Did you love it?" she asked, excitement lighting her eyes.

"Aye, I did."

"You were amazing. I can't believe you've never surfed before," Jenna exclaimed.

"We have nae surfboards at Breaghacraig. We have ocean and we have waves, but none of the clan has ever thought to ride them on a board."

"Well, maybe you can teach them something new."

"The water be much colder than 'tis here. We dinnae swim unless we have to."

"Oh, that's too bad. You could be as good as Dylan with a little practice."

They sat together on the blanket. Jenna remained in his arms and for once she didn't seem to be thinking about running away. He tried not to react as she rested her head on his shoulder and relaxed against him. He couldn't think of anywhere he would rather be at this very moment. Holding her felt right. It was what he had been missing all these years. She fit perfectly against his body and he wanted to have her there always. Only a few days had passed since they met and he was amazed that things were going as well as they were. He hadn't thought it possible. Now he had to convince her to go back with him. He hoped it would be easier than he first anticipated, but he knew it wouldnae be. He had his work cut out for him, but progress had been made. He needed to keep it going in the right direction.

# TEN

Dylan and Jesse joined Cormac and Jenna for a quick lunch before heading back into the water. Jenna had been right. She'd packed just enough food to feed Cormac and Dylan, along with a very hungry Jesse. Smiling to herself, she watched the three scarfing down food like they hadn't eaten in days. Cormac had been most complimentary of her sandwich making skills. He claimed to have never had a sandwich before. She humored him and went along with pretty much all of the crazy stuff he was spouting today. Something about being at the beach felt very liberating to Jenna. She stopped analyzing everything he said and did, instead determined just to enjoy his company.

After the last of the sandwiches were gone, Jenna asked, "Cormac, would you like to go for a walk on the beach with me?"

"I'd be honored to accompany ye, Jenna."

Jenna couldn't help but notice the surprise in his expression. "It's just a walk, nothing else," she warned.

"What else could a walk be, lass?" he quizzed her.

She stood up and grabbed two peaches to take with them. She put her other hand out to Cormac to help him up. Who was she kidding? He didn't need any help, she just wanted to hold his hand. He took it and stood. He seemed puzzled by her actions, but followed as she grabbed Chester's leash, turned on her heels and headed towards the water's edge. They walked in a companionable silence for a while and then Cormac asked, "What are those that ye carry in yer hand, lass?"

"Peaches. It's the end of the season for them. They're my favorite fruit, but they're only fresh and local in the summer. I brought one for you." She handed him the peach and he rubbed the furry skin with his fingers.

"Thank ye. How does it taste?"

"Sweet and juicy." Jenna took a bite out of hers and the juices ran down her chin.

Cormac stopped Jenna in her tracks and turning her to face him, he stared at her with such intensity her knees turned to jelly. He reached out and wiped the juices from her chin in a most seductive manner, and then licked his fingers, never taking his eyes away from hers. He smiled that amazing smile of his and Jenna self-consciously wiped at her chin and offered him a bite of her peach. Cormac accepted and as the juices ran down his stubbly chin, Jenna found herself standing on tiptoes, licking the peach juice from his face as he groaned low in his throat, letting her know he was completely turned on by what had just happened.

"You know, I have really got to stop doing that," she said, as she turned her face away from him, hoping he wouldn't see how embarrassed she was.

"Why? Do ye make a habit of licking a man's face?" he teased.

"No! I don't," she cried indignantly. "It's your fault. I don't seem to be able to control myself around you. I'm really not that kind of girl. I've never in my life been the one to initiate kissing and, and…" She waved her hand around in the air finding herself unable to complete her thought.

"I like it, lass. I like the way ye go after what you want. Dinnae stop. I'm happy to let ye do what ye will with me," he said playfully.

Cormac had tipped his head to the side to get a better look at her face and he looked so sweet that Jenna had to fight with herself not to reach up and kiss him again. *Jenna, what are you doing?* She warned herself. *I just want to jump his bones. I've got to get a grip. He is a visitor to our country and he is only here for a few more days. You know you can't ever do anything part way - and when he leaves you'll be miserable. So, don't go there. Well, maybe just a little.*

Cormac could see the indecision on Jenna's face. He truly wanted her to come to him because she wanted to, and not because he'd pushed her, but one thing he was sure of was that the next time they kissed, he was going to be the one to start it. He reached out to hold her hand and she let him lead her as they continued their walk down the beach. Progress. She had been allowing him to hold her and touch her all day. He didn't want to frighten her back into her shell, so he'd settle for the small successes he was having and not go any further while they were here at the beach.

The waves lapped at their shins and ankles and a few times, a larger wave crashed against them, sending Jenna laughing into his arms. The sounds of the waves, the feel of the sea breeze and the smell of the salty air would all be burned into his memory forever. This was a good day. He was glad he was here with her, but he wanted so much more. More time with Jenna, more Jenna herself and the hope of a life together at Breaghacraig. He wanted her to become part of his large extended family, his clan. He didn't dwell on how he could make that happen, for now he merely wanted to enjoy this moment, the light shining in her eyes as she gazed into his, the feel of her hand holding tightly to his own and the way she seemed to be allowing him to take care of her for this little while.

They had walked for what seemed to be many hours and yet, not enough. In fact, it had been under an hour. They stopped occasionally to watch a pod of dolphins playing just offshore. Seals, sea otters and pelicans also made appearances to the evident delight of Jenna, who was practically jumping up and down at the sight of them. It did Cormac's heart good to see Jenna so happy. He had doubted it was possible the first day he met her, and yet here she was, holding his hand, smiling, laughing, and seemingly very happy to be with him. He wasn't sure what had brought about this change in her, but he would accept it and be grateful. The sun was dipping lower in the sky, and its light played softly across the surface of the water. Chester had been loping along beside them, barking and biting at the waves.

"We should probably head back," Jenna sighed.

"Aye. We've walked a long way."

"I wish we could stay here forever. It's so peaceful and beautiful," she replied.

"Then we should stay," Cormac replied matter-of-factly.

"Unfortunately, we can't. Dylan is probably wondering where we are by now. Come on, let's go," Jenna said as she reluctantly headed back the other way. Cormac followed along with Chester, who was completely soaked by the waves. "Chester, look at you," Jenna observed. "You're going to need a bath when we get home."

Cormac chuckled as he watched Chester continue to enjoy himself in the water. This really had been the perfect day. He wondered what the evening would hold in store for him. He was hopeful it would turn out to be as lovely as the day had been.

~~~

Jenna was walking backwards, gazing up at Cormac. He gave her one of his bone-melting smiles, showing a row of nearly perfect teeth. He was perfection as far as she could see and Jenna drank in the sight of him. She turned around and proceeded to run through the waves breaking on the shore, hoping that Cormac would join her. She peeked back to see him in hot pursuit. She didn't get far before he picked her up in his arms and began to carry her back towards their blanket.

She threw her arms around his neck and enjoyed the moment; something she didn't allow herself to do very often. She set skeptical, untrusting Jenna aside and went with her gut, which told her Cormac was not going to hurt her and it was okay to let herself enjoy her time with him. So what if he wasn't going to be here very long? Maybe they could keep in touch via e-mail after he left. She could even take a trip to Scotland to see him and while she was there, maybe she could find

Ashley. If only she could remember, what she did with the name of that inn Ashley had mentioned. She made a mental note to search for it, when she had a chance. All too soon they reached the blanket. Cormac didn't seem to want to put her down and stood holding her as her cousin Dylan ran up from the water with his surfboard.

"Hey, you two, I was wondering where you were."

Jenna wriggled out of Cormac's arms. "Time to head home?"

"I hate to leave, but the sun will be setting before long and we should get back, I've got a hot date tonight," Dylan boasted.

"They're all hot, Dylan." Jenna rolled her eyes. "Let's get packed up."

They gathered the blanket, towels, cooler and chairs and headed back up to the truck.

"Jenna, would you mind driving? I'm beat," Dylan asked.

"Sure, give me the keys." Jenna took the keys from Dylan's hand and unlocked the doors. They stowed most everything in the bed of the truck and Dylan once again got his surfboard in place for the long drive home.

"I'd like to try driving," Cormac stated, eyeing the driver's seat with interest.

"Have you got a driver's license?" Jenna questioned, already knowing the answer.

"A driver's license?" As she'd suspected, Cormac looked completely baffled.

"I'll take that as a *no*," Jenna laughed. "You can't drive unless you have a license."

"And how do I get one?" he asked.

"It's a long process, especially if you have no driving experience at all. Do you drive back in Scotland?"

"Och, nae," he answered, as if she should have known the answer. "Me horse gets me where I need to go."

"Maybe if you were staying longer I could teach you, but you're going to be leaving soon, so we wouldn't have enough time." She secretly hoped that he wanted to learn badly enough that he'd give up his plan to leave. She poked him in the ribs. "Get in."

Dylan had already settled in the back seat with Chester and appeared as if he would be asleep before they hit the freeway.

Cormac watched everything Jenna did as she settled into the driver's seat and prepared for the return trip home. *He probably thinks I can't drive*, she thought. "Don't worry, Cormac, I'm a really good driver. Probably better than Dylan. You'll see."

She started the truck and headed for home. Sideways glances at Cormac confirmed that he was uncomfortable with her behind the wheel, so she did her best to reassure him with a smile.

The drive home was quiet. Dylan and Chester snoozed in the back and Cormac had finally relaxed enough to enjoy the scenery and let go of his death grip on the dashboard. Jenna was delighted that Dylan was leaving her home alone with Cormac tonight. She thought about what the evening might entail, anticipating a night spent in his arms, when traffic suddenly came to a dead stop in front of her, and she had to slam on the brakes to avoid hitting any other cars.

"I'm sorry about that," Jenna apologized.

Dylan didn't move. Chester opened one eye and when he was satisfied that all was well, closed it again. Cormac seemed to be the only one at all rattled by the event.

"What happened, lass? Did ye nae see them stopping?" Cormac asked, concern written all over his handsome face.

"I was day-dreaming. Sorry, I didn't mean to scare you. Are you alright?" she asked.

"Aye, I be fine, especially if ye dinnae do that again," he teased. "What were ye day-dreaming about?"

She knew he was fishing to see if she had been thinking about him, so she fibbed. "I was wondering what to make for dinner. That's all."

Traffic started up again and they crawled past a wreck on the side of the road. Cormac's eyes grew wide with interest. "What has happened here?" he asked Jenna.

"Looks like an accident," she stated, as the lanes in front of them began to open up, allowing her to increase back up to the speed limit. "The highway patrol was there, but no ambulance, so no one was hurt."

"Highway patrol?" he questioned, lifting one eyebrow.

"The car with the flashing lights on top. They patrol the freeways, making sure people are obeying the rules of the road and helping motorists who've had accidents or breakdowns."

Cormac nodded in acknowledgement, and appeared concerned. She was quite certain he didn't understand any of what she had shared. *He must really live in the boonies*, she thought, *either that - or he's a good actor*. "Who makes sure people follow the rules where you come from?" she asked innocently.

"'Tis Robert who does," he answered.

"You work for Robert, right? So, do you help him with that sort of thing? Are you like the highway patrol?"

Cormac nodded. "Aye. When there is trouble, we handle it."

She wanted to know more, but decided she'd approach the subject slowly. She had to figure out if he was delusional, doing a fine acting job to prank her, or last and least likely - telling the truth.

"I'll need to hit the grocery store. Would you like steak for dinner tonight?"

"I be happy to eat whatever you cook, lass. Do ye have a bow I could use?"

"What would you need that for?" *Wait, was he talking about a bow, like for your hair, or a bow-and-arrow bow?*

"So I can go hunt for our dinner. Ye will have to show me where yer game is located, but I have no doubt I can bring back meat for our meal."

Jenna tried hard not to roll her eyes at that crazy pronouncement. "No need to hunt when we have a grocery store nearby. You can come with me and see how we get our food here in *my* time," she announced, with a hint of sarcasm.

"'Tis no trouble at all, lass." Cormac responded seriously, as if he'd completely missed Jenna's cynicism.

"We don't hunt around here, Cormac. I mean, some people do, but you'd have to drive quite a way and you'd need a hunting license, if it's even hunting season right now." Her lack of hunting acumen was showing.

"I see," Cormac said, but she knew he really didn't. "Another license," he muttered.

The rest of the drive was uneventful and they made it back home without waking Dylan or Chester.

"Hey, Dylan, why don't you hose Chester off before he comes inside? I'm going to take a quick shower before I head to the store; you probably should too, Cormac."

"Aye, aye, Captain," Dylan teased, lifting his arm into a mocking salute. "Right away!"

Dylan took Chester around to the side yard and Cormac helped Jenna unpack the truck.

With everything put away, they went their separate ways to shower and agreed to meet back in the living room in thirty minutes to go shopping. Jenna just hoped she could resist the urge to meet Cormac in his bedroom, instead.

~~~

The trip to the grocery store turned out to be quite amusing, as far as Jenna was concerned. Cormac couldn't have looked more shocked if he'd tried. She could see that he wanted to act as if this was no big deal for him, but his facial expressions and the way he wanted to examine absolutely everything was a dead giveaway.

She was bombarded with question after question about the packaging, the products and most of all, the meat. She realized she was woefully lacking in her knowledge of food production.

"Ye mean ye dinnae even know where yer food comes from?" he asked in surprise.

"Well, I know where some of it comes from, but mostly it comes from big companies, I guess," she tried to explain.

"What are 'big companies'?"

"You know what, let's not ask any more questions. Can we just get the things we need and get out of here?" She was missing Dylan about now. He never tired of answering Cormac's many questions. Dylan might not even know what he was talking about at the time, but he always gave him some sort of reasonable answer.

They got the grocery cart through the checkout stand without incident. She could tell Cormac was biting back his queries and it made her giggle to herself. All in all they managed to survive the grocery store and made it home, where they unloaded the groceries and Jenna set about getting dinner started. Cormac sat at the kitchen counter and watched her every move. She felt a little as if she were on display, but had to admit to herself that she kind of enjoyed his undivided attention.

"Can I help ye with that, lass?" he asked.

"Sure, can you cut up the salad stuff?"

"I believe I can," he smiled that heart-stopping smile of his and she sighed. It was becoming more and more difficult to ignore her growing attraction towards him.

Jenna directed him on what she wanted cut up and how to cut it and he did an excellent job. He put everything into the salad bowl and watched as Jenna made the dressing.

"I've never had salad," he offered. "As a matter of fact, I dinnae even ken what any of these vegetables are."

"Really? What kind of vegetables do you have where you're from?" she asked curiously.

"Carrots, parsnips, peas," he listed.

She had already assumed he'd never been to a grocery store, and now she was certain he was unfamiliar with a lot of the produce she'd purchased. "Hmmm…"

She was baking potatoes on the grill and they were almost ready when she started cooking the steak. The air was filled with the aroma of barbecuing beef, which she left for a few minutes while she set the table outside. Cormac sat in the spot she indicated. She observed that he seemed quite relaxed and happy, which made her feel the same. It was just the two of them tonight. Dylan was out on his date and he'd informed her that he wouldn't be back until tomorrow morning. The only company they had was Chester, who was pretty much glued to Cormac's side. The dog loved him and Jenna was beginning to think she might just understand why.

Candles lit the table as they ate their food. Cormac was very complimentary about her cooking. In fact, he couldn't seem to tell her enough how grateful he was for the wonderful meal she had prepared. Jenna watched with a smile as he tasted and enjoyed all of the unfamiliar foods that were in his salad. She was sure to keep his wine glass full of the delicious cabernet she had opened.

"This has been a beautiful night, lass," Cormac stated.

"It has been, but it's not over yet. Help me clear the table and clean up a bit and I'll serve our dessert."

Cormac was a good helper and had no problem doing his part in the kitchen, unlike Jonathan, who'd thought Jenna should be serving him and cleaning up after him all the time, despite the fact that he had no job to take up his time. Jenna was finding more and more things to admire about the man who had appeared out of the fog. If only she knew the truth about him. The story both Cormac and Dylan had told her couldn't possibly be accurate. Although nothing was impossible in her mind, it was surely improbable - but she couldn't totally discount his story. She'd decided to reserve judgment for now and enjoy his company.

Jenna grabbed a large bowl and filled it with ice cream from the freezer. She added crushed up cookies and chocolate syrup, and two spoons, carrying it to the cozy sofa outside. She lit the gas fire pit and motioned for Cormac to take a seat. He sat in the corner, arms extended over the back and Jenna nestled herself in next to him, tucking her feet up under her backside. She held the bowl between them and took a spoonful of ice cream and fed it to Cormac. She wished she had thought to take a photo, because the look on his face was priceless. He closed his eyes in obvious delight, relishing the flavors.

"More please," he requested, with a sheepish grin.

Jenna was happy to accommodate him and realized she really hadn't needed two spoons, because they ended up sharing one. She couldn't remember being this happy, not since long before Jonathan and she sighed, enjoying being completely at ease.

"I like it when ye smile, Jenna," Cormac said, studying her up-turned face.

"I like it, too. I haven't had much reason to smile lately. It feels good."

"What happened to make ye so unhappy, lass? Was it yer husband?"

Jenna really didn't want to bring the subject of Jonathan into what was turning out to be a perfect night, but Cormac had asked and she wanted to be honest with him.

"Jonathan fooled me. At first he was everything any woman could want in a man. He was caring, kind, funny…" Jenna hesitated and Cormac put his arm around her shoulders, drawing her into his side. His warmth and strength poured into her and gave her the courage to continue, even though she was embarrassed by her tale. "I didn't know until after we got married that he has a gambling addiction. He was placing bets on everything, from ball games to horses and he wasn't very good at it. He racked up quite a large amount of debt with a local bookie and couldn't pay him back. Eventually, the bookie came looking for his money and he came here, to my home, and threatened me. I, of course, paid the debt and then confronted Jonathan about it. He swore he would never gamble again and seemed so grateful to me for helping him. He said he was going to get counseling to help him break the addiction. I gave him the benefit of the doubt, thinking that everyone deserves a second chance. Next thing I knew, the bookie was at my front door again looking for money. The guy seemed as embarrassed as I was, and he told me that Jonathan was nothing but trouble and that I should throw his ass out. I was shocked to hear him say that, and I started snooping through Jonathan's things, searching for evidence of what he was involved in. I peeked at his text messages one day while he was napping and I found all the evidence I needed, to know he'd been using me. It started long before he'd even asked me to marry him. He had another woman, whom he had known for years and they'd texted to one another about how he'd only married me to get at my money - and that after a while, he intended to divorce me and get half of everything I had. Then he'd be free to marry her." Jenna's voice tapered off, her bitterness at what Jonathan had done squeezing at her throat.

"I'm so sorry, lass. Do ye still have feelings for the man?"

Jenna managed a watery smile. "Oh, God, no! I immediately lost any feelings I'd ever had for him. I marched right over to my lawyer's office and told him what was going on and he assured me that I could have the marriage annulled, which I did."

"And so he's angry with ye now and he wants to hurt ye," Cormac stated. "Dinnae fash, lass, I willnae allow him near ye ever again. He willnae hurt ye."

Jenna was taken aback by his determined pronouncement, and where it would have riled her just a few short days ago, now she found comfort in his words and in his arms.

"Thank you, Cormac, but you aren't going to be here to protect me for much longer. You have to leave in a few days."

"Aye, I do. Ye can come with me."

Jenna shook her head resolutely. "I can't, Cormac. I have a life here and I'm not sure exactly where it is you want me to go with you."

"To Breaghacraig. To Scotland. Ye'd love it there. I ken ye would."

"Cormac, please, can we just enjoy what little time we have together and not talk about crazy things?" Jenna pleaded.

~~~

Cormac knew it would be foolish to push Jenna. He had made progress with her and he didn't want to send that progress backwards at this point. She was obviously happy to be here with him now and he could only hope that with the few days he had left, he would be able to convince her to leave with him. It wouldnae be easy, but he had more confidence today than he had done when he first arrived.

They sat by the fire and he held her closely in his arms, aware of every breath she took and how her arm had snaked its way around his waist. He enjoyed the sensation of having her hold him like this. She was the one thing missing in his life. He wanted her, more than he'd ever wanted any other woman. She was perfect in his eyes. He even enjoyed her bossiness, and that sharp tongue she used so swiftly. She was a strong woman. A woman who had become stronger because of the unfortunate situation with her husband. Cormac was happy that she had been able to extricate herself from the marriage and from a man who was without honor. Back home, a man like Jonathan would find himself in grave danger of losing his life for the insult he had brought to Jenna. It would be Cormac's duty to defend her honor and he would have no trouble doing just that. Here, however, he was told by Edna that disagreements were settled by other means and he should not resort to violence if he could possibly help it. It was turning out to be a difficult task where Jonathan was concerned, but Cormac would do his best.

Looking down at the lovely woman curled against his side, Cormac realized that she had fallen asleep. He had hoped to kiss those lovely lips again this night, but he could see she was exhausted. He picked her up in his arms and carried Jenna to her bedroom, where he laid her on her bed, kissing her forehead gently. He took one last look and then left her room, closing the door silently behind him.

# ELEVEN

Cormac held onto Jenna's arm tightly, seeming to fear she might be swept away by the great gust of wind created when the monstrous BART train pulled into the Rockridge Station. The platform was filled with people, all heading into San Francisco on this gorgeous Saturday morning.

"This is our train," Jenna said to Cormac. He didn't move, instead staring up and down the line of cars in apparent wonder. She grabbed his arm and pulled him towards the open door of the nearest train car. He hesitantly stepped aboard and Jenna found them seats right away. "Dylan can be so flaky sometimes," she complained. "He sends me a text in the middle of the night to tell me he can't make it to the Children's Hospital Charitable Ball. Since I don't want to go unescorted, he suggested I take you." Jenna glanced at Cormac, who was tightly gripping the seat in front of him as the train left the station. She smiled, reached out and gently released his fingers from their tight grip on the seat back.

"Does everything here move this fast, lass?" he asked, looking uncertain.

"Pretty much," Jenna sighed. "I'm sorry to ask you to be my date to the ball at the last minute like this. I hope you don't mind accompanying me." She turned so she could see his face and smiled reassuring-ly at him.

"Nae. I dinnae mind. I'd be verra pleased to escort ye."

If she could keep him talking, she might be able to get that look of horror off his face - the one that appeared every time he heard the train squeal as it rounded a curve. Before long, they headed into the tube that took the trains under the San Francisco Bay. There was total darkness outside the windows, where moments before it had been bright and sunny.

"Where did the light go?" Cormac asked, looking more and more concerned with each passing moment.

"Don't worry. It's dark because we're passing under the bay. We'll be out soon enough."

"We're under the water!" he exclaimed, disbelief written all over his face.

"Yeah. It's okay, Cormac. Thousands of people do this every day. It's not a problem." The hand she had been holding seemed cold and clammy to the touch. She would never have believed that a big, strong man like Cormac could be frightened by a train. It almost made his whole time travel story seem more realistic. She kept a running conver-sation going with him until they reached their stop at the Embarcadero Station. "This is our stop, Cormac." She scooted over, pushing him to get up. As they left the train, she heard a very audible sigh of relief leave his lips. She couldn't help giggling as he hurried her away from the train.

Leaving the station, they emerged into bright sunshine once again. There were tons of people wandering to and fro on the sidewalks. Many were tourists and many were Bay Area citizens in the city for the day, undoubtedly sightseeing, shopping, going to the theater, or here to indulge in an excellent meal at one of the many amazing restaurants the city had to offer.

"I thought we'd get your tux out of the way first, and then we can grab a slice of pizza somewhere before we head back to the house to get ready."

"What is a tux, Jenna?" Cormac had such a serious expression on his face that it took Jenna by surprise. Maybe they went by a different name in Scotland? It didn't really matter, they were quickly approaching the shop where they would be picking it up and he'd see for himself what it was.

"You'll see, Cormac."

They entered the shop to be immediately greeted by Antonio, the shop owner.

"Jenna! What a surprise to see you here, I was expecting Dylan." Antonio pecked Jenna on both cheeks and did a double take when he caught sight of Cormac.

"Dylan isn't able to go to the event tonight. Antonio, this is Cormac MacBayne, he's going to be my date for the ball. I thought maybe we could have him fitted for a tux, off the rack. He's a little bigger than Dylan, but perhaps you can find something suitable for him."

"Of course, of course! No problem. You know a lot of our local sports stars come here for their clothes," Antonio said proudly. "I'm sure I'll have no trouble finding something. Cormac, please stand over here so I can take your measurements."

Cormac let go of Jenna's hand for the first time since they'd begun their journey. He stood where Antonio directed him and let his eyes wander about the shop.

Antonio was tut-tutting all around Cormac with his measuring tape, and taking notes on a pad of paper as he went. "Okay. Follow me into the dressing room and I'll bring in something I think will be perfect for you."

Cormac obediently went in behind the curtain and gave Jenna a look of desperation just before Antonio closed it on him. "Remove your clothes," Antonio called. "I'll be right back. We'll have you out of here in no time."

Antonio strode through the shop picking shirts, ties, jackets, and pants with the ease of a professional who knew exactly what he was doing.

Jenna sat in a comfortable armchair by the window and waited.

"You are such a busy lady; I'm surprised you have time to come in here with your friend." Antonio said, selecting a bow tie from a nearby rack.

"I took a few weeks off. I needed to get some rest, you know, with everything that's been going on lately."

"You mean, Jonathan, right?" Antonio asked astutely.

"Yeah. He's a piece of work for sure." Jenna forced her shoulders to relax and smiled at Antonio. It was amazing how quickly word travelled in her circle. She rarely saw Antonio, but he knew all about her troubles. "I know I run my parents' foundation technically, but really it runs like a well-oiled machine, with or without my input."

"It's good you can get away. I should tell you, though, Jonathan has been in here recently. He bought some clothes and told me to charge them to your account. Of course, I refused. I told him I couldn't do that without your express permission. He was very angry, but I naturally assumed you wouldn't want him accessing your account, especially after everything that's happened."

Jenna smiled gratefully. "Thank you, Antonio. You did exactly the right thing."

"Well, I'd better get to work, so you can get on with your day." Antonio turned toward the curtain and pulled it open. "Oh, my!" Antonio swiftly pulled the curtain shut again and rushed over to grab a pair of boxer briefs from a nearby rack. "No underwear," he stage-whispered to Jenna - who nearly choked on a giggle. This was turning out to be quite entertaining.

Cormac hadn't uttered a sound and she wasn't sure how he would survive all the attention being lavished on him by an obviously thrilled Antonio. The curtain opened again and Antonio asked, "Shoes?"

Jenna nodded and while Antonio went to locate a few pairs for Cormac to try, Jenna checked her texts on her phone and reconfirmed the time of the Ball on her calendar. Eventually, the curtain opened and she gasped at the sight in front of her. She couldn't believe how amazing Cormac looked in a tux. She stood and walked up to him, looking him over from head to toe. She circled him, nodding in approval as Antonio stood proudly in front of Cormac, hands clasped together as if he would applaud at any moment.

"Wow!" Jenna exclaimed. "You... you look amazing." She turned to Antonio. "That will work perfectly, Antonio. Put it on Dylan's account, please. Maybe that'll teach him not to back out of our plans at the last minute."

Antonio laughed and asked, "Is there anything else we can get for your friend?"

"No. I can't think of anything else he needs," Jenna answered, still checking out Cormac in the tux. Antonio took Cormac by the arm and escorted him back into the dressing room, even as Jenna continued staring.

"I believe I can take care of getting this off, thank you, Antonio," Cormac said stiffly from behind the curtain.

"Are you sure? It's no trouble, really." Antonio sounded hopeful and Jenna chuckled.

"Nae. I'll call ye, should I need yer help."

A visibly disappointed Antonio left the dressing room and headed towards the cash register. A few minutes later, Cormac had his own clothes back on and he emerged from the behind the curtain. Antonio's face lit up when Cormac appeared. "I'll pack your tux and get it ready to go, Cormac. It won't take a moment."

He headed into the dressing room and Cormac wrinkled his brow and shook his head at Jenna.

She just laughed. "It seems Antonio has taken quite a liking to you." She lowered her voice, ensuring only Cormac would hear her words.

"Unfortunately, for the poor man, I only be interested in ye." He gave her a roguish grin that set her heart to beating as if she had a hummingbird trapped inside her chest.

Antonio came back with the tuxedo and other accessories neatly packaged, including the shoes they had found. Jenna was grateful it had only been a one-stop shopping expedition for Cormac's sake.

Antonio followed them as they walked out the door of the shop.

"I hope to see you again, Cormac. It's been a pleasure," he called as they headed down the street.

They rounded the corner and came to another shop, where Jenna picked up her own gown and some accessories, along with her shoes and then they made their way to her favorite pizzeria for lunch.

"I normally only order a slice, but something tells me you'll want more than that." She ordered the house special pizza for Cormac and a Margherita pizza for herself. She figured whatever she didn't eat, Cormac would. She also ordered an Arugula salad to share.

She could tell Cormac was doing his best to appear relaxed and in his element, but it was obvious to her that he was anything but. Jenna wished she could put him at ease, as he seemed so out of place. She didn't know what was wrong with her today, but she couldn't stop smiling at him. She had been disappointed to wake up alone in her bed this morning. She must have fallen asleep out by the fire and Cormac, ever the gentleman, carried her to her bedroom and tucked her in. She hadn't even woken up in the process. Somehow, she had come to a realization about him. It simply didn't matter to her that he was leaving in a few days and that he didn't have a penny to his name. She was going to enjoy every minute she had left with him. Tonight would be fun and she was quite sure she was not going to get drunk or fall asleep before she got to know Cormac MacBayne a whole lot better.

They enjoyed their pizza and salad. As she expected, Cormac ate most of it. He had a very satisfied smile on his face the whole time.

"Never had pizza before, huh?" Jenna queried.

"Nae. 'Twas verra delicious. How do they make it?" Cormac wondered aloud.

"Well, it's really not that hard. You just need to make good dough and have a really hot brick oven."

She could tell he was thinking about that concept.

"What is it made from?" he asked.

"I have a recipe at home. I'll copy it for you and you can take it with you when you go." The thought made her sad, somehow. She didn't want him to go, but she couldn't expect him to stay either. He had told her he missed his family. That wasn't a feeling she had ever experienced. She missed Dylan when he wasn't around for a few days, but her parents were another story. They hadn't been around much since she was a kid. She missed Ashley, who was off wandering around Scotland with her new husband, and she missed Ashley's mother and father, who were both deceased. She'd spent most of her childhood with the Moore's. Of course, her parents had always provided for her, she never lacked for anything, but they were never really involved in her life. They were busy travelling around the world all the time. She couldn't even remember the last time she'd seen them in person. It had been years. She spoke with them often, or at least, as often as she possibly could. Dylan was the only person she could really rely on since Ashley left, but she couldn't expect him to drop everything to babysit her when she needed him. She was going to have to get her act together and get on with her life. Jonathan had destroyed what little faith she had in humanity, but somehow Cormac was giving that back to her. *Damn. Why does he have to be leaving so soon?*

Back at the San Francisco house, Jenna started the preparations for their evening. Cormac didn't have much to do. He just needed to shower and put on his tux. She, on the other hand, had a manicurist coming by to do her nails, a hairdresser for her hair and a makeup artist. She had to look amazing tonight. She was accepting an award for her parents, who had generously donated an entire wing to the Children's Hospital. She was only slightly nervous about getting up there in front of all those people. Her speech had been memorized and would be followed by a video montage of her parents doing good deeds all over the world. She felt guilty, because it bothered her that she had to share her parents with needy children around the globe. She felt selfish and it embarrassed her to even think about it. She had everything she could possibly want, there was no way she was going to begrudge any child the help they needed, when they needed it. If her parents could do that for so many, surely she could suck it up and be grateful to have been born to such giving parents.

Jenna directed Cormac to a spot on the sofa and turned the television on for him. She showed him how to use the remote control and let him flip through the channels to find something to watch that suited him. While he was doing that, she opened the door to the manicurist, who set up shop in the dining room.

Cormac tipped his head back on the sofa to get a look at what was going on behind him. He had been pushing buttons on the remote control Jenna had handed him and found himself more confused than when he'd started searching 'for something to watch' as Jenna had suggested he do. He had many questions for her, but knew from experience she would not believe he didn't know the answers. She had left the thing she called her 'phone' sitting on the table in front of him and it was buzzing loudly. He picked it up and marveled at the small square pictures all over it. He touched one and before he knew what was happening, he was seeing more things he couldn't comprehend. He took the phone with him and got up to see what was causing the odd smell coming from the dining room.

The manicurist practically dropped the open bottle of nail polish when she got a glimpse of Cormac coming up behind Jenna.

"What is that smell?" he asked, wrinkling his nose.

"It's the nail polish," Jenna offered. "Melanie's almost finished, so it'll be gone soon."

"Jenna, yer phone was buzzing like a bee. I know you like to keep it close by, so I brought it to you."

"Oh, thanks. You can put it down over there. I'll check it when my nails are dry."

"Jenna, I must ask ye," he hesitated, looking unsure of himself.

"Yes," Jenna responded. "It's okay. Ask me anything - within reason."

"How did the wee dancing bird get inside of yer phone?"

Jenna burst out laughing, as did the manicurist.

"Cormac, you are so funny. Oh gosh, it's a good thing I haven't had my makeup done yet, I'd have mascara running down my cheeks," Jenna said.

The two women continued giggling, even as Cormac stood there dumbfounded as to what he had done that had them laughing so hard.

"I dinnae ken why yer laughing. I saw the wee bird and wondered how it got into yer phone, and how did it learn to dance? I truly dinnae understand this thing," he said as he waved his hand over the phone and placed it on the table. "Or that thing in there." He indicated the television across the room.

"I'll try to explain it to you later, or you can ask Dylan. He's much better with technology than I am," Jenna sounded different to him today. She hadn't gotten angry with him for his questions. She had laughed, but that was better than yelling, he supposed.

The doorbell rang and Jenna asked, "Can you get that for me, Cormac. It's probably my hairdresser."

Cormac turned and walked to the door. He opened it to a smiling young woman with red hair, who was wheeling a trunk behind her.

"Hi," she said. "Is Jenna here?"

"Aye, lass. She be right in there," Cormac said, pointing towards the dining area.

"I love your accent. Where are you from?" she asked.

"Scotland," Cormac said, wondering why all the women in America were in love with the way he spoke. No one at home had ever said anything to him about it. He followed the nameless redhead as she bustled over to Jenna.

Melanie was packing up her bag and getting ready to leave. "Becky," she gushed as she hurried over to the new arrival and offered her a hug. "How've you been? I haven't seen you in ages."

"I know. Can you believe how long it's been?" Becky responded.

"Becky, this is Cormac. Cormac - Becky." Jenna introduced them and gave Melanie a quick hug. "Thanks so much, Mel. I appreciate you making a special trip for me."

"No problem, Jenna. Have a good time tonight," Melanie said, and she gave Cormac one last, lingering look as she headed for the door.

"Cormac, this won't take long, so maybe you should go and get showered and dressed," Jenna suggested.

"Aye. I'll do that." Cormac headed into the bedroom he'd been using since he arrived and closed the door behind him. He didn't think he'd ever get used to all of the oddities of twenty-first century San Francisco. He sat on the bed and called to Edna. After a few moments she was there in his mind, speaking to him.

"Cormac? Can you hear me?" Edna asked.

"Aye, Edna. I'm here." Cormac responded.

"Is everything alright? I haven't heard from you and I was a wee bit worried."

"All is well, Edna, but I'm not sure I'll be able to convince Jenna to come with me."

"Well, if that's the case, you'll have to leave without her. You still have a few days left. Don't give up."

"I willnae. We're going to an important dinner this evening. I'm worried I will do something to embarrass Jenna."

"Cormac, do not think that way. As I told you, just act like you've seen it all before. If people ask you questions, just give them basic answers. Nothing about witches and time travel, you ken?"

"Aye."

"Good. You are a handsome and charming young man. Don't you forget that. Jenna will see that, I promise. I will contact you again before it's time to leave."

"Thank ye, Edna." Cormac got up and headed into the bathroom, feeling a little more confident about the situation with Jenna and the evening to come.

# TWELVE

Jenna knew she looked good, but the expression on Cormac's face when he saw her was worth a million bucks. Her dress was perfection. A very pale aquamarine silk fabric flowed in soft pleats from a banded empire waist. The strapless, sweetheart neckline and top were covered in beautiful aquamarine crystals. She wore long, dangling diamond earrings and a matching bracelet. Her delicate hand was adorned by a beautiful emerald cut aquamarine ring that matched her dress. Jenna liked the way that her heels made her tall enough to rest her head comfortably under Cormac's chin, if need be. Best of all, were the pair of soft blue eyes staring with lustful appreciation at her and only her.

Cormac strode across the room and took her hand in his, raising it to his lips. His eyes never left hers and a chill of delight covered her from head to toe.

"You are more beautiful than a field of heather in the Highlands. You take my breath away, *a thaisce*," he stated, in a voice filled with desire.

"Thank you. What does it mean?" she asked, not understanding the last of what he said.

"My treasure." He leaned down and softly kissed her cheek, his hands caressing her from shoulders to fingertips.

Jenna could feel herself warming at his words, his touch, and his eyes on her. "You look very handsome. That tux fits you so well," she babbled and self-consciously looked away. "We should go. I just got a text that our limo is waiting downstairs." She grabbed her wrap and purse and hooked her arm through Cormac's as she headed for the door. She smiled up at him and he gave her his most devastating smile right back. This was going to be quite a night.

~~~

The limo pulled up outside the St. Francis Hotel, where the event was taking place. As they stepped from the car, they were greeted by a large group of people who hoped to see a celebrity or two emerge from the row of limousines arriving at the curb. Cormac threaded Jenna's fingers through his own as they made their way up the red carpet. They stopped to have their photos taken in front of a backdrop announcing the event and its sponsors. Cormac wasn't sure what was happening, but Jenna explained and he nodded his understanding. They were shown to the ballroom where the gala was to take place and Cormac was amazed at how beautifully the room was decorated, with flowers everywhere and lights the likes of which he had never seen. They were more brilliant than candles or torches, but still added an ambience to the room which gave the feel of being in a fairy palace. He smiled as he looked around and wrapped an arm possessively around Jenna's shoulders, drawing her closer.

"It's so beautiful," Jenna sighed in delight.

"Aye, 'tis," Cormac answered.

A raven-haired woman, dressed in a long, flowing red gown approached them excitedly.

"Jenna!" she cried. "It's so good to see you again!"

"Angelina!" Jenna let go of Cormac and threw her arms around the woman. "I wasn't expecting to see you here tonight. How have you been?"

"Just fine. I'm in town for a few days and I thought I'd come and support the hospital and hopefully, run into you."

The woman looked over at Cormac and a smile lit her very red lips. "And who is this handsome gentleman?" she asked.

"Oh, I'm sorry. Cormac MacBayne, this is Angelina Woods. Angelina this is Cormac. He's visiting with us for a few days. Dylan couldn't make it tonight, so he volunteered to be my escort."

"It's a pleasure to meet you Cormac. Lucky you," she said looking at Jenna and then to Cormac. "I'm Jenna's aunt. Her mother is my *much* older sister." She smiled at this last bit of information and offered her hand, which he took and brought to his lips. He was surprised at the reaction he got every time he made that simple gesture which was common in his own time, but obviously not done here.

"Oh, Angelina, I'm glad Mom isn't around to hear you say that," Jenna teased.

"Are you accepting the award for them tonight, sweetie?" Angelina asked.

"I am. I've got my speech memorized and I can't wait to get it over with." Jenna replied.

A waiter stopped and offered them each a glass of champagne.

*"Slainte mhath,"* Cormac raised his glass to the ladies. They both smiled and clinked their glasses together.

"What does that mean, Cormac?" questioned Angelina.

"Good health," Cormac replied.

"Gaelic?" she asked.

"Aye."

"He's from Scotland," Jenna offered.

"Nice. I love a good Scottish accent and a good Scot." Angelina winked at Cormac and he nearly choked on his champagne, once again marveling at how very forward women were here in San Francisco. Not that he didn't enjoy the attention, but he didn't want Jenna to be concerned about it.

"I'm going to go mingle. I'll see you at the table. I believe we're seated together." Angelina touched Cormac's hand as she began to walk away and whispered something into Jenna's ear, which made Jenna blush a lovely shade of pink.

"Yer aunt is very flirtatious," Cormac stated. He didn't ask what Angelina had said to get that reaction from Jenna.

"She's a very big flirt, always has been. She goes through men like some people go through water. Come on let's go find our seats," Jenna said.

They found their table number and their seats near the dais. Cormac held out Jenna's chair for her and then sat down beside her. He took her hand and examined her fingers, running his finger over her nails.

"Nail polish. Do you like it?" she asked.

"I've never seen the likes of it before."

"Don't tell me... they don't have this where you're from, right?"

"'Tis correct," he smiled.

Jenna just shook her head at him. He continued holding her hand, as Jenna didn't seem to mind and he was enjoying the sensation of it in his own.

~~~

The dinner was very pleasant, although Cormac had to fend off Angelina's advances throughout. Jenna hid her laughter. She knew Angelina was not a threat. She just really enjoyed men and flirting was second nature to her. Cormac looked a bit uncomfortable and Jenna tried to let him know that it was alright. In fact, she was quite sure that if he flirted back, Angelina would lose interest and set her sights on someone else, but Jenna was enjoying his discomfort, so she'd keep that piece of information to herself.

The award ceremony began and Jenna was called to the stage to accept the award for her parents, amidst loud applause. She wasn't comfortable speaking in front of large crowds, but she took a few deep, calming breaths and began.

"Thank you so much. On behalf of my parents, I'd like to accept this prestigious award. They wanted me to let you know how honored they are to be recognized. Their passion in life has always been helping children, whether here in San Francisco or in the remote jungles of Southeast Asia, South America or on the savannah's of Africa. It was a simple choice to help out the Children's Hospital by donating a new wing to the existing building. It is their hope that with this extra space, the doctors and researchers of San Francisco will work their magic and do what they do best - to come up with cures for some of the more virulent diseases that are affecting children today, not just here, but worldwide. They've put together a brief film to give you an idea of what they have been working to accomplish, through their foundation. Thank you again, and I hope you enjoy it."

The crowd erupted in applause and Jenna left the stage and headed back to her seat.

"Jenna, I am so proud of you," Angelina gushed.

"Aye, lass, that was verra well done," Cormac added.

Jenna smiled at them both and sat back to watch the film. She was proud of the work her parents were doing, even if it meant she never got to see them. She was a grown woman. She didn't need them anymore. She could manage her life on her own, without their help. That wasn't really true. They had helped her with Jonathan and she knew if she asked they would be there for her in a heartbeat. She had never been their main focus though. Growing up, her dad was always busy with his start-up company and her mom had been very involved as well. After they sold the company and made a gazillion dollars in the process, they'd dedicated their lives and time to helping underprivileged children. Dylan had the same issues with his folks. They had followed in the footsteps of Mark and Sally and become world travelers. It was an odd feeling, being both frustrated and proud. She hadn't figured out how to get around it yet, and maybe she never would.

The film ended to a standing ovation and when they were done, people started moving around from table to table to visit with friends and business acquaintances. Jenna turned her head to find Cormac examining her with an expression on his face she couldn't quite decipher.

She squirmed just a little under his intense scrutiny.

"What?" she asked.

"I'm sorry, lass, I dinnae know what yer asking," he responded.

"What's so interesting? You're examining me as if I'm some sort of rare specimen."

"I enjoy watching ye, when yer not aware that I am. Yer expression changed from happy to sad - to something I couldn't quite put my finger on."

"Oh, I guess I was just thinking about my parents."

"What about them?" Cormac asked.

"Why I can't seem to justify the time they spend away from me. I know they're doing a good thing, but most of the time, I don't feel as if I'm their daughter. I could just as easily have been any one of the neighborhood kids when I was growing up."

Cormac appeared sympathetic as he listened to her vent.

"Mayhap they just dinnae ken what it means to ye. Have ye ever told them how ye feel?"

"I used to tell them all the time when I was a child, but they would tell me not to be selfish. They'd tell me I was lucky to have grown up not wanting for anything, that there were many children going to bed hungry, or sick, and kids who had no schools to attend."

"I imagine that would be enough to make ye keep yer thoughts to yerself on the matter," Cormac sympathized.

"It did. I learned early on that no matter what I was thinking or feeling on the subject I should just keep it to myself. And I have, still do, even now."

They were alone at the table now; the others who'd been seated with them were moving about the room and socializing. Cormac reached out and caressed Jenna's cheek with the back of his hand, and Jenna leaned into his comforting touch. There was something about him that put her at ease, even when she was feeling out of sorts. His very presence grounded her and she knew that if she let him, Cormac would be there for her, through any struggle she may have. He'd protect her and care for her and it was very seductive to see him in that light.

Music began to play and Jenna suddenly wanted to be closer to Cormac, to have him hold her in his arms and to feel his warmth shield her from the rest of the world. She held out her hand to him. "Dance with me," she said.

He stood and took her hand, guiding her to the dance floor.

"I'm afraid I'm not familiar with yer music or dances, lass," he apologized.

"Nothing to it. You just need to put your arms around me and move around the floor. It's not rocket science," she laughed.

Cormac lifted an eyebrow. "Rocket science?"

Jenna tipped her head and pursed her lips. She wouldn't ruin this moment with a snarky comment. Instead she moved closer to him. The anticipation of touching him sent zinging sensations across her skin, and from the satisfied look on his face, she knew he was pleased.

"I'd be more than happy to hold ye in me arms, Jenna." Cormac pulled her into his embrace and they swayed around the dance floor, oblivious to the others dancing around them. She rested her head under his chin as she had imagined doing earlier, and let his presence comfort her.

The music was slow, an Etta James song, handled masterfully by the woman singing with the band. Jenna looked up at Cormac and their eyes locked together. She was falling under his spell. She knew she shouldn't, but didn't seem to be able to stop herself. This man, whoever he was and wherever he was from, had worked his way into her heart and she was helpless to stop it. The fact that he was leaving in a few days was distressing, but Jenna wasn't about to go with him. Besides, she wasn't so certain he was going anywhere. There was no such thing as time travel and in her world, witches didn't send people clear across the ocean to collect a wife. How was she going to deal with that aspect of Cormac? Maybe she could get someone to help him with his delusions, if he stayed. She needed to figure this all out. Dylan hadn't been any help at all. He just continued to feed the flame of this unbelievable story Cormac kept spinning. The song ended and Jenna was loathing the need to pull herself away from Cormac - and he didn't seem too eager to let her go, either.

"It's warm in here," Jenna observed. "Let's go outside for some fresh air."

Cormac took her hand and led her to the doors leading outside. As they exited the building and stood on the sidewalk, he turned her to face him and much to her surprise, leaned down and kissed her, quite thoroughly. His lips were soft, his breath warm and his arms wrapped around her, holding her in place. She felt her knees go weak and her heart began to pound. With shaking hands she ran her fingers through his gloriously soft hair and wrapped her arms around his neck. The kiss seemed to go on forever, and she would have loved it if it were true, but all too soon it ended and they stood face to face, unable to look away from each other.

"Well, well, well, who do we have here," a familiar voice chanted.

Jenna started at the sound and released her grip on Cormac. "Jonathan! Oh, my God! Are you following me?"

"Of course not, baby. I just happened to be in the neighborhood, walking down the street, just as anyone has a right to do, and I saw the two of you over here doing the kissy-face thing. You really ought to get a room. You are at a hotel, you know," he laughed, even as he sneered at Cormac.

"I suggest ye just continue on yer way." Cormac glared at him and stood to his full height, dwarfing Jonathan in the process.

"You do, do you?" Jonathan asked, with a hint of a challenge to his voice.

"Aye. This is not the place to cause a scene. I'd be happy to meet you elsewhere, if ye like."

"Cormac, just ignore him. He's just trying to get a rise out of us," Jenna growled, tugging on the sleeve of Cormac's jacket.

"I have places to go and people to see, sweet cheeks, so I'll get out of your hair... for now." Jonathan leaned in and kissed Jenna's cheek and Cormac lunged at him. Jenna grabbed Cormac before he could make contact with Jonathan.

"Don't, Cormac. It's exactly what he wants." Jenna stood between the two men who continue to glare menacingly at each other. "Good-bye, Jonathan."

Jonathan strutted away, with a cocky look on his face.

Cormac glanced down at Jenna, his eyes questioning. "Are ye sure ye dinnae still care for him, lass?"

"God, no! Cormac, I've already told you that. I'd say my feelings for him come closer to hate."

"Then why do ye not allow me to knock him on his arse? I've no doubt he'd stop bothering you if I did," Cormac assured her.

"I know him and I know what he's trying to do. He wants you to punch him. When you do, he'll have you arrested and then he'll try to coerce more money out of me, to get the charges dropped. I can't let that happen to you. I'm going to call my lawyer tomorrow and get a restraining order. Then he'll have to stay away from me."

Cormac appeared confused and she chalked it up to the language barrier. He obviously didn't understand many of the American terms she used. Jenna put her arms around his waist, very aware of the well-muscled physique under his tuxedo. "Come on," she coaxed. "Let's not allow him to spoil our night, okay?"

"Aye," Cormac agreed as he hugged her close.

Jenna shivered and laughed. "I was warm and now I'm cold."

Cormac took her hand and they walked back inside to the fairy-land atmosphere of the gala.

~~~

The music and dancing continued long into the night and Jenna seemed to be relaxed and enjoying herself. Cormac was sure to stay close and kept a watchful eye on their surroundings to be sure that Jonathan didn't appear again. It hurt his pride that he was unable to protect Jenna from the threat that Jonathan presented. A man in his time would have ensured her safety by removing the threat, but in this time, it was apparently frowned upon. So many of the things he had seen since his arrival were perplexing to him, and he had no choice but to accept them. He would do it to keep the peace with Jenna - unless things worsened, of course.

Cormac stood guard in the hallway outside of the ladies room, when Jenna visited it, waiting for her to reappear. The scowl on his face went a long way towards keeping people at arm's length.

"Is everything alright, Cormac?" Jenna's Aunt Angelina laid a gentle hand on his arm to catch his attention. "You look fit to kill someone," she teased.

"Aye. I'd like to, but Jenna will nae allow it," Cormac answered, tension written all over his face.

"Why, what's going on?" Angelina asked.

"Jenna's former husband is making her miserable. We had words outside earlier." He clenched and unclenched his fists in frustration. "I just dinnae ken why Jenna willnae allow me to take care of him. It wouldnae take much to get him to leave her be."

"Unfortunately, Cormac, you'd end up in jail." Angelina fussed with her dress and glanced at the line of women waiting to use the ladies' room. "She's lucky to have you to protect her."

"She doesnae want my protection, Angelina. She has told me not to interfere and I have honored her request, although it chafes to do so. I can protect her and if he tries to hurt her, he will regret it, but I'm only here for a short while. I must return to my home. I've asked Jenna to come with me, but she willnae."

"I see. Well, you *have* only known each other a short time, right? Maybe after she knows you a bit better she'll change her mind."

"I cannae stay, I must go back. Mayhap she'll change her mind before then. It's a fine life I can offer her, but she doesnae trust me yet."

"Cormac, I can see you're an honorable man. Jenna deserves that. Especially after what she's been through with Jonathan, but this might all be happening too quickly for her. When do you have to leave?"

"I have a few more days here," he answered.

"That's a shame. It would do Jenna good to get away for a while. Maybe you could convince her to go for a short vacation."

"Vacation?"

"Oh, dear, I'm sorry. For rest and relaxation," Angelina said.

Cormac continued to look puzzled.

"Sorry I took so long." Jenna approached them from the ladies' room. "I'm always amazed at the wait."

Angelina laughed and Cormac nodded, even though he wasn't sure what the wait was for.

"'Tis nothing to apologize for, lass," Cormac stated.

"Shall we go back to our table?" Jenna asked.

"Aye," Cormac said, as he took her hand. Angelina joined them, following along beside Jenna.

"Jenna, Cormac told me that Jonathan has been bothering you. Why didn't you say anything to me about it?" Angelina sounded concerned.

"It's no big deal, really. I'm going to call Bill tomorrow and get a restraining order. He'll have to stay away from me then. Besides, he doesn't scare me. He thinks he's intimidating, but he's actually just very annoying." Jenna rolled her eyes and snickered.

"I ken ye dinnae believe he'll hurt you, lass, but I'm nae so sure. I'd feel better if ye'd let me threaten him with bodily harm if he doesnae stay away from ye," Cormac said.

"Cormac, stop being such a caveman!" Jenna exclaimed.

"He just wants to help, Jenna," Angelina said.

"Aye, lass. Ye ken that dinnae ye?" Cormac asked, not wanting to upset her.

"I know. I'm sorry. I didn't mean that. You're not being a caveman. You're just being kind and I appreciate that, but you needn't worry. My lawyer will take care of it and if he comes near me, I'll call the police. Let them take care of it, Cormac. I don't want you to get into trouble." Jenna looked contrite and Cormac decided it would be best to drop the subject.

"It's getting late. Maybe we should head back to the house. Angelina, do you need us to drop you off somewhere?" Jenna asked.

"No, sweetie, I'm staying right here in this hotel. Thanks for asking though." Angelina smiled sweetly at both of them. "I'd think twice about letting this one get away, Jenna." She leaned in and kissed Jenna's cheek as she grasped Cormac's hand. He adeptly raised her hand to his lips, kissing the back of it. "I rest my case," she laughed. Cormac and Jenna watched as she walked away and then they headed for the valet parking.

# THIRTEEN

The air outside was crisp and cool after being in the crowded ball-room. Jenna held tightly to Cormac's arm as they waited for their limo to appear. She even felt comfortable enough to rest her head on his upper arm. She was rewarded with a crooked grin as Cormac pulled her into his arms and held her close. The limo pulled up and the driver exited, coming around to open the door for them. Cormac guided Jenna into the back and then followed as the driver closed the door and then took his place behind the steering wheel.

"Did you have a good time, Cormac?" Jenna wondered aloud.

"Aye. I was with ye - and that was all I needed to enjoy the evening."

Jenna smiled and snuggled a little closer. His body emitted a great amount of heat and she doubted she would ever need much more than him, to keep her warm on a chilly night. He undid the bow tie and the top few buttons of his shirt to reveal a stretch of muscular chest. Jenna lifted her nose and nuzzled his neck, enjoying the scent of pine and musk that had been set loose to assail her senses. She felt so comfortable with him. Once again she found herself wishing he was staying. She should be able to convince him, shouldn't she? She relished the feel of his arm around her back holding her close, the rise and fall of his chest beneath her cheek. This moment was perfection and she didn't want it to end. She felt safe and treasured. She had a realization at that moment. *This is the way a man should make a woman feel.* Jenna wished she had known this before. If she had, she might not have married Jonathan. She had been his safety net and he had never offered her the same courtesy in return.

The limousine continued across the city, stopping at the occasional red light on its way to Jenna's home. The two passengers remained comfortably silent as they pulled to a stop in front of Jenna's place. Jenna looked up into his glorious blue eyes and smiled sweetly, waiting for the door to be opened by the driver. As it did, Cormac exited the vehicle and put his hand inside the door to take Jenna's and help her out onto the sidewalk. They thanked the driver and hurried up the steps. Jenna fumbled through her evening bag for the keys to unlock the front door. The beep of the alarm system reminded her to reset it once they were inside and the door was closed and locked. She had butterflies fluttering around in her tummy, not sure what to do next. She hoped Cormac was on the same wavelength as she was and then, before she could give it a second more of her attention, Cormac took her into his arms and lowered his head to hers. He kissed her gently at first and then with more passion as his lips lingered on hers. Jenna came up for air and smiled, drunk with desire. She realized that up until this night, she had been the one making all the first moves and she was elated that Cormac had taken the lead this time. She decided that she would let him continue to do so.

~~~

Determined to kiss her before she kissed him, Cormac was pleased with the result. Jenna looked radiant and he knew that his kiss was the cause. The path to winning her heart was a treacherous one. He was uncertain how to proceed, but he let his instincts take control, leading her into the living room and the large, yet cozy chair set by the fireplace. Jenna reached over and flicked a nearby switch and the fireplace came to life. Cormac did his best not to seem awestruck by the sudden appearance of flames licking at what was obviously not a real piece of wood. He focused his attention back on Jenna, sitting comfortably on his lap. His fingers traced the line of her jaw seductively, then continued up to her parted lips. Jenna sucked his finger into her mouth and he knew he was lost. Dipping his head once again his tongue flicked out and teased her lips. His hands gently cradled her head, fingers tangled in her silky hair. She moaned softly, urging him on. The kisses were sweet and hot, soft and passionate. Coming up for air, Cormac changed tactics, kissing her chin, her throat, and up to her sweet little ears. She reached up to remove her earrings, which were impeding his progress. Soft mewling sounds came from deep within her throat and she wrapped her arms around his neck, pulling him closer.

"I really must get out of this dress," Jenna panted, as she pulled away.

"Aye, ye must." Cormac had a wicked twinkle in his eye. "Shall I help?"

"Please… I'd like that." She smiled coquettishly. "And while we're at it, you need to get out of that tux."

Cormac was completely enamored with Jenna. All he had to do was look at her beauty and his rigid manhood made itself known instantly.

"I'm going to get a bottle of champagne and some glasses," Jenna said, getting up from his lap. "I'll meet you in my bedroom."

"Nae. I'll wait for ye. I dinnae wish to take my eyes off ye. Ye are so beautiful." He reached out and grasped her fingers in his hand as she backed away towards the bar. Cormac stood and adjusted his painfully tight pants. He followed Jenna with his eyes, watching her every move. When she returned, she handed him the bottle as she took his other hand and they headed for her room. Cormac swallowed deeply, wanting to savor every single moment of this night.

~~~

They entered the bedroom and Jenna turned on the lights. "Oh, too bright!" she said. She immediately set about lighting the candles, which were on every flat surface all over the room. "Much better," she smiled, as she turned off the lights. The candles cast a sensuous glow throughout the room, setting the mood for romance.

Cormac popped the cork on the bottle of champagne and Jenna set the glasses down on her dresser for him to fill. Picking up one of the filled flutes, Jenna spoke. "To us."

"To us," Cormac repeated, clinking his glass with Jenna.

They sipped their champagne, eyes locked on one another. Cormac set his glass down first and drew Jenna into his embrace. Wrapped in his strong arms, Jenna could feel the muscles rippling as he stroked her back. His large hands encircled her waist as he stepped back and spun her around so her back was to him. He skillfully unzipped her dress, which glided over her soft, curvy figure ever so slowly as it headed for the floor, leaving Jenna in nothing but her tiny lace thong and high heels. Cormac's sudden intake of breath told her he obviously liked what he saw. She cupped her breasts with her hands as she turned to face him shyly. His hands rested on her shoulders momentarily and then his fingers brushed across her chest. He gently put his hands over hers, moving them out of his way.

"I would like to see ye, Jenna," he said, his voice husky with passion.

She gazed up into the deep blue depths of his eyes, watching as they took in every inch of her from head to toe. He led her to the bed, where she sat as he knelt in front of her and began to remove her shoes.

"I dinna believe I've ever seen shoes like these," he smiled up at her, holding one of the strappy heels in his hand. "I like them verra much. I like them, almost as much as yer tall boots," he added, with a mischievous glint in his eyes. He placed the shoes on the floor by the bed and standing, removed his jacket. Jenna sat watching what was turning out to be a very seductive striptease. His shirt came next. She realized she had been holding her breath and gasped for air at the sight of his glorious physique. He kicked off his shoes and removed his socks. Her eyes were riveted to the waistband of his pants, knowing what was about to happen. Cormac unbuckled and unzipped his pants, letting them drop to the floor. Jenna gasped and her eyes went wide at the sight of a fully naked Cormac standing within easy reach.

"Did I frighten ye, lass?" Cormac teased, with a knowing grin on his face.

"No. No, not at all," Jenna teased back. "Let's just say, I'm pleasantly surprised."

He knelt down in front of her again and she wrapped her legs around his torso. "Just making sure you don't try to get away." She smiled alluringly.

"I dinnae believe ye need worry. I dinna intend to go anywhere, but right here." Pushing her back onto the bed, Cormac unwrapped her legs and hooked a finger on either side of her panties, pulling them off and tossing them away. Rising from his knees, he lowered his body, covering hers easily with his large frame. Jenna looked up at him as he rested himself on his forearms. She gently touched his face, examining each feature, committing it to memory. If he was leaving in a few days, she wanted to be sure that this moment and the moments to come were readily available for her to recall this special night. Her hands went around his neck again and she pulled him down closer to her lips, which she grazed across his chin. His hot breath tickled her ear as she brushed her face against his razor stubbled cheek. Her own breathing was becoming ragged at the feel of his hands caressing her sides and her hips. His lips kissed a trail from her cheek down to her breasts, where he took one and then the other into his warm mouth, swirling his tongue across and around her pebbled nipples. The pulsing between her thighs was becoming insistent with need as she wrapped her legs around him once again, this time nestling the hardness of his swollen manhood against the softness of her moist center. She thrust her hips against him and he threw his head back and growled, coming back to nuzzle her neck with his nose.

"Dinnae tempt me, Jenna, or I'll take ye right now," he groaned.

"I'd like that," Jenna gasped.

"Aye, I ken ye would, but I believe ye'll like this as well." Cormac winked at her as he slid down her body, his kisses tickling her waist, her hips, and her thighs as he guided his fingers into her warmth. Jenna's breath came in gasps and her heart beat wildly in her chest. His thumb grazed her sensitive nub and she closed her eyes giving herself up to the sensations running rampant through her body. She opened her eyes to see Cormac watching her. "Do ye like it, Jenna, love?"

She couldn't answer him, because her whole body was vibrating, humming with emotions. Jenna was under his spell. She felt his mouth on her, and her frenetic breathing increased as she slipped over the edge and was flooded with the most amazing sensations she had ever had.

Cormac slowly climbed up Jenna's body, a smug smile lighting his face as his hands found her breasts and his lips met hers in a crushing kiss. It couldn't get much better, Jenna thought, but somehow it was. Cormac's rock hard shaft pressed into Jenna's satiny folds, which were so sensitive she jumped at his touch. She could feel his smile on her lips as his tongue entered her mouth, playing languidly with her own. He thrust himself further into her and rested momentarily before beginning a sensual dance. His long dark hair hung like a curtain around Jenna's head. The staccato of his movements brought her close to release one more time as his frenetic pace increased and he relentlessly pounded into her. She cried out and Cormac answered her with a husky growl and one final thrust. Jenna held tight to Cormac, and they both panted from their efforts, as he rolled onto his back. In heaven, she rested her head on his solid chest, her body covering his as she closed her eyes and sighed happily.

~~~

Having Jenna here in his arms was merely a dream when he first arrived; a dream, which he was pleased to note, had finally come true. His feelings for her had blossomed over the last few days and he suddenly felt confident Jenna would join him when he returned to Breaghacraig in two days' time. A satisfied smile made its way across his handsome face. He'd found the woman who would be his wife. He would be sure to thank Edna when next he communicated with her. Cormac propped himself up on a pillow, pulling Jenna closer and covering them both with a soft blanket.

His gaze lit on Jenna's face just as she opened her eyes and gazed up at him. "Jenna, my Jenna," was all he could say.

"Cormac," she breathed, a shy smile lighting her lips. She reached her hand up, fingers brushing his lips. He captured her hand in his and softly kissed it. She scooted up a little higher and kissed his cheek. "You were wonderful," she said. "When can we do it again?" Jenna giggled brazenly.

"Whenever ye'd like, love." Cormac's heated gaze let her know he was ready at a moment's notice.

"How about now?" Jenna asked.

Cormac didn't need further invitation as he seared her lips with another burning kiss.

# FOURTEEN

The smell of bacon and coffee tickled Jenna's nose. She slowly opened her eyes, to find that Cormac was wide-awake and watching her and she suddenly remembered what she'd been doing all night and with whom. A lazy smile crossed his face as he reached out to caress her cheek.

"Good morning," Jenna managed to mutter as she stretched and sat up. The aromas from the kitchen had her mouth watering and her stomach grumbling. "If you're here and I'm here, who's cooking breakfast?"

"I heard yer cousin Dylan come in a short time ago. At least I believe 'tis he, based on the singing," Cormac teased.

"What time is it," Jenna looked around frantically, in search of the answer to her question.

"Oh, my gosh, it's almost eleven! I never sleep this late!"

"I dinnae think ye did much sleeping, love." Cormac had his eyes trained on her suggestively. "Do ye not remember?"

"How could I forget," she giggled. "But I have to get up. I have to call Bill about the restraining order and then I thought I'd take you across the Golden Gate Bridge to Sausalito. Maybe we could have dinner there."

"I'd like that, but are ye sure ye wish to leave this bed?"

"Well, as much as I'd rather not, we really should get up. Besides, we'll be back here tonight," she smiled at him saucily.

"Ye are a woman after me own heart." Cormac lunged at her and before she could dodge him, he had her in his arms and was kissing her senseless. When he was done, he hopped out of bed, grabbed his kilt and adeptly had himself wrapped up and ready in seconds. "I'll shower after breakfast, aye?" Jenna was left breathlessly glassy-eyed by his kisses. "Are ye well, Jenna? I'm verra hungry. Come, let's go see what yer cousin and Chester are up to." He pulled the blankets off her and taking her by the hand, helped her out of the bed.

Jenna was speechless, but not in a bad way. Cormac was an amazing man and she was coming to appreciate him more and more with each passing day. Now she just had to convince him to stay. *After last night, I should be able to do that, no problem.* She threw on a pair of yoga pants and a t-shirt and followed Cormac out to the kitchen.

"Dylan, 'tis good to see ye, lad," Cormac announced boisterously.

"Wow! Someone's in a good mood this morning," Dylan answered, slapping palms with Cormac.

"Chester, I've missed ye," Cormac said, watching as Chester wriggled all over the kitchen in excitement.

"That dog sure loves you," Jenna observed. "At first I thought sure you were wearing bacon cologne, but I can see that even with the smell of real bacon in the room, Chester is totally interested in only you."

"Bacon cologne?" Cormac wrinkled his nose at the thought.

"What are you doing here, Dylan?" Jenna asked.

"Well, I didn't mean to interrupt you two love birds, but I felt bad about bailing on you last night and I wanted to make it up to you, so I thought I'd come over and make you breakfast. Besides I have a ballgame to go to today."

"Ah, the truth comes out. You didn't really feel bad about last night," Jenna accused.

"No, but I knew you'd probably be happy to go with our Scottish

GQ model here," he winked at Cormac.

"GQ model?" Cormac repeated.

"I'll show you what I mean." Dylan left the kitchen and came back momentarily with a copy of GQ. He opened it to a page with a cologne ad and a model in a tux. "GQ - Gentlemen's Quarterly," he explained, handing the magazine to Cormac.

Cormac looked at the magazine, touching the pages as he turned them, and then back up at Dylan, with a puzzled expression on his face. "I've never seen a book like this before."

"Technically, it's a magazine, but I guess you probably don't have these where you're from." Dylan went back to cooking their breakfast and Cormac continued to examine the magazine carefully.

"I have to go call Bill," Jenna said. "I'll be back in a minute, babe." She rubbed Cormac's back and walked from the room, leaving Dylan and Cormac alone with Chester.

~~~

"Why did she call me babe?" Cormac wondered aloud.

"It's a term of endearment, like honey or sweetie," Dylan offered. "You made some progress last night, my man. She hasn't looked this relaxed and happy in forever. I don't expect you to tell me all the gory details, but did things go well?" Dylan queried.

Cormac was baffled by his choice of words. Mayhap gory meant something different in this time. "Aye. They went verra well. I believe Jenna will come with me now. Edna was right after all."

"Congratulations, dude! I'm excited for both of you," Dylan announced. "You still have a couple of days left though, right?"

"Aye. Jenna is taking me to..." His voice trailed off when he couldn't remember the name of the place she'd mentioned.

"Sausalito." Jenna appeared in the doorway. "Well, that's all taken care of. Jonathan won't be bothering me again."

"Why, what happened?" Dylan wanted to know.

"He showed up last night outside the gala. I think he was hoping to get Cormac involved in a fight," Jenna explained.

"You kept things cool, I take it," Dylan stated.

"Yep. No fight occurred and I decided immediately I would call Bill this morning and get a restraining order. I don't know why I didn't think of it before."

Dylan tossed some bread into the toaster oven and then put the cooked bacon on some paper towels to drain. "How would you like your eggs?"

"Scrambled, please," Jenna answered.

"Cormac?" Dylan asked.

"I'll have whatever you're making," Cormac stated.

"Okay then, I'll whip up a batch of my famous veggie scramble."

"I'll get the dishes and pour us some coffee," Jenna offered.

"May I help?" Cormac asked.

"No, you just take a seat at the breakfast bar and let us do the rest," Dylan said.

Cormac watched the cousins as they moved around the kitchen, Dylan expertly cooking and Jenna getting dishes, cups, silverware, and napkins. She poured the coffee into three mugs and set one in front of Cormac, along with the cream, sugar, and a spoon for stirring. She set a cup next to Dylan and taking hers, added cream, and sugar.

Before long, they were seated side by side at the breakfast bar enjoying Dylan's wonderfully cooked breakfast. Chester was happily munching on a piece of bacon, which Cormac had handed him surreptitiously.

"Thank ye for breakfast, Dylan. 'Twas delicious," Cormac said.

"You're welcome. I'm glad you liked it," Dylan answered.

Cormac rose from his place and headed towards Jenna's room.

"Hey, where are you going?" Jenna questioned.

"Shower," Cormac replied.

"I'll join you." Jenna followed close on his heels. "Dylan, you can handle the dishes, right?"

"Sure," Dylan snickered.

Cormac was a bit surprised when Jenna announced she'd join

him. Did she mean to shower with him? If so, he had no objections to the plan. In fact, he thought it a fine idea. She put her hands on his waist as she followed him down the hallway. He couldn't believe the shift in her attitude from day one of his arrival, to this moment. He was so happy he thought he'd burst. Cailin and Ashley would be so surprised to see Jenna when he brought her home with him.

~~~

The hot shower filled the bathroom with steam and Jenna thought her life was pretty perfect right at this moment, and it would be even more perfect once she convinced Cormac not to go back to Scotland. Sure, he did have some issues they'd have to deal with. He couldn't go around thinking he was from the sixteenth century and that a witch had sent him to the present day, but she'd get him some help and he'd be fine, because he was amazing in every other way. She still wasn't quite sure that Dylan hadn't been involved in some elaborate practical joke on her, but both Dylan and Cormac assured her that wasn't the case. Could she believe them?

"Are ye joining me, love?" Cormac asked from inside the shower.

"Oh, yeah, sorry. I was just thinking."

Cormac's hand extended from behind the shower glass to pull her in with him. "And what were ye thinking?" he asked, water running in rivulets down his body and making Jenna quiver with anticipation.

"I was thinking how amazing you are." They stood face to face in the large double shower, the length of their bodies touching. "Here, let me turn on some of the other nozzles." She reached behind him and turned a knob which had water spraying them from every angle. "How's that?"

"'Tis good," Cormac said, watching her closely.

Jenna grabbed the soap and began lathering Cormac's chest. The feel of his skin under her hands was making her crazy with desire. She looked down and discovered it was having the same effect on Cormac. She made her way down to his abs, which rippled under her touch and then further still until she grasped his hard length in her soapy hands. Cormac groaned in apparent delight.

"I believe I may have died and gone to heaven, lass." He leaned back against the shower wall and Jenna took full advantage of his obvious enjoyment. She seductively stroked his thighs, all the while lubricating her hands with soapy bubbles.

"Turn around so I can wash your back," Jenna ordered.

Cormac did as he was directed and she proceeded to wash his back and very shapely butt.

"Okay, all done," Jenna announced a few minutes later.

"I dinnae believe I am done, Jenna." Cormac scooped her up and she wrapped her legs around his waist as he backed her into the shower wall and drove into her, exactly as she'd hoped he would.

Jenna couldn't remember ever being this turned on. There was something about this man that got her all hot and bothered, just from looking at him. This was the icing on the cake. She held on tightly to his shoulders, but she knew he wouldn't drop her. He was giving her the ride of her life. The sensations overtaking her body left no room for further thought and she let herself get lost in the pleasure.

"Jenna. Jenna." He breathed her name, his hot breath tickling her ear as his pace increased and she felt him pulsing deep within her at the very moment that she let go, burying her head in his shoulder to stifle the scream that wanted to escape her lips.

# FIFTEEN

"I have to stop in at the office for a minute or two. Just to drop off my parents' award." Jenna announced as they prepared to leave the house a short while later.

Cormac nodded, not sure what or where the 'office' was. He followed Jenna downstairs into a room, with a small *car* inside it. It was the color of silver and something about it proved very appealing to Cormac. He walked around the car, examining and admiring every detail from all sides.

"You like it, huh?" Jenna noted with a grin. "Most guys do. Come on, get in." She motioned for him to open the passenger door.

Cormac watched Jenna open her own door and he strode around to the other side and opened his. He climbed into what was a very small car, but he discovered that despite its size, he fit perfectly. He remained silent, busy studying the seats, the windows, the roof and every other aspect of the vehicle.

Jenna hit a button on the dashboard and the garage door opened. Cormac watched as she turned the key and the *car* came to life with a roar. This was very different from Dylan's *truck*. He really wanted to learn how to drive one, but Jenna had told him he couldnae, because he needed a license.

"Ready?" Jenna asked.

"Aye," Cormac was excited to go out with Jenna today. He was feeling a strong bond with her and he hoped she felt the same. It seemed that she did, based on the last twenty-four hours. He would be leaving soon, and he was determined to take her with him. After the night and morning they had shared, he didnae believe he would have any trouble convincing her to go with him.

~~~

As they pulled out of the garage, Jenna's heart was singing inside her chest. A few days ago, she would never have believed she'd find herself falling for Cormac. Especially after the way he came into her life and even more so, after she had sworn to steer clear of men following the Jonathan fiasco. She loved the way everything seemed so new to Cormac. He looked at the world around him with awe and a sense of disbelief. Things must be very different in the part of Scotland he came from.

She laughed to herself and shook her head.

"What's so funny, lass?" Cormac asked, drawing his attention away from the car for a moment.

"I was just thinking about how far we've come, since that morning on the Marina Green."

"Aye. It seems so long ago," Cormac smiled in agreement.

Jenna drove through the streets of San Francisco, stopping at every red light, which was one of the headaches that came with driving in the city. Fortunately, once they'd finished in the Financial District where they would be dropping off the award they were off to Sausalito and the traffic would thin out.

Jenna pulled up in front of The Sinclair Foundation building and they were met by the valet. "Miss Sinclair, it's good to see you," the valet said as he opened her door.

"Thanks, Jimmy. We won't be too long." Jenna smiled brightly at the valet patting his arm before leading Cormac in through the sliding doors of her parents' building. She stopped at the elevator bank and pushed the call button.

While they stood waiting, Cormac looked at the doors of the elevator, seeming baffled. "What is going to happen?" he asked.

"We're just waiting for the elevator, to take us up to the top floor," Jenna answered.

The doors to the elevator opened and Jenna motioned for Cormac to follow her inside. As the doors closed behind them, Cormac jumped and Jenna found herself once again amazed at his seeming lack of worldliness.

"Don't worry, it'll be okay. It's faster to take the elevator, than to walk up the stairs," Jenna reassured him, placing a hand on his arm.

Arriving at the top floor, the doors opened and they entered the executive suite where they were greeted by Susan Mitchum, the executive assistant to the Sinclair family.

"Hi Susan," Jenna greeted her warmly.

"Jenna, I wasn't expecting to see you today!" Susan's eyes wandered across to Cormac who stood behind Jenna quietly. "I see you've brought a guest."

"Oh, yes - Susan, this is Cormac MacBayne. Cormac, this is Susan Mitchum. She's our very capable executive assistant."

"'Tis a pleasure to meet ye," Cormac said politely.

"And you," Susan smiled, returning her attention to Jenna. "Can I help you with anything, Jenna?"

"I'm just dropping off the award from last night. Do you want to take it?" Jenna asked.

"Sure. I'll put it in the display case." Susan took the award from Jenna. "It's beautiful. You never know, sometimes they look like football trophies," she laughed. "By the way, Jenna, I have some papers for you to sign. Your Dad asked that I have you sign them when you next came in."

"Oh, sure. I'll just be in my office." Jenna took Cormac by the hand and led him into a large room, beautifully decorated and with an incredible view of the city from the floor-to-ceiling, wall-to-wall windows. Jenna went and sat behind the desk. She glanced at the mail that was sitting there, waiting for her attention and then opened her laptop to check for e-mails. While she was busy responding to them, Cormac walked over to the windows and stood silently, awestruck by the view.

"'Tis incredible. I can see all the way to the water from here."

"It's one of the best views in the city," Jenna stated proudly.

"Here are those papers, Jenna." Susan walked in with a stack of folders and placed them on Jenna's desk.

"What are all these?" Jenna wondered aloud.

"Some contracts, letters, and proposals. Your Dad has already approved all of them. Here's his e-mail, explaining everything." Susan pointed to the top piece of paper.

Jenna quickly glanced over the e-mail and then grabbed a pen and went to work signing the various forms. Cormac hadn't left his spot by the window. Jenna made quick work of the papers and then handed them back to Susan. "Here you go. Thanks, Susan."

"No problem. Where are you off to now?" Susan asked.

"We're heading over to Sausalito. Cormac's visiting from Scotland, so I wanted to show him some of the sights," Jenna said.

"You should go through Muir Woods, too. It's so beautiful. Those giant redwoods aren't found everywhere, you know," Susan suggested.

"That's a good idea, I think we'll do that. Thanks again, Susan. Either Dylan or I will be in soon. You never know." Jenna got up from the desk. "Cormac, we should go."

Cormac turned from the window with a look of wonder on his face. A crooked grin lit his face as he headed towards Jenna and Susan. "I cannae wait to tell my family back home about all the wondrous things I've seen here."

"Well, there's more to see before you go." *If you go,* Jenna thought.

The Golden Gate Bridge was unusually traffic-free as Jenna guided the car across. Cormac looked to be enthralled by all that lay before him. The sun was glinting off the water, which was dotted with the tiny white sails of boats slicing through the waters of the bay below the bridge on this beautiful day. Besides the cars, there were pedestrians strolling along and taking in the view, along with those riding bikes and running. Jenna was feeling relaxed and happy. She hadn't had this feeling for a long time and had almost forgotten how it felt. She was actually enjoying the view. It was fun to see it through the eyes of another. Especially someone who was so obviously excited by it all.

"Ah, Jenna, I feel like a daft idjit every time I open me mouth. This place, this time is so verra beautiful! Words fail me." Cormac threw his hands up in apparent exasperation at his own lack of words to express his thoughts.

"It is beautiful! I understand completely how you feel," Jenna said. She removed one hand from the steering wheel and gently laid it on his arm.

"Aye, but no matter how beautiful, 'tis not nearly as beautiful as Breaghacraig," Cormac professed.

"Well, I guess I'm going to have to see that for myself someday," Jenna conceded.

"Ye could see it with me sooner than someday, lass," Cormac offered quietly.

"Cormac, let's not go there, please," Jenna said. She didn't want to spoil the day and hoped to avoid this discussion for now.

"Jenna, ye'd like to see where I live, ye said so yerself. Why do ye nae come with me when I leave? It may be yer only chance to do so."

"That may be true, but I'm not going with you when you leave. We'll keep in touch and maybe in a month or so, I'll come to Scotland and you can show me around."

"'Twill be too late. Ye must join me when I leave, or not at all." Cormac looked utterly dejected by her refusal.

Jenna was starting to feel more like her prickly old self. *How dare he tell her what she must do?* "Cormac, we've been having a really nice time. Don't ruin it now with all this talk about me going to Scotland! We hardly know one another, I'm certainly not up and leaving to travel to a foreign country with you without giving it some more thought!"

Cormac sat back in the car seat and harrumphed in annoyance, while Jenna removed her hand from his arm and drove on over the bridge in stony silence.

~~~

Cormac wasn't quite sure how things had gone so terribly wrong in such a short time. He'd merely suggested that Jenna come with him, as she herself had said she would like to see Breaghacraig. Now she wasn't speaking to him and he felt as if the wall he had worked so hard to demolish was building back up. He needed to do something, before he was back where he started with her.

"I'm sorry, Jenna. I didnae mean to upset ye. Yer right. We've been having a lovely time together. Can ye forgive me? I couldnae help meself. I'd be a fool not to want ye to come with me, but I willnae speak of it again. I can see that ye've made up yer mind on the subject."

He sat perfectly still, awaiting her response, and was just about to give up when she looked over at him wearing the saddest expression he had ever seen. His heart hurt. Had he caused that pained expression? If anyone else had dared to cause Jenna to become so sad, Cormac knew he would turn into the caveman Jenna had spoken of, but it was he himself who was making Jenna so unhappy. He didn't deserve her love. Perhaps 'twas best he go home and forget about her.

"Cormac, of course, I forgive you. You have to understand why I can't go with you, not right now. We've known each other for less than a week and even though we've grown close, it just wouldn't be smart for me to drop everything and head off with you. I've learned some hard lessons recently and I need to be extra careful, especially with you. You do get that, don't you?" Jenna asked.

"Aye, I do." He didn't really, but he was so relieved that she was speaking to him again, he had no intentions of rocking the boat.

"Okay, good," Jenna said, sounding relieved. She pulled the car into a vacant parking space. "We're at our first stop. This is Muir Woods."

Cormac got out of the car and made his way around to help Jenna out, but she beat him to it. "No need to worry about me, Cormac, I can get out of the car on my own."

"Of course ye can, lass." Cormac felt a bit wounded by her reaction. He knew she could get out of the car on her own, but he wanted to do the courteous thing and assist her. He certainly had a lot to learn about women of this century. Jenna stood waiting for him with her hand outstretched. Cormac took it and they walked along the path that led through the trees. Cormac had never seen anything like this place, the size of the trees was impressive.

"This is a grove of Coastal Redwoods. They are between 400 and 800 years old and some of the trees are as tall as 250 feet. Amazing, huh?" Jenna, sounding like a tour guide, shared her knowledge of Muir Woods with Cormac, who craned his neck back as far as it could go, so that he could see to the very tops of the trees.

"These trees were here and growing in my time," he said, feeling rather awestruck.

"Right," Jenna rolled her eyes at him.

"I ken ye dinnae believe me, Jenna, but 'tis true," he announced quietly.

She didn't respond, but instead stood with her hands on her hips and a perplexed expression on her face. Cormac thought it best to change the subject and began asking her questions about Muir Woods. "Muir, 'tis a Scottish name, aye?" he asked.

"Yes, John Muir, the man these woods were named after, was a Scottish naturalist. He was born in Scotland and came to America when he was a child."

"Is he still living?" Cormac asked innocently.

"You really need to stop this, Cormac! It's starting to get old," Jenna snapped.

"Stop what, lass?"

Jenna raised an eyebrow and looked very angry.

"I really dinnae ken if he is alive or dead," Cormac commented quietly.

"He passed away a long time ago, Cormac. Look, can we set some ground rules for the rest of the day. I don't believe you're from the sixteenth century and I don't believe a witch sent you to find me, so can you please stop this crazy game you're playing."

"As ye wish, lass, but 'tis not a game."

"Thank you."

He took her hand and brought it to his lips. Jenna tipped her head and smiled sweetly. They continued walking among the giant trees. Cormac was a bit homesick and walking in the woods was soothing his heart. This was as close to home as he'd seen, since being here. He could imagine walking in the woods back home, holding Jenna's hand and showing her his world. He had one day left to convince her and it wasn't looking good. Jenna wouldnae even allow him to bring the subject up.

# SIXTEEN

Battery Spencer was the best place to see the sunset, as far as Jenna was concerned. She guided the car to a parking spot and they both got out. Cormac leaned on the hood of the car while Jenna leaned back into him and waited for what turned out to be a kaleidoscope of colors - pink, orange, gold, purple. It was magnificent and it was even better watching it from the shelter of Cormac's strong arms. Jenna was beginning to realize that their relationship was going to be very short lived. If she wanted it to continue, she was going to have to broach the subject of him staying. She'd do it tonight and hope she could convince him.

Cormac dipped his head and nuzzled her ear. "That was almost as beautiful as ye, Jenna."

Jenna leaned into the nuzzle. "That's sweet of you to say."

"I wouldnae say it, if it werenae true."

Jenna spun in his arms and wrapped hers around his neck. "You are quite the romantic, Cormac MacBayne." Standing on tiptoe, she rubbed her nose on his and scooted a little closer into his strong embrace. There was a fluttering in her belly, as she thought of the previous night, which they'd spent wrapped around each other.

Cormac's eyes twinkled when he looked into hers. "Where have ye gone to, love?"

"Nowhere, really," she lied. "I was just thinking that we should go get dinner."

"Dinner, aye?"

"Yes, dinner. You haven't eaten since our late breakfast. You must be hungry."

He seemed to think about that for a moment before he responded. "Aye, that I am."

"Well, let's go then." Jenna pulled out of his embrace and felt a chill at the loss of his heat.

Cormac put his hand to the small of her back and gently guided her toward the driver's door, which he opened before she could protest. She got in and got herself situated and Cormac closed the door and strode around to the passenger side. Jenna watched as he easily folded himself into the compact space beside her and gave her another breathtaking smile. She was so enthralled by him that she literally forgot to breathe for a minute. Getting herself under control once again, she started the car and headed off in the direction of Sausalito and her favorite waterfront restaurant.

"Hi Casey," Jenna greeted a tall, slender brunette woman who was waiting for them, just inside the doorway of the little seafood restaurant that sat perched right on the water's edge.

"Do you have a table for us?"

"Of course, right this way. How've you been? I haven't seen you in a while." Casey said, as she led them to the outdoor patio and a table that overlooked the San Francisco Bay. "Are you doing okay since the annulment?"

"I'm fine. I'm getting on with my life. I'm finally free of the anchor that would have been holding me down. I was lucky to get out when I did."

Cormac pulled Jenna's chair out for her and as she sat down, Casey handed them both menus. "I know I probably don't have to ask you what you want, Jenna. The usual?"

"That would be great, Casey. What about you, Cormac? I'm having the seafood pasta. It's to die for, right Casey?"

"It is the house specialty," Casey happily agreed.

"Then that's what I'll have," Cormac said.

"Drinks while you wait?" Casey asked.

"I'd like a Sunset Margarita, no salt, please," Jenna said. She glanced at Cormac, who seemed a bit bemused by the drink menu. "He'll have the same. And can we get an order of fried calamari, too?"

"Sure. I'll put your order in and be right back with your drinks." Casey confirmed, as she started back inside.

"I love this place. I've been coming here since I was a little kid. My best friend, Ashley's parents used to bring all of us, including Dylan, for a special treat." Jenna looked wistfully at Cormac who had a very strange expression on his face. He cleared his throat and took a huge gulp of water, avoiding Jenna's gaze. "Is everything alright?" she asked.

"Aye. All is well, lass. Dinnae fash."

Jenna persevered. "It's just that you had a really strange expression on your face. Was it something I said?"

"Nae. I just had a tickle in me throat. 'Tis all."

Casey came back with their drinks. "Here you go. Enjoy."

"Thanks, Casey." Jenna smiled at the restaurant's hostess, who was also serving as their waitress.

"Thank ye, lass," Cormac offered, when Casey placed his drink in front of him.

"You're welcome." Casey turned and looked at Jenna, before she mouthed the words, "He's hot!"

Jenna laughed and Cormac gave her a questioning look as Casey walked away.

"She thinks you're hot," Jenna said.

"Nae. I'm fine, lass. The weather is perfect."

Jenna laughed again. "Not that kind of hot. She thinks you're very handsome."

"'Hot' means handsome?" Cormac questioned.

"Yes, except when it means hot," Jenna was having fun messing with him, and she was amused that he was preening like a peacock at this news.

Jenna raised her glass in a toast. "To your hotness," she giggled. They clinked glasses and took a sip.

"What's in this drink, love?" he asked, studying the contents of the glass with interest.

"Tequila, triple sec, lime juice and the sunset part is provided by grenadine."

"I've not had any of those things before. 'Tis verra good."

"Actually, you have. You tasted mine at the karaoke bar, remember? It didn't have the grenadine, though."

Their calamari arrived and Cormac examined it quite carefully, poking it with his fork as if he expected it to jump off the plate. "What is this calamari?" he asked.

"It's squid. A little tiny octopus," Jenna explained. When Cormac still looked puzzled, she spoke again. "Never had it before, huh?"

"Nae, I havnae." He looked very uncertain, picking one up between his fingers.

"Here, dip it in the sauce." Jenna showed him what she meant, dipping a piece of calamari in the sauce before she popped it in her mouth. "I like the tentacles the best," she smiled.

"Tentacles?" Cormac asked, following her lead and indulging in his first calamari.

"The little squiggly things." She picked one up and showed it to him. "What do you think? Do you love them?"

"Aye. They are verra good. The cook at Breaghacraig has never made anything such as this."

"You've been missing out," Jenna teased. Cormac continued devouring the calamari, much to Jenna's delight. She was happy to share some new experiences with him - and even happier that he was enjoying it.

Their main course arrived and plates were set in front them, along with a basket of freshly baked bread for the table. Jenna once again observed Cormac looking totally confused by the food. He turned his attention to her and said, "I recognize the seafood, but what is this?" He picked up a strand of pasta.

"It's pasta. Your cook doesn't make this either, does she?" Jenna shook her head. "No, don't bother to answer the question. I get it. This is all new to you. Let me show you how to eat it." Jenna took her fork and spoon and showed Cormac how to twirl the pasta onto the fork. He gave it a try and failed miserably. "Keep trying. You'll get the hang of it," she giggled.

Determination was written all over Cormac's face as he went to work mastering the pasta twirl. After a few tries, he was finally getting the pasta from the plate to his mouth without dropping it and he appeared to be enjoying it very much. As she ate, Jenna kept checking on Cormac to see if he needed any help, but based on how quickly the food disappeared from his plate, she didn't think he was struggling. When she was full, she offered him the rest of hers and he gladly accepted. It vanished in a heartbeat.

Jenna paid the check and said goodbye to Casey as they left. "Thanks, Casey. Everything was great."

"Hope to see you in here again soon," Casey replied, as Jenna and Cormac made their way out the door.

"Let's walk around a little and then stop for some ice cream or candy - or both," Jenna smiled. She took Cormac's arm and snuggled up close to him as they walked along the waterfront towards the more touristy shopping area. "It's pretty busy tonight," Jenna observed. Cormac didn't seem to hear her; he was so busy trying to look around at everything at once. She pulled on his arm to gain his attention and he stopped walking and turned to her. Jenna took a deep breath before she spoke. "Cormac, what would you think about staying here with me?" she asked cautiously.

His expression dropped, and she saw the indelible sadness on his face. "Jenna, I cannae stay. I want to be with ye, but I dinnae belong here. I must return home to my family, I am needed there." She knew he was speaking from the heart. It was obvious from his demeanor that he wanted to stay, but he simply couldn't. Disappointment and heartbreak washed over her like the waves at Mavericks. "I'm so sorry, Jenna. I believe I have fallen in love with ye in this short time I've been given to spend here. Edna was right. Ye are the one for me, and I will spend the rest of me days regretting the loss of what could have been. I have asked you to come back with me, but ye willnae."

Jenna wanted to cry on hearing that he'd fallen in love with her. Life was full of cruel surprises. Cormac arrived in her life in a less than conventional way and he had grown on her. At first she was snarky and rude to him, but he never let that stop him from wanting to be with her. Now, she was going to have to say goodbye to him, just when she was understanding that she loved him too. Could she just pick up and leave? No, of course not. What did she really know about him? When she thought about it, not much more than he had present-ed to her. She couldn't go. She had to know him better before she could possibly make such a monumental decision, be sure she wasn't going to regret it as she had with Jonathan.

"Jenna, look at me." Cormac held her face in his hands. "Please, come with me."

"Cormac, I don't trust myself to make good choices when it comes to men. Past experience has shown me that I'm pretty bad at it. I know everything seems perfect right in this moment, but what about a week from now, or a year from now. I just can't do it." She felt tears pricking at her lashes and brushed them away before Cormac could see them.

Cormac gazed down into her eyes. "Have faith, love. All will be as it should be."

Jenna rolled her eyes skyward. What was this New Age mumbo jumbo he was spouting? She knew better than to put her faith in love. It could really come back to bite you in the butt. They continued walk-ing and found themselves in front of the ice cream shop. Putting aside their situation for the moment, they decided to share a cone, which meant that Cormac got most of it. Not that Jenna minded, she was feeling a bit out of sorts and didn't have much of an appetite left, even for ice cream. Next stop was the candy shop. "Cormac, let's go buy some candy, for you to take back for the little ones," Jenna suggested.

"Jenna, I have no money to buy it and I cannae ask you to spend more money on me than ye already have."

"I want to do it. You can tell them it's a gift from me."

Cormac pulled her close and placed a kiss on top of her head. "Ye are a sweet one. They'll be verra happy."

"Let's go then," Jenna smiled, trying to be as cheerful as possible, even though she was struggling internally.

The candy shop was full of families buying candy, which only saddened Jenna even more. She couldn't help but remember her time spent here with the Moores. All these happy people made her wonder, if she would ever have a family herself. She found herself thinking about Cormac and what a great Dad he would be. The fantasy of happily-ever-after was calling to her. Mentally she shook her head, knowing she'd better not listen.

Jenna picked up a basket at the front of the store and led Cormac around, explaining what all the different candies were. He picked a little bit of everything - lollipops, chocolate, jellybeans, and taffy. They came to a basket of peach gummy candies and Jenna said, "My friend Ashley and I used to come here whenever her family brought us to Sausalito. We always stocked up on candy, but Ashley's favorites were these peach gummies."

Cormac picked up one of the candies and examined it. "She really liked these best?" he asked, sounding strangely as if he knew Ashley and was surprised by this information.

"She sure did. She'd fill the basket as much as she possibly could, before her parents would tell her she had enough."

"Hmmm... I think I'll get some of these," Cormac announced. He started filling the rest of the basket with handfuls of the peach gummies.

Jenna laughed. "I certainly hope you like them."

"They're not for me, love."

"Oh..." Jenna wasn't sure who they might be for, but she was a little jealous that whoever it was obviously held a special place in Cormac's heart. She hoped it wasn't another woman. There was nothing she could do about it though. She wouldn't go - and he wouldn't stay. They were at an impasse and it didn't seem either one of them would change their minds.

At the cash register, Jenna paid for the candy and asked them to put it into two bags, because Cormac requested the peach gummies be separated from the rest. Again, she had the odd feeling that Cormac had gotten the peach candy for someone special. The curiosity overcame her and she had to ask. "Cormac, who are you getting the gummies for?"

"For me brother Cailin's wife."

Jenna was a little taken aback by his response. "I see," she said, but she didn't really.

They walked out of the store and down the street in the direction of the car. Jenna was deep in thought. She didn't like the way she was feeling. Hadn't she promised herself not to get involved with anyone? And hadn't she already broken that promise? She was at her wits end. She tried not to sound too possessive or clingy when she asked, "Cormac, what are your plans for the future?"

Cormac, who had been munching on a piece of candy, stopped and gazed directly into her eyes. "For me, the future is back home. I ken that it willnae be with ye, even though I had hoped that it would be different. I wish to get married and have a family and to spend the rest of me days with them. Now, I'm not sure." He seemed very contemplative. "What of ye, Jenna? What do you plan for the future?"

Jenna shrugged. "I don't know. I have my charity work and the foundation, I guess. I once thought I had my life all mapped out, but I have absolutely no plans now. Sad, huh? I can't blame Jonathan completely for what happened. I wasn't blind, but I didn't want to see. I wanted to be married so badly and consequently I made a terrible choice. I wouldn't listen to anyone when they told me I was making a mistake. I purposely didn't see or hear what was obviously happening right in front of my face. I'm as much to blame as Jonathan is."

Cormac pulled her in close and wrapped her in a hug filled with warmth and caring. She melted into it, but in true Jenna fashion she pulled away and started walking again, with Cormac hurrying to catch up with her. She couldn't let him know how much she wanted him. He had turned down her offer to stay and she had to think about getting on with her own life. They reached the car and she quickly opened her own door and got in, closing the door before Cormac could reach it. Distance was what she needed. She had let herself get too close and now she was deeply regretting it.

Cormac opened the passenger door and got in. She could tell he was confused by her abruptness, but she wasn't in any mood to explain. She started the car and sped off towards the freeway. She just wanted to get home and put some space between herself and the man she so desperately wanted to be with.

~~~

Surrounded by nothing but the hum of the car, the silence emanating from Jenna was a reminder that he hadn't been able to win her over. That his trip to San Francisco had been a failure. Cormac couldn't think of what to do or say to lift Jenna's spirits. She had been acting oddly for the past few hours. He had one more day in San Francisco and he wanted to spend it with her. Despite her prickly side, he found Jenna to be fascinating. She was smart and beautiful. She made him laugh and her warmth and caring were apparent, even though she tried her best to hide it.

"Jenna, what is wrong, lass?" he asked, knowing his concern was written all over his face. Not that Jenna would have noticed, she didn't take her eyes from the road in front of her.

"Nothing's wrong," she replied.

Cormac wasn't convinced. "Are ye sure? Ye've not said a word in quite a long time."

"I'm fine… really. Just concentrating on driving."

"Aye. I can see that." He waited a beat and when she didn't respond, he hopefully asked, "What will we do tomorrow, Jenna, love?"

"Well, I don't know what you're doing, but I have things I have to catch up on. I've taken enough time off to spend with you, and now I need to get back to my own life."

"I see. It's my last day here tomorrow. I hoped you could spend it with me. We dinnae need to do anything special. I just want to be with you." He hoped he wasn't sounding as desperate as he felt. Why was she pushing him away? This had been the most wonderful week of his life and he thought she was enjoying it too. Perhaps not. He tried another tactic. "Jenna, I will go with ye, to help with whatever it is ye need to do."

Jenna kept her gaze focused on the windshield, much to Cormac's frustration. "No, that wouldn't work. I just need to be by myself."

"Is that what ye really want, Jenna?"

"Yes. Yes it is."

Silence again. He wouldn't fight her on this, she had obviously made up her mind. He would just see how the day went. He'd wait for her to come to him. He felt certain she would, eventually.

Jenna pulled into the garage and they both got out of the car. Jenna locked up and they headed upstairs to the kitchen entrance. Dylan was sitting at the counter and he glanced up when they entered.

"Hey, there you are! I was wondering what happened to you two. Thought you might have run off and eloped!" He laughed at his own joke.

Jenna scowled at him and headed off towards her room.

"Jenna," Cormac called after her.

"I can't do this right now, Cormac. Good night," she said and he heard the slam of her bedroom door.

"Okay, what did you do now?" Dylan wondered aloud.

"I did nothing, Dylan, I promise. We had a lovely day. I dinna ken why she is behaving this way."

"Did you have a fight?"

"Nae. As I said, everything went verra well." Cormac thought back on the day and realized that the only time Jenna had turned away from him was when they discussed his leaving. "Perhaps she is upset with me because I am leaving. She did ask me to stay, but when I explained that I couldnae she seemed upset. She was back to normal for a short time and then she went back to not speaking with me."

"Hmmm… That's not good." Dylan scrunched his eyebrows and asked, "Cormac, is there a reason you can't stay?"

"Edna told me that if I didnae return at the appointed time, I might not be able to return at all. She hasnae ever sent anyone away from their own time to such a distant place. I cannae risk that. I have my family back home and I wouldnae wish to live without them in my life. If there was a way for me to stay a while longer, I would. Jenna willnae return with me and I am truly saddened by that, but I understand why she must stay. She doesnae feel she knows me well enough to leave all this behind and truth be told, I find I dinnae ken her all that well either."

Cormac paced restlessly across the kitchen floor. "What am I to do, Dylan? I have one more day here and I want to spend it with her, but she says she willnae, she has other things to do."

"I'll try talking to her. Not right now though. Sometimes she just needs a little time to think and then once she realizes she's being unreasonable, she's back to normal."

"Do ye think that will happen?" Cormac asked. Dylan shrugged his shoulders and Cormac was not convinced even Dylan believed it would work. "I'll be off to bed then. I'll see ye on the morn."

"Good night, Cormac."

Cormac headed to his room. He wanted to stop at Jenna's door, but he didn't want to make her angry. When she was angry all he wanted to do was make her happy. Seeing her smile was like watching the sunrise. Her face glowed and her eyes sparkled and they did that for him, because of him. Perhaps he didn't deserve a gift so wonderful.

# SEVENTEEN

Flinging her pillows across the room wasn't making Jenna feel any better. *Damn it! How could I have fallen in love? That was definitely not in the plan!* She curled up in a tight ball on the bed, pillow clutched to her chest and let the tears she had been holding back fall. *Damn! Damn! Damn!* She was being such a baby. This was not the way to treat the man who had done nothing more, than want her enough to ask her to go home with him.

She couldn't go. She needed to stay in San Francisco. Tears and pouting were not something she did. At least not until Cormac Mac-Bayne made an appearance in her life. She'd cried angry tears plenty of times with Jonathan, but sad tears were a rarity in her world. She didn't allow herself the luxury of feeling sorry for herself, but that was exactly how she was feeling now. Her emotions fluctuated between sadness, hopelessness and irritation that this should happen to her. If Cormac hadn't arrived out of the fog that morning, she wouldn't be facing a future of wondering *what if*. What if she went with him? Would she regret her choice? Would they both wake up one morning and realize they made a terrible mistake? Jenna wanted to run down the hall to Cormac's room and throw herself into his arms, but that wouldn't solve anything. It would just muddle things even more. She needed a

150

clear head to deal with his departure. She'd stay in her room tonight and instead of thinking with her heart, she'd think with her head. Jenna took a deep breath and decided that in the morning she'd let Cormac come with her. She had lied about having things to do. At that particular moment, she hadn't wanted to be around him. She knew that if she were, she'd never be able to deal with what was inevitably going to happen. Tomorrow would be tough, but she was tough, too, and she could handle it. It would definitely be the hardest thing she'd ever have to do in her life, but she would spend the day with him and then the next morning she would take him to the Marina and say goodbye.

Her eyes grew wide. What was she thinking? If he wasn't going to the airport and getting on a plane, he wasn't going anywhere. She had let herself get all worked up, when in actual fact, he wasn't really leaving. Maybe tomorrow she could get him to tell her the truth. Maybe it *was* all a practical joke, just as she'd suspected from the beginning. If it was, it was the cruelest joke anyone had ever played on her. With that thought in her head, Jenna fell into a fitful sleep.

In her dream, Jenna was wandering through a forest shrouded in mist. The trees were all gnarled and the branches were like arms, reaching out to grab her. She was afraid, yet she continued walking. Suddenly, right in front of her, she saw a yellow-eyed wolf. He was baring his teeth and Jenna was terrified. She backed away, but the wolf moved towards her. She took another step back and stumbled over a large root, falling backwards into a tree. Jenna searched her surroundings for a way to escape. The wolf stood before her now, not more than ten feet away. "Cormac, Cormac, where are you?" she cried. "Help! I need you. Help me!" The wolf lunged for her as she threw her arms up to protect her face.

Jenna woke with a start, perspiring heavily and gasping for breath. She brushed the tears from her damp cheeks and sat up, hearing a knock at her door.

"Jenna are ye alright? May I come in?" Cormac sounded concerned.

"I'm okay, Cormac, I just had a nightmare. You can go back to bed."

"I heard ye calling me. Are ye sure ye dinnae need me?"

"I'm sure. I was calling to you in my dream, but I guess I was talking in my sleep. I'm sorry I woke you."

"Dinnae fash, lass. I'm here if ye need me."

She didn't answer him and the silence stretched on until finally she heard him retreat down the hallway. *What kind of crazy dream was that?* Jenna lay back onto the pillows and tried in vain to fall back to sleep. She rolled over, checked her clock, and discovered it was only four a.m. Jenna tried closing her eyes, but each time she did, she kept seeing that wolf, his teeth dripping with saliva, his hot breath fanning over her skin and his eyes boring holes through her. Jenna was glad she awoke when she did. She couldn't imagine what would have happened next in her dream, but it surely wouldn't have been good. She shuddered just thinking about it. It had felt so real.

Turning on the light, Jenna searched the room. Something didn't feel right and she got up and padded to the bathroom, where she switched on another light. That nightmare had really spooked her. *You look like hell, Jenna.* She leaned on the sink and gazed into the mirror, noting the dark circles under her eyes. *Nothing a little makeup won't fix.* "I might as well get up 'cause there's no way I'm falling back to sleep." She threw on her robe, grabbed a blanket and headed for the living room. Watching reruns of old sitcoms always helped when she couldn't sleep and she hoped it would do the trick this time as well. Jenna curled her legs underneath her and covered herself with the blanket, pulling it up tight around her ears.

"Jenna, may I sit with ye?" Cormac appeared in the room, bare chested and wearing a pair of Dylan's sweatpants. "Ye obviously cannae sleep," he stated.

Jenna scooted over to make room for him on the couch and he sat down, pulling her into his arms. She rested her head on his chest, deeply breathing in his scent - pine and musk - and the uneasiness that had been following her since the nightmare vanished. He didn't say a word, just held her, kissing the top of her head. The warmth of his body reassured her and made her feel safe. Nothing could harm her when she was in his arms. What would she do when he was gone? The thought had her wrapping her arms around his waist, anchoring him to her. She didn't want to let go. A tear slid down her cheek and landed on Cormac's chest.

"Jenna, are ye crying?" he asked. Her answer was a sniffle. "I'm here, lass. I'll watch over ye. Sleep."

~~~

He held her close as she closed her eyes and drifted off to sleep. He would protect her while he was still in San Francisco, but he couldn't help but wonder how she would fare after he was gone. Would she be alright without him here? Would Jonathan continue to harass her? He didn't want to think about those things, so instead he thought about the soft, sweet woman in his arms and he too, drifted off to sleep.

~~~

"Good morning, sleepy heads," Dylan greeted. "And just why are we sleeping on the sofa? Rumor has it that a bed is much more comfortable."

Jenna yawned and stretched, accidentally hitting Cormac's chin. "Good morning," she managed as she blinked the sleep from her eyes. Reaching out she gently massaged Cormac's chin. "I'm sorry, Cormac, I didn't mean to pop you."

"Dinnae fear, love, it would take more than that to hurt me," Cormac reassured her. He released his hold on Jenna and she sat up.

"I hope you two made up," Dylan said, with a teasing glint in his eyes.

"We weren't fighting, Dylan," Jenna said. "Or, I guess I should say, Cormac wasn't fighting." She repositioned herself on the sofa and wrapped the blanket closer around her shoulders. "I'm sorry, Cormac.

It seems like I'm always saying that and before you tell me that it's okay, I'm going to tell you that it's not. I don't know what's wrong with me; I don't seem to have any control over my emotions lately."

"I willnae tell ye it's *okay*, instead, I'll accept yer apology, if ye promise me that today ye will not be angry with me."

"I think I can do that. I promise." She smiled shyly at him. "Okay. We've got one more day together and we should enjoy it. How about if we just spend time together. I don't have any specific plans. Let's just see where the day takes us."

"I believe that will be fine. I just want to spend the day with ye." Jenna could see the love in his eyes and her heart ached at the thought of not seeing him again after tomorrow.

"I just have one question for you and I want you to be honest with me," she stated. "I've been told more than enough lies lately."

"What is it, love?" Cormac asked.

"I need you to tell me the truth. Have you and Dylan been playing a practical joke on me?" she demanded quietly.

"Jenna, I ken yer not able to believe what I've told ye, but ye can believe that I am nae trying to fool ye about anything."

"He's telling the truth, Jenna. There's no practical joke," Dylan added. He seemed rather serious, which Jenna knew was not typical for Dylan. If he was joking around, he surely wouldn't have been able to keep it going for a whole week. But that left her with an even bigger conundrum. Time travel? Witches? She might not believe it, but both Cormac and Dylan apparently did. She'd try to keep an open mind and let this play out as it would. What else could she do?

"Okay. I believe you," she said, even though she was still struggling. "I'm not going to give it another thought. Let's make today a day that neither one of us will forget."

"A day to remember, aye?" Cormac nodded.

Chester padded into the room, looking sleepy-eyed. "Chester, where have ye been?" Cormac fluffed his ears and ruffled the fur on the dog's back. Chester responded by licking Cormac's face and wriggling his delight from head to toe.

"I'm going to take Chester for his morning walk. I'll be back a bit later. You two have fun," Dylan winked in their direction as he leashed Chester and headed for the door. "Should we all have dinner together tonight, or would you rather be alone?"

"Together," Cormac said, much to Jenna's disappointment. "But only for dinner. After that I'd like to spend my final evening here with Jenna alone."

"No problem, bro. I'll leave you alone after we eat," Dylan continued with a grin, opening the door.

"I'll cook," Jenna said. "We'll go shopping for groceries while we're out."

"Okay. See you later then." And with that, Dylan and Chester were gone, leaving Jenna alone with Cormac.

"We should get dressed," Jenna announced, as she headed for her room. "Let's go get some coffee."

"And food?" Cormac asked hopefully.

"Of course," Jenna answered. Cormac appeared very happy with the response, clearly he must have been starving. "I'll meet you back out here."

~~~

The coffee shop was quite crowded and Cormac couldn't believe that all these people were waiting in line for coffee. He didn't understand it. Coffee was good, but he didn't think it was so good that it warranted stores on every corner and lines out through the door. People in this time seemed to always have a cup of coffee in one hand and their phone in the other. They were completely unaware of what was going on around them. Dangerous to be sure. Why only this morning, he had seen two people almost hit by the speeding wagons people used to get around. They barely looked up from their phones to notice their near demise.

Jenna paid for the coffee and pastries and led the way to a corner table for two. She ordered herself a drink with a verra long title and he got his coffee black. After drinking it with cream and sugar, he had discovered that he preferred it black. It had tasted bitter at first, but after getting used to it, he discovered he enjoyed the flavor of the coffee. Everything here was either too sweet or too salty to his taste buds. Jenna handed him a *bagel and cream cheese*.

"Thank ye, Jenna. What do I do with this?" he asked, holding up the small container of cream cheese.

"It's to spread on your bagel, silly," she smiled sweetly at him. He watched carefully as she spread cream cheese on her own bagel. He immediately followed suit and took a bite and then another. If this was his breakfast, he was going to be hungry again verra soon. He sipped his coffee and admired Jenna as she ate. She was so ladylike and dainty in her movements. Exactly the woman he had imagined would be his wife. He deliberately pushed the thought away. It would do nothing but serve to sadden him.

Cormac perused the people in the room. Since his arrival, he had taken great pleasure in observing those he saw around him. He tried to imagine what their lives were like. He knew not everyone lived as Jenna and her cousin did. He had seen people, who in his time, would likely be merchants or artisans. There were plenty of poor and homeless. He had seen evidence of that daily. At Breaghacraig everyone was well cared for and had what they needed to live a good life. He knew that wasn't the case in all parts of Scotland in his time, but those the MacKenzies were responsible for had no complaints to speak of. He felt sorry for those in San Francisco whom he'd seen sleeping in doorways and being passed by as if they didn't exist. He was just about to ask Jenna about it when there was a scuffle outside the coffee shop. An older woman was wrestling with a much younger man, who was attempting to steal her purse and her phone. Cormac immediately rose from his seat and before Jenna could stop him, he was outside.

The man had managed to snatch both objects and was running down the street.

"Cormac, wait!" Jenna called. "Don't go after him. He might have a gun!"

Cormac didn't heed her warning, instead, charging off down the street after the thief. The man quickly turned a corner and Cormac flew after him. They were running down an alley now and Cormac was right on his heels. Turning, the thief flashed a knife and Cormac quickly grabbed his arm, forcing the man to drop the knife. Cormac grabbed the man by his shirt and threw him up against the nearest wall.

"I believe ye have something that doesnae belong to ye," Cormac growled fiercely.

"Here, take it," the man's voice quivered as he held out the purse and cell phone. "Just let me go."

"I'm afraid not, lad." Releasing the man from the wall, Cormac grabbed his arm and started back down the alley. The man's feet barely touched the ground as he was dragged along. At the corner, a breathless Jenna had just turned her ankle and fallen to the ground. "Dinnae move or ye'll regret it," Cormac warned the thief. The man nodded and stood perfectly still while Cormac scooped Jenna off the ground. "Ye shouldnae have come after me, Jenna."

"I was afraid he'd hurt you," Jenna said.

Cormac laughed. "Ye were afraid that this wee man could hurt me? 'Tis not likely." He renewed his grip on the man's arm, placing him in front of him while also carrying Jenna in his arms and heading back to the woman whose purse had been stolen. All along the street, people were applauding Cormac and as they approached the coffee shop, they were met by two police officers and a paramedic.

"Cormac, you can put me down now," Jenna whispered.

He gently placed Jenna on her feet and noticed she was obviously favoring her ankle. The paramedic, who had been tending to the other woman's bruises, led Jenna to the back of another strange-looking wagon, where he examined her ankle.

"Sir, that was very courageous of you." One of the men in blue uniforms was talking to Cormac. "You can release your hold on this guy. We'll take it from here."

"I have a few questions for you, sir," the other man in blue said. Cormac watched as the man was led away to the backseat of a black and white wagon with flashing lights on top. Much like the one he had seen that day, on their way home from the beach.

"Aye. What would ye like to know?"

"I just need to get your statement. What you saw, etc."

"Thank you so much," the older woman gushed as she threw her arms around Cormac. "You're my hero." She continued holding onto him, despite Cormac's attempts to extricate himself.

"Sir I need to know your name and address, etcetera. If you could just fill out this form for me I'd appreciate it. You can sign it down at the bottom," one of the men said.

Jenna hobbled back to his side and whispered, "I'll help you with that. Officer, can we take this back into the coffee shop to fill it out?"

"Sure. We'll be out here for a while."

"Ma'am, you'll need to let go of my friend," Jenna said politely to the bag theft victim.

"Oh, I'm so sorry. I just can't thank you enough."

Cormac peeled the lady's arms from around his waist and set her away from him. Her bright smile belied the fact that she had just been the victim of a crime. Cormac moved to pick Jenna up again, but she waved him off. "I can walk, thanks." She limped to the door of the coffee shop and Cormac opened it, ushering her inside. They sat back down and Cormac stared at the papers in his hand. "Here, let me see that," Jenna offered.

Cormac handed the papers to her and Jenna produced a pen from her purse. "What is that?" Cormac wanted to know.

"It's a police report. I'll fill it out for you and then you can sign it on the bottom. I'm sure that's all they'll need, although they might need you to testify in court."

"When will that be?" Cormac asked.

"Oh, it won't be for a while, I'm sure."

"I'm leaving tomorrow, lass. I'll nae be here."

Jenna looked disappointed, but she began filling the paper out. When she was finished, she handed the pen to Cormac and pointed to a spot on the paper for him to sign.

"Okay. That should do it. Let's go give this to them and then we can leave," Jenna said.

Cormac handed the papers to the police officer and they checked to make sure they had his contact information. "Thank you, sir. We're grateful for your help. We'll be in touch."

"'Twas no trouble at all," Cormac replied.

They started to walk away and Cormac noticed that Jenna was still favoring her ankle. He swept her up into his arms and the people who had gathered to witness the incident broke out in applause again. Jenna buried her head in Cormac's chest. "You really don't have to carry me, you know. I can walk," she said in embarrassment.

"Not verra well, lass. I'm going to take you home to rest," Cormac raised an eyebrow as he answered. "Believe me, 'twill be quicker my way."

"Let me call a cab, please."

"Dinnae waste yer time, lass. We've nae got that far to go." He felt her relax in his arms and knew she wouldnae continue to resist.

# EIGHTEEN

"San Francisco has a new hero tonight and from the response to this cell phone video taken earlier today, he's setting hearts across the Bay Area aflutter." The evening news was on and Jenna and Cormac sat in total amazement as the news anchor continued. "Earlier today, a woman was robbed of her purse and cell phone outside a local coffee shop. The victim tells us that a man wearing a kilt ran after her assailant, and not only retrieved her possessions, but also captured the thief, disarming him of a knife."

Cormac recognized the woman he helped when she appeared on the screen. She was smiling brightly as she described what happened. "His friend ran after him, turned her ankle and fell. He picked her up and carried her back, all the while holding my attacker by the scruff of the neck. It was unbelievable, like something you'd see in a movie." The video continued, showing the woman hugging Cormac tightly around the waist and followed their every move, even as far as Cormac picking Jenna up and carrying her away as the crowd applauded.

"Oh my God," Jenna said. "You're on the news!"

Cormac's mouth had dropped open as he watched the television disbelievingly. "Jenna, how did I get inside the box?"

"You're not in the box, Cormac. Someone took a video of the

whole event with their cell phone."

"I dinnae ken what ye speak of."

Jenna pulled her cell phone out of her pocket and held it up, waving it in front of him. Cormac nodded his head at her, but was still deeply puzzled. "It takes photos and video," Jenna said. Cormac shook his head and shrugged his shoulders. "Watch, I'll take a picture of the two of us. Come closer and look at the phone." Cormac did as he was instructed and Jenna held the phone up in front of them. He could clearly see himself in the phone's glass screen. "Okay. Smile." He glanced at Jenna and saw her smiling brightly. He did the same and she took the photo before turning the screen back towards him. "Now look. See, there we are."

"Is it magick?" Cormac questioned, studying the screen carefully.

"No, silly, it's technology. I can't believe you've never seen a cell phone. You must be the only person left on the planet who hasn't."

Cormac nodded slowly, still fascinated by the photo. "Aye. Ye may be right."

"So, if I push this button, it takes a video." Jenna pointed the cell phone at Cormac, who furrowed his brow.

"What is it doing now?"

"You'll see." She stopped the video and played it back for him.

"If I didnae see it with my own eyes, I wouldnae believe it." He took the cell phone from her hands. "Can I see it again?"

"Sure. Touch the arrow on the screen," Jenna showed him how to replay the video. "So you see, someone at the coffee shop had their phone out and recorded everything. I don't know if that's a good thing or not. If they find out where you are, they'll be camped out on our doorstep wanting to talk to you." Jenna reached over to the coffee table and picked up her laptop. She tapped on the keys and brought the news video up online. "Wow! That video's gotten thousands of hits already, and it's only been up for an hour. Looks like it's going viral."

"Viral?" Cormac was more confused than ever.

"Don't worry about it. Hopefully no one I know will see it. If they do, and they alert the media... well, you don't want to have to deal with that."

Someone was bound to recognize her and that could spell trouble for Cormac. He hadn't exactly been truthful with her and she was afraid that any extra scrutiny he might receive would bring up uncomfortable questions. If he answered them the way he had answered Jenna's questions, it would be bad for Cormac. Jenna's cell phone vibrated in her hands. She checked the caller ID and not recognizing the caller, decided to let it go to voicemail. Her phone vibrated again, almost instantly. This time it was a text from Dylan. *Just saw the two of you on the news. Stay in tonight.'*

"Jenna, is all well?" Cormac seemed concerned.

"Oh, yeah, it's just Dylan. He says he won't be able to join us for dinner." The phone buzzed yet again. "And we should probably stay in tonight." She smiled brightly, trying to reassure him. "I wasn't planning on going out anyway." Instead of responding, Cormac lifted her foot in his hands and gently probed her ankle. "It doesn't hurt anymore," she reassured him. "I just turned it. No big deal."

"Good. I'd not want to see ye hurt, lass." The expression on his face told her he cared a great deal, about what happened to her.

"I'm fine. No need to worry about me," she said, although she was secretly delighted at his attentiveness. "We'll just stay home and relax."

"Jenna, tell me about yer life here in San Francisco. I ken that ye dinnae spend all yer time at the beach, or attending feasts. What do ye do that makes ye happy?"

Jenna thought long and hard about the question. She realized that Cormac must think she was a spoiled rich girl. She hadn't shared the details of her life with him. She'd been enjoying a vacation from her everyday life and had been happier than she had been in a long time. "Hmmm… that's a good question. Mostly, I work at my parents' foundation. You know they do a lot of charitable work involving children and since they're away all the time, Dylan and I handle matters here at home. I also work with the local homeless shelters and battered women shelters. I have lots of friends in the restaurant business, and I see to it that at the end of the day, they collect any food that's left over and donate it to both groups."

"Does that make ye happy, Jenna?" Cormac asked.

Jenna frowned, considering the question. "I haven't had much to be happy about this past year. Don't get me wrong, the work I'm doing is very rewarding. It makes me feel good to know we're helping so many people. My own happiness is the last thing I think about."

Cormac brushed his hand across hers. "Ye deserve to be happy, lass."

Jenna rolled her eyes. "Happiness is overrated," she lied.

Cormac raised an eyebrow at her. "What do ye mean by that?"

"I don't know if I can explain it. It's hard to be happy. I guess I have moments of happiness, but it can't last forever." She reached her hand out to Cormac and he took it. "You know, you've made me very happy this past week."

"Aye, you've done the same for me."

"What makes you happy, Cormac?"

Cormac grinned. "Lots of things make me happy. A smile on your face makes me happy."

"Not here in San Francisco with me. What makes you happy when you're at home?"

The grin grew even wider, and his eyes sparkled with joy. "Ah... so many things. My family, my home, the people of my clan. Riding my horse through the MacKenzie lands and feeling the cool breeze on my face. The green grass, the forests, the ocean - the feeling that I belong there. There is much more, but I dinnae wish to bore ye."

"You're not boring me, Cormac. I love listening to you talk. Your home sounds like a wonderful place, I wish I could go with you. And before you say I could," she paused, thinking of how she could possibly explain it to him. "I know I can, but I also know I can't. This is all so new to me - *you're* so new to me. I'm afraid of making another terrible mistake. Afraid my heart will be broken. I wish I was the kind of person who didn't care about this kind of stuff. I wish I was the type of person who could just leave everything behind and go, but I'm not.

I tried it once, with Jonathan, and I've regretted it every day since. You understand, don't you?"

"Aye." Cormac remained silent for a moment, his eyes travelling across her hair, over her face. "I don't want to forget ye, love. I want to always be able to think of ye and remember exactly how beautiful ye are. I want to remember the touch of yer hands, the smile on yer face, the sound of yer voice in me ears, the taste of ye on my lips."

Jenna found herself speechless. It was truly the most beautiful thing anyone had ever said to her and it brought tears to her eyes. Cormac noticed and brushed them away with his thumb. He ever so gently brought his mouth down on hers. Jenna met his kiss with all the sadness, hunger and longing she was feeling. Her senses drank him in. She couldn't tell where she ended and he began. He felt so right, but somehow she knew it had to be wrong. Jenna would let herself forget all about that for now. She wanted to be with him, to go with him. How could she not? She cleared her mind of all doubt and gave herself up to this man, to this moment.

In the darkness of the room, Cormac lay awake, Jenna secure in his arms. *Edna, are ye there? I must speak with ye.*

*Aye, Cormac, I'm here. Are ye ready to leave tomorrow?* The sound of Edna's voice in his head was reassuring. Cormac was still anxious that he might not be able to return home tomorrow, despite a part of him not wanting to go.

*I am. Jenna willnae be returning with me. Of that, I am certain.*

*I'm so sorry, Cormac. You couldn't convince her? What reasons does she give?*

*She doesnae trust me enough. She has been hurt too recently by her idjit husband and cannae believe I won't do the same.*

*Do you love her? Because if you do, there is always hope. It is always possible she will change her mind. You do not know what tomorrow will bring. Be at the appointed spot at first light and wait for the fog. You will be home before you know it.*

*Thank ye, Edna. I do love her and I believe she feels the same for me, but it may be asking too much of her, to expect her to leave her life here.*

*Go to sleep now, my dear. The morning will be upon you before you know it.*

*Things will work out exactly as they were meant to. I promise.*

And then Edna was gone. Cormac lay on his back, staring up at the ceiling. How could things work out the way they were meant to? Jenna was not going to leave with him. She didnae even believe him. She most likely thought he was out of his mind. Amazingly, she still wanted to be with him, just not together at his home in Scotland. Taking a deep breath, Cormac tried to relax his mind and sleep. Tomorrow he would have to say goodbye to Jenna. It would be the hardest thing he'd ever had to do in his life, but he had nae other options.

~~~

The morning light peeked through the curtains and Jenna stretched her arms overhead. She turned to look at the man lying next to her and was surprised to find him wide-awake and gazing at her with the saddest expression in his eyes.

"I must go, Jenna," he said. "I must be at the place where we met verra soon."

"Oh, no. I don't want you to leave," Jenna cried.

"I have no choice. If I dinnae leave today, I willnae be able to go back."

Jenna was absolutely baffled by his insistence that a witch had sent him to San Francisco and a witch was going to return him to his home. It went without saying that the fact he believed his home was in sixteenth century Scotland was simply beyond being rational. Despite her disbelief, Jenna decided she'd humor him and when he found he was still here later this morning, she'd do her best to help him overcome this delusion.

"I understand. I'd like to come with you." On seeing the brilliant smile that broke out on his face, Jenna corrected him gently. "Not back to Scotland, just down to the Marina, to say goodbye."

Cormac's face fell and she felt terrible to cause him such disappointment. "I'd like that verra much," he said quietly.

"I guess we should get dressed and get your things together then,"

Jenna suggested.

"Aye."

Silence descended upon them as they got out of bed and dressed. Cormac gathered the bags of candy he had purchased and put them in the leather bag slung across his body. The bag had been a gift from Jenna.

"Come, lass, let's be off," Cormac said when he'd completed his preparations.

They headed down the hall and into the living room, where Jenna was surprised to see Dylan waiting for them on the couch.

"I couldn't let you leave without saying goodbye." Dylan stood up and wrapped Cormac in a bear hug, which was returned in kind. "It's been a pleasure getting to know you. I wish you could stay longer, but I know you have to get back. I hope I'll be able to get there for a visit myself, someday."

"I'll speak to Edna about it, she may be able to arrange it," Cormac suggested as he clapped Dylan on the back. "And ye Chester, I will surely miss ye." Cormac squatted down to pet Chester and the dog practically knocked him over in his attempts to lick his face. The dog's body was wriggling left and right as he displayed his love for Cormac. "Yer a good dog. I wish I had one like ye, back home."

Dylan walked with them to the door. Jenna found herself amazed to think that Dylan genuinely believed Cormac was going somewhere. She kept her thoughts to herself, however. This was going to be difficult, but she'd be there to soften the blow once Cormac realized he wasn't going anywhere.

They reached the Marina and Jenna sat on a bench. Cormac knelt in front of her and looked so serious, it nearly broke her heart. He took her hands in his. "Jenna, love, I'm sorry to leave ye. I wish things could be different, but they cannae." He leaned forward and kissed her. The sweet taste of his lips on hers almost had her changing her mind and saying she'd go with him, but she knew he wasn't going anywhere. She'd get to kiss him again, she was certain of it. Cormac said his goodbyes and walked solemnly across to the spot where Jenna had first spotted him. He stood there, very still, and waited. Nothing happened, but he stayed in place.

Jenna felt so badly for him. He really seemed to believe he was going somewhere. Tears filled her eyes as she thought about how terrible he must be feeling. His delusions were obviously still firmly in place and she didn't know how she could convince him otherwise.

"Edna!" he called suddenly. "Edna, are ye there?"

Jenna couldn't take it anymore and she went over to him. "Cormac, it's all going to be okay," she said soothingly.

At that precise moment, the wind picked up and the fog began to swirl around them. "Cormac, I'll help you." The next words out of her mouth were impossible for either of them to hear. The roar of the wind in her ears was incredible.

"Jenna, ye must get back away from me," Cormac shouted.

"No, Cormac. Please, listen to me!" She grabbed his hands and tried to pull him in the direction of the bench, but the swirling fog wouldn't allow it. Jenna wasn't sure what was happening, but she knew she needed to get Cormac out of there.

"It's too late, Jenna. Hold on to me. I dinnae wish to lose ye." Cormac pulled her in tight to his body and held her in a vise-like grip. What happened next was too unbelievable for words. The fog continued to swirl and little pops of light burst around them. The ground seemed to drop out from under her feet and she felt herself moving at a high rate of speed.

"What's happening?" she screamed, but the wind ate her words and the fog swirled around them like a tornado.

# NINETEEN

Jonathan walked into Joe's Diner and sat at a vacant table. He thought he'd have some breakfast, before heading over to Jenna's to confront her about her latest stunt. He couldn't believe she'd had the nerve to get a restraining order against him. He'd show her, no restraining order was going to keep him from getting to her and completing his plan. She'd ruined his future when she got the annulment, but what she didn't know would definitely hurt her, and he'd be rolling in the dough soon enough.

"Hi, my name's Sophia, can I get you some coffee," the waitress asked when she sidled up to his table.

"Hey, Sophia, yeah, I'd like that very much."

"I'll be right back with the coffee, and then I'll take your order." She smiled sweetly at him.

He winked at her. He loved to flirt, and this waitress was just his type. She might come in handy as an aide to his future plans, too.

Sophia brought his coffee over and took his order. "Come back and sit with me," Jonathan offered with another suggestive wink.

She thought for only a moment before she responded. "Okay, my shift is just about over anyway. You're my last customer," Sophia said.

"I hope I can be more than just your customer," Jonathan pretended to sound hopeful, and he could tell Sophia was falling for it.

She brought his order back a few minutes later and sat down opposite him, pouring herself a cup of coffee. "I don't often get invited to join people at their tables. Thanks for asking." Sophia was obvious about giving him a head to toe perusal, and he could tell she was definitely interested.

"I'm happy you agreed to it. What are you doing after you're done here?" he asked casually.

"Not much. I was going home to do some laundry," she said.

"Laundry! That's no fun. Why don't you come with me, I could use your help."

"What do you need my help for?" she asked.

Jonathan could see she was intrigued and he wanted to make her feel at ease. "I know you don't know me, but I'm a fine upstanding citizen. Everyone around here knows me, so if you want to check my references, you can start by asking Joe. He's known me for years."

"I've seen you here before. I'm not worried about you."

"Okay. Then let me tell you what I'm up to. You can help me out and I'll take you to dinner later. How's that sound?"

Sophia considered for a moment before she responded. "Well, I guess it depends on what you need me to help you with."

"I just need you to be my arm candy." Jonathan smiled his most charming smile and he could see it was making Sophia feel special by the way she sat up a little straighter in her seat and brushed her hair back from her face. "My ex lives nearby and I'm going to pay her a little visit. I need her to think I've moved on… with you. Do you think you could be convincing in that role?"

Sophia nodded, but he caught the hesitation in her eyes. "Sure, but why do you need her to think you've moved on?"

"Don't you worry your pretty little self with the details. I'm completely over her and I have been for a long time, but she won't let me near her and I'd really like for us to be friends, after all, we were together for a long time. So, I thought if I showed her I had a beautiful lady like yourself, she'd be more receptive to my friendship. It would make our lives a lot easier, if there was no tension between us."

"I can understand that. I've got friends who got divorced and they hate each other. It's made their lives hell for years," Sophia said. She sipped her coffee thoughtfully, and Jonathan was certain she was going to agree.

"Yeah, so you can see what I mean. Good. You're not only beautiful, but you've got brains, too. I find that very attractive in a woman."

Sophia blushed and Jonathan knew his ploy was definitely working. He finished his breakfast, making small talk with Sophia and sent her obvious signals that he was interested. She was eating it up. He paid the bill and then waited while Sophia went in the back and changed out of her uniform and into her regular clothes.

"Wow! Look at you. Even more beautiful out of your work clothes. I'm a lucky guy." Jonathan was laying it on thick, but again, she didn't seem to notice. "Let's get out of here."

They walked the few blocks towards Jenna's house. He used to live there too, and the thought that she'd thrown him out and cut him off was a bitter pill to swallow. But he had a plan and this was merely step one.

They stood across the street while Jonathan checked his watch. He'd wait a few more minutes - it was still early. He knew Dylan was there and was positive he'd follow his usual schedule of walking Chester, the devil dog, himself. Once he was gone, he'd be able to talk to Jenna without interruption. If he could convince her he was over her and he wasn't angry about the money, then he was home free. She'd let her guard down and drop the restraining order.

The door opened and Jenna came out, holding Cormac's hand. He heard Sophia gasp when she saw them. "Is something wrong, Sophia?"

"No. It's just that I know them. That's Jenna and he's Cormac. He was flirting with me at Joe's and Jenna was pretty jealous," she announced, with a malicious grin on her face.

"Is that going to be a problem? Will you still be able to help me?"

"Sure. No problem. It'd serve her right if she thought I had both of you interested in me."

Jonathan cocked an eyebrow. "You don't like her much, do you?"

"No. She's one of those girls who looks down her nose at people like me. It'll be nice to get some respect."

Jenna and Cormac were headed off down the street. Jonathan didn't know where they were going at this hour, but he was determined to follow them. "Come on," he said as he grabbed onto Sophia's hand and pulled her down the street with him. "Looks like they're heading for the Marina. We'll hang back a bit and see what they're up to and when the timing's right, we'll approach them."

"Okay. Whatever you say," Sophia said.

When they got to the Marina, Jonathan was surprised to see Jenna sitting on the bench, while Cormac looked to be saying goodbye. This was perfect. Jenna was a much easier target without that Scottish bastard in the way. Cormac moved to a spot on the green and just stood there.

"What's he doing?" Sophia wanted to know.

Jonathan motioned for her to be quiet. The air around them changed. It seemed to be charged with an electrical current. He watched in fascination as Jenna went to Cormac and he embraced her just as a whirlwind of fog began swirling around them. Weird lights were flashing and the wind had picked up. His curiosity got the better of him and he started to head in their direction. Sophia followed along, gripping his hand. As they reached the outer band of the fog, Jenna and Cormac were no longer visible. "Where'd they go?" Jonathan wondered. "I can't see them." He pulled Sophia deeper into the fog and before he knew what was happening he felt himself falling. Where there once had been solid ground, now there was nothing but air rushing past as if he was being hurtled through space. He could hear Sophia's screams as she clawed her way into his arms. "Hold tight," he yelled, but he really didn't have to, he was wearing Sophia like she was a second skin. He felt her go limp in his arms, but he held on to her, not sure what would happen next. Fear was lodged in his throat and he didn't want to go wherever he was headed, alone.

~~~

When the swirling stopped, Jenna found herself still anchored in Cormac's arms. They hit the ground hard, but Cormac took the brunt of it as Jenna landed atop him.

"What just happened?" Jenna asked, searching the unfamiliar sites surrounding her.

"Jenna, yer not going to like what I have to tell ye, lass." Cormac looked like a man who was sure he was in trouble.

"What do you mean? Where are we?" She could feel herself losing control of the fragile grip she had on reality.

"We're back in Scotland, in my time. There's the bridge, right over there."

Jenna looked in the direction he was pointing and was surprised to see the bridge he spoke of was not the Golden Gate Bridge, but a small stone bridge spanning a stream. Panic filled her and she wanted to run, but where? She had absolutely no idea why she wasn't on the Marina Green. The only answer was standing right in front of her.

Cormac had gotten to his feet and he was holding out his hand to help her up. She batted it away. "You, you kidnapped me! I don't know how you did it, but you brought me here against my will!"

"I'm sorry, Jenna. I didnae mean to bring ye. Ye grabbed on to me just as the fog arrived. I was afraid if I let go, ye might end up in another time and place, all alone. I wasnae willing to take that risk."

"I can't believe this! Am I awake? This isn't possible." She was rapidly losing her equilibrium. "You need to take me back, right now!"

"I'm afraid I cannae do that. I don't know *how* to do it. Edna will have to help ye."

"Edna!" Jenna called, circling around on the grass. "Edna! Where are you? When I get my hands on you…"

"Jenna, I know this is a shock, but try to be reasonable. Look, over there, Edna left my horse. We can ride to Breaghacraig and try to contact Edna once we're there."

"No! I'm not going anywhere with you! This is beyond ridiculous.

I can't believe you did this to me." She got up and started stalking towards the bridge. Maybe if she crossed the bridge, she'd be able to get back.

"Jenna, where are ye going? Ye must come with me. This is not San Francisco and ye willnae be safe on yer own. Please, listen to me. I ken yer angry with me, but ye must understand that I didnae mean for ye to come with me!"

Jenna stood with her hands on her hips and for the first time, noticed that her clothing was different. "What happened to my clothes? And your clothes?" she asked in total confusion. She found herself wearing a long medieval-looking dress and cloak. She checked her feet and much to her surprise was delighted to find she still had her tall boots on. That might become a problem if she had to do a lot of walking, but at least she had one thing to hold onto from her life in San Francisco. Cormac was still dressed in a kilt, but gone was the leather jacket and t-shirt. In its place he wore a linen shirt with laces and the kilt looked different as well. He still wore boots, but not the one's he'd worn in San Francisco. The leather satchel still hung across his body and despite the difference in his clothing, he still looked amazing to her, but she was furious with him. He had taken her away from everything she knew and brought her to an unfamiliar place, and according to him, *time. Get it together, Jenna. You need him to help you.* Her heart was racing in her chest and she was starting to hyperventilate. She took a deep breath and did her best to relax. Jenna was shaking uncontrollably as she walked back towards Cormac. He reached out to pull her into his arms, but she stood away from him. "Don't touch me. Don't you ever touch me again!"

Cormac held his hands up in surrender. "I'll not touch ye lass, but it might be near impossible because we have to share my horse."

"I'm not getting on that horse. No way. I hate horses," she yelled.

"Lass, it's a long way to Breaghacraig. Ye cannae walk all that way, especially in yer tall boots." He smiled and she knew exactly what he was thinking.

"Stop it. Grrr… I can't believe this. When I meet this Edna, she's going to be one sorry witch. I can't even believe I just said that. Witch! Time Travel! Scotland! I'm going to be sick." Jenna started to feel nauseous and dizzy. "I think I might be going to faint." Abruptly, she shook her head determinedly. "No! No, I will *not* faint." She was determined to get a grip on her escalating fear and she would ride out the sick feeling that was overtaking her, and not let it overwhelm her.

"Jenna, please, calm yerself. I will help ye, but I cannae do it here. We must go. It is a long way from here to my home."

Cormac went to get his horse "Saidear," he said softly, as he stroked the massive bay's neck. The horse nickered and nudged Cormac with his nose. "Come my friend," Cormac said. As he approached Jenna, she backed away. "I told you. I'm not getting on that horse. I'll walk. Which direction are we heading in?" Cormac pointed towards the path and she headed off at a determined pace. She could sense him behind her, but she certainly wasn't going to soften her stance. Had he planned on kidnapping her all along? She wanted to scream in frustration, but what good would it do? As aggravated and angry as she was, Jenna knew that her only chance of getting back home lay with Cormac.

The sound of hooves pounding along the pathway behind them caused both Jenna and Cormac to freeze in their tracks. Glancing back, Jenna saw a man dressed completely in black, riding atop the largest horse she had ever seen. He galloped past them and then reined his horse in and turned in their direction.

"Is that Cormac MacBayne I see?" the man questioned. He had an obviously English accent.

"Aye. 'Tis." Cormac answered sullenly. There was an intense, angry expression on his face as he quickly made his way to Jenna's side. "How did ye get back here?" he demanded of the other man.

"Good question. I've been waiting for quite some time, but today was apparently my lucky day. The fog happened to be swirling at the bridge and I was able to ride through. Who is this lovely woman you have at your side?"

"'Tis not your concern. I warn ye, Richard, stay away from Mac-

Kenzie land, or ye'll pay the price."

"Ha! I have other things to attend to MacBayne, and none of them include the Mackenzie's. At least not at this particular moment." Richard sneered down at Cormac and gave Jenna an appraising once over, before turning his horse and galloping deeper into the woods.

"Who was that?" Jenna asked.

"That was Sir Richard Jefford. He is an enemy to my clan," Cormac watched intently as Sir Richard disappeared into the trees. "We must get back to Breaghacraig at once. We must warn them."

"Warn them about what?" Jenna wondered aloud.

"Warn them that Sir Richard is back. He's been in the future for these past few months. We were told he'd been jailed. I didnae ever expect to see him again, but he is back and nae doubt he will cause trouble."

"So the future is back that way - and you're leading me away from it!" Jenna was beside herself with fury. "I'm heading back to the bridge, and don't you dare try to stop me!"

Cormac reached out to grab her arm, but she shook him off. "Jenna, you don't understand. The fog must be there, and it is gone now."

"Then how did he get here? He said the fog was there. You're lying to me," she barked.

"I wouldnae lie to ye, lass. Ye cannae go back right now. The fog is fickle. It is only there when someone is waiting on the other side. Do ye nae ken? If there is no one waiting for you, in the future, the fog willnae appear for ye."

"Was someone waiting for him? I didn't see anyone else when we arrived. How did we get here?" Jenna demanded suspiciously.

"My horse was awaiting our arrival. The fog disappeared as soon as we got here. I dinnae ken how Richard arrived. I'm not the one in charge of the bridge. If Edna were here, she could answer yer questions, but I cannae." Cormac was sounding increasingly frustrated with Jenna. He raked his fingers through his hair and stared up at the sky as if seeking divine intervention. "Now, come with me... *please*. We must hurry."

Jenna glared at him, hands fisted at her sides. *Damn, damn, damn him... and Edna!* "Fine, let's go." She again headed off down the path, Cormac following close behind. She'd figure this out, without his help.

Cormac had been so busy trying to appease Jenna that he almost missed the low murmur of voices coming from their left. Jenna was babbling on and on, in a most disagreeable manner. "Shhh..." Cormac put his finger to his lips to silence her. She was about to protest when she obviously heard the sound as well. She threw him a questioning look and Cormac held up his hand for her to stay put. "I'll be right back," he whispered.

Leaving his horse and Jenna behind, Cormac made his way silently through the trees toward the voices.

"Where are we," the woman's voice questioned.

"How the hell would I know?" The man responded with an angry growl.

"Hey, don't get mad at me! It's not my fault something weird just happened."

Creeping closer, Cormac was able to make out the figures of a man and woman standing in the clearing. They had their backs to him, but he could tell they were from the future. Their clothes were a dead giveaway. They searched the area, looking both confused and out of place. As they turned in his direction, Cormac dove low into the cover of some brush. He peeked over the top and was amazed to see Jonathan and Sophia, not more than ten feet away. *How did they get here?* He was just about to approach them, when Sir Richard appeared in the clearing.

"Hello, fellow time travelers. I'm Sir Richard Jefford. May I be of service? You appear to have just arrived."

"Time travelers?" Jonathan questioned suspiciously.

Sophia crept closer to Jonathan's side, but he offered her no protection. "Where are we?" she asked.

"You find yourself in Scotland. The year 1514." They looked shocked and Sophia teetered on her feet. "I'll let that sink in for a moment." Sir Richard sat atop his horse and waited before speaking again. "Where are you from?"

"San Francisco. 2014," Jonathan answered.

"Do you know how you got here?" Sir Richard asked.

"I'm not too sure…" Jonathan glanced down at Sophia, as if she might know the answer.

"We were following Cormac and Jenna when we walked into a fog bank. Next thing we knew, we were here. Do you know how we can get back?" Sophia appeared to be rapidly regaining her composure.

*Why were they following us?* Cormac didn't like the sound of that. Perhaps if he listened longer, he might have his answer. He was concerned for Jenna, but felt certain she'd stay where he left her, as he'd requested.

"Did you say Cormac and Jenna? I just saw them. Or at least, I assume the young woman with him was Jenna. Cormac did not introduce us. They are most likely heading back to Breaghacraig. What do you want with them?"

Jonathan perked up when he heard this information. "I need to get Jenna back to San Francisco. She's going to help me get some money I need."

"I thought you said you wanted to convince her to be friends with you," Sophia interrupted.

"Yeah, well, I didn't get any money when she annulled our marriage, so I have to get it somehow." Jonathan defended his actions.

"You have an ulterior motive, it seems. Do you wish this woman harm?" Sir Richard asked.

"I don't know how any of this is your business," Jonathan retorted.

"It's only my business because she's with Cormac MacBayne, and he and his family… let's just say we're not on the best of terms. What is his relationship to this Jenna?" Richard asked.

"They're definitely an item," Sophia offered.

"An item?"

"They like each other… a lot," she explained.

"I see. Well, then perhaps we can help each other," Sir Richard suggested.

Cormac had heard enough to know that Jonathan was planning to find Jenna and bring her back to San Francisco and not with good intentions, and that Sir Richard was still up to his old tricks. He had to get Jenna away from here. He left Sophia, Jonathan and Sir Richard to their plotting and hurried back towards Jenna.

# TWENTY

At first, Jenna had thought it a good idea to head off on her own. After all, Cormac seemed to be taking a really long time getting back to her. This might be her only opportunity to escape from him. She decided to head back the way she had seen Sir Richard coming from, in hopes of finding some fog to swirl her back home. No such luck. She had been wandering about for what seemed like hours and had only succeeded in getting herself hopelessly lost. Her feet hurt and her ankle was starting to ache. The woods were spooky, too. The limbs of the trees were covered in moss and they seemed to be reaching out to grab her, even though she knew it was only her imagination. A chill raced through her body and she kept glancing back over her shoulder. Hearing the sounds of twigs breaking, she stopped and whirled around. Nothing. Jenna knew she was just extra jumpy. *I have no idea where I am or how to get back to Cormac. Why am I so stubborn? I really need to learn to think before acting.*

Cormac had been so patient with her, but then again, he *had* kidnapped her. Jenna couldn't depend on him to help her get back to San Francisco. She was going to have to do this on her own. With renewed purpose, Jenna continued trudging through the woods. Her heels kept puncturing the soft forest floor, which was making it very difficult to make progress. *That's probably why Edna let me keep my boots! She knew I'd never be able to walk very far in them.* Maybe she should take them off, but then her feet would freeze. The trees blocked the sun's rays and the longer she walked, the colder she was getting. If she didn't find help soon, she'd find herself suffering a case of hypothermia.

At the sounds of howling animals, Jenna's head jerked up. She scanned the area around her and saw nothing, but had the distinct impression she was being watched. Were those coyotes or wolves? Did they even have wolves in Scotland? There weren't many creatures who howled, so the choices were limited. They sounded very close, but she couldn't really tell. She'd never been one for trekking through the woods, especially on her own.

Exhausted and feeling increasingly hopeless, Jenna leaned her back against a nearby tree and slid to a seated position at its base. She was exhausted, scared, and cold. Not a good combination. Tears began to form in her eyes when she realized she might die out here. The how of her demise was up for grabs. She would either freeze to death, or be eaten by a wolf. Jenna began to shake uncontrollably. Head in hands, she called out into the forest. "Cormac! Cormac! Help me!" Silence punctuated by howling was all she heard. Sensing a presence in front of her, Jenna lifted her head. "Cormac?" Her breath caught in her throat and panic seized her as she looked into the face of a very large and scary wolf. A wolf just like the one she'd seen in her dream.

~~~

Cormac arrived back to find that Jenna was missing. He'd told her to stay put, but apparently she'd decided to wander off in search of a way home. As silently as possible, Cormac mounted his horse and headed off in search of Jenna. He hadn't been gone that long, so she should be close by. He headed back towards the bridge, assuming that would be her destination. Tracking was usually his specialty, but he wasn't seeing much to help him in his search. He made it all the way back to the bridge and couldn't find her. His heart sank as he realized she might have managed to return to San Francisco. He couldn't be certain though, so he decided to keep searching. Cormac turned his horse back the way he'd come and looked around more carefully for signs that Jenna had been there. If she had made it back to San Francisco, he'd be happy for her, but if she was still here, he needed to find her before she came to some harm. The weather was changing and he knew she'd be cold, and if it started to rain, as it looked like it might, that would be an even bigger disaster. It was imperative that he find her quickly.

Cormac finally saw something that he knew would lead him directly to Jenna. Her high-heeled boots were making holes in the ground as she walked. She had taken a side path and Cormac guessed she'd gotten turned around. If he hadn't blindly headed towards the bridge, he would have noticed and found her more quickly. He hoped he would reach her soon. He'd heard the sounds of wolves in the area and knew them to be excellent hunters. As he rode, he listened carefully and was finally rewarded by the sound of Jenna calling his name.

"Jenna," he called back. "I'm here." He broke into a canter and headed in the direction of her voice. He realized he was also heading in the direction of the howling wolves. As he broke through the trees, he saw a terrified Jenna backed up against a tree with a lone wolf ready to lunge at her. "Jenna. Dinnae move, lass." Cormac spurred his horse forward, right at the wolf.

As he approached, his horse reared and struck out, clipping the wolf's hindquarters. The wolf snarled and spun in Cormac's direction. Saidear bravely snorted and ran at the wolf, which yelped and ran off.

Jumping down from his horse, Cormac pulled Jenna to her feet and into his arms. "Dinnae fash, lass. Yer with me now, I'll not let him harm ye."

Jenna was sobbing uncontrollably. Cormac cooed soft words in her ears and held her close. When she calmed, he held her away from him. "Did he harm ye, lass?"

"No," she hiccoughed. "I'm okay."

"Come. We must get away. He'll be back with his pack. They are not one's to give up on a meal."

Jenna shuddered. "I'm sorry I ran away. I just wanted to go home. I got so lost. I didn't think I'd ever see you again."

"I'm here. I found ye. I would search for ye forever if need be," Cormac reassured her. "Come. I ken ye dinnae care for horses, but ye'll need to ride with me if we're to make any progress. The sun is setting and we'll need to find a place to stay for the night."

Jenna shook her head anxiously. "I'm afraid of horses. I can't."

"Ye can. Saidear is a good horse, he'll take care of ye. And I'll be holding on to ye, so ye'll be safe. Come." He motioned with his hand for her to follow.

Jenna hesitated, but Cormac took her hand and gently pulled her towards his horse. He lifted her up into the saddle and she sat frozen with fear. Hoisting himself up behind her, Cormac wrapped one arm around her, anchoring her to his body and with the other hand gathered the reins and started his horse on a slow walk until he began to feel her relax.

"I'm going to take Saidear to a gentle lope. Ye willnae fall. It will be a soft, rocking motion. Ye'll see." The horse moved off smoothly under Cormac's guidance. "Why are ye so afeared of horses, Jenna?" he asked.

Voice shaking, Jenna explained. "When I was a child, I went for a riding lesson with Ashley. My parents said it was okay for me to go. We were riding around the arena when something startled my horse and he bolted for the gate at the entrance. I didn't know if he would stop or try to jump. I was so scared, all I could do was hold on tight and hope he wouldn't go over the gate. He didn't, but I did. I landed on my shoulder and broke my collarbone. I've never been on a horse since. Not until today."

"Ye had a most unfortunate accident and I can see why ye'd be frightened. When we get to Breaghacraig, I'll find ye the quietest horse in all of Scotland and I'll teach ye to ride. It will take time, but ye'll lose yer fear, and when I'm done, ye won't even need a license to ride." Cormac tipped his head to gauge Jenna's reaction. He was pleased to see she was smiling at him.

"Very funny, Mr. MacBayne. I don't suppose you need a license for much around here."

"Nae. I dinna have a single license to my name," he chuckled and Jenna relaxed even more in his arms. He was relieved. Now he had to get them to a safe place to stay for the night.

Jenna sat on a log next to the blazing fire Cormac had built for them. They would be sleeping outdoors tonight. She wasn't looking forward to that prospect, but at least she was still alive. Cormac had gone off in search of food and returned with a rabbit for them to share. Jenna wasn't used to this kind of thing, she preferred to buy her food at the grocery store, but she was so hungry that her stomach was growling and she was actually shaking. She'd eat whatever was presented to her at this point. He'd found some oats and a griddle in his saddlebag and had whipped up some bannocks as well.

"Are ye enjoying yer meal, Jenna?" Cormac asked. "I know this isnae what yer used to at home."

"It's good, thank you." Jenna continued to eat in silence. Cormac was so much more at home here. She'd noticed in San Francisco that he always seemed a bit uncomfortable and out of place. He had done a very good job of trying to hide it, but here, he was in his element. He took control of their situation and no matter how grumpy she'd been with him, he never let it get to him. He knew exactly what to do and how to do it to keep them safe. He'd built them a little shelter, which he lined with a plaid he kept in the saddlebag. It was long enough to wrap them both up comfortably for the night. He kept the fire blazing. He explained it would keep them warm and keep the wolves away. Apparently they had been following Jenna and Cormac, not willing to give up on their quarry. Cormac had also removed her boots and wrapped some warm stones in yet another plaid, then he'd massaged her feet and placed them on the stones, swathing them in the remainder of the fabric. It felt amazing and she had to control herself to keep from moaning in pleasure.

"Jenna, I dinnae wish you to be angry with me. I truly didnae know ye'd get swept up in the fog along with me, but when you touched my hands, everything started moving and I knew that if I didnae hold onto you, you might be lost forever in a different time and a different place. Can ye forgive me?"

"I'll think about it." She wasn't quite ready to give up the idea that he'd purposely kidnapped her and dragged her back to Scotland with him.

"I'll accept that," he responded with a sweet smile.

Raindrops began plopping down on them. It was just starting, but within minutes it would be a downpour. Cormac carried Jenna inside the shelter and bundled her up in the plaid. He had been warming more rocks on the fire and he poked them out of the flames with his sword. "We'll need these to keep warm," he said as he gathered them up in his kilt. They were still quite hot, but he managed to get them under the plaid where they would emanate warmth for some time to come. He had unsaddled his horse and placed the saddle in their shelter, along with anything else that needed to stay dry.

"What about your horse?" Jenna asked. Saidear was nibbling on some grass and didn't seem to mind that he was getting wet.

"He'll be fine. 'Tis not the first time he's been caught out in the rain." Cormac lay down beside Jenna, resting his head on his saddle. "May I hold ye, Jenna, lass? Ye told me not to touch ye, and I ken that I have done so since, but here in our shelter, I don't want to presume too much."

"It's okay," Jenna said. "We need to stay warm. Here," she said as she held the plaid up for him to crawl under. "For survival purposes, you can hold me." She turned her back to him and he pulled her in to the curve of his body. Before long she heard the sound of his steady breathing, letting her know he had drifted off to sleep. She only hoped she could manage to do the same.

~~~

A drop of water landed in Cormac's ear, waking him from what had been a very peaceful sleep. Jenna's eyes remained closed and he hoped he could get up and start the fire again to warm her before they left for Breaghacraig. He gently slipped his arm out from under her head. She didn't wake and he was relieved. He wrapped the plaid tightly around her and made his way out into the open. Taking a quick look at the fire, he realized it would be impossible to get it going again. Everything was pretty well drenched. There was a small amount of food left from the night before and it would have to do until they reached his home.

"Cormac," Jenna called from inside their shelter.

"Aye. Jenna, I'm here." He peeked inside and was rewarded with a smile.

"I was afraid you'd left me."

"I would never leave you, Jenna. You have nothing to fear."

"Are the wolves gone?" she asked.

"Aye. They no doubt sought shelter from the storm. We should go as soon as possible though."

"How long will it take to get to your home?"

"A wee bit longer. We should arrive there this afternoon."

"Okay." Jenna unwrapped herself from the plaid and emerged into the early morning light. It looked like rain was still a possibility. She hoped not, it would make the rest of their journey miserable. "I have to pee. Is there somewhere safe to do that?"

Cormac choked back a laugh. Jenna was not the least bit shy in her speech. "Of course, come with me." He led her to a stand of nearby trees. "How does this look?"

"Fine. You're not going to stand there, are you?"

"Nae. I'll give ye yer privacy, lass. I'm just over here if ye need me." He walked away and left her.

Cormac was verra happy to be back in his own time. He knew exactly how Jenna felt. This was neither her time nor place. The only difference between them was that he had willingly gone to San Francisco. He had gone to find her. When he went to the Marina Green with her yesterday morning, Cormac was certain he'd never see her again. Had

Edna orchestrated this whole thing? He had tried to contact her since his return, but she was not responding. If Jenna didnae want to stay, then he was honor-bound to see that she returned safely to her own time. How he would do that was another question, all together.

"Okay. I'm ready to go." Jenna was back and looking better than she had yesterday. She seemed to have accepted her current situation and Cormac was happy she would not be harping on him all day - or at least, he hoped that would be the case.

"Here. There's some food left from last night. Eat. You will need your strength."

"What about you, you need it more than I do," Jenna protested.

"We'll share," Cormac said. "You first."

Jenna took a bite out of the leftover rabbit and ate one of the bannocks. "That should be enough for me. Your turn."

"Take another bite of the rabbit, Jenna." Cormac told her with his eyes that he would not take no for an answer. She did as he requested and handed him the rest. He ate as he gathered their things, few though they were, together. He saddled Saidear and repacked the saddlebag. He had completely forgotten that he had a whole bag of candy draped across his body. Reaching in, he picked out a piece for Jenna and one for himself. "Here." He offered Jenna a piece of chocolate.

"Oh… thanks. I forgot all about the candy we bought. I don't usually eat candy for breakfast, but in this case, I'll make an exception."

Cormac hoisted Jenna up onto his horse and mounted behind her. They set off at a trot, which must have been a bit jarring for Jenna because she spoke after a few minutes. "Could we go faster, please? It's not quite as bouncy."

"As you wish, m'lady." Cormac offered her a mock bow and urged Saidear forward into a canter.

"That's better," she smiled.

They followed the path that would lead them to Breaghacraig without incident. Cormac could tell that Jenna was relaxing as she allowed herself to sink back into his chest and the closeness of his body.

"Jenna, something strange has happened." Cormac wasn't sure how to bring this subject up, but it was time she knew what he'd discovered yesterday. "When I left you to check on the voices I heard, I came upon Jonathan and the waitress, Sophia."

Jenna twisted in the saddle to look at him in disbelief. "You're kidding right?"

"Nae. I'm afraid not. I heard them talking to Sir Richard. They had been following us back in San Francisco and somehow got pulled into the fog and transported here."

"But why didn't we see them then?"

"I'm not sure. I imagine they didn't arrive at the same time we did, but shortly after. That would also explain how Sir Richard managed to get across the bridge and back to this time. They must have arrived at exactly the same moment. Richard most likely rode right past without seeing them."

"Then how is it that you saw him talking to them?"

"He surely doubled back for some reason, mayhap to follow us, and came across them in the clearing. Jenna, Richard asked Jonathan to work with him. Jonathan wants you to return to San Francisco - he said something about money and Richard would be more than happy to have help destroying the MacKenzie's."

"But I have a restraining order against Jonathan."

"Your restraining order is of no use here," Cormac explained grimly. "We must get back to Breaghacraig. Ye will be safe there."

# TWENTY-ONE

Jenna pondered what Cormac had just told her. What was Jonathan up to? He knew he was not supposed to go anywhere near her, or contact her in any way. She had a momentary thought that perhaps he might intend to hurt her. His relentless efforts to get more money out of her or the family were wearing. He should know by now that he wasn't going to get any more. It was bad enough she had to worry about him in San Francisco, but now, here in sixteenth century Scotland he had apparently found two allies to help him. But help him to do what? That was the question. An involuntary shudder ran through her limbs.

"Jenna, are ye warm enough?" Cormac asked, concern written all over his handsome face.

"Yes. I'm fine, Cormac," she lied. "I was just wondering why Jonathan thinks he can get more money out of me. The annulment was final and we're not married anymore. I don't owe him a thing."

"I dinna ken what his plans are, but I fear he may wish you harm."

Jenna didn't respond. Cormac had just voiced her own deepest fear. She had never said a word to anyone, not even Dylan, but she was secretly worried that Jonathan's motives could only be dangerous for her. She needed to get back to San Francisco and hire someone to keep an eye on him. She mentally shook her head. What was she thinking? If she went back home and Jonathan was stuck here, she might not need to deal with him again. She did feel badly for the waitress. Surely, Sophia could have no idea what she had gotten herself into. Jonathan was very convincing and had probably charmed her into helping him by lying.

"Cormac, do you think we should try to help Sophia?" Jenna asked.

"I was wondering the same thing," Cormac said. "She doesnae seem to be the kind of woman who would willingly do Jonathan's bidding."

"I'm sure he lied to her, or she wouldn't have gone along with him," Jenna said.

"Dinnae fash, lass. When we get to my home, I'll speak with Robert and Cailin. We'll find a way to help her."

Jenna didn't really like the idea of Cormac being anywhere near Sophia. She knew the waitress had wanted him and the thought made Jenna jealous. Although why she was jealous was beyond her - she'd made up her mind she wasn't interested in staying here in this godforsaken place. She needed to go home and Cormac needed to stay here. She really shouldn't concern herself with jealousy. It would do nothing to help her return home. If Sophia wanted to stay here, she had every right to go after Cormac, if she wanted. Jenna's back stiffened and anger rose in her chest again. "How much longer is this going to take?" she asked testily.

"We're almost there, lass. Relax. All is well." Cormac sounded maddeningly calm.

"What does 'almost there' mean in sixteenth century time? An hour? Two?" Jenna much preferred being able to put things in perspective and thought for some reason that being angry at Cormac right now would assist in that regard.

"Jenna, are ye angry with me, lass?" Cormac sounded puzzled by her sudden change in demeanor.

"What do you think? I'm on a horse, which I told you I didn't want to do. I'm in the sixteenth century, which I also told you I didn't want to do - and now, I find out that your little friend, Sophia, is in league with my ex and some crazy English guy and they have it in for me. Yeah. I'm pissed."

"Jenna, I really dinnae believe that Sophia had any idea what Jonathan was really up to. She seemed surprised by what he was saying to Richard."

"Fine. Whatever. I can't wait to get off this horse and find out when I can go home."

"Soon enough, Jenna. Soon enough." Cormac didn't seem bothered by her behavior and she irrationally worried that he wanted to be rid of her, as much as she wanted to leave.

They continued their ride through the Scottish countryside. Jenna had to admit it was beautiful. Mist hung low to the ground and moss grew everywhere, making everything around them the most beautiful shade of green. Raindrops started pattering on them and Jenna was just about to complain again, when they came to a slight rise and before them, a beautiful castle appeared.

"That is Breaghacraig, Jenna." Cormac pointed unnecessarily towards the castle, which appeared to be the only thing for miles around along with a few small cottages.

Jenna was scrunching herself into as small a target as possible, to avoid the pelting raindrops. Cormac reached into his saddlebag and pulled out a plaid, which he expertly wrapped around her, to shield Jenna from the weather.

"Thank you," she muttered through the layers of fabric. She almost laughed when she imagined that Cormac had purposely covered her mouth, so he didn't have to listen to her complain any longer.

"Yer most welcome, lass. Now, let's get to Breaghacraig before ye catch yer death." He urged Saidear forward into a ground-eating canter and before she knew it, they were at the gates of the castle, which opened wide to allow them entrance. As they passed through, she was amazed to see many people scurrying about. The rain was not deterring them from attending to their tasks. Two boys ran to them when they finally came to a stop and took Saidear's reins from Cormac, who had hopped down and was reaching up for Jenna. She was wrapped up so tightly that she had no choice but to allow Cormac to lift her from the horse. As she stood by his side, he gave direction to the boys on Saidear's care. He wrapped a protective arm around Jenna's shoulders and guided her towards the massive doors of the castle. They were still quite a distance away when the doors opened and a petite woman with dark auburn hair and a tall dark-haired man came through and the woman stopped dead in her tracks.

The man said something to her, but she continued to stare at Jenna, who watched as the woman called her name and began running towards her. For a split second, Jenna wasn't sure, but then she recognized her best friend, Ashley. The man grabbed Ashley's arm to stop her and gave her a stern talking to. "Oh, my God, that's Ashley!" she said to Cormac. "Who's that crazy fool who's holding her by the arm?"

"That daft idjit is me brother, Cailin. Ashley is his wife."

~~~

Cormac caught Jenna as her legs went out from underneath her. "Damn this stupid blanket!" she cursed, trying unsuccessfully to disentangle herself. She'd almost fallen flat on her face in her rush to reach Ashley.

"Jenna, let me help ye," Cormac said calmly, as he unwrapped her from the plaid. He had no sooner removed it than she bolted towards Ashley.

"Leave her alone!" Jenna shrieked at Cailin.

Cormac couldn't help but laugh. The expression on his brother's face was priceless. He obviously had no idea who this woman was, or why she might be telling him to leave his own wife alone.

Cailin glanced at Ashley and then returned his gaze to Cormac, who had just arrived at Jenna's side. "Brother, who is this wee spitfire ye have with ye?"

"She is Ashley's good friend, Jenna." He watched as his brother took in the scene in front of him. Jenna and Ashley were hugging fiercely, laughing, and crying. It almost brought a tear to Cormac's own eyes to see how happy they both were to be reunited. "We should get them inside out of the rain and I'll tell ye the whole story."

Cormac's sister Irene was standing in the doorway with her husband Robert. They both appeared puzzled, but remained silent. Cormac and Cailin pried the girls apart and led them inside, past those who had gathered to discover what was happening. Once inside, the great hall was warm and inviting. A huge blaze burned brightly in the fireplace and torches had been lit throughout, to make up for the dark and dreary day outside. Cormac was relieved to have finally returned home. He prepared himself to tell those gathered where he had been over the past several days, but before he could speak, Irene had a question. "Who is this lass ye've brought home with ye, Cormac? She seems to know our Ashley."

"Aye. She does, Irene. 'Tis Ashley's friend, Jenna, from San Francisco," Cormac explained.

"What is she doing here? Where did ye find her?" Irene asked.

"'Tis a long story and one I'd be happy to share with ye, but we are both verra hungry and wet. Irene, do ye have something dry that Jenna could wear? She's had a long journey and has a tendency to be prickly as a thistle when she is uncomfortable." Cormac hoped Irene would take care of the food and clothing and be satisfied to wait a bit for his story.

"Aye. I'll help the lass get dry and we'll see to it that ye both are fed," Irene said. "Go on then. Go get yourself changed and come right back. I'll not want to wait long to hear yer story." Irene swatted his backside to send him on his way.

"Jenna, go with me sister, Irene. She'll see that ye get some dry clothes and I'll meet ye back here for some food."

Jenna glanced up from her conversation with Ashley and nodded. Ashley smiled a huge smile of thanks in his direction and blew him a kiss. He looked from his sweet sister-in-law to Jenna and Irene, who were sizing each other up. They were a lot alike and Cormac watched as Irene headed Jenna's way, hoping that the two would get on well.

~~~

Jenna stood her ground, holding on to Ashley's hands, as Irene approached. She was a black haired, blue-eyed beauty, who obviously was the one in charge here.

"Jenna, I'm pleased to meet ye," Irene introduced herself. "Cormac is me brother and yer friend Ashley is as good a sister to me, as if she had been born into our family."

"Nice to meet you," Jenna said, extending her hand to Irene, who looked a bit confused by the gesture. "Oh, I'm sorry, I guess you don't shake hands here." Jenna pulled her hand back in embarrassment.

"Jenna, let's go get you something dry to wear," Ashley said. She had happy tears in her eyes as she took Jenna by the hand and they followed Irene up the stairs.

"We'll give her yer old chamber, Ashley. Right this way, Jenna." Irene directed them to a room on their right and said, "I'll be right back with a dress for ye."

Ashley opened the door to the room and ushered Jenna inside. "Jenna, I can't believe you're here. I'm so happy. I didn't know if I'd ever see you again." Ashley was crying happy tears again and Jenna gave her another big hug.

"I know. When you called and said you were getting married, you omitted the part about time travel and my never seeing you again. You should have told me, Ashley." Jenna pulled back and gazed earnestly into Ashley's eyes.

"I should have, but I thought you wouldn't believe me and the last thing I wanted was for you to come over here and try to find me." Ashley couldn't take her eyes off her friend. "Jenna, tell me how Cormac found you. How did you get here?"

"It's a long story, and I'm sure you won't believe me," Jenna hesitated for just a moment. "Cormac kidnapped me." There, she'd said it.

Ashley seemed shocked, but Jenna was just telling her the truth.

Ashley shook her head in denial. "What do you mean? Cormac would never do anything like that."

"Well, he did. He showed up on the Marina Green and told me Edna sent him to get me. That I was supposed to be his wife. I thought he was crazy, but Dylan really liked him and insisted that we let him stay with us. Long story short, I guess he had to be back at the Marina exactly seven days after he arrived and poof, here I am."

"So he forced you to go to the Marina with him?" Ashley asked.

"No, of course not. He tricked me. He stood there, looking all lost and upset, and I went to him, thinking he was losing it and that he wasn't going anywhere. I no sooner put my hand on his arm than the fog came in and started swirling around us. He grabbed me and held on to me so I couldn't get away - and next thing I knew I was here."

"Jenna, I think Edna had a little something to do with that. I can't imagine Cormac would want you to come with him against your will. He's not like that." Ashley defended her brother-in-law. "I am confused about one thing though. How are you supposed to marry Cormac? You're already married to Jonathan."

"A lot has happened since you've been gone, Ashley," Jenna spat out bitterly. "You and everyone else were right about Jonathan. He was only interested in me for my money. I had the marriage annulled."

Ashley gasped and took Jenna's hand in her own. "I'm so sorry, Jenna. That's not something I wanted to be proven right about. I know how much you loved him."

"I *thought* I loved him, but when it came right down to it, I realized it had never been right between us, not from the very beginning. He swept me off my feet, but somewhere deep down inside I think I knew he was pulling the wool over my eyes and I'm angry with myself that I let it happen."

Ashley didn't respond. Jenna knew her friend wanted to try to make her feel better, but Ashley also knew Jenna well enough to know that she wouldn't accept sympathy. Instead, they continued talking and Jenna poured her heart out to Ashley, who had many questions for her. She filled her in on everything that had happened since she'd been gone and then had just as many questions of her own for Ashley, but she'd have to wait to ask them because Irene arrived with a lovely dress for her to wear.

"Let's get you out of those wet things and into something dry," Irene suggested. Irene motioned with her hand for Jenna to turn around and Jenna just stared at her. "You'll need help getting out of your gown. If you prefer, Ashley can help you."

"Oh, yes, I'd prefer to have Ashley help me. I'm uncomfortable undressing in front of someone I've just met."

Irene didn't look very happy with Jenna, but she turned her attention to Ashley and smiled warmly. "Ashley do you mind helping your friend and then we'll see ye back downstairs when yer done."

Ashley smiled brightly at Irene and nodded in agreement.

"That woman doesn't like me," Jenna observed after Irene slipped out through the door and closed it quietly behind her.

"Don't be silly. She just doesn't know you yet. She's very protective of her brothers." Ashley said.

Jenna shook her head in disbelief. "I can't believe I'm here. I can't believe *you're* here."

"Come on; turn around for me so I can undo your gown. Who helped you into it?" Ashley wondered aloud.

"That would be Edna. Somehow, when I arrived I was already dressed like this. Oh, but she did let me keep my own boots."

Ashley just giggled at that announcement. "Oh, that Edna! She must have something in mind for you. She probably really believes you and Cormac belong together." She continued unlacing Jenna's gown and when she was done, Ashley helped Jenna step out of it and into the silky lavender one Irene had delivered.

Jenna couldn't help but admire the workmanship. "This is beautiful, Ashley."

"Irene made it. She's an amazing seamstress. She's made, or helped me make practically every gown I have."

"She's very talented."

Ashley picked up a pair of matching slippers and handed them to Jenna. "You can wear these, or keep your boots on if you like."

"Cormac would probably prefer if I kept the boots on, but I'm going for comfort. I'll take the slippers."

Ashley studied her friend with curiosity. "So what's going on here, Jenna? You like him, don't you?"

Jenna didn't want to look up, for fear she'd give herself away, but when she eventually did, she saw Ashley was examining her as if she was a specimen under a microscope. "Yeah. I can't lie to you. I do like him. A lot. But I can't forgive him for taking me out of my own time. I told him I couldn't go with him and he didn't want to stay in San Francisco. He should have just accepted my decision and not forced me."

"You have to know, deep down in your heart, that he wouldn't do anything to hurt you, Jenna."

"I do know. But I don't want to be here," Jenna cried.

Ashley appeared hurt by that comment. "I'm sorry, Jenna. We'll find a way for you to return home. Don't worry." She turned and headed for the door. "Let's join the others. You must be starving."

~~~

Cormac was waiting for them at the bottom of the stairs.

"I haven't properly welcomed you back, Cormac," Ashley said, hugging Cormac and planting a kiss on his cheek. "I missed you. Shame on you, for not telling us where you were *really* going."

"I was *really* going to go to Edinburgh to search for a wife, but Edna called to me and told me she knew the perfect lass for me." He looked lovingly at Jenna, who deliberately turned away. He sighed heavily. "So, I made a detour and went where Edna directed me. She sent me to San Francisco and when I arrived, Jenna was the first person I saw."

"You'll have to tell me all about it at dinner," Ashley smiled. "I want to know what you did, where you went... everything."

"I will share it all with ye. I promise." He offered Jenna his arm, but she walked right past him and into the massive dining room. Cormac rolled his eyes skyward, seeking divine intervention, but when none was forthcoming, he offered his arm to Ashley instead, and she walked with him towards the table.

"Where's Cailin?" Ashley asked.

"He'll be here shortly. He's still upstairs." Cormac guided Ashley to her seat and pulled out a chair for Jenna. He sat sandwiched between the two women. He was initially going to let Jenna sit next to Ashley, but he suspected he'd have a better chance of speaking with her if he didn't. Watching her now, he wasn't so sure his seating arrangement was going to work to his advantage because Jenna was deliberately avoiding looking in his direction.

Cailin joined them and sat on the opposite side of Ashley. He kissed her gently on the cheek as he sat down and held her hand as they waited for the food to arrive.

Cormac leaned in towards Jenna. "I'll explain everything to you, don't worry."

"I know how to eat, Cormac. I really don't think there's anything you need to talk to me about," she replied curtly.

For about the millionth time since he'd met this woman, Cormac questioned Edna's choice and his own sanity. He wasn't sure he wanted to spend his life with such an ill-tempered woman. He tried to remember those moments when she had been the total opposite. When she had been sweet and caring, but he had to question where that woman had gone. He caught a glimpse of Jenna out of the corner of his eye and realized that she must be feeling completely lost. He felt much the same way when he'd been in San Francisco. He knew he needed to be more understanding of her predicament. He would continue to try to contact Edna and when he did, he would take Jenna back to the bridge so she could return home. He didn't want her to stay in Breaghacraig unless it was her own choice and at this stage that didn't seem a likely outcome.

Food was placed on the table in front of them. It was really quite a feast. Cormac was starved and he was sure Jenna probably was, as well. They hadn't had a decent meal since they left San Francisco. Everyone helped themselves, but Jenna sat stiffly, watching everyone else and eyeing the food suspiciously.

"Jenna, please, allow me to help ye," Cormac said quietly. She didn't respond and he took that as his answer. He picked up a platter of food and started placing various items on her plate. When he was done, he filled his own plate.

"Jenna, don't worry, it's not going to bite you," Ashley laughed. "Just pretend you're at some new restaurant in the city. Everyone's been raving about it and you can't wait to try it."

Jenna glanced her way and made a face that had Ashley giggling. Cormac watched as Jenna took her first bite and then another. *She'll be fine,* he thought to himself.

"Cormac, would you mind if we switched seats?" Ashley asked. "I'd like to speak with Jenna. We've got a lot of catching up to do."

"Of course," Cormac was actually relieved to trade places. The icy way in which Jenna was ignoring him had left him looking for any excuse to get away from her. He moved Ashley's plate and helped her into her new seat, before taking his own.

"So, brother, tell me all about yer adventure," Cailin sounded excited to hear Cormac's tale.

"'Twas amazing," Cormac answered. "Everything about it was beyond belief. It is a world filled with magick." Cormac had the attention of everyone at the table, with the exception of Ashley and Jenna. "Cailin, you've been there. You understand what I mean."

"Aye. I do, brother. Did ye enjoy the food? What did ye eat?"

"The food was so different. Many fruits and vegetables that we do not have here. I had coffee, pizza, pasta and many other things I'd never heard of. Cailin was nodding his head and smiling at this announcement, obviously recalling his own adventure.

He settled in to telling his family all about the journey. They were full of questions and he answered every single one. Glancing towards Jenna, he noticed that she and Ashley were deep in conversation and he was happy to see Jenna looking more relaxed. He remembered what Dylan had told him and he hoped he was right. Mayhap by the morning, she would no longer be angry with him.

# TWENTY-TWO

The hall was a very lively place. Everyone was talking, eating, and generally having a good time. Jenna had been grateful to Cormac for switching seats with Ashley. She and her friend had a lot to catch up on and talking to Ashley was making her feel better. She could hear Cailin and Cormac trying to one up each other on the things they'd seen and done in the twenty-first century.

"So, does everyone here know about time travel?" Jenna wondered aloud.

"Not everyone, but the immediate family and a few others. We try to keep it to ourselves. It might cause problems if the wrong people knew," Ashley explained quietly.

"Who are the few others? I don't want to make any mistakes while I'm here. You know, say the wrong thing to the wrong person."

"Sure. Well, Helene, she's my ladies' maid and her man, Dougall, they both know. You don't have to worry about saying anything in front of them. That's Helene and Dougall over there. Helene is the pretty blonde and Dougall is the handsome highlander sitting beside her." She pointed in their direction and when Jenna looked across the room, she saw Helene waving and smiling at them. "Some of the men know, but not all of them. Those who do have been sworn to secrecy, but to be on the safe side you should just avoid speaking about it with anyone other than the family, or Helene and Dougall."

"And they're really okay with it? I just can't imagine. I was a total nonbeliever when Cormac told me. I thought he was nuts."

"I can imagine. What did Dylan think?"

"He believed Cormac right from the start, but then Dylan is a bit of a sci-fi geek and it was like a dream come true for him. I wasn't on board until I found myself on my way to Breaghacraig."

"You didn't believe him, when he told you about me and Cailin?" Ashley asked.

"He never told me about you." Jenna's relaxed posture began to stiffen. "He lied to me. There are so many things I just can't get past, right now."

Ashley took Jenna's hand in her own. "Jenna, you have to believe me when I tell you Cormac is a great guy. If he didn't tell you about me, it was because he had a good reason. You need to ask him about it. He'll tell you the truth."

"That's what he always says. He always tells me that if I ask him something, he'll always tell me the truth."

"He's a man of his word, Jenna. So are Cailin and Robert. You'll see. Just give them a chance."

Jenna rolled her eyes in frustration. "I don't seem to have much choice in the matter, Ashley. I'm stuck here."

"Jenna, you know I wish you'd stay here with us, but I understand if you want to leave. We'll help you contact Edna… I promise. In the meantime, just enjoy the experience. You might be surprised at how much you like it."

"I doubt it, but I'll do my best," Jenna smiled warmly at her dear friend.

"And don't be so hard on Cormac. I don't want to see either one of you get hurt."

*That might be unavoidable.* Jenna pulled Ashley into a hug, dreading the time she'd have to say goodbye to both her and Cormac.

Jenna avoided contact with Cormac for the rest of the evening.

She needed time to process everything that had happened and letting him get close would just muddy her thinking. Exhaustion was creeping up on her and she really needed to get some sleep. The others in the hall were laughing and talking together and she felt very out of place. She couldn't think of a thing to say to any one of them. She could feel Irene's eyes boring a hole through her. Irene didn't trust her, Jenna could tell and she looked angry. Jenna didn't think she had much of a chance of winning her over. Strangely, Ashley seemed to fit right in. She was tucked up under her husband's arm and they seemed like two people who were completely in love. Jenna suffered a pang of jealousy, but she also felt a great sense of happiness for her good friend. Ashley had been pretty down the last time Jenna saw her, but now here she was, practically glowing with joy. Jenna hated to disturb them, but she really wanted to go to bed.

"Ashley, I'm really tired. I'm going to go upstairs," Jenna said. "Good night, Cailin. It was a pleasure meeting you."

"Good night, lass. I'm so happy yer here. My Ashley has missed ye a great deal." Cailin's smile brought to mind the smile of another handsome man. A man she didn't want to think about, right now.

"I'll get Helene to help you with your gown," Ashley said, and hurriedly continued when she saw Jenna was about to protest. "Don't say no, you're going to need help." Ashley turned from her and waved to Helene, who hurried in their direction.

"Helene, this is my best friend, Jenna. She came back with Cormac."

"Pleased to meet you, Lady Jenna," Helene said.

"Lady Jenna? What…" Jenna was baffled by the greeting.

"Just call her Jenna, Helene. No need for formality, you know that," Ashley said.

"Of course, come with me… Jenna." Helene led her away towards the stairs.

"Thank you, Helene, I appreciate the help," Jenna said.

"'Tis my job. I help Ashley and Lady Irene every day."

"I'm just adding to your work load," Jenna protested. "I can probably get out of this dress on my own, really." Jenna didn't want to be a burden. She was very capable of taking care of herself and didn't want to cause a fuss.

"Please, Jenna, let me help ye. 'Tis no trouble. 'Twill take but a moment."

They reached the door to Jenna's room and Helene opened it and went inside. Jenna stepped through the doorway and shivered. "Ooh… it's chilly in here."

"Dinnae fash. I'll get a fire started right away," Helene offered.

"Can you show me how to make a fire, Helene? You know, in case you're not around and I'm cold."

Helene nodded and Jenna watched as she expertly started the fire in the hearth. "Do ye think ye can do it on yer own?" she asked when the fire was burning brightly.

"I'll just do what you did, I'm sure I can manage."

Jenna caught a look of skepticism on Helene's face but the young woman got to her feet and reached for Jenna's shoulder, gently turning her around. "Let me help ye get yer gown off. Lady Irene has left ye a nightdress."

A quick glance towards the bed revealed a pretty muslin gown, adorned with pink ribbons and embroidered flowers had been left on the bed for her. Helene undid the laces of the lavender gown with nimble fingers and helped Jenna step out of it. "I'm not used to getting undressed in front of strangers," Jenna admitted uncomfortably.

"'Tis naught for ye to be concerned with. I've seen many a lady in this castle as naked as the day they were born." Helene giggled as she assisted Jenna into the nightdress. "There, ye'll be nice and warm now that the fire is blazing and ye have many beautiful furs to cover ye while ye sleep."

"Thank you, Helene. It was very kind of you to help me."

"As I said, 'tis what I do. Good night." Helene headed out through the door, closing it behind her.

Before climbing into bed, Jenna stood in front of the fire for a few minutes, enjoying the warmth and the flickering and crackling of the flames. She felt completely and totally alone. Jenna stretched and yawned as she got under the covers. This was a luxury she didn't have at home. The furs were incredibly soft and would definitely keep her warm during the night. Lying in bed, she thought about Cormac. She wished she hadn't been such a *prickly thistle,* as he liked to call her. She'd have to sleep alone because of her moodiness, and having his warmth and comfort would have made it easier to fall asleep, but she had been her own worst enemy once again and completely shut him out. *One of these days, Jenna, you're going to figure it out.* Ashley's mother used to tell Jenna regularly that 'You catch more flies with honey than with vinegar.' Jenna had been nothing but vinegar today and Cormac had been nothing but a gentleman. *You are such an idiot,* she thought to herself. *One of these times, he's not going to forgive you.* She snuggled down deeper into the furs and yawned again. She was exhausted. Maybe things would seem better tomorrow.

"Jenna…" a voice called out to her in the darkness.

"Who's there?" Jenna searched the dark corners of the room, trying to locate the source of the voice.

"Jenna, it's me… Edna."

Jenna sat up in bed. "Edna? Where are you? I can't see you."

"No. You cannae see me, because I'm not there in Breaghacraig."

"What do you want?" Jenna asked suspiciously.

"I want ye to know that I'm aware it was not yer choice to go to Breaghacraig. But ye have to understand, it was nae Cormac who brought ye. He was prepared to leave without ye, but I couldn't let that happen. I knew ye'd eventually go to him and when ye did… well, that's when the magick happened."

"But, he held onto me! He wouldn't let me go."

"And it's a good thing he did. Ye might have ended up even further back in time and all alone. Ye should be grateful to him, for saving ye from that fate."

Jenna crossed her arms furiously. "How dare you! You knew I didn't want to go with him and yet you forced me to! Edna, you should be really happy that you're not standing in front of me right now."

"I'm aware of that, my dear. Now, let's get down to business, shall we?"

Jenna nodded, but wasn't certain Edna could see her, so she spoke instead. "Okay, I guess. How do I get back home?"

"Well, for starters, ye are going to have to spend some time at Breaghacraig. Ye'll get to know Cormac better, ye can visit with my dear sweet, Ashley, and ye can learn a little about life in sixteenth century Scotland. Cormac stayed in San Francisco for seven days and you will stay at Breaghacraig for seven days. I'll contact ye again when it's time to leave and Cormac will take ye to the bridge. From there, ye can go home, if that's what ye decide."

"Great! Torture me again. I guess it wasn't bad enough the first time we had to say goodbye to each other."

"Ye needed more time together and I'm a hopeless romantic. I think ye belong together. Seven days isnae verra long, but it will be long enough for ye to realize ye are exactly where ye need to be."

"You're crazy and manipulative. I am not staying here. Yeah, I'll stay for the next seven days, but after that I'm going home and you can't stop me."

"Well, I think I could, but our agreement is seven days and seven days it will be. Tomorrow is day one. Make good use of yer time, Jenna. Take care now, my dear, and I'll be in touch at the end of yer stay."

Abruptly, all Jenna could hear was the crackling of the fire and any sign of Edna having been there disappeared. She was spooked by what had just happened, but she was not going to go wandering around the castle all alone, searching for Ashley. She'd talk to her about it tomorrow. Right now, she needed to sleep. This had been the weirdest two days of her life and it had taken a lot out of her.

# TWENTY-THREE

A light tapping on the chamber door told Jenna she wasn't completely alone. She had been awake for hours and though it was definitely morning, Jenna wasn't sure what she should be doing. The room was freezing and she really didn't want to get out of bed to get the fire burning again. Nothing but embers and ashes remained from the fire Helene had started the night before.

Another knock sounded, this time louder and Jenna realized that Helene must have returned to help her get dressed. "Come in," she called.

The door opened and Cormac peeked his head inside. "Good morning," he said quietly. "May I come in?"

"Sure." She shivered and pulled the furs up more tightly around her chin. "The fire's gone out and I was too cold to get up and start it again," Jenna explained.

Cormac immediately went to the fireplace and started a fire with little effort. "There, that should warm the room quickly. Do ye need any help getting dressed?" he asked. "I'll send for Helene."

"No. Cormac I need to talk to you. Maybe you could help me get dressed while I tell you about what happened last night."

Cormac looked a bit apprehensive. "Are ye sure ye want me to help ye?"

"Yeah. You've seen me without my clothes before. I'm sure we can manage to put a dress on without having to call Helene. Unless, of course, there's some rule against it here."

"As ye wish, lass, I'll be happy to help ye." Cormac held out his hand and she reached for it, enjoying the familiar sensation of warmth spreading through her limbs. She stepped out of bed and he pulled her closer to the fire.

"My dress is over there," Jenna pointed to the lavender gown draped over a nearby chair and Cormac retrieved it. Turning her back to him, she let the nightgown drop to the floor. Cormac's sharp intake of breath told her he was paying close attention. He wrapped his arms around her, holding the dress so she could easily step into it. The closeness of his body and the hardness of his wanting as it pressed against her back had Jenna trembling. Maybe this hadn't been such a good idea. She steadied her breathing and did her best to pretend she was merely feeling the cold. Cormac quickly pulled the dress up and she put her arms in the sleeves. He then expertly did up the laces and when he was done, he stepped away from her. She immediately missed the warmth of his body and turned to look at him for the first time since he'd entered her room. He was more handsome than words could express.

"Thank you," she managed.

"Yer welcome, lass. Is there anything else I can help ye with?"

"No," she answered. "I really wanted to tell you about what happened last night when I went to bed."

"I'm listening."

"Edna was here. Not physically, but I could hear her in my mind."

"Ah…" Cormac seemed disappointed, probably because he suspected that meant she'd be leaving.

"She told me that I have to stay here for seven days. Just like you had to stay in San Francisco for seven days."

"Did she say why?" Relief was tangible in his voice.

"Just that I needed to take the time to get to know you better. She said at the end of the seven days, if I still wanted to return to San Francisco, she'd send me back."

"I see. How do ye feel about that, Jenna? Do ye want to get to know me better?" He seemed anxious, like a little boy awaiting his punishment.

"Yeah. I do want to get to know you better, but I don't think it will matter. I'm still going home," she said firmly.

"Well, then, I guess we should get started. I'd like to show ye my world, just as ye showed me yers." He watched her with one eyebrow cocked, waiting for her answer.

"Okay. Can we start with breakfast first? I'm starving." She gave him her most brilliant smile. It wasn't faked, but very real. She really was happy to have the opportunity to spend time with him. Once Edna took the choice of leaving immediately, away from her, Jenna realized she probably would enjoy this experience, just as Ashley had suggested. "Cormac, I'd like to apologize. I know, I know, I'm always apologizing for my behavior, but I unjustly accused you of kidnapping me. Edna set me straight and I wanted you to know that I am so sorry I doubted you."

"'Tis nothing for ye to concern yerself with. I understand why ye would think those thoughts and I dinnae hold it against ye."

"Good. So we're okay, then?" she asked hopefully.

Cormac nodded. "Aye, we are."

Jenna threw her arms around his waist and hugged him for all she was worth. She felt Cormac's arms wrap around her and an audible sound of relief escaped his lips.

"Breakfast?" she asked.

"Aye."

Cormac was so relieved to have the Jenna he loved back, he could hardly contain his excitement. Everyone was already seated and eating when Cormac and Jenna arrived in the great hall. Irene looked up, with surprise written all over her face. He knew she was concerned about him; she had shared that much with him last night. She wasnae sure Jenna was to be trusted with Cormac's heart. He understood Irene didnae wish to see him hurt, but he was not a little boy anymore and he was capable of handling anything life threw his way, including the possibility that Jenna would end up breaking his heart. If that was to happen, so be it. He wouldnae allow that to ruin the next seven days with her.

"Good morning," Jenna greeted everyone cheerfully. "I'd like to apologize for my behavior yesterday. I was very tired and I felt out of place, so I wasn't on my best behavior. I hope you can all forgive me."

"Of course we can, lass. Shall we start by properly introducing ourselves? I be Robert, the laird of Clan MacKenzie and I'm happy to know ye." Robert stood and came around the table to take Jenna's hand in his. Raising it to his lips, he gently kissed her knuckles. Jenna turned a becoming shade of pink. Right behind him was Cailin, who also took Jenna's hand and kissed it. Jenna had already met everyone, but this was their way of letting her know that she was welcome among them, even if she hadn't been at her best on their first meeting.

"I be Cailin, Cormac's brother and husband to Ashley, but ye already ken that." Cormac saw Cailin wink conspiratorially at Jenna.

Irene sat silently, her face a stony mask. "I believe ye met me sister Irene when we arrived yesterday, and ye already know Ashley," Cormac said.

"I'm very happy to meet all of you and I'm looking forward to getting to know you better," Jenna said shyly.

"Jenna will be staying with us for seven days and then she'll decide if she wants to return to her home." Cormac wanted them to know what was taking place, so they would all be comfortable with each other.

"Why seven days?" Irene asked.

"My trip to San Francisco was for seven days and Edna thought it would be a good length of time for Jenna to get to know me better and to get to know all of you. It will also give her time to spend with Ashley."

"That's exciting news, Jenna! It makes me very happy," Ashley bubbled.

Taking Jenna's hand, Cormac led her around to her seat beside Ashley. "I will use the time to show Jenna around Breaghacraig and while she's here, I will teach her to ride a horse."

Jenna immediately protested. "Cormac, I don't think that's a good idea. I'm only going to be here for seven days, I really don't need to know how to ride."

"Jenna's afraid of horses. She had an accident when she was a child," Cormac explained to the others.

"That's right," Ashley chimed in. "I remember that day you came to the barn with me and took a lesson. You never wanted anything to do with them after that."

"And I still don't," Jenna said firmly.

"Cormac I believe there's a mare in the stables that would be perfect for Jenna," Robert offered. "She's verra sweet. Ye'll love her, Jenna."

"I don't know," Jenna began anxiously.

"Lass, I told ye I'd find ye the most gentle horse in all of Scotland and I believe ye'll fall in love with her. I won't let any harm come to ye," Cormac assured her.

"I know, but horses are so big and I don't know how you can stop it, if it wants to toss me off," Jenna worried.

"Let's eat breakfast first and we'll talk about it later. How does that sound?"

Jenna smiled in agreement and helped herself to some food. "This is so good." She started eating and Cormac relaxed and did the same. The family discussed their plans for the day as they ate breakfast. Cormac took suggestions on things he should share with Jenna while she was visiting and Jenna seemed agreeable to most of them. He was going to have to overcome her fear of horses for some of the activities. It wasn't that he minded sharing his horse with her, but Cormac felt sure if she could ride a horse of her own, it would build up her confidence, and she could begin to see Breaghacraig as the beautiful place he knew it to be, instead of something to fear.

So far, Jenna was feeling better about being at Breaghacraig this morning. She decided she was going to try and be open to new experiences - with the exception of learning to ride. Cormac was crazy, if he thought he was going to convince her to try it. She still had memories of her fall years before, and the fear and pain it had caused. He'd have to be extremely persuasive to convince her and she doubted that would happen.

After breakfast was finished, Jenna went walking with Cormac and he showed her around the castle. They had already done a tour of the interior and now they had moved outdoors. Cormac had shown Jenna the postern gate, which led out through the back of the castle grounds, the barracks, the blacksmith and now they were heading towards the stables.

Jenna didn't have a good feeling about this idea. Stopping dead in her tracks, she tried to divert Cormac in a different direction. "What's over there?" She pointed vaguely off into the distance.

"Where?" Cormac asked.

"Over there," she pointed again.

Cormac sighed heavily. "Jenna, we've already been over every inch of the inner courtyard. Let's go into the stables. There's something in there I'd like to show ye."

When she didn't budge, he tried grasping her hand and tugging. Still no movement. Jenna was quite determined she was not going into that stable and she appealed to him with wide eyes. "I can't go in there, Cormac, there are horses in there."

"Jenna, ye're always so brave. Please, trust me, I won't let them harm ye," Cormac coaxed quietly.

Jenna stared up at him with obvious fear in her eyes.

"I promise," he said.

"If anything happens to me, I'm going to be so angry with you," she snarled.

"I'll take my chances. Come." He led her in to the darkened stables. The smell of horses, sweet hay, and leather assailed her nostrils. It wasn't a bad smell, just different to what she was used to. Adjusting to the lack of good lighting, she also noticed how quiet it was. The only sounds she could hear were those of the horses, munching on hay in their stalls. She was surprised at the peaceful feeling that came over her.

"I know this is all new to ye, but Jenna, I want to share the things from my world with ye. Just as ye did with me, in San Francisco."

"Okay, I get it," Jenna said, relenting a tiny bit.

Cormac led her down the line of stalls. Each one they passed held a horse, whose head bobbed up with a mouthful of hay when they passed. It seemed the horses were curious about who was visiting the stables. As they approached the last few stalls, Saidear, popped up and nickered at Cormac. Jenna approached the horse with caution, holding out her hand for him to sniff. "Hello, Saidear," she whispered. "It's good to see you again." The horse snuffled against her hand and stuck his nose further out to sniff her hair. She could feel the warmth of his breath against her face. Feeling a bit braver, Jenna touched his soft nose and let her hand glide up to his forelock, which she fluffed with her fingers. Cormac stood beside her, not saying a word. She knew he was letting her experience this at her own pace.

Cormac handed her an apple. "For Saidear," he said.

Jenna looked questioningly at him. "You want me to feed him?"

"Aye. Put it in yer hand like this." He showed her how to lay her palm out flat and place the apple on it. Then he held her hand out in front of Saidear, who scooped the apple up and happily munched away on the sweet treat.

Jenna giggled. "I did it! He didn't bite me."

"Jenna, come see this lovely mare over here."

She turned to the stall across from Saidear. A beautiful little black horse stood there. She had soft, licorice eyes and a sweet demeanor. Her ears were pricked forward in Jenna's direction.

"What's her name?" Jenna asked.

"Rose. Like the flower."

"Hello Rose, like the flower." Jenna held her hand out to the mare, who gently sniffed it. "I'm sorry. I don't have an apple for you. Saidear ate it all."

"Here, love. I have one for her." Cormac handed her another apple.

Rose was very dainty in her approach to the apple, unlike Saidear; she took her time and delicately bit a single bite instead of taking the whole apple. Jenna looked up at Cormac with wonder in her eyes. This wasn't so bad. These horses were actually very sweet and gentle.

Cormac put a halter on Rose and handed a lead rope to Jenna, who looked at him questioningly. "Here you go. Let's go for a walk with her." They walked out of the stables and into the sunshine and Jenna had to blink several times to adjust to the brightness. "This way," Cormac said, leading them through the gate that led out of the castle.

"Where are we going?" Jenna asked, with a tinge of apprehension in her voice.

"Don't worry. We're nae going far and I'll nae have ye get on her today. Just get to know her for now. Ye must learn to trust each other."

Jenna smiled and breathed a sigh of relief. She wasn't going to be coerced into riding today. Thank goodness. She wasn't prepared for that idea, but she could take Rose for a walk. As they strolled, Cormac explained different things about Rose that Jenna needed to know. He explained how a horse's ears were a good way to tell what they were thinking. Pricked straight forward, they were paying attention to something ahead of them. Pinned back and they were showing displeasure. One ear forward and one ear back suggested they were listening to their rider and paying attention to what was in front of them. He gave her lots of useful information and she realized what a wonderful, patient teacher he was with her. She knew she had not been quite as patient with him when their circumstances had been reversed. She felt badly about that. "Cormac, I'm sorry for all the times back home when I was impatient with you. You know, when you were asking me questions and I'd tell you to ask Dylan. I was rude and you didn't deserve that."

"Lass, don't trouble yerself. I ken ye thought I was playing a trick on ye. Now ye ken I wasnae. Dinnae fash. I have thick skin." He gave her one of his blindingly brilliant smiles and Jenna knew all was forgiven.

"I like Rose," Jenna said, surprising herself with the admission. "She's very sweet."

"I'm happy ye like her. Mayhap tomorrow, ye'll feel comfortable enough to get on her for a wee ride."

"Maybe. We'll see." Jenna was softening her stance regarding the whole riding thing, feeling as if she could do anything, as long as Cormac was by her side.

They continued walking and Jenna was quite taken with the beauty of the surrounding area. It was so picturesque. It was also very quiet. She hadn't realized just how much noise was constantly being made in her own time. No cars and no planes here in medieval Scotland. No cell phones either and if she was honest with herself, she wasn't missing it. This truly was a new experience.

"I'm happy yer here, Jenna," Cormac said. "I was hoping I would be able to show you Breaghacraig and I'm pleased to do so now."

"It's beautiful, Cormac. Everything about it is…" Jenna struggled to find just the right words. When she couldn't she said, "It's so different. I like it."

Cormac's whole face lit up. He reached an arm out and pulled her towards him, lifting her in the air, and twirling her around. Jenna shrieked and laughed at his antics. He put her back down and held her close, tipping her chin up so she was looking directly into his devastating blue eyes.

"Ye make me so happy, Jenna." And then he kissed her, sending her head spinning and her legs wobbling. She kissed him back with a heart full of passion.

Their lips parted and Jenna said, "You make me happy, too, Cormac." She snuggled in closer to him, resting her head on his chest. With her eyes closed and feeling at peace with her situation, Jenna was surprised to feel whiskers tickling her cheek, followed by soft, warm horse breath in her ear.

"I think Rose is feeling a wee bit jealous," Cormac laughed.

"I forgot all about her." Jenna had dropped the lead rope without thinking when Cormac picked her up and Rose had been happy to graze the nearby grass. "I'm sorry, Rose, I didn't mean to ignore you," Jenna apologized to the horse, who put her head back down and continued to graze.

"We should head back," Cormac suggested. They had been out with Rose for quite a while, but Jenna was not at all bored. In fact, she had begun to wish this day could last forever.

"Do we have to?" she asked.

"I'm afraid so. I promised Ashley I wouldn't keep ye out too long. She would like to spend some time with ye herself."

"You don't mind, do you?" Jenna wanted to be certain it was okay with Cormac. If he said he wanted to spend the rest of the day alone with her, she was more than happy to do so.

"Nae. She is yer good friend and it has been a long time since ye've seen her. I have duties to attend to and I'll see ye later at the evening meal."

"Cormac. I have to ask you a question."

"Anything, lass. I've told ye, I'll always answer ye truthfully."

"I know. But you were less than truthful with me in San Francisco. You never told me about Ashley. I don't understand why."

"It may not make any sense to ye, but I didnae tell ye because I wanted ye to come back to Breaghacraig with me. But *I* wanted to be the reason ye came. If I told ye Ashley was here, ye would have returned with me, but for her, not for me." He paused and waited for Jenna to speak. When she didn't he continued. "I hope ye can understand and forgive me for not telling ye the whole truth."

"I probably wouldn't have believed you anyway. I thought you and Dylan were playing some elaborate joke on me. And besides, it turned out to be the best surprise."

"Aye. It was a surprise for the both of ye."

# TWENTY-FOUR

"Ashley!" Jenna called to her friend from across the courtyard and saw Ashley wave and smile a greeting.

"Jenna," Ashley headed her way. "I see you took Rose out for a walk. How was it?"

"It was wonderful. Rose is very sweet and Cormac was so patient with me. I learned a lot today." Jenna smiled up at Cormac, who leaned down and gave her a quick kiss.

"I'll leave ye to yer friend," Cormac said. Ashley stood on tiptoe and gave Cormac a kiss on the cheek.

"We'll see you later, Cormac," Ashley said, watching as he strode away towards the barracks. "Oh, and Cormac!" Ashley called. He turned back to see what she needed. "Thank you again for the peach gummies," she announced, popping one into her mouth.

"Where's he going?" Jenna asked curiously.

"Probably to the practice field with the other men. They work there every day."

Jenna raised an eyebrow. "Doing what?"

"They practice with their swords and bows. It's fun to watch. Sometimes I go up on the battlements and take a peek." Ashley giggled at revealing her guilty pleasure. "Come on. I'll show you."

Ashley took Jenna by the hand and headed for the stairs leading up to the battlements. They reached the top and made their way past the guards, who were stationed at regular intervals around the perimeter.

Ashley seemed to know them all by name. She exchanged greetings with them and continued to drag Jenna along until they came to the overlook of the practice field. "Here." She pulled Jenna closer and pointed down to a field filled with shirtless men in kilts. They all wielded some sort of weapon, and looked utterly amazing while doing so.

"Wow! This is quite the sight," Jenna gasped audibly. "Where's Cormac?"

"There," Ashley pointed to the figure of a tall, handsome, and extremely well built man whom Jenna recognized immediately as Cormac. "Try not to drool, my dear."

Jenna giggled self-consciously. "Is Cailin out there, too?"

"Mmhmm. And Robert."

"And Dougall," another female voice announced from behind them.

"Oh, hi, Helene," Ashley greeted the other young woman.

"And what are you two ladies doing up here, might I ask?" Helene asked with a mischievous grin.

"I dare say we're doing the same thing you are, missy," Ashley teased.

Jenna returned her gaze to the men in question. She had to admit, they were a seriously good-looking group of men. She'd never seen anything quite like it back at home. "Do they know we're up here?"

"I'm sure they do, but they're busy trying not to get bonked over the head with a sword," Ashley laughed.

"Dougall teases me about it all the time. I told him I'd nae come up here again and he admitted that he liked knowing that I was watching him."

"It's true. I know Cailin enjoys it. And it makes for some pretty amazing sex later on."

"Ashley!" Jenna was shocked at her friend's honesty.

"What? I can't help it if I have the hottest husband in all of Scotland."

The three women burst out laughing and Jenna had to admit that this was better than any sporting event she'd ever been to. Ashley handed out more candy. It was Helene's first taste and her facial expressions went from surprise, to deep concentration, to joy. She held out her hand for another.

"Are you and Dougall married, Helene?" Jenna wanted to know.

"Nae yet, but I'm hoping he'll ask me soon," Helene blushed.

Jenna returned her focus to Cormac, who was looking amazingly hot. She couldn't take her eyes off him and was disappointed when Ashley suggested they head back down for some tea.

"Come on. They do this every day. We'll come back tomorrow if you like," she coaxed.

"Okay." She begrudgingly let Ashley tear her away from their spot on the battlements.

Once inside the castle, Helene went off on her own to see to some work and that left Ashley and Jenna alone. They went and sat beside the fire, where they warmed their hands after the brusque weather outside.

"I'll go get us some tea and see if there are any sweet cakes around. I'll be right back," Ashley announced.

Jenna was about to offer to go along with her, when Irene entered the room. The tension was thick between them and Jenna was uncomfortable.

"Hi, Irene. I'm going to get some tea. Shall I have them bring some for you, too?" Ashley asked.

"That would be lovely, Ashley. I'd be pleased to sit with Jenna while yer gone," Irene said.

"Be right back," Ashley said as she headed out of the room.

There was an awkward silence, and Jenna stared down at her hands rather than look at Irene. The look on Irene's face when she'd first come into the room told Jenna that she was probably not Irene's favorite person.

"Well, Jenna, how are ye enjoying yer stay at Breaghacraig?" Irene suddenly asked.

"I'm enjoying it very much. Thank you for your hospitality."

"Of course. Me brothers are very important to me and if Cormac wants you here, then you are welcome here." Irene sat stiffly across from Jenna, with a serious expression on her face. "Jenna, I hope that ye willnae break me brother's heart. It is obvious to me that he cares deeply for ye. I dinnae wish to see him hurt."

Jenna sighed heavily before she responded. "I don't wish to hurt him, Irene. This is an awkward situation for the both of us. A meddling witch was certainly not something I ever believed I would come across. When Cormac arrived out of the fog in San Francisco, I had no idea he was from another time. I didn't believe it. Coming here with Cormac was not my doing, so if you have a problem with it, I suggest you speak with Edna. Cormac and I are just the unfortunate recipients of her matchmaking scheme." Jenna was feeling a bit defensive as she sat here with Irene's eyes boring holes right through her.

Irene softened her tone a bit. "Jenna, I dinnae mean to accuse ye of anything. I understand this was nae yer choice, but I ask ye not to give me brother false hope."

"I care deeply for Cormac, too. I would never purposely hurt him. I don't want to be hurt either, but I'm not sure how to avoid that at this point. I will be leaving when the time comes and I will be very sad to leave him behind, but I cannot stay here."

"Why?" Irene asked.

"Why? How could I? I, I... I'm used to my life in San Francisco." Jenna knew her response didn't sound very convincing. Surely, she could come up with something better than that. Irene had her feeling off-kilter and that was the problem.

"Ashley did it. She came from San Francisco and she has fit right in here with us. I believe you could, as well. We would welcome you here, just as we've welcomed Ashley. She is a loved member of our family now."

"I'm not Ashley," Jenna said firmly.

"I know that ye aren't. I just ask that ye take the time ye've been given to consider a life here at Breaghacraig."

"The tea's coming and I managed to get some sweet cakes, too," Ashley announced, walking in and settling into a chair by the fire. She glanced from Irene to Jenna and back again, lifting an eyebrow. "What are you two so serious about?"

"Oh, nothing. We were just talking about Breaghacraig," Jenna replied breezily.

The servant arrived with the tea and cakes and served the ladies while they sat by the fire.

"Don't you just love it?" Ashley asked. "I'm certain Breaghacraig is the most beautiful place on earth."

Jenna didn't answer. Instead, she sipped her tea and carefully examined the sweet cakes on the tray in front of her.

"I have something to share with the two of you," Ashley said excitedly. "I haven't told a soul. Well, I've told Cailin, but I swore him to secrecy."

"What is it?" Irene questioned.

"I'm pregnant," Ashley blurted out. "I think I'm about three months along, but I wanted to be certain before I said anything."

"Ashley! That's amazing news! Congratulations!" Jenna gushed.

"Ashley, I am so pleased to hear yer news," Irene took Ashley's hand and rubbed it gently between her own. "You are going to be a wonderful mother."

"How are you feeling? Have you had any morning sickness?" Jenna questioned.

"No. None at all. That's why I wasn't sure. I've always heard stories of women being really nauseous all the time and I've been so lucky so far. Not even sick once." Ashley was beaming. "I wanted you two to be the first to know. Cailin has been a bit over-protective though. He won't let me carry anything heavy and he's always right at my elbow, making sure I don't fall down. I mean, honestly, I've been walking practically my entire life. Does he think, all of a sudden I'm going to forget how?" Ashley laughed at the silliness of it all.

"He's just concerned for yer safety, 'tis all," Irene said. "He loves ye so much, Ashley."

"I'm sure he'll lighten up, once he realizes that you won't break," Jenna agreed. Thinking back to the day she arrived, she couldn't help but wonder. "So the day I got here, he was trying to keep you from running over to me. I guess that was because he was afraid you'd fall?"

"He's so sweet and concerned. I can't get mad at him about it. I think he's going to tell Cormac and Robert today. He's just about bursting with keeping the secret."

"So, in six more months, my best friend is going to be a Mommy. I can't believe it!" Jenna said.

"The way my life was going last year, I wouldn't have believed it either," Ashley said. "But now, I'm the happiest woman on the planet!"

"Ashley, we'll have to start making baby clothes, don't ye agree?" Irene seemed to be calculating in her head just how many things they could manage to make before the baby was due.

"I hadn't thought about that, but you're right," Ashley agreed.

"Maybe someone could throw you a baby shower," Jenna suggested.

"A what?" Irene asked.

"Oh, you know - a bunch of women friends get together and bring gifts for the baby and they play games and eat. In 2014, that's what we do," Jenna explained. "That way, the new Mom has everything she needs when her baby arrives."

"We could do that, Ashley. We would invite Lady Lena, Kenna, Helene and the other women of the clan," Irene agreed enthusiastically.

"I would love that," Ashley beamed with delight.

Jenna suddenly felt very sad. Her very best friend in the world was going to have a baby and she wouldn't be around to celebrate with her.

"Is everything okay, Jenna," Ashley queried.

"Yeah, I'm okay. I just wish I could be here when the baby is born," Jenna explained quietly.

"Then stay," Ashley begged. "Please, I'd feel so much happier knowing that you were going to be here with me."

"I can't, Ashley. I just can't." Jenna was determined she was not going to have this conversation. She was leaving and nothing anyone could say would make her feel differently.

Irene grasped Ashley's hand a little tighter when Ashley seemed visibly deflated by this announcement. "Dinnae fash, love," Irene comforted her. "Ye'll have many to help ye. All will be well, ye'll see."

A sense of not belonging began to overwhelm Jenna. "I think I'm going to lie down for a while. I'll see you later." She was miserable and needed to distance herself from her friend and from her own emotions. There was no way she could even begin to explain to anyone how she felt - jealous, angry, sad, lost, confused and as if she needed to get as far away from Breaghacraig as possible.

~~~

"So, brother, what is this news ye have for us?" Cormac asked.

"Ashley has finally given me permission to tell ye," Cailin started.

"Why do ye need yer wife's permission to share a story with us?" Robert interrupted with a knowing smile.

"I'm sure ye know why, Robert," Cailin answered.

"Well, come on, out with it." Cormac was impatient to hear the news.

"Ashley is with child," Cailin announced proudly and he immediately found himself being pounded on the back by both men.

"Congratulations to ye," Robert said. "When is the happy event to take place?"

"Ashley says 'twill be in about six months," Cailin beamed.

"Brother, 'tis wonderful news. I am so happy for ye both," Cormac added.

"Thank ye, Cormac," Cailin said. "I must admit, I've been a bit worried about leaving Ashley's side. She is a stubborn lass and would do many things that might nae be good for the bairn."

Robert laughed at that. "Cailin, dinnae fash, Ashley will be fine. I've been through this enough times to know it."

"Aye, now that I think on it, I dinnae believe I ever saw Irene allow Robert to carry her up and down the stairs," Cormac teased.

"If I had tried to hold her back from hurrying about the castle, she'd have taken me head," Robert agreed.

"Yer right. Ashley willnae put up with it for much longer, I fear. I will try to stop meself from being over-protective."

The three had left the practice field and were walking towards the stables. "A ride would do ye good," Cormac suggested.

"Aye," Cailin agreed.

"I have some business to attend to inside, so I'll leave ye both here," Robert said. He clapped Cailin on the back one more time and was off.

"Cormac, what of this lass ye brought home with ye? Do ye think she'll stay?"

"I dinnae think she wishes it," Cormac reported sadly.

"Ye must try to convince her then."

"'Tis what I plan to do, but I dinnae hold out much hope that she'll change her mind."

"Let's get our horses and mayhap we'll come up with some brilliant plan to get her to stay," Cailin said with confidence.

They brushed and saddled their horses and were out the gate and on their way in less than thirty minutes. They travelled at a leisurely pace past the little cottages that were scattered along the path to the castle. Happy clan members greeted them as they passed. Many offered food or drink if they'd care to stop and talk. The brothers politely refused, after making sure that there was no serious need for their help. They had just arrived at the tree line and were about to enter the woods when movement off to their right caught both their eyes. Cormac froze in his saddle at the sight before him.

"I dinnae believe it," he said, as he urged Saidear into a canter. Cailin followed suit with Cadeyrn, his massive chestnut stallion.

"Who are they?" Cailin wanted to know.

"They're from the future. 'Tis Jenna's former husband and a waitress named Sophia."

"How did they get here?"

"'Tis a long story, but the last I saw of them, they were with Sir Richard."

"Sir Richard? When were ye going to tell us about him?" Cailin asked, concern written all over his handsome face.

"I'm sorry, Cailin. I guess it slipped my mind. I was so happy to be home and I've had Jenna on my mind almost constantly."

"When we get back to Breaghacraig, I expect to hear the whole story," Cailin demanded.

"Of course," Cormac agreed as they came up beside Jonathan and Sophia. "What are ye doing here?" Cormac demanded.

"Thank goodness you found us, Cormac," Sophia said. "We've been wandering around in the woods ever since we got here."

"We need some help to get back home," Jonathan said.

Cormac couldn't help but be wary of Jonathan's motives. He didn't mention Sir Richard to them, instead waiting to see what they were about.

"Ye'll have to come with us," Cailin said. "No decisions will be made out here. The others must know of yer arrival."

"Sure thing, dude," Jonathan said.

Cormac smelled a rat. He knew they were up to something. He looked around for Sir Richard, but he was not visible anywhere nearby. "Just keep heading towards the castle. We'll be right behind ye."

Sophia looked up at Cormac adoringly and spared an appreciative glance for Cailin. She started walking and Jonathan fell into step beside her. Cormac held back and let them get a good distance ahead of them before he spoke to Cailin.

"Something's not right here," he said. "They were with Sir Richard and they were speaking about getting Jenna back to San Francisco. I'm afraid Jonathan means to harm her."

"We cannae allow that, Cormac," Cailin stated firmly.

"Nae. We willnae. When we get back to Breaghacraig, I'll question them about Sir Richard. I'm certain he's involved in this."

They continued to follow Jonathan and Sophia and when they arrived at the gate, they called out to the guards to let them know there was nothing to be concerned about. They passed through and Cailin and Cormac dismounted, handing their horses off to the stable boys.

"Let's go inside," Cormac extended his hand in the direction of the door.

"I appreciate the help, man. I know we didn't get off on the right foot, but you know Jenna was my wife. I guess I was just a bit jealous seeing you with her," Jonathan explained smoothly.

Cormac didn't respond. Sophia sidled up next to him and clung to his arm as they entered the great hall.

"Who is this ye've got with ye?" Irene asked, eyeing Sophia suspiciously.

"This is Jenna's former husband, Jonathan and a friend of his, Sophia. They somehow find themselves in need of our help," Cormac explained.

Irene set about making them feel comfortable in the Great Hall. "I be Lady Irene, me husband Sir Robert is Laird of Breaghacraig. Ye must be verra tired after yer journey. Did ye walk all the way here?" she asked.

"Yes, ma'am," Sophia said. "My feet are killing me."

"I imagine they may well be. 'Tis quite a long walk all the way from the bridge. But how is it that ye find yerselves here?" Irene wanted to know.

"We were out walking on the Marina Green the other morning. Sophia and I had an early morning breakfast date," Jonathan smiled slyly and looked to Sophia for confirmation. "We saw Jenna and Cormac in this swirling mass of fog. We lost sight of them and were worried, so we walked into the fog to see where they'd gone and the next thing we knew, we arrived here."

"I see. Cormac, do ye think Edna knows about this?" Irene questioned.

"I dinnae think so, but I havenae heard from her since we've been back," Cormac stated coldly.

"I'll get our guests some food and find a place for them to rest. Ye can speak with Robert about what's to be done with them," Irene said, taking charge as she usually did. "Please have a seat by the fire to warm yerselves."

"Thank you, ma'am," Sophia said politely as Irene left the room.

"Jonathan, I believe ye may have met Sir Richard out in the woods near the bridge," Cormac said.

"Sir Richard," Jonathan hesitated and then screwed up his forehead, as though he were trying to remember something. "Oh, Sir Richard... yeah, we did. He's an odd guy, isn't he? He was asking us to join him, or something. I don't know what he wanted from us, but Sophia and I got a bad vibe and decided we'd be better off on our own."

"I see. So yer not working with him in any way?" Cailin asked.

"No!" Jonathan almost shouted his denial. "Absolutely not. He seemed like he had it in for you all, didn't he, Sophia?"

"Oh, yeah... he did," Sophia hesitated for just a moment before answering.

"How did ye manage to find Breaghacraig then?" Cormac wondered.

"Sir Richard pointed us in this direction, before he left to go back home. Where did he say he was from babe?"

Jonathan was obviously up to something, Cormac could tell from his demeanor. He had only had a few interactions with him, but he was behaving very oddly.

"I think he said he was going home to England?" Sophia seemed unsure.

"Cailin, I need to speak with ye for a moment. Please excuse us." Cormac led Cailin far enough away so they would not be overheard. "I must warn Jenna that they are here. Will ye stay with them until I return? Jonathan isnae to be trusted. I don't believe Sophia is one to be concerned over, but don't let them out of yer sight."

"Aye. I willnae. Go see to Jenna then." Cailin walked back over to their guests and Cormac headed upstairs, hoping to find Jenna in her room.

# TWENTY-FIVE

Sleep had not come easily to Jenna. She was physically and emotionally exhausted, but somehow, no matter how hard she tried to nap, she couldn't seem to shut her mind off. Thoughts of a life without Cormac and without Ashley were leaving her with numerous questions. Could she stay here? Would she want to? What if Ashley needed her during her pregnancy? The questions kept coming and she didn't seem to have any answers.

A quiet tap at the door let her know she had a visitor. "Come in," she said.

The door opened and Cormac came in, closing the door behind him. Jenna's heart began to race and her breathing became shallow at the sight of him. She hid her trembling hands beneath the furs.

"Jenna, I have news," Cormac started.

"Oh, I know. Ashley already told me."

"Ashley. How could she know?" he asked.

Jenna gave him a 'have-you-lost-your-mind' look. "She's the one who's pregnant. Of course she knows."

Cormac looked confused, but continued. "I know Ashley's with child, but that's not what I'm speaking of."

"Oh, well, what are you speaking of?" Jenna teased.

"Jonathan and Sophia are here at Breaghacraig. Cailin and I found them walking towards the castle while we were out riding."

"What?" Jenna's face paled. "How did they get here? Why?" She had a million questions floating through her head. It seems all that was in her brain - were questions, but no answers.

"I hope to find out the answers soon. I didnae want ye to come downstairs and stumble upon them."

"Cormac, I'm getting a bad feeling about all of this," Jenna said worriedly.

He came to her side, settling on the edge of the bed. "Dinnae fash, love. They are only two and we have many to protect ye." Cormac stroked her cheek and did his best to calm her. "They are staying here as our guests at the moment, but we willnae leave them alone at any time. Do ye wish to come downstairs and see for yerself?"

Jenna wasted no time in getting to her feet. She slipped on the soft shoes Irene had given her and straightened her dress. The time to face her fears was now and she could ask for no better guardian than Cormac. She held her hand out to him and he stood, taking it and walking her to the door. "Are ye ready for this?" he asked softly.

"Let's go. There's no time like the present, right?" She smiled up at him and seeing the strength and determination in his beautiful eyes, all her fears vanished. They made their way downstairs and into the Great Hall.

"Jenna, I'm so happy to see you. I was worried about you," Jonathan simpered, and it was obvious to Jenna he was lying.

"I'll bet you were," Jenna replied sarcastically.

"I was, babe. I wouldn't want anything to happen to you." From the expression on Jonathan's face, there was no doubt that he wished for the exact opposite. "Look at you, already fitting in. Great dress."

Jenna ignored him and turned to the young waitress. "Sophia, how did you get mixed up with him?"

"We met at the diner and he asked me if I wanted to go for a walk with him. I didn't know it would involve time travelling." She was speaking to Jenna, but staring at Cormac. Jenna thought Sophia would start drooling at any moment and the jealousy she had suffered at the diner came crashing back into her.

"I'll bet you didn't. Who would? You and Jonathan do make a cute couple," Jenna said sarcastically. "I'm glad you found someone, Jonathan." Jenna kept a close eye on both of them, to see if they would slip up.

"You know me, I don't like to be alone for long," Jonathan responded drily.

"I know. Sometimes you actually double up, so there's not a minute in the day when you're alone." Jenna was referring to the woman Jonathan had been seeing, both before and during their marriage. She had no idea if the woman was still in the picture, but she knew Sophia was easy prey for a man like Jonathan.

"If you're talking about Liz, she's long gone. After you left me penniless, she couldn't find a single reason to stick around. But that's old news; you aren't thinking of staying here, are you?" Jonathan asked.

"No. I'm planning to return to San Francisco soon," Jenna was uncomfortable stating her intentions in front of Cormac. She knew he would be upset by it. She gave him a quick glance and sure enough, his eyes were focused straight at her and Jenna couldn't help but see the pain there.

"Okay. Good. So you know how to get out of here then. Sophia and I were worried we'd be stuck here forever." Jonathan glanced to Sophia for back up and didn't get any support. Sophia was obviously smitten by every man she saw. She hadn't been able take her eyes off Cormac and then Cailin and now Robert, who had entered the room.

"What have we here?" Robert asked. "I hear ye've come from the future. Is that true?"

"Yes, sir," Jonathan answered, showing uncharacteristic respect for someone other than himself.

"I be Robert MacKenzie, the laird of the MacKenzie Clan. Yer welcome in our home. Irene wishes ye to join her in the kitchen where she has some food for ye and then she will lead ye to yer sleeping chambers."

"Thank you, sir," Jonathan replied.

"Cailin, would ye show them to the kitchen, please?" Robert asked.

Cailin led them out of the room and Robert waited until they were gone before explaining to Cormac and Jenna that Jonathan and Sophia would be under constant surveillance. "We have arranged beds for them in the barracks and the woman's solar. There will be someone keeping an eye on them at all times." He looked to Jenna. "Ye needn't fash, lass. We will see to it that ye are well protected."

"Thank you, Robert, I appreciate your help." And she really did.

"Now, if you'll both excuse me. I have duties to attend to." With that, Robert left them alone.

Jenna turned to Cormac, anguish apparent in her eyes. "What am I going to do, Cormac? When I leave, do I have to take them with me?"

"I dinnae ken if Edna knows of this. Mayhap she will have an answer for ye. At any rate, I dinnae like the idea of Jonathan being in the same century with ye, whether it be here or back in yer own time."

"Me either. I really think he's up to something. I don't know what it is, but it can't be anything good. Did you see the way he tried to pretend that he was worried about me? And Sophia, what's her deal? I can't believe she has any idea what kind of guy he is."

"I dinnae believe Sophia is aware of his plan. Not completely. Mayhap she believes he is interested in her."

"I suppose that's possible, but I don't get it. Her eyes are about to pop out of her head every time she sees you, your brother, or Robert." She's obviously not that interested in him. I'd love to know what he told her, to get her to leave the diner with him. Maybe I can speak with her alone and find out."

"Be careful around either of them, Jenna," Cormac warned.

"Don't worry, I don't have any intention of letting Jonathan get the better of me… again," Jenna assured him.

~~~

The evening meal brought everyone together once again. Jenna sat next to Cormac, who was attentive, as always. Ashley and Cailin were deep in conversation and Jenna thought Ashley was more beautiful than ever with her pregnancy glow. Robert and Irene were speaking with some of their guests as they made their way to the table. All seemed normal, at least until Jonathan and Sophia entered the room. The room lapsed into silence as all eyes turned their way. Someone had gotten them appropriate clothing and as was normally the case for Sophia, she looked like she just might pop out of her gown, as her breasts were practically overflowing the bodice. Jonathan caught sight of Ashley and practically ran across to greet her, as if she was a long-lost friend. For her part, Ashley gave Jonathan an 'I-can't-imagine-you-think-I-believe-this' look, before turning to Cailin and completely ignoring Jonathan's attempts at friendliness. Sophia's expression was of someone who was lost, confused and definitely out of their element. One of the nearby men came to her rescue, offering for her to come and sit with him for the meal. He offered her his arm and Sophia looked relieved as she accepted it. Sophia glanced Jonathan's way and then shrugged her shoulders dismissively, sitting down at a table with a group of highlanders who all seemed very pleased to meet her.

"Who's that," Jenna asked Cormac of the young man who had taken Sophia's arm.

"'Tis Latharn. He's one of Cailin's men," Cormac responded. "Dinnae fash, love, he's a good man."

"Good. I guess we'll just have to hope Sophia won't lead him astray," Jenna responded, and she knew she sounded a bit more snarky than she had intended. Cormac tipped his head and gave her a quizzical look, before Jenna shook her head and laughed. Cormac joined her and before they knew it, everyone at the table was looking at them with a question in their eyes.

"'Tis nothing," Cormac reassured those turned their way.

Jenna watched Jonathan's reaction when he found that Sophia

was already seated at a full table and he was now without a dining partner. No one seemed in any hurry to help him out, but he eventually found a spot at a nearby table filled with couples. Jenna watched as he turned on the charm and made himself at home while the food was served.

"Jenna, are you okay?" Ashley asked quietly.

"Yeah, I'm fine, I just don't trust him. You never know what he might be up to."

"I'm amazed he'd actually think I believed his false show of friendship. He hated me in San Francisco, I'm not certain why he would think that would have changed," Ashley quipped.

"How could anyone hate ye, my love," Cailin asked. "He must be a fool."

Jenna smiled at that. Cailin truly loved her friend and she was so happy for Ashley. Happy that she had found a man who could appreciate her for all of her wonderful qualities. Jenna turned her gaze to Cormac, who as always, only had eyes for her. His brilliant smile and smoldering blue eyes turned the heat way up. She could feel it, all the way from her head to her toes and every place in between. Jenna had to look away, so she could catch her breath. Maybe she could be as lucky as Ashley had been. Maybe she had found the perfect man for her. Maybe Cormac could love her, the way she had always dreamed of being loved. Or, maybe she was living in fantasyland. A sigh escaped her lips. *It doesn't really matter. I'm not staying here and he's not going to come back with me. It's all just a dream I'll wake up from, before too long.*

"Is something wrong, Jenna?" Cormac questioned.

"No. Everything's fine, just fine," Jenna lied.

"I dinnae believe ye," Cormac smiled warmly, searching her eyes for the truth.

Jenna wondered if he was a mind reader. He always seemed to know exactly what she was thinking. "Suit yourself, then," she answered, taking a bite of her dinner. Maybe if she kept her mouth full of food, she wouldn't have to tell Cormac what she'd been thinking. For his part, Cormac kept an eye on her, but Jenna could tell he was content to let it slide for the time being. It was a good thing, too. She'd hate to admit to him what she'd been thinking.

~~~

Cormac knew Jenna was avoiding his question, but he'd get the truth out of her later. He was sure Jonathan and Sophia had upset her, but he wasn't exactly certain why. Was it because she was wary of their plans, or was it because she might have to take them back to San Francisco when she went… *if* she went. Cormac still had time to convince her to stay, but then what would happen? Would Jonathan and Sophia be able to get back to San Francisco, or would they be cursed with Jonathan's presence at Breaghacraig forever? He'd speak with Robert about it, later. There had to be a way to get him out of their lives and far enough away, so he couldn't bother Jenna ever again. Cormac watched Jonathan as he ingratiated himself on his tablemates. They were all smiling and laughing at whatever story he was telling them. He could see how Jonathan had managed to fool Jenna into believing that he loved her. If he didn't know him better, Cormac might even have believed Jonathan was a decent human being, but he had met the more sinister Jonathan in San Francisco and knew he would need to protect Jenna from him, at all costs. He didn't like having him here, this near to Jenna, but it was better to keep him close. Cormac would just have to remain vigilant.

Everyone sat at the table for much longer than was usual for them. They had a lot to talk about and Robert was intent on toasting Cailin and Ashley's good fortune. Cormac was happy for them. His brother had found the woman of his dreams and they were about to start their family together. He wished them all the best. He just wished he could be so lucky. He thought he was, but Jenna had other ideas. She was not an easy one to deal with. He would have to work hard to prove his love to her, but she was definitely worth it. He wanted her in his life, even though she could be as *prickly as a thistle*; he knew she was the one for him. And he knew if she left, he would spend his days lamenting the loss and regretting his inability to keep her here as his wife.

"Cormac, now I'm the one asking… is everything okay?" Jenna asked.

"Aye, love. I was just thinking," Cormac responded. His eyes fell lovingly on her beautiful face. Her soulful brown eyes drew him into their depths and he wished he could linger there forever.

"About what?"

"About ye… about how beautiful ye are. About how happy I'd be if ye were to stay here with me."

Jenna seemed saddened by his admission, but didn't respond. Instead, she reached for his much larger hand and squeezed it with her own.

"I'd like to share something with ye, Jenna. Would ye come with me?" Cormac asked.

"Of course," Jenna answered.

He stood and pulled Jenna's chair out for her. "We're going for a walk," Cormac announced to the table.

"Have fun," Ashley smiled and winked at Cormac.

"We will, dinnae fash," Cormac answered, eyes twinkling with mischief. "Come, let's go, Jenna." They left the noise of the hall for the contrasting silence outdoors. "Are ye warm enough?"

"I'm fine. The fresh air feels good and besides, I happen to know that, if need be, you'll keep me warm." Jenna poked Cormac in the side and when he tried to return the favor by tickling her, she squealed with delight and tried to run. Cormac wrapped his arms around her waist before she could get away and lifted her off the ground.

"Dinnae think ye can escape," he chuckled. "We're going this way." He led her to the steps to the battlements.

"Oh, I've been here before. Ashley brought me up here."

Cormac lifted an eyebrow. "Did she? Whatever for?"

"I'm not sure I'm supposed to say. It might be a secret," Jenna said with a mysterious smile.

"Dinnae make me tickle it out of ye, lass," Cormac teased.

"Okay, okay… she showed me a place where the women go, to watch you guys at work on the practice field."

"I see. And what did ye think?"

"I was impressed," Jenna admitted.

"And what precisely were ye impressed with?" Cormac thought he knew the answer to his question, but he wanted to hear Jenna's response.

"Well, there was this one guy…" she started.

"Aye. And what is his name? I'll be sure to work him extra hard tomorrow."

Jenna giggled at that. "I think his name is… Cormac MacBayne. Do you know him?"

"Aye. I do. I hear he fancies a lass named Jenna. Have ye heard it too?"

"I think I might have heard that rumor going around," Jenna teased him back.

Managing to draw her attention away from Cormac, Jenna was amazed by the darkness of the sky and by the bright dots of lights that were scattered across it. "This is beautiful, Cormac. Thank you for bringing me here."

"'Tis my pleasure. Ye shared yer favorite places in San Francisco with me and I wanted to do the same for ye."

"I'm so happy that you did," Jenna replied, as she snuggled closer to Cormac. "I'm feeling a little cold. Could you warm me up, please?"

"Ye dinnae have to ask me twice." Cormac pulled her close and wrapped her in his strong embrace. "Is that better, love?"

"Yes. It's perfect."

# TWENTY-SIX

The morning air was chilly, but Jenna was focused on the fact that she was about to mount a horse and take her first riding lesson since her accident as a child.

"Dinnae fash, Jenna. I willnae allow anything to happen to ye," Cormac reassured her.

"Okay. It's just that I'm afraid and I know Rose can sense it. Are you sure I won't make her nervous?"

"She is a verra quiet mare. Many a child has learned to ride on her. Now 'tis yer turn."

Jenna tentatively stepped up next to Rose and laid her hand on the horse's neck. "Hi, Rosie. Be good to me, okay?" Cormac helped her mount the horse and then took the lead rope and walked Rose around the circular pen near the stable.

"'Tis important that ye learn to balance yerself," Cormac instructed. "I'll hold onto Rose and ye can concentrate on yer seat."

Jenna did as she was instructed and Cormac had her first walking, and then trotting around without holding onto the horse or the saddle. He taught her how to sit, where to keep her legs and most of all how to relax on her mount. Rose for her part, was a star. She never once took a wrong step and she seemed as concerned as Cormac that Jenna stay safe in the saddle. Rose was a very placid horse and if she felt Jenna's weight shift, she seemed to push herself instinctively to that side, in order to save Jenna from falling. Jenna's confidence grew with every passing minute and she found herself smiling and enjoying herself.

"Shall we take her to a canter, Jenna?" Cormac asked.

Apprehension lit Jenna's face. "I'm not so sure that would be a good idea."

"Try it for me. Have Rose and I not taken good care of ye today?"

"Yes, you have," Jenna said. She squared her shoulders and sat up straight and tall. Taking a deep breath, she said, "Okay. Let's do it."

"Jenna, put yer right foot back and squeeze," Cormac instructed.

"Oh, my…" Jenna squealed when Rose broke into a gentle canter. She grabbed for the saddle for balance.

"Ye can hold onto the saddle if ye like, Jenna. Dinnae be afraid. Yer doing verra well, lass."

Jenna held the saddle with both hands for a minute or two and then, she put first one arm and then the other straight out to either side and relaxed into the saddle and the rhythm of the horse without holding on for support.

"Jenna, we're going to go back to a trot and then to a walk."

As Rose slowed to an eventual walk, Jenna's face lit up with a glorious smile. "I did it, Cormac! I did it!" Stopping Rose, Cormac scooped her from the saddle and she wrapped her arms around his neck, kissing him soundly on the lips before alighting on the ground.

"Ye did it! I'm so proud of ye. Thank ye for trusting Rose and me."

"I can't wait to tell Ashley. She'll never believe it."

"Tomorrow I'll take ye off the lead and ye can do it on yer own."

She couldn't believe it, but she was actually excited about overcoming her fear. It felt so good to be in control of something that had been a constant source of stress all these years.

"You're the best teacher, Cormac. I love you," she blurted the words before she could stop herself.

Cormac appeared stunned by the admission. "Do ye, Jenna?" he responded quietly.

"I do, Cormac," she said, realization dawning. She really did. Back in San Francisco, she thought she might be falling in love with him, but she'd just confirmed it in her own mind. It wasn't a romantic dream she'd been having. It was something so much more. "You're everything I've ever wanted, Cormac. You're kind, you're patient, and you're fun to be with. You make me feel so special. I've never had that before. I didn't think it was possible for me to fall in love again and I've been denying it ever since we met. I thought I was a really bad judge of character because of what happened with Jonathan, but you've proven me wrong."

Cormac seemed speechless. The love in his eyes was apparent. After a moment, he said, "Ye fill my heart, Jenna. It feels ready to burst with happiness. Does this mean ye'll stay? Please, stay, Jenna. Ye can't leave now."

The euphoria Jenna had been experiencing vanished as she realized that this was not going to work. She had just told Cormac she loved him and she'd made the mistake of letting him think they had hope of a future together. Irene was right. She was going to break his heart and hers was going to be broken as well.

"Jenna?" Cormac sounded worried. "What's wrong, lass? Ye were so happy and now ye seem..." His voice trailed off. He must have guessed exactly what Jenna was thinking.

"I'm sorry, Cormac. I shouldn't have said any of those things to you. I'm a terrible person. Please forgive me." Tears welled up in Jenna's eyes as she realized what a dreadful mess she had made. "I'm so, so sorry."

Cormac hugged her tightly to his chest. "Dinnae greet, Jenna, love. I understand. I truly do. 'Tis a terrible trick that has been played upon us. 'Tis nae yer fault. There is nothing for me to forgive."

Jenna sniffled and gulped for air. Tear filled eyes gazed into Cormac's and she saw that he too had eyes full of sadness. Why had this happened to them? She silently cursed Edna and once again was thankful she wasn't standing in front of her. If she had been, Jenna might have knocked her on her ass. Cormac put one arm around her and holding the lead rope in the other hand, led Jenna and Rose back to the stables. Jenna was inconsolable as he handed Rose off to the stable boy.

"Come, Jenna, we can't have the others see ye like this. Let's sit for a moment." He led her to a bench just outside of the stables, but hidden from the view of any passersby. There they sat, each in their own world of hurt. Each wanting something they knew was not going to be possible. It took a while, but eventually they were able to express their feelings.

"I'm sorry, Cormac. I've made a complete mess of things," Jenna apologized again.

"Jenna. Ye must not feel that this is yer doing. 'Tis not."

"I know. I guess on some level, I wish I could stay here with you. Not go back home. I'd have you and Ashley."

"Ye'd have much more than just the two of us. Ye'd have my family, my clan."

"I don't think your sister likes me very much. I don't know that I'd fit in here."

"Irene and ye are verra much alike. She is my sister and she believes 'tis her role in life to take care of Cailin and me. Ye'd think she had enough to do with looking after her own bairns, her husband and being the Lady of the castle," he chuckled. "You may not have brothers, or bairns, but ye have Dylan. Ye take care of him and ye'd be verra suspicious of any woman who was in his life for more than a mere night. Ye love him as though he were yer brother. Ye have yer friends and yer life in San Francisco. I cannae ask ye to give all that up for me and as much as I love ye, Jenna, I dinnae believe I could survive in San Francisco. I fear I would be lost and that I'd become a burden to ye. I couldnae live with that."

"You'd never be a burden to me, Cormac. But, you're right. It would be much too difficult for you to jump ahead by five hundred years and fit comfortably into life there. It was a fun vacation, but living it every day is something else altogether."

"Well, then, I think we agree that we only have a few days together. So, I'd like to spend them with ye, Jenna. But I want to see yer smiling face and know that we are making the most of every second we have together. Agreed?"

"Agreed," Jenna smiled for the first time since they'd sat down.

"Then let's go see what mischief we can get into, shall we?"

He took Jenna's hand and they wandered off towards the castle doors.

~~~

Cormac opened the doors to Breaghacraig and peeked around in search of his sister. It was totally silent inside. No one was around to disturb them. When he'd suggested that they see what mischief they could get into, both he and Jenna knew exactly what he meant. He wanted to be alone with her, but he had a few things he needed to get in order first.

"Wait for me up in yer chambers, Jenna. I willnae be long, I promise."

"I hope not. I can't get out of this dress on my own, Mister," Jenna playfully eyed Cormac as she headed for the stairs.

Cormac laughed as he headed off to find someone to help draw a bath for them. Well, technically it had to be for Jenna. He couldn't exactly tell anyone it was for both of them, but what they didn't know couldn't hurt anyone. He rounded up the tub, the largest one he could find, and the boys to bring the hot water. He also found some of Robert's fine wine and two goblets. Cheese and fruit were next and for good measure, he went out to the garden and picked a beautiful red rose for his love.

Arriving upstairs in Jenna's room, he found her waiting patiently for him in a chair by the fireplace, where he presented her with his treasures.

"I tried to start a fire, but I'm not very good at it," she admitted.

"I'll take care of that for ye, my sweet." Cormac got the fire started and it was blazing merrily before long.

"Don't you think that might be a bit too much heat?" Jenna asked.

"Not at all, love," Cormac replied. There was a knock at the door and he opened it up to a troop of young boys with buckets of hot water and a large tub, which they set by the fire. Jenna seemed to be catching on as her tongue darted out to wet her lips.

"A bath would be very nice. Thanks for thinking of me," Jenna said.

Cormac waited impatiently for the lads to finish filling the tub and then closed and locked the door behind them. He hesitated for only a moment before turning back to Jenna. "Shall we?" He motioned towards the tub.

Jenna glided across the room and was in his arms in a heartbeat. Their lips met in a tangle of tongues and lips. Their physical yearning for each other had reached its limit and Cormac could hardly wait to get Jenna out of her gown. He made fast work of the laces and had it pulled off her as quickly as possible. He admired her from head to toe and then led her to the tub. She stepped in and settled down into the water, sinking in up to her chin and staring at him wantonly. Cormac disrobed to Jenna's appreciative stare and joined her, sloshing water out of the tub as he got in and sat across from her. Jenna leaned forward and kissed him gently, her tongue tickling his lips. Her hands went to work below the water line and Cormac threw his head back in ecstasy. He knew this had been a good idea. Perhaps the best one he'd ever had. He loved that Jenna was so uninhibited. She was so unlike any of the women he'd been with in the past. She was a beauty beyond compare and she was his. His for this short time and he would enjoy every minute he had with her. From the looks of her, Jenna was enjoying it as well. She scooted forward and lowered herself onto him. A moan escaped her lips and Cormac was lost to the incredible sensations that assailed him as Jenna slowly rocked up and down. His hands found her hips and guided her movement, just as their lips locked on one another. Cormac growled deep in his throat and quickened his movements within Jenna.

"Oh, Jenna, Jenna," Cormac cried out as Jenna called his name in response, each reaching their climax and seeing it in one another's eyes.

"That was fun," Jenna said breathlessly. "I like your idea of mischief." Jenna sat with her back nestled into Cormac's chest. They stayed that way until the water was no longer warm.

"The water's getting cold, aye. Let's get out and under the covers."

They got out of the tub and dried each other off. Jenna scurried across to the bed and Cormac grabbed the food and wine, bringing it with him. He climbed in next to Jenna and poured them a goblet of wine each, and then placed the bottle on the floor. The plate of food sat in his lap.

"This is a very romantic way to spend an afternoon, Cormac," Jenna batted her eyelashes playfully at Cormac.

"Aye. I have a bit of romance in me, love."

"You certainly do," Jenna seemed to have forgotten her woes for now, happily wrapping herself in Cormac's embrace.

They finished their wine and set everything aside. Jenna yawned heavily and lay her head on Cormac's chest.

For Cormac's part, he was content. If only he could find a way to make this moment last forever.

# TWENTY-SEVEN

"Ashley, are you sure this is a good idea?" Jenna asked for the umpteenth time, as they walked along the path to visit one of the outlying cottages.

"Jenna, it's fine. I do this all the time. Don't be such a worrywart," Ashley chided gently.

"Okay. But I don't want to be around when Cailin finds out we're gone," Jenna warned.

"I want you to meet this sweet little family. They were among the first I met when I got here. You'll love them."

Jenna wasn't so sure about that. They had been walking for what seemed like an hour and her feet were starting to hurt. She wasn't sure at all that it was what a pregnant Ashley should be doing. They rounded a curve in the road and before them sat a small cottage. Smoke was coming from the chimney and the sounds of children playing were evident in the otherwise silent surroundings. Jenna just wanted to spend some time with Ashley and the rest of her time with Cormac. She didn't really care about meeting people, but she couldn't seem to get that message across to Ashley. It was apparently really important to Ashley that she get to know these people. Ashley had explained that Heather and Finn were not aware of the whole time travelling thing, so

Jenna was going to have to be careful not to give anything away. The basket of goodies she'd been carrying was getting heavy and Jenna would be happy to hand it over once they arrived.

"Lady Ashley!" A young sandy-haired boy came running towards them with a dog by his side.

"Willliam!" Ashley called and opened her arms to welcome him into her embrace. "How are you, William? I haven't seen you in a while."

"I be fine, Lady Ashley. Me mum will be happy to see ye." Jenna caught his questioning gaze when he looked her way.

"I'm Jenna," she offered. "I'm a friend of Lady Ashley's."

"Are ye from America, too?" he asked.

"I am." She handed him the basket. "We've brought some American surprises with us."

"Thank ye, Lady Jenna. We be verra grateful."

By now, the other children were headed their way. Each greeted Ashley with a hug, the youngest, Mary, climbing into her arms. She threw her arms around Ashley's neck and hugged her tight. They were all introduced to Jenna, who found herself, surprisingly, enjoying the chance to meet them. As they walked towards the cottage, a man and woman came out and waved to them.

"That's me Ma and Da," William announced.

"Heather and Finn," Ashley added.

"Good day to ye, Lady Ashley," Finn said as they approached. "How be ye, this fine day?"

"I'm fine, Finn. You all look to be doing well," Ashley said.

"Aye. That we are," Heather responded. "'Tis good to see ye." Heather came forward to embrace Ashley.

"Heather, Finn, this is my good friend Jenna. She's just arrived from America."

"Ye must have had a long journey, Lady Jenna."

"It wasn't too bad," Jenna responded. She didn't get the whole Lady Jenna thing, but Ashley had told her to go along with it.

"Are ye from the same place in America as Lady Ashley?"

Heather questioned.

"Yes. We grew up together."

"Will ye be staying for a while then?" Finn asked.

"Unfortunately, no. I have to return home soon."

"Please, come inside. I'll make us some tea," Heather offered.

They entered the tiny cottage, which despite its lack of space was tidily kept and there seemed to be room enough for everyone. They sat at a table near the rear window and Heather poured them all some tea. Finn excused himself, saying that he had some sheep to check on. Jenna could hear him calling to the dog as he walked out the door.

The children were all hunkered down on the floor, sifting through the contents of the basket Ashley and Jenna had brought with them.

"And what is all of this?" Heather asked.

"Some treats from San Francisco," Jenna answered. "I hope you don't mind that we gave them to the children, without asking you first."

"Nay. Of course not. They get precious few treats, so 'tis nothing for ye to worry over," Heather assured her.

"Heather, I have some news I wanted to share with you," Ashley said.

"What is that, Lady Ashley?"

"I'm expecting my first bairn, in about six months," Ashley proudly stated.

"Is that true? Oh, my! I am so happy to hear it. Cailin must be over the moon," Heather beamed with delight.

"I believe he is," Ashley giggled. "I'm so excited."

"I'm feeling privileged that ye wanted to share yer good news with me," Heather looked genuinely surprised by this revelation.

"Of course. Your family is very special to me. I love your children and seeing them made me realize how much I wanted bairns of my own."

"Thank ye, Lady Ashley. Ye are too kind," Heather looked a bit embarrassed. "Let me get ye some of the fresh batch of bannocks that I've made." She retrieved a platter of bannocks, some butter, and honey and brought them back to the table. "Can I get ye any more tea?" she asked, before sitting down again.

"No, this is wonderful," Jenna said. "They look very delicious."

"Well, try one then," Ashley said. "I think you'll find they taste delicious, too."

Ashley and Heather chuckled and Heather offered Jenna a bannock. "This is really good," Jenna said, swallowing her first bite. "The best I've had since I've been here." Bannocks seemed to be a staple at every meal. Cormac had even made them for her when they were on their way to Breaghacraig, but these were truly the best she'd had.

"Thank ye, Lady Jenna. 'Tis me secret recipe," Heather smiled proudly.

Ashley and Jenna spent another hour at the little cottage, enjoying tea, bannocks, and conversation. The children loved their treats and Jenna was happy to see they'd emptied the basket for the return trip. As they got up to leave, the children lined up for hugs, but not just from Ashley. They wanted to hug Jenna as well. She couldn't resist. They really were very sweet children and the little one, Mary, was the sweetest of all. The way she nestled into Jenna's arms and then touched her face and hair, was very precious and had Jenna melting.

"'Twas so good to see ye both," Heather said. "I wish ye all the best with the bairn, Lady Ashley. If I can be of any assistance, please let me know, won't ye?"

"You know I will, Heather. You have a lot more experience than I do. I was told that you might be able to help me with the birthing. Is that true?"

Heather looked a little embarrassed by the praise, but said, "Aye, I have helped many of the women of Clan MacKenzie with their births. I'd be happy to do the same for ye."

"Good. That makes me feel better." Ashley had confided to Jenna that she was nervous about giving birth here in sixteenth century Scotland. Jenna had tried unsuccessfully to convince her to go back to San Francisco to have the baby, but Ashley wouldn't hear of it. She was not going anywhere. She couldn't possibly leave her husband and all the people she loved behind, even for a short time. Jenna was happy that Heather had helped to make Ashley feel better about the whole thing and now understood the reasoning for bringing Jenna to meet her. Jenna was sure Ashley would be in good hands when the time came, because truth be told, she was nervous about it, too.

~~~

"What do ye think he's up to?" Cailin asked Cormac.

"I dinna ken what he's doing, but I'm happy Robert has someone watching him at all times," Cormac responded.

The two men were just leaving the practice field when they noticed that Jonathan had been watching them.

"Wow! You guys really go at it out there," Jonathan said when they approached.

"We must always be prepared for battle," Cormac responded.

"Would ye care to join us when next we practice?" Cailin offered.

"That might be fun. I could stand to work off some of this stress," Jonathan said.

"Fine then. We meet here every day at the same time. You're welcome to take part," Cormac responded.

They walked away from Jonathan and headed toward the stables. "Why did ye ask him to join us on the practice field," Cormac asked.

"'Tis better to know your enemy's capabilities - dinnae ye think so, Cormac?"

"Aye. Yer right. We can see what his skills are and be prepared should he try anything."

"Look, Ashley and Jenna are returning from their walk. I hope she didnae tire herself." Cailin said worriedly.

"Dinnae fash, brother, she is verra able to take care of herself."

"That is what I'm for, Cormac, to take care of her," Cailin protested.

"Ye apparently dinnae understand these women from San Francisco. They are fine on their own."

"That's what they say, but I dinnae believe it." Cailin headed off towards the women and Cormac quickly followed behind.

"Ashley, are ye well, love? Where have ye been?" Cailin asked.

"We just took a walk to Heather and Finn's," Ashley responded. "And before you say anything, I am not going to break, Cailin. I'm just having a baby and I feel wonderful. There is no need to worry. If there is, I'll let you know." With that pronouncement, she stood on tiptoes and kissed his nose.

Cailin seemed to have had all the wind taken out of his sails. He just stood there looking as though he was searching for a good reason to disagree with Ashley, but instead he smiled down at his lovely wife and took her arm to lead her inside.

"How was your walk, Jenna?" Cormac asked.

"Good. Ashley wanted to take some treats to the children and to ask if Heather would help her when it comes time for the baby to be born."

"And will she?"

"Yes. She said she'd be happy to help. I think that put Ashley's mind at ease. I'm sure I don't have to tell you, but giving birth in these times can be dangerous for a woman."

"But not in your time?"

"Not so much," Jenna assured him. "I tried to convince Ashley to come back to San Francisco to have the baby, but she wouldn't hear it."

"I would think not. Her life is here now. She wouldnae leave Cailin," Cormac stated firmly.

"I know. That's what she told me," Jenna said. "Don't worry; I'm not going to try to steal her away with me when I leave."

"I hope not, love. It would kill me brother." *Just as it will kill me, when you leave.*

Jenna scrunched up her nose and stuck her tongue out at him.

"I can think of better things to do with that tongue, love," Cormac teased.

"I bet you can," Jenna responded.

"You'll have to wait until later, as today is the day you ride Rose all on yer own."

"Ugh, not today," Jenna whined.

"Today." Cormac started striding towards the stable. He looked back and noticed that Jenna had not moved, so he stopped and waited for her to join him.

"Okay. Okay. I'm coming." Jenna grabbed his arm with a frustrated huff and followed along to get Rose.

~~~

Jenna was pleased with her riding lesson. She didn't know why she'd ever doubted Cormac when he'd told her he'd have her riding Rose on her own. She was proud of herself and feeling very accomplished, when she ran into Sophia just outside the stable doors.

"What are you doing here?" Jenna asked. She searched around to see who was watching Sophia and saw Latharn leaning against the wall of the blacksmith's shop. He nodded at Jenna, to let her know he was keeping an eye on the situation, when Cormac emerged from the stables.

"Are ye ready, love?" Cormac stopped short when he saw Sophia standing there.

"I was just about to tell Jenna, that I was going in to look at the horses," Sophia confessed.

"Do ye ride, lass?" Cormac asked.

"I've ridden before. Not a lot, but I think I did pretty well when I did."

"Mayhap ye can convince Latharn to take you out for a ride. I'm sure he'd be pleased to go with ye." Cormac nodded in Latharn's direction and Latharn headed towards them. "Latharn, ye should take the lovely Sophia out on one of the horses. She may enjoy it."

Sophia looked up at Latharn with a huge smile. "I'd love it, actually."

"I'll get some horses saddled up then." Latharn seemed complete-ly smitten with Sophia, and it seemed the feeling might be mutual.

The two walked into the stable together, leaving Jenna and Cor-mac alone outside.

"That was weird," Jenna observed.

"Weird?"

"You know… not normal," Jenna explained.

"Latharn will keep an eye on her."

"Okay. Is it bath time, yet?" Jenna picked up her skirts and started to run for the castle doors.

"I believe it is," Cormac said. He took off in pursuit of her, catch-ing her just as she got to the steps of the Keep. "Wait for me, love. It wouldn't do for me to be chasing ye through the doors. What would me sister think?" Cormac chuckled at the thought of what his sister would say, if she knew what they were up to.

Jenna straightened her dress and fixed her hair, putting on a show of regality, and stifling a giggle, she tucked her hand in the crook of Cormac's arm and let him guide her through the doors and upstairs, to what was fast becoming their afternoon ritual.

# TWENTY-EIGHT

Jenna could hardly believe her stay at Breaghacraig was almost over. Here it was, Day Four, and she had to admit that she wasn't looking forward to leaving. She'd thought when she first arrived that she couldn't wait to go home, but the last few days had taught her that she enjoyed life at Breaghacraig. She loved seeing Ashley every day and she definitely loved being with Cormac. Day Seven was going to be torturous. But that was still a few days off. She'd done a good job of not thinking about it and she planned to keep it that way.

Cormac had saddled up their horses after breakfast and they were going to go for a ride down to the beach. Jenna was really looking forward to it. Rose was turning out to be a quiet, calm horse and her gentleness was infectious. Jenna relaxed and enjoyed riding her. They made their way through the castle gates and rode side by side down the path that led them to the nearby shoreline. Cormac had explained to Jenna that in times past, this beach had been the landing site of smugglers. They'd bring goods from other European ports and sell them here at Breaghacraig.

"That would explain where a lot of the beautiful things in the castle came from, then," Jenna observed.

"Aye. Some of it came from the smugglers, but some also came from travelling vendors and from journeys that the MacKenzie's took to Edinburgh and London."

"Do people here know that there's a land on the other side of the ocean?" Jenna wondered aloud.

"Aye. Some have travelled there. But 'tis not called America in our time."

"So, I guess Columbus didn't really discover America," Jenna observed.

"Who do ye speak of, love?"

"It's not important, really. It's a lovely day, isn't it?"

"Any day I can spend with you is lovely," Cormac answered, a serious look in his eyes.

"Don't make me jump off this horse and onto your lap, you sweet talker, you," Jenna teased.

"Teaching ye to ride was a good thing, but I think I liked it better when ye rode with me," Cormac said.

"Me, too," Jenna answered.

They rode to the edge of the bluff and dismounted. Cormac removed the saddles and let the horses graze on the abundant grass surrounding them.

"This way, Jenna." He held out his hand and guided her down the path to the beach. He had brought an extra plaid and a basket of food with him. "We can spend some time here, if ye like."

"I like," Jenna agreed.

Cormac spread the plaid in the sand, and placed the basket down beside it. He helped Jenna down onto the plaid and sat next to her.

"This is such a nice way to spend the day," Jenna said.

"I'm happy you approve," Cormac replied. He moved closer to Jenna and placed his arm around her shoulders.

Jenna sighed and leaned her head on his shoulder while she took in the beauty of the beach and the water. The smell of the ocean brought her memories back to the waters of San Francisco Bay and a childhood spent with Ashley and her family, and Dylan. Those were happy, happy times for Jenna. Her life had not been quite so happy over the last few years. Of course, she'd had a period of false happiness with Jonathan and the more she thought about it, the more she realized the happiness she enjoyed with Cormac was the real thing. It was the same sense of happiness she remembered from her childhood. It was carefree and easy. She knew she was safe, protected, and loved. What more could a girl ask for?

"Cormac, this is perfect. Thank you for bringing me here," Jenna said.

Cormac didn't respond. He let the moment rest on Jenna's words. She liked that about him. He cared what she thought, how she felt, if she was cold or tired. She would never take that for granted. Until this point in her life, no one had ever cared about any of those things and she would have said that it didn't matter because she *knew* what she thought and how she felt. If she were cold, she'd get a jacket. If she were tired, she'd go to bed. She'd never had the luxury of anyone else caring about those things. Sure, people said they cared, but they didn't really. Cormac really cared and that was quite a gift he had presented to her, but one she could not accept. Before she started to feel sad about her circumstances, she quickly stood up and offered Cormac her hand.

"Do you want to go for a walk down the beach?" she asked.

"I'd love nothing better," he replied.

~~~

"Did you two have fun?" Ashley queried, as soon as they walked through the door.

"Aye. I believe Jenna enjoyed the beach as much as you do," Cormac said.

"I love the beach. It's my favorite place," Ashley agreed.

"Me, too," Jenna added.

"Well, I'll leave you with Ashley, then, love. I cannae keep ye all to myself." Cormac kissed Jenna softly on the lips and let his fingers caress her cheek before he went back out the door.

"He's a keeper, Jenna, I'm telling you. You need to rethink this whole going home thing," Ashley insisted.

"I know he's a keeper, but Ashley, I've already told you I can't stay."

"Don't be so stubborn, Jenna. You know you don't have anything waiting for you back home that you need to hurry back for," Ashley argued.

"What about Dylan? And Chester? They need me. And my parents' foundation. Who'd take care of that? And all my charitable work. I have to go back, Ashley."

"No. You don't have to go back, Jenna. You and I both know it. Dylan and Chester will be fine. And there are plenty of people to look after your parents' foundation and the charitable work. You need to think about Jenna right now. Don't do something you'll regret for the rest of your life."

Jenna shook her head in denial. "Ashley, I don't want to argue with you about this. I'm only here a short time and I don't want to spend it with the two of us being pissed off at each other. So, enough about me staying. Okay?"

Jenna could tell Ashley didn't want to cave so easily, but after a minute or two, Ashley nodded her head in concession. "Okay. Let's hug it out," Ashley said, pulling Jenna into a bear hug and giggling the whole time.

"You know, for a tiny little pregnant woman, you're pretty strong," Jenna teased.

"I can still kick some ass if the need arises, so don't you forget it." Ashley flexed her arm muscles for Jenna.

"Very impressive, my friend."

"Hey, we're having a big to do around here tomorrow night. There's going to be music and dancing. It'll be lots of fun."

"Am I invited?"

"Don't be silly; of course, you're the guest of honor. I should give you one of my pretty gowns to wear. That one's starting to look a bit tired," Ashley chuckled.

"Guest of honor? You're kidding, right?" Jenna thought it would be highly unlikely that anyone here would be celebrating her visit.

"Nope. I'm not kidding." Ashley stated.

Jenna continued to appear skeptical, but decided to go with it. "Okay, then. I'll definitely need a gown. Should we go see what you have in your closet?" Jenna linked arms with her friend, they headed for the stairs, and up to the chambers Ashley shared with Cailin.

"I miss shopping with you," Jenna admitted. "I guess this is the next best thing." They had pulled every gown out of Ashley's armoire and thrown them on the bed. Jenna was trying on a lovely green dress, when her eyes lit on a pale aquamarine gown, not unlike the color of the dress she'd worn to the gala she attended with Cormac in San Francisco. "Oooh... I like that one." She pulled the gown from the pile and held it up against her body.

"Oh, me, too," Ashley agreed. "Try it on. I'll bet that's the one."

Jenna stepped out of the green gown and into the blue one. Ashley did up the back for her and tipped her head from side to side to get a better look.

"What do you think?" Jenna questioned breathlessly.

"You look stunning," Ashley said. "You have to wear that one."

"Okay. It's settled." Jenna took the gown off and got dressed again. "Let's take this one to my room and then go downstairs for some tea."

"You know, you're beginning to sound like you live here," Ashley teased.

"Well, you know me. I'm pretty good at making myself at home, wherever I am."

As they left Ashley's room, Jenna noticed Irene coming down the passageway towards them.

"What are ye two ladies about?" Irene asked.

"We were just picking out a gown for Jenna to wear tomorrow night."

"Is that the one ye've chosen? Let me see," Irene said. Jenna held it up and Irene nodded her approval. "Ye'll look lovely in that color," she said. "It suits ye."

Jenna was stupefied. Irene had not said much to her since the talk they'd had the other day. Jenna was surprised that Irene was actually trying to be nice to her. "Thank you. We're going to go downstairs to have some tea. Please come with us," Jenna offered.

"I think I will. I'm going to check on the children and then I'll be down," Irene said and she headed down the passageway to the nursery.

Jenna was puzzled and it must have shown on her face because Ashley patted her arm. "She's one of the most giving and loving women you'll ever meet. Give her a chance and you'll see," Ashley explained.

"I'm trying. That's why I suggested she join us for tea. It might be a good opportunity for us to get to know each other better. You can be the referee," Jenna giggled at her own joke.

They continued on their way to Jenna's chambers to deposit the gown, eventually making it downstairs, where they found tea and sweet cakes waiting for them. Irene had beaten them by a few minutes and got everything prepared and set out by the fire. They all sat down and Jenna took a sip of her tea.

"I'm excited about tomorrow night, Irene. What are you celebrating?" Jenna asked.

"Well, it is customary when we have a guest to invite the members of the Clan and some of our neighbors to join us. We couldn't do it any sooner, because we had no prior notice of your arrival and it took us a few days to get the word out to those who live further away, ye see."

"You're doing this for me?" Jenna was shocked and surprised; she'd thought Ashley had been joking earlier.

"Of course, we are happy to have ye here as our guest and it is the perfect opportunity to have a celebration of sorts. I hope ye will enjoy yourself."

"I'm sure I will. It's just so unexpected. Pleasantly so," Jenna explained. Imagine that, they *were* having a party for her. "Does Cormac know?" she wondered.

"No. We've kept it a surprise until now. He'll find out soon enough."

The three women continued drinking their tea, eating the delicious sweet cakes and chatting. Jenna would never have imagined that Irene would be so warm and accepting of her. She had seemed so angry with her when she first arrived. She assumed Cormac and Ashley must have spoken to Irene and assured her that Jenna would never intentionally hurt Cormac and that she was not going to steal him away to the twenty first century.

~~~

Cormac arrived to the sounds of the women laughing and talking. He walked in to find Irene, Ashley, and Jenna all chatting like old friends. He was relieved that his sister had softened her stance on Jenna and was trying to make amends.

"Ladies, you all seem to be enjoying yerself. Are there any extra sweet cakes?"

"You can have the rest of mine, Cormac," Jenna offered.

"There are more in the kitchen, brother. We were just discussing tomorrow evening's festivities. I'm sure Cailin has told ye of the celebration we are having in honor of Jenna."

Cormac's mouth dropped open and he tried to hide his surprise by quickly snapping it shut. "No, he hadnae mentioned it to me." He quickly sought out Jenna's gaze and was happy to see she was smiling brightly at Irene. It didn't seem false at all. "That was verra thoughtful of ye, Irene."

"Ashley is letting me borrow one of her dresses," Jenna beamed. "It's very pretty."

"Jenna, ye can make the plainest dress beautiful just by virtue of wearing it." He meant every word of it. He had never seen her look anything but beautiful. He rested a hand on her shoulder and she covered it with her own. Her eyes, shining with happiness, focused on him.

"Why don't you join us, Cormac," Jenna suggested.

"Yes, please do," Ashley added.

His eyes searched out his sister's approval and when she nodded, he knew it was all right for him to stay. "Only for a short while. I have duties to attend to before the day is done." He sat next to Jenna and she reached a hand over to place it on his arm. He loved the feel of it, the heat emanating through his sleeve. Despite the fact that the ladies had asked him to join them, the conversation had come to a standstill. He didn't want to be the reason for the silence. "So, sister, who have ye invited to this celebration?"

"All of the usual guests, brother. I have sent word to all the Clan, including Lena and Ewan and some of our neighbors. I hope they will be able to attend on such short notice." Irene took another sip of her tea. "Cormac, would ye care for some tea? Some cakes?"

"Nay, Irene. I can only stay for a moment longer. I must speak with Cailin and Robert about the festivities tomorrow evening. As a matter of fact, I should be on my way now," Cormac rose and bid the ladies goodbye. He leaned in to kiss Jenna's cheek. "I will see you when I return, Jenna."

~~~

Cormac sought out his brother. He knew he needn't worry about the festivities, but he wanted to be sure that everything was in place to protect his family and Jenna.

"Cailin, ye didnae tell me about tomorrow evening's celebration."

"Aye. I forgot to mention it. I apologize," Cailin said, looking contrite.

"I'm concerned about Jenna's safety. A celebration is an opportunity for our unwanted guests to cause trouble."

"Dinnae fash, brother. We are prepared. Latharn has his eyes on Sophia at all times and Jonathan is being watched by Donal and Fergus. So far, they have not done anything to raise suspicions."

"Latharn seems quite taken with the lass," Cormac observed.

"Aye. That he does and she with him."

"She is nae the one I'm worried about. 'Tis Jonathan. I dinnae trust him."

"I ken ye dinnae, brother. He is only one man and we are many."

"Yer right," Cormac admitted. "And we've nae had any sign of Sir Richard since they've been here?"

"Nay. We've sent riders in search of him and from all accounts, Sophia and Jonathan were telling the truth. He seems to have returned to England."

"Good. We have enough to worry about without him causing us more problems."

"Cormac, tomorrow night is a celebration for Jenna. You can relax and enjoy yerself. Let the rest of us handle any difficulties that may arise."

"As you wish, Cailin," Cormac replied, clapping his brother on the back and then extending an arm around his shoulder. "Irene tells me there are sweet cakes for the taking." Cailin cocked an eyebrow at that and the two headed off in the direction of the kitchen.

# TWENTY-NINE

"What do you suppose those two are up to?" Jenna asked Ashley. She was about to go upstairs to get dressed for the party, when she noticed Sophia and Jonathan huddled together in one corner. She and Ashley had gone for a brief ride and they had just handed their horses to the stable boys, when Jenna spotted Sophia and Jonathan in close conversation near the postern gate. Looking around she could see Latharn, looking none too pleased at the exchange, but he, along with Donal and Fergus were giving them their privacy. For a brief moment, she thought she noticed Jonathan handing something to Sophia, but she was too far away to see clearly and assumed she might be just imagining things.

"Forget about it, Jenna. They've got plenty of people keeping an eye on them. We need to go in and get cleaned up and into our gowns for the party," Ashley said, pulling Jenna along with her.

"Okay. Okay. I don't trust Jonathan though. He's up to something. I can feel it," Jenna realized that if she'd been paying more attention, she might have noticed he wasn't to be trusted long before she married him. As they approached the stairs, Jenna was beginning to feel a bit like Cailin. "Ashley, slow down. There's no need to run up the stairs. You're pregnant, remember?"

Ashley rolled her eyes at Jenna. "Don't you start, too."

"I'm sorry, but I'm starting to understand Cailin's concern. We've got plenty of time to get ready and Helene will help us, I'm sure."

"I know she will. I'm just so excited to have you here for this celebration. It'll be like when we went to the prom. You remember? We fixed each other's hair and makeup."

"There's not really any makeup here, Ashley," Jenna pointed out.

"That's where you're wrong. I have some in my room. Edna sent it to me in my magick backpack."

"Your what?"

"My magick backpack. I've had it with me since I got here and I'm always finding things in there that weren't there before. Edna has a bit of a guilt trip going on about almost getting me killed."

"Wait a minute. What are you talking about? How did she almost get you killed?" Jenna couldn't believe her ears.

"Well, it's a long story, but the condensed version is that she tricked me into going over the bridge, where I met Cailin. By the way, it was the best thing that ever happened to me. Then later, after I was kidnapped by Thomas and Sir Richard, I was almost raped and killed. I got sliced up by a sword and broke my arm. I don't hold it against her though. She didn't know it was going to happen."

Jenna's head was swimming. "She tricked you, you were kidnapped, almost raped, and sliced by a sword, and you don't hold any of that against her?"

"Everything worked out in the most unbelievably magical way. I'm alive, the man who tried to rape me is dead, and I survived my wounds."

"I have to admit, I've never seen you happier," Jenna conceded.

"That's because I've never been happier. Someday I'll tell you the whole story, but for now, let's get dressed."

Jenna couldn't help but be swept up in Ashley's excitement. "Okay, you win. Let's get ready."

~~~

Cormac scanned the room as he waited for Jenna to make her entrance. Everything seemed to be in order. Cailin had men stationed around the room and at all the entrances and exits. He could relax and concentrate on Jenna, who was taking a good deal of time to join him. He went and stood by the stairs and was greeted by every single person who entered the Great Hall. Irene and Robert were already inside and the room was buzzing with activity. Cailin joined him to wait for Ashley.

"What is taking so long?" Cormac wondered.

Cailin chuckled. "Ashley is almost always the last person down the stairs, and now she has a friend to help delay her even further."

At that precise moment, the two men looked up to see their lovely ladies heading towards them. Ashley was first and greeted Cailin with a deep kiss. She took his arm and they entered the Great Hall.

Jenna was next and she took Cormac's breath away. "Jenna, ye are so beautiful." It was all he could manage to get out.

"Thank you, Cormac," Jenna said, as she placed her hand in the crook of his arm. "Shall we?"

They made their entrance and the room seemed to stand still as everyone stopped what they were doing to look at them. Or more precisely, to look at Jenna. They were all curious about this newcomer and it made for an uncomfortable moment or two of silence.

Irene and Robert rushed to their rescue. "Everyone, we'd like to present the Lady Jenna," Robert said with a flourish. All those in the room turned to face them, bowed, and curtsied as they walked past. Jenna appeared to be very nervous, which was unusual as far as Cormac was aware. She had seemed very much in control at her gala in San Francisco. He understood though, this was different. She didn't really know quite what was expected of her here in his world. He wouldnae leave her side this night. He whispered in her ear, "I'm here, all is well." She leaned into him for support, he imagined. If he had said that to her in her own time, she would have been angry with him. She always let him know that she was perfectly capable of taking care of herself. He knew that to be true, but he also knew her standoffish demeanor was a ruse. It was a show she created, to keep people where she wanted them - just far enough away, so she could escape if need be.

~~~

Jenna had a firm grip on Cormac's arm and was not going to let go. They reached the head table where they sat facing the other guests. Platters of food made their way from the kitchen to each table and Jenna was impressed with the selection. She was completely unfamiliar with most of the food, but had no trouble trying new things. They had eaten very well since she'd been at Breaghacraig, but tonight Irene had gone above and beyond for their guests. Jenna forced herself to relax; after all, she had attended many dinners in her own time and some she had attended where she'd been the guest of honor. This was no different she kept telling herself.

Cormac was very attentive, which she appreciated. He knew she was out of her element and he let her know he was there to provide support for her. Ashley was on her other side and was in the midst of an animated conversation with Cailin. Jenna loved and admired her friend so much. She had been brave enough to make a place for herself in an unfamiliar land and time. Not only that, but she was making it work. She was married and very much in love with her husband and she was expecting their first baby. Jenna suffered a bout of overwhelming sadness, knowing she couldn't have the same thing. Once she got back home, she knew it would take time, but she'd get over Cormac - at least enough to carry on with her life.

*Who was she kidding?* She didn't honestly believe she'd ever get over Cormac. How could she? He was the best thing that had ever happened to her. Tears formed in her eyes and she fought to control them. She surreptitiously wiped away any hint of them with her napkin.

Across the room, she kept a careful eye on Jonathan and Sophia. Latharn appeared to be very upset. He apparently didn't appreciate

Sophia spending the evening beside Jonathan, but to his credit, he didn't interfere. Instead, he sent Jonathan a death glare from his corner perch. Cormac was laughing with Dougall, who had stopped in front of the table to speak with him. She hadn't been paying attention and missed the joke.

"Lady Jenna, I hope you are enjoying your evening," Dougall said.

"Very much so, Dougall. You seem to be enjoying yourself, as well," Jenna smiled.

Dougall dipped his head in agreement. "You must excuse me, Helene will be waiting." He wandered off into the crowd of people who, having finished their meal, were milling around the outer edges of the room. The servants appeared and began clearing the tables and before long, Jenna understood why. The Great Hall was being transformed from a dining room to a dance floor. Musicians entered and set themselves up in a nook by the door. The music began and it took only seconds for the floor to be filled with happy faces, as couples began twirling and dancing around the room. Jenna was amazed to see almost everyone out on the dance floor. Those on the sidelines had mugs of ale and whiskey in their hands.

"Would ye care to dance with me, love?" Cormac looked so handsome standing there in front of her that she could hardly refuse.

"I'm not sure I know what to do," Jenna said, glancing around the room warily.

"Dinnae fash, love, I will show ye, much as ye showed me what to do at yer gala in San Francisco."

"Yeah, but that wasn't a very complicated dance. This seems much more complicated."

"Just follow me. Ye cannae go wrong and if ye do, not a soul would notice or care."

Jenna took his hand and followed him out to the dance floor. She glanced around and saw Ashley having a serious discussion with Cailin. Ashley obviously wanted to dance and Cailin was apparently doing his best to keep her from it. Jenna laughed as she watched the two of them. She knew who would win and it certainly wasn't going to be

Cailin.

"Cailin should just give up and let Ashley dance," Jenna observed.

"He will," Cormac stated. "Yer doing verra well, Jenna.

"Thank you, I'm not sure I'm doing it right though." She was enjoying herself and realized that it didn't matter to anyone but her how she danced. Cormac whirled her around the dance floor, her feet flying beneath her. She had no fear of falling as Cormac held her in place with strong arms and a strong hand on the small of her back, guiding her left and right and around and around. "This is so much fun, Cormac. Thank you for this," she said with heartfelt sentiment.

The dancing continued and she switched partners, dancing with Cailin and then Robert. She met Robert's brother Ewan, for the first time. He and his wife Lena had been seated at the far end of the table and she hadn't had a chance to speak with them until now.

"I'm verra happy to meet ye, lass," Ewan said. He was a handsome one. He looked very much like his brother and had the sweetest dimples when he smiled.

"And I you," Jenna replied.

"I'm sure Ashley has told ye that me wife, Lena, is also from yder time," Ewan said.

"No. She didn't tell me. Is she, really?" Jenna was amazed to find that there was someone else living here from the twenty first century.

"Aye. She is."

"Is she from San Francisco, as well?" Jenna was curious to know more.

"Nay. She is from Glendaloch. Her mother is Edna, the witch," Ewan explained.

Jenna didn't say anything for a minute. She needed time to digest this information.

"I imagine Ashley forgot to tell ye. It is normal for us, you understand," Ewan continued.

"I'd be very interested to speak to Lena," Jenna said. "It's not normal for me, so I have lots of questions."

"Of course, I'm sure she'd love to meet ye." Ewan surveyed the room. "There she is, dancing with Robert. Let us make our way over to them." He guided Jenna through the crowded dance floor, never once breaking step with the music, until they were right next to Lena and Robert.

Lena smiled at her and seemed to be able to read Jenna's expression. "I'm Lady Lena and you must be Lady Jenna," Lena said. "Robert, if you and Ewan would excuse us, I'd like to have a chance to get to know Jenna."

"Of course, my love," Ewan responded and he and Robert disappeared into the crowd.

"I just discovered that you're Edna's daughter," Jenna said.

"Please don't be angry with me," Lena teased. "I had nothing to do with your being here. My mother fancies herself to be a bit of a matchmaker."

"No worries. I'm not angry with you. I just wondered how you got here. Did your mother send you to meet Ewan?"

"No. I found my way here all on my own. It was a case of a willful teenager ignoring her mother's warnings to stay away from the bridge. Obviously, I didn't, but I wouldn't change a thing, even if I could. I've been verra happy here."

Jenna sighed heavily. "I guess I'm the only time traveler who hasn't wanted to stay."

Lena arched an eyebrow. "No?"

"No. I plan on leaving when my time here is up."

"I'm sorry to hear that. Cormac obviously hasn't been able to convince you to hang up your time-travelling boots," Lena asked.

"He hasn't. Not for lack of trying though."

"Well, you know what's best for yourself and there's no point in staying, if you'd rather be elsewhere."

Lena was the first person who hadn't tried to convince her she belonged at Breaghacraig. Jenna was surprised by that, but was happy to have someone finally in her corner.

"How much time do you have left, Jenna?" Lena asked.

"Today's my fifth day, so I guess I'll have to leave tomorrow in order to get back to the bridge in time to go home. Your mother is pretty accurate with her timing, isn't she?" Jenna suffered a moment of worry.

"Some of this time travelling stuff is new to her. Cormac is the first person she's sent from here to another time and place, but I'm sure if she did it once, she can do it again. I wouldn't worry if I were you. Besides what's the worst that could happen?"

Jenna didn't want to think about that idea. She could end up in the wrong place and the wrong time, completely alone - no Cormac, no Ashley and no Dylan. The thought of it had her feeling a bit woozy.

"I'm going to go find Irene and see about getting something to drink. Would you care to join me?" Lena asked.

"No. I'll stay here. Thanks though." She watched as Lena went off in search of Irene. Jenna scanned the room and couldn't see Cormac anywhere. Cailin was missing as well. Where could they be, she wondered? She was headed for the doors, thinking to look outside for them, when a hand reached out and grabbed her, pulling her into an outer passageway. Jenna almost screamed, but stopped when she realized who it was.

"I'm sorry, I didn't mean to scare you, Jenna," Sophia said. Jenna searched for Latharn, but he was nowhere in sight.

"What do you want?" Jenna snapped.

"Don't be mad at me, Jenna. I need your help," Sophia explained.

"Help? With what?"

"It's Latharn. There's something wrong with him. I think he's sick. I looked around for Cormac, but I couldn't find him. Please, I'm really worried about him."

Jenna searched the great hall once again for Cormac or Cailin, but they weren't there. "Okay. Lead the way." She reluctantly followed Sophia, all the while on the lookout for someone else from the castle that could help. She hesitated when she noticed that surprisingly, none of the men she'd seen earlier were at their posts.

"Hurry, please," Sophia pleaded, grabbing her arm and dragging her outside to the courtyard.

At first, Jenna couldn't see. It was so dark outside and the few torches placed here and there around the courtyard gave off very little light. "Where is he?" she asked as her eyes slowly adjusted.

"This way. In the stables," Sophia said, sounding frantic.

"Are you sure?" Jenna asked. Something was wrong. She could feel it in her bones, but Sophia seemed so distraught. Jenna had to help her.

"Yes, please hurry, there's not much time."

"I don't understand. What happened to him that has you so worried? Did he injure himself?" Jenna was trying to make sense of this situation, but Sophia wasn't listening to her. Instead, she was practically dragging Jenna in through the stable doors.

The sight that met Jenna's eyes immediately filled her with terror. Standing over the very still body of Latharn was Jonathan, a gun in his hand.

"Nice of you to join me, Jenna," he said.

"What are you doing, Jonathan?" Jenna gasped.

"I'm waiting for you. We're going to steal a few horses and we're going to ride back to that bridge so we can go home to San Francisco."

"You're crazy, if you think I'm going anywhere with you," Jenna yelled.

"You're the crazy one, Jenna. We're leaving and you're coming with us." Jonathan stated.

Jenna looked at Sophia who was now sobbing uncontrollably. Obviously, this was not her doing. "No. I'm not leaving."

"Okay, but poor Latharn here is going to have to die, if you don't. Next on the list after him will be your man, Cormac."

"Cormac isn't going to let you leave here with me. He'll stop you and you know it," Jenna stated.

"He might have stopped me, but Cormac, Cailin, every guard, and anyone else I thought might be a threat got a little surprise in their ale tonight."

"What did you do to them?" Jenna was beginning to panic.

"I drugged them. They'll all get a good night's sleep and won't know anything's amiss until tomorrow morning when they wake up."

"Sir Richard gave Jonathan a vial of some potion he said would make everyone sleep." Sophia cried. "Jonathan made me put it in the ale. He said he'd kill Latharn if I didn't."

"Jonathan, you're even more devious than I gave you credit for." Jenna looked down at Latharn who was completely knocked out. He obviously wasn't going to be any help and from the sounds of it, no one else would either.

"Devious. Yeah, that's me. You're a smart woman, Jenna. Get your horse and let's get out of here. You too, Sophia." Jonathan ordered.

Jenna knew she didn't stand a chance of escaping. If she tried, he'd surely kill Latharn and then, as he said, Cormac would be next. She'd do as she was told and hope there was a chance to escape sometime during the night.

Jonathan, Sophia and Jenna mounted their horses and headed off through the gates. "We'll have to hurry," Jonathan said, as he urged his horse into a gallop, whacking Rose on the rump as he went by. Rose jumped forward into a dead run and Jenna almost lost her seat, but Rose, true to form, slowed just a bit until Jenna was solidly seated in a balanced position. From that point on, they were off down the path and into the woods, riding for all they were worth and as if the hounds of hell were on their tails. Jenna kept alert, waiting for an opportunity to escape, but Jonathan made sure he stayed right with her at all times. Sophia hadn't stopped crying once and Jonathan was getting quite irritated with her.

"Shut up, Sophia. I'm getting tired of your wailing."

"Leave her alone, Jonathan," Jenna shouted. "She's worried about Latharn!"

"He'll be fine when he wakes up, but he'll probably never forgive Sophia for drugging him," Jonathan laughed cruelly.

Jenna lapsed into silence at that. She really wasn't interested in engaging Jonathan in conversation anyway. She prayed that Cormac would find her before Jonathan got them to the bridge, but deep down, she didn't believe it would happen. Especially if, as Jonathan said, they wouldn't wake up until the morning.

After hours of riding, Jonathan slowed and came to a stop. "I think we're safe to rest here for a while," he said. He dismounted and waited for Sophia and Jenna to do the same. "No fire. We don't want anyone to see us," he commanded.

"We'll freeze," Jenna complained furiously.

"Too bad," Jonathan barked.

Jenna wasn't the least bit surprised by the Jonathan she was seeing. Sophia wouldn't meet Jenna's eyes, instead keeping her eyes focused anywhere but in her direction. Rose was covered in sweat and Jenna did her best to wipe her down with a plaid she found in her saddlebag. "Rosie, I hope you're going to be warm enough," she whispered to the horse. "I'm sorry you got dragged into this."

"Who are you talking to, Jenna?" Jonathan demanded.

"No one. I'm just making sure Rose is okay."

"What do you care? You can't take her with you. Besides, she's just a dumb animal." Jonathan kicked some pine needles into a flat spot at the base of a nearby tree, making a bed for himself. "I never understood your thing with animals. Take Chester for instance. That dog should be locked away in the pound. He's the meanest pooch I've ever seen. Yet you and your dumbass cousin love him."

"Chester is a very good judge of character. He didn't like you. It's as simple as that," Jenna snapped.

"Yeah, well, if it were up to me. He'd be long gone."

Sophia sat quietly, her back resting against a huge tree trunk. The expression on her face was a troubled one. She met Jenna's eyes in a silent show of support. Jenna joined her and they sat as close together as possible, to ward off the chill of the night. Jonathan had wrapped himself in the plaid Jenna had used to wipe down Rose, leaving Sophia and Jenna to freeze. It wasn't long before he dozed off and they could hear soft snores emitting from him, as he lay on his bed of pine needles.

"Sophia," Jenna whispered. "We've got to get out of here. Now's our chance while he's sleeping." Sophia appeared too frightened to move and Jenna felt bad for her. "Come on Sophia let's go - unless you'd rather stay here."

"I'm coming," Sophia said softly.

There were good reasons for them to be afraid of Jonathan, and this could be their only opportunity to escape. Jenna decided they should head back to Breaghacraig, and hope Jonathan would sleep through their departure and long into the night. That would give them the time they needed to get safely away from him. Sophia put her finger to her lips and the two women got up and moved towards the horses, as quietly as possible. They continued to check on Jonathan every few feet, to make sure he was asleep. Once they reached the horses, Jenna motioned to Sophia that they should take Jonathan's horse along with them. Sophia nodded her understanding and reached for one of the leads. They had all three of the horses and were beginning to creep away when Jenna heard the unmistakeable sound of a pistol being cocked.

"Where do you ladies think you're going?" Jonathan was standing up and had the gun pointed in their direction. "You really didn't think I'd be fool enough to fall asleep around you two, did you?"

Jenna and Sophia huddled together miserably. "Jonathan, put that gun away. You aren't going to use it." Jenna tried to sound strong and determined, despite the fact that she wasn't.

"I guess you don't know me very well then. I'll do whatever I have to do, to get you back to San Francisco. Once we're back, you're going to be so distraught over our breakup, you're going to decide to kill yourself."

Jenna stared at him in disbelief. "What are you talking about? I'd never kill myself."

"No. You probably wouldn't, but I certainly would. You see, I took out a life insurance policy on you, while we were still married. The only way I can collect on it, is if you're dead. I thought about killing you here in this medieval hellhole, but that wouldn't work. You'd just be missing back in our time and then I'd need to wait seven years to collect. I can't wait that long, I'm afraid. I need the money now."

"Jonathan, think about what you're saying! I can give you money! You don't have to kill me. I'll give you as much money as you want, I promise," Jenna pleaded desperately.

"Sorry, babe. You had the chance to do that already, but you blew it. Now, get back over here. Leave the horses," Jonathan ordered.

Jenna exchanged a 'better-do-what-he-says' look with Sophia. They dropped the reins and went back to sitting beneath the shelter of the tree. This time, when Jonathan lay back down, he faced them and kept the gun in his hand. "I'm a light sleeper. Don't try anything," he threatened.

# THIRTY

Head throbbing, Cormac tried to stand up, but his legs had a mind of their own and insisted that he stay seated. "What happened," he groaned. Off to his left, he heard the sound of another groan.

"Cormac," Cailin rasped.

"Aye, brother, I am here. What goes on here? I'm having difficulty remembering."

Cailin sat up, just as a frantic Ashley made her way to his side. "Cailin, are you alright?"

"Nay," Cailin responded.

"What happened? I was so tired that I decided to retire for the evening. I just woke and realized you hadn't come to bed."

"Ashley, where's Jenna?" Cormac said, his head pounding with the force of a thousand drummers drumming against his skull.

"I haven't seen her. I lost track of her during the evening and I thought she was with you."

"Something's not right here," Cailin stated the obvious.

"I'm going to search for Jenna. You two should try to get up. Did you drink too much last night?" Ashley asked.

"Nay. Not enough to have this effect," Cailin answered.

"The last thing I remember is Sophia refilling my cup with ale," Cormac rubbed his head and squinted. "Cailin do ye think she gave us a sleeping draught?"

"Aye. Mayhap she did, but why?"

"We'd best see if we can find Jenna." Cormac had a bad feeling about this. Panic seized him as he forced his way up from the ground. His legs swayed beneath him, but he fought to maintain his balance and won.

Ashley reached down to help Cailin up. "Cailin, we have to find her. Let's check the guards and see if they've seen anything. Where are Latharn, Donal and Fergus? They were supposed to be keeping an eye on Sophia and Jonathan."

The three began their search and were not surprised to find that Latharn, Donal and Fergus, along with all the guards, were in the same state. Worse, nobody had seen Jenna, Jonathan or Sophia in hours.

"I'm sorry, Cailin. I've let ye down. Sophia filled me cup with ale and I stupidly drank it," Latharn apologized.

"As did Fergus and I," Donal added.

It seemed that all the guards were telling the same story.

"Where would she get a sleeping draught from?" Cormac wondered aloud. He felt a bit nauseous from the aftereffects of the drink and abject fear for Jenna's safety. The other men all seemed to be experiencing similar symptoms and swayed precariously on their feet.

"Sir, Sir!" one of the stable boys came running over to them, breathing heavily. "Sir, someone has stolen three of the horses!"

"Are ye sure?" Cailin asked.

"Aye. I went in to feed them this morning, and they were gone."

"Which horses are missing?" Cormac demanded.

"Rose, Sir, and Donal and Fergus' horses are both gone, too."

Donal and Fergus both let loose with a guttural curse.

"Saddle up my horse, lad. I must go after them," Cormac announced.

"Cormac, you don't look very good," Ashley said doubtfully. "Maybe you should take a few minutes to rest. Get some food in your stomach. You all should," she insisted.

Cormac shook his head impatiently. "We dinnae have time for that. They must be headed for the bridge. We have to stop them. We cannae allow Jonathan to take Jenna back to San Francisco." Cormac was almost overwhelmed with worry and unanswered questions. Did Jenna go with them willingly? Surely not? Or had Jonathan kidnapped her? How much of a head start did they have? Standing around was not going to locate her. He needed to act now.

"I'll come with ye," Cailin stated.

"We will all go," Latharn volunteered and Donal and Fergus nodded in agreement, although it was obvious that it made their heads ache to do so.

"Let's be off then. Ashley, go back inside and tell Robert what has happened. Make sure the other guards are looked after."

"Okay, but you all be careful. Jonathan is a sleaze bag," Ashley said.

"A what?" Cailin asked, his eyebrows rising almost to his hairline. Cormac exchanged a long look with his brother that confirmed they both chalked it up to twenty first century slang.

The horses were brought out, everyone mounted swiftly, and they galloped out through the gates in search of Jonathan, Sophia, and Jenna.

Jonathan stretched and yawned. "Happy you two didn't decide to make a run for it again. Smart. Let's get on those horses and head for the bridge."

"Do you even know where it is?" Jenna questioned curtly.

"I do. I happen to have a perfect sense of direction. It's not too much further." He mounted his horse and ordered Sophia and Jenna to do the same with a wave of the gun.

"I'm so sorry, Jenna," Sophia said unhappily.

"I know. I believe you wouldn't have been involved, unless Jonathan threatened you." Jenna wasn't interested in blaming Sophia for her predicament. She blamed herself - for being stupid enough to become involved with Jonathan in the first place. Jenna mentally shook her head, warning herself that laying blame would do little good at this point. She could remind herself of all the warning signs that were blatantly obvious to her now, but what good would that do? She was in trouble right now. She had to believe that Cormac would come searching for her. But what if he didn't. Then what? The thought terrified her. She might have to plot her own escape. And where was Edna? She'd been all about getting Jenna to Breaghacraig. Why wasn't *she* helping out? Grrr...

"Jenna, are you okay?" Sophia asked quietly.

"Yeah. I'm just thinking."

"Well, don't think too hard, babe. You might hurt yourself," Jonathan barked, a crazy laugh escaping his lips.

"Jonathan, could we stop for a minute," Sophia pleaded.

"No."

"I've gotta pee... please, Jonathan," Sophia begged.

Jenna wasn't sure if this was a ploy to buy them more time, but she was grateful that Sophia would even attempt to delay their movements.

"Fine. Make it fast. And you," he pointed at Jenna. "Stay where you are."

Sophia disappeared behind some bushes, and when she didn't reappear in a reasonable amount of time, Jonathan's frustration started to show.

"Sophia!" he yelled. "Get your ass back on that horse. We've got to go! Believe me, I don't have a problem leaving you here all alone."

Jenna believed him. "Sophia, let's go," she suggested anxiously.

"Okay," a voice came from behind the bushes. "I'll be right there." The rustling of the leaves let them know Sophia was on her way back as she appeared out of the bushes and headed to her horse.

"I didn't know you knew how to ride, Jonathan," Jenna commented.

Jonathan shrugged nonchalantly. "Nothing to it. I watched some of the guys at the castle and figured I could pull it off."

"And what about you, Sophia?" Jenna asked.

"My family had a ranch out in the central valley. We had horses, cows, and chickens. I learned to ride almost before I could walk."

"I've just learned," Jenna said. "Cormac taught me."

"Awww… isn't that sweet? True love at last. So sorry you won't get to enjoy it," Jonathan said derisively, and then laughed that maniacal cackle again. It sent a chill down Jenna's spine. "Oh, wait. I'm not sorry."

"I didn't think you would be. You know, Jonathan, no matter how much money you get from that insurance policy, it's never going to be enough, if you don't stop gambling."

"I don't need you to tell me what I should do. It'll last me long enough and then I'll find another rich bitch to take advantage of," Jonathan sneered.

After hours of riding and getting lost, despite Jonathan's supposed excellent sense of direction, they were approaching the bridge and Jenna couldn't think of a single thing she could do to slow them up further. She could only hope the fog wouldn't appear.

"What if the fog doesn't show up?" she asked.

"We'll wait," Jonathan stated.

"Cormac is bound to come looking for me," Jenna said.

"Well, he can look all he wants. I've got the gun. Gun trumps sword, every time."

Jenna shuddered to think what would happen if Cormac did show up. She suddenly hoped he wouldn't. She didn't want to see him hurt or worse, killed, trying to save her. She suddenly found herself praying he'd stay away.

"Sophia, do you think Cormac and Latharn will be okay?" she asked.

"I hope so. Jonathan gave me the sleep potion and I poured it into the ale I was serving the men. It was just supposed to knock them out," she explained. "That Sir Richard… I don't know what his deal is, but he hates the MacKenzies. He said he didn't want to get personally involved in Jonathan's fight, but he didn't mind helping from afar. He said he knew it would kill Cormac to lose you and he seemed pretty happy about the idea." Sophia explained everything that had transpired between Jonathan and Sir Richard after they ran into him.

"Cormac told me Sir Richard had it in for the MacKenzies. You're certain he went back to England?" Jenna asked quietly.

"He said he was. He rode off in the opposite direction, after he showed us how to get to Breaghacraig."

"Jenna, what's the secret to getting the fog to show up?" Jonathan demanded restlessly.

"I don't know. It shows up on its own," she replied honestly.

"Don't lie to me! You know and you'd better tell me," he threatened.

"Edna makes it happen," Jenna said. "I'm not lying. I don't know anything else."

"Who's Edna and where is she?" Jonathan was starting to look frazzled, as if he might lose it at any moment.

"She's a witch and I don't know where she is." Jenna hoped he would believe her.

"A witch! Ha! You expect me to believe that," he spat furiously.

"Jonathan, you travelled back in time - believing in a witch doesn't seem that farfetched, does it?" Jenna's patience with Jonathan was hanging by a thread. She knew she was walking a fine line and should avoid provoking him, or she might find herself dead sooner rather than later.

"Point taken," he said. Jonathan began pacing back and forth at the foot of the bridge, when a shimmering light suddenly appeared on the other side. "What's that?" he moved back away from the bridge.

The figure of a woman with blue hair appeared in front of them. She looked like a hologram, but Jenna knew it must be Edna. Jenna dismounted and moved as far away from Jonathan as possible.

"Young man," Edna said. "I am afraid I am not in a position to send ye back home."

Jonathan stared at her in disbelief. "What do you mean? You brought me here and now you're going to send me back. And I'm taking Jenna with me."

Sophia suddenly looked frightened and started shaking like a leaf. Jonathan was not planning to take Sophia back with him, Jenna realized. His plan had been to leave Sophia behind all along.

"Ye don't seem to understand. Ye brought yerself here. I had nothing to do with it," Edna explained carefully. "Ye went into the fog, looking for Jenna and were trapped by it and brought here. I cannot undo that which was not done by me. I'm sure ye understand."

Jonathan pointed his gun at Sophia. "If you don't send me back, I'm going to kill her."

"Don't be rash," Edna said calmly. "Ye'll need to give me some time, to see what I can do."

"You better hurry up, I don't have all day here," Jonathan snapped.

"I'll do my best, but put the gun down for now."

Jonathan refused to do as she asked and instead stood silently watching Edna as she closed her eyes and threw back her head, arms flying out to the side. He was so mesmerized by the spectacle that Edna was creating that he didn't notice when Sophia came up behind him intent on stealing his gun. They struggled for it and as they did, the fog began to swirl around Jenna. Jonathan saw what was happening and threw Sophia to the ground, trying to reach Jenna before she disappeared. Sophia stuck her leg out as he ran and tripped him. Jonathan quickly got back to his feet and turned on her, gun in hand.

"You've done it now, bitch. You're not going to stop me again." He started to pull the trigger as Cormac and Cailin came crashing through the brush. Jonathan fired the gun at Sophia while simultaneously turning in their direction. The shot missed her as she dove for the dirt. Sophia managed to get to her feet, running at him and knocking him to the ground. Jonathan grappled with Sophia for the gun and regaining possession of it, aimed it at her once again, but before he had a chance to fire the weapon, Latharn appeared out of nowhere and ran him through with his sword. The gun fell from Jonathan's hand as he toppled to the ground, blood pouring from the wound he clutched with his hands. Seeing that he was obviously mortally wounded and no longer a threat, all eyes focused on the fog as it swirled up and away. Cormac leaped from his horse and tried to reach Jenna before she was gone, but he was too late, everything seemed to have happened in a split second of time. Jenna had left him, vanishing before his very eyes. He stared across the bridge to the spot where he'd last seen Edna, but she too had disappeared from sight. He sank to the ground in despair at the cruel twist of fate, which had taken his love from him before he could say a last goodbye.

# THIRTY-ONE

Jenna landed with a thud and when the fog receded, she realized she was back in San Francisco. She hoped she was in the right time. Everything seemed right, but after the events of the last few weeks, she wasn't certain. The last thing she remembered before the fog swept her away, was seeing Cormac watching her with a pained expression on his face. Everything had happened so quickly, Jenna could hardly believe it. She'd had one more day to enjoy with Cormac in Breaghacraig. One more day. Jenna was grateful to Edna for saving her from Jonathan, but why had she sent her back early? She hadn't been given the opportunity to say goodbye to Cormac. Would he know she hadn't wanted to leave him?

Realization struck Jenna like a ton of bricks. She hadn't wanted to leave him. Not when she did, and not if Edna had waited until the following day. She knew now, she would have stayed and made a life there with Cormac, Ashley and the MacKenzies. And instead, here she was, back in San Francisco. She'd screwed up the only good thing in her life. Could it be fixed? Only Edna could help her and there was no guarantee she'd ever show up again.

"Are you okay, Miss?" An elderly woman had stopped and was staring at Jenna.

Jenna nodded, and brushed off her clothes. "Yeah. I'll be fine."

"Did you fall? I was walking along the marina and I didn't see you, and then all of a sudden, there you were. Of course, my eyes aren't what they used to be," the woman said.

"I guess I did fall. Thanks for your concern. I'll be okay now," Jenna offered her a weak smile.

The woman walked away, leaving Jenna alone. Tears began to fall as Jenna started walking towards the home she shared with Dylan and Chester.

"Dylan!" she cried, when she walked through the front door. "Dylan, I'm home!" Silence greeted her. *Where could he be?* The last thing she wanted was to be reminded of just how alone she was without Cormac.

She wandered into the kitchen and saw a sink full of dirty dishes. "At least I know he's in the city," she said to herself. She went into her bedroom and sank sadly onto the bed. "I can't do this without you, Cormac," she cried. She picked up her cell phone, which was on the end table next to the bed and pulled up the photo she'd taken of the two of them together. Staring at it, she saw two very happy faces looking back at her. Next, she watched the short video she had of Cormac. *I can't believe this. I'm such an idiot.* "Edna, if you can hear me. I want to go back. Please, let me go back."

Nothing. This was it. This was her life. She'd have to figure it out. If no one was going to help her, she'd have to do it on her own. She'd find a way to get back to him. She had to.

Jenna heard the front door open and she ran out of her bedroom to find Dylan and Chester staring at her in disbelief. She ran straight into Dylan's arms and he held her and let her cry until she had no tears left. Chester was leaning into her legs, trying to get as close to her as possible. He'd always hated to see her cry.

"Jenna, tell me what happened. Why are you back?" Dylan questioned.

"I don't really know why I'm back. I mean, I guess I know, but it wasn't what I wanted. It's just what happened."

"Tell me all about it," Dylan guided her towards the living room where she sat beside him on the sofa. "Are you okay? Can you talk about it?"

"Yeah. It's all so unbelievable. I thought you were pulling a prank on me, but you weren't."

"I told you I wasn't," Dylan said.

"I know. I know. You have to admit though, time travel seems like something that only exists in fictional stories and in the minds of sci-fi geeks. But now I know it's true. I experienced time travel myself."

Dylan ran his fingers through his hair. "I'm jealous. I wish I could have been with you."

"I saw Ashley, Dylan. She's there! She's married and she's having a baby! Can you believe it?"

"Cormac told me she was there, but I didn't know she was pregnant."

Jenna smiled wistfully. "She is and she's so happy. I've never seen her so happy."

"What about you? Were you happy there?"

"Yes. I was, but I didn't want to admit it to myself. I just wanted to come home, but now that I'm here, I realize this isn't my home anymore. My home is with Cormac. What am I going to do, Dylan? I don't want to live my life without him."

"Jenna, I don't know how to fix it for you," Dylan replied sadly. "Maybe we can try to find Edna. She's a real person, isn't she?"

Jenna sat up straighter and a hopeful expression spread across her face. "She is a real person, and she's a twenty first century person! She lives in Scotland." She jumped up from the sofa. "We have to find her, Dylan. You will help me, won't you?"

"You know I will, Jenna, I want you to be happy. For now though, I think you need to rest and then you can tell me everything that happened. I want to know every detail. Okay?"

"Okay. I am tired. I didn't sleep very well last night and this has all been so draining."

"You go lie down and I'll try to remember if Cormac ever told me anything that might help us find Edna."

Jenna pulled her cousin into a hug. "I love you, Dylan. I want you and Chester to come with me."

"I think we'd like that very much, but for now you go rest and then we'll try to find Edna."

~~~

"Edna! Edna, where are you?" Cormac called. He had been in his room trying to contact Edna ever since they had returned to Breaghacraig without Jenna. She wasn't answering him and he wasn't sure if yelling her name into the emptiness of his chambers was going to work. Edna was in another century, so he couldn't go riding off to find her. Mayhap Lady Lena could help. They arrived back at Breaghacraig to find that she and Ewan had returned home. Cormac would leave as soon as possible to speak with her. He had to get Jenna back, or at the very least make sure she had arrived back in her time without incident. He'd been angry with Sophia initially, but when she explained that Jonathan had forced her to help him, Cormac couldn't blame her. Jonathan had planned to kill Jenna in San Francisco, to collect some more money from her. Sophia had explained that she led Jenna to believe she needed her help with Latharn and Jenna had gone with her, only to be taken against her will by Jonathan. Cormac hoped that she knew how much he loved her. He hoped she had seen him, when he arrived at the bridge with every intention of saving her from Jonathan.

With his mind made up, Cormac went to the stables and saddled up Saidear. He was determined to find Edna and convince her to at least let him be able to see Jenna one more time.

"Shall I come with ye, brother," Cailin appeared in the doorway of the stables.

"Nay, Cailin. I'd nae be verra good company. I'm going to see Lena. I hope she can help me to reach her mother. I must speak with Jenna one more time. I need to tell her that I love her."

Cailin squeezed his brother's shoulder. "Cormac, I'm sure she knows."

"Aye, but I must try to find her," Cormac knew he was behaving irrationally, which was most unusual for him. He was usually so calm and reasonable. His love for Jenna was driving him mad. He hadn't slept or eaten since they'd returned from the bridge, and grew more agitated by the hour.

"Cormac, please allow me to go with ye. I'd verra much enjoy seeing Lena and Ewan. I dinnae care if ye speak to me even once on the journey." Cailin went to retrieve Cadeyrn. "I don't know why I'm asking you. I dinnae need yer permission, if I wish to pay a visit to Lena and Ewan, I shall."

Cormac relaxed a bit and laughed at his brother's determination to join him. "Fine. Ye may ride with me, but I've already told ye I'm nae verra good company."

"I'll be ready in no time at all," Cailin said.

"Do ye nae need to tell yer wife where yer going?" Cormac asked.

"Nae. She already knows. She doesnae wish to see you travelling alone."

Cormac realized he was a lucky man - he had a wonderful family. They were always there for him and he could count on it. Now, he needed to find a way to get Jenna back. Once outside the stables, Cormac and Cailin mounted their horses to begin the trek. They were met by Ashley and Irene who came bearing food, which they packed into the saddlebags.

"Cormac, good luck," Ashley said warmly.

"Bring her back with ye," Irene added.

"That is my plan, sister. I'll see ye soon." Cormac spurred Saidear forward and Cailin followed, catching up with him just outside the gates.

~~~

"Dylan, we've got to be able to find something to lead us to Edna." Jenna had been exhaustively searching the internet, looking for anything which might help them locate the woman.

"She's not the only Edna in Scotland, Jenna. It's not that easy. We need a little more to go on. A last name... *anything.*"

Jenna sifted through the cobwebs in her brain. There had to be something she was missing. She had a nagging feeling that the key to finding Edna was right under her nose. What could it be?

And then it suddenly came to her. "Ashley... Ashley met Edna in Scotland! I remember, she told me if I needed to contact her, I should look Edna up. She gave me the name of the inn Edna owns. What did I do with it?" Jenna began searching the kitchen frantically, rifling through drawers and cabinets. "It's times like this that I wish I wasn't such a neat freak. I probably threw it away in one of my cleaning frenzies," she lamented.

"Don't give up so soon. We'll just have to search every room. Do you remember where you were, when you talked to Ashley?"

"No. I should be able to remember. She called me and said she had been staying at this little inn. What was the name of it? Urgh... I can't remember!"

"Just relax, it'll come to you. You're trying too hard. Let's go get something to eat and unwind a bit. Maybe if you put it out of your mind for a while..."

"Okay. Let's go get some food," Jenna agreed. Dylan was right, she'd been totally consumed with finding Edna for the past few hours. A little food and some wine might be just what she needed. She grabbed her purse and headed for the door and Dylan had to run to catch up with her.

They walked up the hill to a little Italian restaurant, which was one of Jenna's neighborhood favorites. Everyone at Massimo's Cucina knew her and she always felt like a welcomed family member. Massimo himself greeted them at the door and showed them to a corner table, where they could dine without interruption. "Wine?" Massimo asked.

"Whatever you recommend," Dylan answered. He watched Massimo disappear towards the bar before he leaned forward and spoke. "So, Jenna, if you find the name of the inn, what are you going to do? Are you going to call them?"

"Actually, I think I'll just fly over there. I'd like to meet this Edna in person."

"I'm coming with you," Dylan stated determinedly.

"Don't be silly, Dylan. You don't have to come with me, I can do this on my own," Jenna responded and then she realized she was doing it again. She was giving the impression that she didn't need anyone else, and for a time that had been true, but she'd made a decision not to live like that anymore. If people wanted to help her, she was going to learn how to let them. "I'm sorry, Dylan. I'd love you to come with me, but what about Chester? Who'll take care of him?"

"We'll take him with us." Dylan announced. He appeared relieved that Jenna had changed her mind.

Massimo brought two glasses and a bottle of his best Pinot Noir to their table.

"Perfect," Jenna said, smiling. She was beginning to feel a bit more hopeful. Now, if she could just remember what she had done with the information Ashley had given her.

"We'll have two specials," Dylan suggested to Massimo, who nodded and went to put their order in.

"Dylan," Jenna suddenly sounded very excited. "I think I know where it is!"

Dylan waited for her to continue and when she didn't, he prodded. "Where? Is it at the house?"

"Yeah! I put it in my journal. I remember I was writing in my journal when Ashley called and I just jotted the information down on the first blank page I came to. It's in the nightstand next to my bed. I don't think I've written anything else in it, since that phone call." Jenna took an appreciative sip of the wine. "Mmm… this really is good. Massimo has the best wine selection." She was relaxing now, enough to enjoy the wine and her dinner. Everything was going to work out. It had to.

~~~

Ewan rode out to meet them before they arrived. "Cailin, Cormac... to what do we owe this honor?" Ewan asked, as he drew his horse to a halt.

"I need to speak with Lena," Cormac said. "About Jenna."

"Did ye not find her?" Ewan sounded concerned.

"We found her, but it was too late. Edna had already sent the fog to take her back home. By the time we arrived, there was naught we could do, but watch as she disappeared before our verra eyes."

"I'm so sorry to hear it. Do ye wish Lena to contact her mother?" Ewan turned his horse and the three rode through the gates and into the courtyard.

"Aye. I must speak with Edna. She doesnae answer me, so I thought mayhap Lena could help," Cormac explained.

"I'm not so sure she can. She hasnae really had much success in contacting Edna. For the most part, Edna comes to her in her dreams. But we will see. Perhaps she can try," Ewan said doubtfully.

Dismounting, the three handed their horses over to the stable boys and headed inside. Lena was waiting for them as they came through the large wooden doors. This was the home Cormac and Cailin had grown up in and now it was home to Lena, Ewan and their sons, Ranald and Rowan. The two red-haired whirlwinds whizzed past as Lena greeted her guests.

"Cormac, Cailin...'tis good to see you. Is all well at Breaghacraig?" she asked, concern visible on her face.

"Aye. All is well," Cailin assured her. "Cormac needs yer help."

"Is that true, Cormac? What could you possibly need my help with?" Lena asked, turning to him.

Cormac explained how Edna had sent Jenna back to San Francisco a day earlier than had been agreed upon, but he was sure she had done it to save her from Jonathan, who planned to kill her. Cormac explained that Sophia had told him the whole story on the ride back to Breaghacraig. She had apologized repeatedly, but Cormac could not find it in his heart to blame her. She had been threatened by Jonathan and she too had tried to help Jenna escape. Cormac poured his heart out to Lena, who listened with sympathy in her eyes.

"Cormac, I am so sorry. I dinnae ken whether I'll be much help. My mother always contacts me. I havenae had much experience in trying to reach her. I will do my best, though."

"You will try?" Cormac was relieved.

"Yes, but dinnae get yer hopes up. It may not work," Lena said cautiously.

"Cailin, mayhap ye'd like to come with me and see what we've done with the place ye once called home," Ewan suggested.

"Aye. I'd like that," Cailin answered.

Cormac and Lena sat in the Great Hall and conversed for quite a long time. Lena had many questions and wanted to know every detail, so that if she were able to speak with her mother, she'd be able to tell her what Cormac wished to accomplish. Cailin and Ewan returned and they all sat at the table for the evening meal. When they were done, Lena explained that she was going to retire to her room. "I'll try to contact my mother. Don't wait up for me. It may take me quite some time, if I'm successful at all. I'll see you all in the morning."

"Good night, then," Cormac said. "And thank ye."

Lena kissed her husband and laid a gentle hand on Cormac's shoulder, giving it a reassuring squeeze. "Ye'll have yer answer in the morning, if there is one." She left the men all seated around the fire, sipping whiskey and morosely staring into the flames.

# THIRTY-TWO

In Jenna's mind, the plane ride to Scotland took forever. She slept through a good portion of the flight and she dreamt Cormac was frantically searching for her along the wooded path that would eventually lead him to the bridge. She could see him riding Saidear and repeatedly calling her name.

"I'm right here, Cormac," she shouted, but he couldn't hear her. "I'm on my way. I'll be with you soon." She woke up feeling guilty, for causing Cormac such tremendous pain. What was done, was done. She couldn't change it. The only thing she could do was try to get back to him as soon as she possibly could. That's where Edna would need to work her magic. There was no doubt in Jenna's mind that Edna would help her. She had to - there were no other options.

Dylan rented a car, and with Chester happily ensconced in the back seat, they made their way from Edinburgh to Glendaloch. Jenna's first thought on seeing the little town was that it was lovely. They traveled down the main street and almost immediately came to The Thistle and Hive Inn. She couldn't wait to get out of the car and inside.

"You go ahead, Jenna. I'll get the bags and Chester," Dylan said agreeably.

"Okay." Jenna was already opening the front door of the inn and she searched the lobby, hoping to see Edna. Instead, she saw an attractive young woman standing behind the reception desk.

"Checking in, Miss?" the young woman asked.

"Yes. I mean, no. I don't know," Jenna conceded unhappily.

"We're checking in," Dylan came through the door with their bags and Chester. "Do you have two rooms?"

"Yes, we do. My name's Maggie," the young woman said, her eyes never leaving Dylan.

"Nice to meet you," Dylan said. "I'm Dylan Sinclair and this is my cousin, Jenna. And this is Chester. I hope you allow dogs." Jenna watched him putting on the charm for this lovely green-eyed redhead.

Maggie had come around the desk and was petting Chester. "Of course. He seems verra well behaved. My aunt willnae mind."

"Who is your aunt?" Jenna asked eagerly.

"My aunt and uncle own The Thistle and Hive. They are Edna and Angus Campbell. Now, if you dinnae mind filling out the registration forms, I'll have ye in yer rooms in short order," she smiled, once again focusing all of her attention on Dylan. "How long will ye be staying with us?"

"Well, that depends on your aunt," Dylan said. "We need to speak with her urgently."

"I see. She's not here today, nor is my uncle. They've headed off to Edinburgh for the weekend. They'll return the day after tomorrow."

"Can you call her," Jenna asked anxiously. "It's extremely important that I speak with her."

"My aunt doesnae carry a cell phone with her, but she may check in with me later. I'll tell her ye wish to speak with her. She's had a trying time of it lately and Uncle Angus thought she could use a break."

"Thank you." Jenna felt deflated. She had hoped to meet Edna and then be on her way back to Cormac immediately. Now she knew she was going to have to wait.

Dylan finished the paperwork and Maggie handed them the keys to their rooms. "They'll be at the top of the stairs. Let me know if I can be of any help. Dinner is served in the dining room shortly, if ye're interested in a meal." Jenna noticed that Maggie was speaking to Dylan again, as though he were the only one in the room.

"Thank you," Dylan said. "I'm sure we'll be down once we get settled in. I'll need to take Chester for a short walk. Is there a pet store here in Glendaloch?"

"Aye. It's right up the street," Maggie said. "I'd be happy to show ye where, when ye're ready."

"I'd like that," Dylan answered warmly.

Jenna stood back and watched the exchange taking place and thought Dylan was seeming awfully interested in this girl. She took one of the keys from his hands and wearily made her way up the stairs to her room.

Once Jenna got herself settled in, she tapped on Dylan's door to see if he was ready for dinner. No response. *He must have taken Chester for a walk,* she thought, as she headed downstairs. Maggie didn't seem to be in the lobby anywhere and Jenna was just about to walk into the dining room when the door to the inn opened and a laughing Dylan and Maggie walked through.

"Hey, Jenna. Maggie just walked down to the pet store with me. I picked up some food for Chester." Dylan held out the bag of dog food as proof.

"I was wondering where everyone was. I was going to go in to get something to eat. Are you hungry?" she asked Dylan.

"Yeah. I'll take Chester upstairs and I'll be right back down. Would you care to join us, Maggie?" To Jenna's eyes, Dylan seemed very hopeful that Maggie would say yes.

"I'd like that," Maggie answered. "Jenna, if ye'll follow me, we'll get ye seated and pour ye some wine."

"Wine would be amazing," Jenna agreed, as she followed Maggie into the dining room and the young woman led them to a cozy booth near the window.

"I'll be right back, then," Maggie said, making her way over to the bar. Jenna's view was of the quaint little main street through the window. The streetlights glowed and reflected off the damp sidewalk. It had started to drizzle since their arrival, and the few people she saw had their collars turned up and umbrellas out. The dining room was only partially filled with guests. There were empty tables here and there, and only the slight murmur of voices, giving the room an almost churchlike atmosphere. Maggie headed back Jenna's way and stopped to exchange a few words with some of the diners.

"Thank you," Jenna said, accepting the glass of wine Maggie presented. "Have you worked here long?"

"Not really. I was working at my family's teashop in the next town over, but Auntie needed me here. Ye see, she doesnae get much time off, what with all her responsibilities. So she asked me if I would come to work here and she'd teach me what I need to know in order to take over for her."

Jenna wasn't sure she should ask Maggie about Edna being a witch. Maybe Maggie didn't know. She decided to keep that information to herself. Maggie's face lit up and Jenna saw that Dylan had just entered the dining room. He lifted his hand and waved, making his way over to sit with them.

"Would ye care for some wine?" Maggie asked.

"I'd love some. This is a great little place. So unlike the places back home. Isn't that right, Jenna?"

"Very different," Jenna agreed.

Maggie retrieved two more glasses - one for herself and one for Dylan - along with a bottle of wine. "I decided to bring the whole bottle," she winked and smiled.

"Good plan," Dylan said, with a wink of his own.

*What the heck is going on here?* Jenna almost laughed aloud. She couldn't recall ever seeing Dylan wink at anyone.

"I'll go see what chef has going on in the kitchen and I'll bring back his best dishes, if ye don't mind."

"Not at all," Jenna said, before Dylan could wink at Maggie again. He sat transfixed by the young woman. Jenna had to wave her hand in front of his face to get his attention.

"Hello… anyone home?" she teased.

"I'm sorry, did you say something," Dylan managed to focus on

Jenna for the first time since he'd sat down.

"No. Just wondering where you'd gone off to."

Dylan chuckled at that. "Isn't she something?" he asked.

"Yeah. She seems like a lovely girl," Jenna agreed.

"You must be disappointed that Edna's not here," Dylan noted.

Jenna shrugged her shoulders. "Not much I can do about it. At least I know she's coming back. So I'll just have to wait."

Maggie returned with a tray of food, which she placed on the table. "I thought we could all share and if there's anything ye are particularly in love with, I'll get more." There was roast beef with gravy and vegetables, a pasta dish, and chicken with lemon and capers.

"It all looks delicious," Jenna admitted, helping herself.

"Maggie. Tell me about your Aunt Edna," Dylan suggested.

"There's not much to tell. She's been a fixture in this town forever. She was born here and she opened the inn with her husband, quite a long time ago."

"She's a witch, right?" Dylan said, in between bites.

"Dylan!" Jenna glanced apologetically to Maggie, who didn't seem fazed by his question.

"She is," Maggie agreed calmly.

"Do you know anything about this time travelling thing she does?" Dylan continued. Jenna kicked him under the table. "Ow! Jenna, what are you doing?"

"I'm so sorry, Maggie. You'll have to forgive Dylan for being so blunt."

Maggie shook her head. "No trouble. I'm just curious how ye came to know about it."

"She sent Jenna back to the sixteenth century with my friend Cormac. Jenna would like to go back."

Maggie smiled apologetically. "Aunt Edna has been teaching me lots of things, but we haven't gotten that far yet. Ye'll have to wait for her to come back. I'm sure she'll help you."

"So... you're a witch, too?" Jenna said, wondering how on earth she'd gone through her whole life without ever meeting one - and now she knew two.

Maggie just nodded and sipped her wine. "It's a family thing."

"Wow!" Dylan exclaimed.

Maggie laughed at that and sent Dylan a sweet look.

The caliber of the food was right up there with any five-star restaurant Jenna had dined in, and as a result, they managed to eat everything Maggie had delivered to the table and polished off another bottle of wine. Jenna retired to her room early, leaving Dylan to get to know Maggie better, while they shared dessert. She hoped Dylan would behave himself and not do his usual *love 'em and leave 'em* thing. Somehow, she didn't think he would. He had behaved very differently around Maggie. Maybe her cousin was finally growing up. Jenna settled in front of the fire in her room and thought wistfully of Cormac. "I'll see you soon," she said, and hoped she was right.

~~~

Jenna awoke feeling more exhausted than when she'd fallen asleep, thanks to her dreams, which were a mishmash of Cormac, Edna, swirling fog and frustration. The last coming from her inability to be seen or heard by anyone in her dreams. She could see and hear the other people clearly, but no matter how hard she tried, or how loudly she spoke, no one looked her way. Cormac was at a different castle - not Breaghacraig. Cailin was with him and they were with Lena and Ewan. It had to be their home she was seeing. Cormac appeared as frustrated as Jenna felt. Above it all was Edna, waving her arms frantically at Lena, who didn't seem to notice her, either. Jenna wondered what it all meant when she heard a knock at her door. Thinking it must be Dylan, she threw on her robe and padded to the door. She opened it to find a blue haired woman with sparkling green eyes staring daggers at her.

"Edna?" Jenna questioned warily. "I thought you weren't coming back until tomorrow."

"I had no choice in the matter. My daughter, Cormac and Maggie have been pummeling me with messages since yesterday. So, I cut my weekend short, to find out exactly what was going on back here."

Jenna chewed on her lip anxiously. "I'm sorry. I didn't mean for you to return early. I was willing to wait until tomorrow."

"Really, my dear?" Edna asked, with a hint of disbelief in her voice. Not waiting for an answer, she continued. "What are ye doing here? I sent ye home because that was what ye wanted!"

"I thought it was what I wanted, but when I saw Cormac arrive at the bridge, I knew I wanted to stay with him. I'm sorry I've caused you so much trouble. I realized a little too late that I was being a fool."

"Aye. I ken that ye were," Edna responded sarcastically.

Jenna was taken aback by Edna's stern demeanor. "Would you like to come in?" Jenna opened the door wider and Edna came into the room. She immediately went to the fireplace and snapping her fingers, started a roaring fire.

"That's better. I hate a chilly room," Edna explained.

"Thank you. I was a little cold." Jenna surveyed Edna for a minute and wasn't certain her request to return to Cormac would be accepted by this woman. She didn't know what to do except ask, but Edna beat her to it.

"I assume yer here because ye want to go back. I expect ye've learned yer lesson. I only hope I'll be able to communicate with Lena or Cormac, to get him to return to the bridge. Ye see, ye can't go back, unless there's someone waiting for ye."

"Yes. So I've been told."

"And I know ye have another request as well. Ye'd like your cousin and his dog to return with ye."

Jenna lifted an eyebrow in surprise. "Yes. How did you know that?"

"I met him downstairs, he was having breakfast with Maggie and he explained it all to me."

"Is that possible?"

"Aye. I believe so."

"So what do I do? How do we make this happen?"

"Patience, my dear. I've only just arrived back. Let me have a few moments to gather my thoughts. I must try to reach Lena, which may take some time. She hasnae been practicing her abilities as I've asked her to, and it may be that the only way I can reach her is when she's asleep."

"You mean through her dreams? But I thought you said you knew she was trying to contact you?"

"Aye. Exactly, but communicating back and forth has been a challenge for her."

"You were able to contact Cormac before though, weren't you?"

Edna nodded and let out an exasperated sigh. "Aye, but magick is a tricky thing and my darling daugher hasnae always been open enough to communicate."

"I tried to contact you, from San Francisco, but you didn't hear me."

"I heard ye, Jenna, but I wanted ye to realize that this is nae a game I'm playing. I truly know that ye and Cormac are meant for each other and I wanted ye to know it as well. So, ye had to work hard to find me, but it will be worth it in the end, if everything works out. I'll leave ye now. Why don't ye get dressed and head downstairs for a bite to eat? Ye can explore Glendaloch while I see what I can do about contacting either Lena or Cormac."

~~~

Cormac was seated in the Great Hall when Lena appeared. "I've been trying and trying to reach her, Cormac, but she doesnae seem to hear me. It's been days now."

"Maybe she hears ye, but doesnae wish to speak with ye," Cormac suggested, immediately regretting his words. "I'm sorry, Lena. It's just that I'm worried I'll never see my Jenna again. I'm sure yer mother wishes to speak with ye, but perhaps something is preventing it."

"That something could be me. I've not done as she asked. If I had, this would all be easier," Lena lamented.

"Dinnae fash. If ye dinnae mind having us here, Cailin and I will stay a while longer. At least until ye tell us there's no hope left."

"Alright, then. I feel as if I'm on the brink and then the feeling leaves me. Mayhap when I sleep tonight, she'll call to me."

Cormac graced her with an encouraging smile, but he didn't feel it in his heart. What could he possibly do? Cailin and Ewan had gone off again, leaving him alone to sip his whiskey by the fire. It was a verra quiet night. In his mind, he could hear the sound of Jenna's voice speaking softly to him. "I'll see you soon," she said.

*Jenna... Jenna...* He reached out to her from within his mind. She was somewhere nearby, he could *feel* it. He stood up and began pacing back and forth. Mayhap he just wanted her so badly, he was starting to imagine things. That must be it. He sat down again and this time he heard Edna's voice. Not distantly, as Jenna's had been, but as if she were in the same room with him. He relaxed his breathing and closed his eyes, mentally welcoming Edna to speak to him.

"Cormac? Can ye hear me lad?" Edna said.

"Edna? Is it really ye?" Cormac was astounded, he'd gotten so close to giving up hope and yet, here was Edna speaking to him again.

"Aye. Of course 'tis me. As I've told ye before, who else do ye know, who can speak to ye in yer head?"

"Edna, I'm so happy to hear yer voice. I must speak with ye."

"I ken ye must. That is why I'm here."

"Edna, ye must help me find Jenna. She left without saying goodbye. I just want to see her one more time. I ken she doesnae want to stay here, but I must tell her some things."

"And ye shall. Meet me at the bridge as soon as ye can. Do not cross it. Stay on yer side, do ye understand?"

"Aye. Aye, I do, Edna. Thank ye, thank ye so much!" Cormac could hardly contain himself. He was going to see Jenna again. His heart hadn't felt this light for days.

"Until then..." Edna's voice faded away, leaving Cormac in silence once again.

"Lena!" Cormac called out. "I've spoken with Edna!" He was up from the chair and about to leave the Great Hall when Lena entered, accompanied by Ewan and Cailin.

"Did ye say ye've spoken with my mother?" Lena was incredulous. "Why can ye speak with her and I cannae?"

"I dinnae ken the workings of it, Lena. But she was here." He pointed to his head, laughing with happiness.

"What did she say?" Cailin demanded.

"She said I'm to meet her at the bridge, as soon as I can get there. She said nae to cross, but to stay on this side."

"When do ye plan to leave?" Ewan asked. He had his arm draped across Lena's shoulders and gave her a little squeeze. Cormac could see Ewan was trying to make Lena feel better about her inability to communicate with her mother.

"Right away," Cormac replied. "Cailin, ye can stay here if ye like. I'll be fine on me own."

"Nae. I wouldnae miss this for the world, brother. I'm coming with ye," Cailin stated firmly.

"Alright then, we'll be on our way." Cormac kissed Lena on the cheek. "Thank ye for trying, Lena. And thank ye Ewan, for your gracious hospitality."

"Yer family, both of ye. Yer welcome here at any time," Ewan said. "I'll have the boys get yer horses ready and Lena will get some food prepared for yer trip."

"Ewan, they may need another horse. Could ye see to it," Lena said, a twinkle in her eye. "My mother says ye should bring one." She beamed at them.

Cormac was happy for Lena, glad that she had been able to receive a message from Edna. But he was happier for himself that she wanted him to bring another horse. That could only mean one thing. *Jenna.* "Can ye make it a quiet one, Ewan?"

Ewan grinned. "Of course, a quiet one 'twill be then."

The following morning as they approached the bridge, Cormac felt as light as a feather. The weight of the past few days had been lifted from his shoulders and he knew in his heart that he would see Jenna again.

"We wait here," Cormac announced to Cailin. They both sat and silently waited for something to happen. It was a quiet morning, but they could still here the birds chirping happily in the trees and the sound of the stream rushing over rocks as it passed underneath the bridge.

Dismounting, Cormac motioned for Cailin to do the same. "I think we should make ourselves comfortable. We dinnae ken how long this will take." They let the horses graze and sat under the shade of a nearby tree. Leaning their backs against its sturdy trunk, they waited.

~~~

"Are ye ready, lass?" Edna asked Jenna. "Silly question, I know. Ye've been ready since before ye left San Francisco." Edna chuckled at that one.

Jenna grabbed her leather tote and headed for the door of the inn. On her way out, she hugged Angus, who she'd found to be a very sweet man. He obviously had a soft spot in his heart for Ashley. He handed Jenna a wrapped gift and asked if she would be sure to give it to Ashley when she returned to Breaghacraig.

"'Tis something for the wee bairn," Angus explained.

Jenna also said goodbye to Maggie. Not that she'd seen all that much of her, not since their dinner the other night. Maggie seemed to be spending all of her time with Dylan, who was leaving with Jenna.

"It's been so nice getting to know you," Jenna said to Maggie.

"And ye," Maggie replied, leaning in to kiss Jenna's cheek and give her a brief hug. "With any luck at all, my Auntie will let me come visit ye." She glanced at Edna, who rolled her eyes. "And ye, ye handsome man," Maggie said to Dylan. "I'll see ye soon, I hope."

"I hope so, too," Dylan said. Jenna occupied Edna and Angus, so Dylan could sneak in a goodbye kiss without an audience.

"How far is it to this bridge, Edna?" Jenna asked.

"Not far. It's a lovely walk and ye'll have company, so the time will pass quickly."

Chester sat patiently by Jenna's side, waiting for Dylan and Maggie to finish their farewells. Angus cleared his throat as a signal that everyone was waiting on the young couple.

"Okay. Let's go," Dylan said, obvious excitement in his voice.

Edna gave them instructions on where the path to the bridge was located and Dylan assured her that they wouldn't get lost. They set off down the road, looking back to wave a final goodbye to the Campbells.

~~~

"Cailin," Cormac admonished. "Ye'll eat everything Lena gave us and then we'll have nothing for the return trip to Breaghacraig!"

"I'll not eat it all," Cailin said, rummaging through the saddlebags. "Lena gave us enough food to feed ten people. I imagine Edna told her we'd be needing extra."

"Aye. Yer probably right, but just in case, mayhap ye should stop."

The two were busy arguing about the food and didn't notice a change in the atmosphere surrounding them. The wind had picked up and the fog was swirling nearby. Cormac stopped and listened. He could hear the popping sound and saw the colored lights appearing. "It's here," he shouted to Cailin, over the sounds of the whirlwind spinning in front of them. The horses stopped what they were doing and pricked their ears towards the fog and Cormac and Cailin stood perfectly still, waiting breathlessly.

~~~

Jenna, Dylan, and Chester arrived at the bridge just in time to see a whirlwind of fog spinning on the other side. "That's for us," Jenna said.

"Are you sure?" Dylan asked, concern in his voice.

"Yeah. The same thing that took me from San Francisco. Come on. Hold on to my hand and to Chester," Jenna instructed.

Dylan did as he was told, but not wanting to take any chances, he lifted Chester into his arms, and Jenna looped her own arm through his. They walked forward cautiously. Chester was focused on the fog and started to wriggle in Dylan's arms. "He sees something we don't," Dylan said. They walked into the fog and stood immobile, as it swirled around them.

~~~

Cormac couldnae believe his eyes as a very excited Chester came bounding towards him. Cailin took a defensive stance, but Cormac put a hand on his shoulder in warning.

"Chester," Cormac exclaimed as the dog leaped into his arms and licked his face. "I wasn't expecting to see you, my friend." He put the dog down and Chester immediately went to Cailin, who had apparently never seen a dog quite as ferocious-looking as this one. The dog wagged his stubby little tail and Cailin visibly relaxed. A moment later, Jenna came out of the fog, looking even more beautiful than Cormac remembered her and by her side was, Dylan, whose face lit up when he saw Cormac.

"We did it! We're here. We travelled through time, didn't we?" Dylan asked excitedly.

Jenna was in Cormac's arms in the blink of an eye. "Cormac, I'm so sorry. I didn't mean to leave you. I realized as the fog was taking me that I was making the worst mistake of my entire life. It took me a while to find Edna, but Dylan, Chester and I flew to Scotland to get her to help me."

Dylan hugged them both together. "I'm so happy to see you, Cormac. I hope you don't mind that I tagged along."

Cormac was so happy he couldn't speak. Instead, he hugged the two of them even more tightly. The sound of Cailin clearing his throat got their attention. Cormac stepped back and grinned. "I'm sorry, brother. Let me introduce ye to Jenna's cousin Dylan and I believe ye've met Chester."

"Aye. This is an amazing creature. I've never seen a dog like this before and I'm pleased to meet ye, as well, Dylan."

"Same here, dude," Dylan said, sizing up Cailin. "Strong family resemblance," he observed.

"Aye. We've been told we look enough alike to be twins," Cailin agreed.

Jenna and Cormac were so wrapped up in one another that they hardly noticed anything going on around them.

"Cormac, we should get going," Cailin said. We can make good progress if we leave now. We'll make camp later," he explained to Dylan, "but we've got plenty of food and we'll make a fire to stay warm overnight."

"Sounds great," Dylan replied enthusiastically.

"Cormac, Dylan should ride the extra horse Ewan lent us and Jenna can ride with ye. Chester," he said to the dog, "ye'll have to walk, I'm sorry to say."

"He'll be fine," Dylan said. "He likes to go for long walks."

Cormac could see that his brother was forming a friendly bond with Dylan already. He was happy about that, because when he married Jenna, which he planned to do as soon as he possibly could, Dylan would be part of the family.

"Shall we then?" Cormac asked.

"You ken, this reminds me of a similar ride I took back to Breaghacraig with Ashley," Cailin smiled.

"I'd love to hear that story," Dylan said, mounting the spare horse.

Cormac and Jenna made themselves comfortable on Saidear and were oblivious to anything but each other.

Cailin rolled his eyes at them. "Well, I'd be happy to share it with ye, Dylan. It looks like ye and I will have much time to get acquainted." With Chester trotting happily along beside them, the sound of Cailin's voice rang through the woods as he told his tale.

# EPILOGUE

Jenna was standing in the middle of her chambers, feeling like the luckiest woman on earth. She was surrounded by her best friend, Ashley, her sister-in-law to be, Irene, along with Lena and Helene. She felt a special bond with all of these women and looked forward to a lifetime of their friendship.

"You look gorgeous," Ashley observed. "Irene, you did an amazing job on this gown."

"Well, I didn't mean to presume anything, but I knew ye'd be back to marry me brother and so I started work on it right away. Do ye like it, Jenna?"

"Irene, it's perfect. I'm in awe. To think you made this just for me and in just a few short weeks. It's unbelievable," Jenna gushed, running her hands over the beautiful golden gown.

"'Twas my pleasure. I know we didn't start off on the best of terms, but I want ye to know that yer me sister now."

Jenna was touched by Irene's admission. She reached out to grab Irene's hand and pulled her in for a hug. "I'm so very happy." Tears threatened to spill and she got herself under control. She didn't want Cormac to see her with red puffy eyes, even if they were the product of happy tears.

"Are we all ready then?" Helene asked.

Jenna nodded and Helene opened the door, leading the procession of women as they made their way down the stone steps and into the Great Hall, which was filled to the brim with the MacKenzie clan and their neighbors. Dylan and Chester were waiting nearby. Dylan gave her the thumbs up as she passed. In the midst of it all, stood a very handsome Cormac MacBayne. The sight of him took Jenna's breath away, just as he always did. Jenna glided across the room and straight into his arms. The other women went to stand with their respective partners as Cormac led Jenna to stand in front of the priest, who had arrived especially for their ceremony. They stood hand in hand and listened intently as the priest spoke. They exchanged their vows and Cormac presented her with a beautiful amethyst ring. The band was adorned with silver thistle leaves and the stone itself was set to resemble a thistle flower. As he slipped it on her finger, he whispered in her ear, "Yer my beautiful thistle, Jenna. I'll love ye forever and ever."

# ABOUT JENNAE

Jennae was born and raised a New England girl, just outside of Boston, Massachusetts, where her imagination was always bigger than she was. Her large, extended Irish and Italian families were a great source of support, inspiration and humor. Laughter, love and food were never hard to find in her home. Jennae grew up surrounded by nostalgic, historical landmarks, which fed her love of history and creative writing.

She has worn many hats over the years. From owning her own typing service and horse boarding facility, to operating an embroidery/t-shirt business, her entrepreneurial spirit was strong and thriving. Determined to do something she truly loved, her vivid imagination took over again and she decided to follow her literary dream of writing stories that tapped into her love of magical people and places.

Jennae now lives in the San Francisco Bay Area with her husband, where they've raised two beautiful and talented children. Along the way they've gathered a menagerie of pets, including dogs, cats, chickens and horses to make the family complete.

You can contact Jennae at her website: www.jennaevaleauthor.com

Facebook: www.facebook.com/jennaevaleauthor

Twitter: @jealil

jennaevaleauthor@gmail.com

Dear Reader,

Thank you for reading Jenna and Cormac's story. I hope you enjoyed reading it as much as I enjoyed writing it. If you enjoyed it and you'd like to help other readers find my books, I'd be grateful if you'd leave a review on Goodreads or at the retailer where you purchased A Thistle Beyond Time. If you'd like more info on book releases, cover reveals, giveaways, etc., please sign up for my newsletter here: http://www.jennaevaleauthor.com/-!news-and-events/c1pz

Thank you again,

Jennae Vale

## Books in The Thistle & Hive Series

A Bridge Through Time (Book 1)

A Thistle Beyond Time (Book 2)

Separated By Time (Book 3) To be released in 2015

www.ingramcontent.com/pod-product-compliance
Lightning Source LLC
Chambersburg PA
CBHW051409170626
46809CB00006B/2092